I Had Wild Jack For A Lover

I HAD WILD JACK FOR A LOVER

MEREDITH MARSH

Coward, McCann & Geoghegan, Inc.
New York

Copyright © 1977 by Meredith Marsh
All rights reserved. This book, or parts thereof, may not be reproduced in any form without permission in writing from the publisher. Published on the same day in Canada by Longman Canada Limited, Toronto.

Excerpt from "Crazy Jane on God" from The Collected Poems of William Butler Yeats reprinted with permission of Macmillan Publishing Company, Inc. Copyright 1933 by Macmillan Publishing Company, Inc., renewed 1961 by Bertha Georgie Yeats. Also reprinted by permission of M.B. Yeats, Miss Anne Yeats and the Macmillan Company of London and Basingstoke.

PRINTED IN THE UNITED STATES OF AMERICA

To Grem and Pudd, who in creating their own world, made room in a very splendid one for me.

Crazy Jane on God

That lover of a night
Came when he would,
Went in the dawning light
Whether I would or no;
Men come, men go,
All things remain in God.

Before their eyes a house
That from childhood stood
Uninhabited, ruinous,
Suddenly lit up
From door to top:
All things remain in God.

I had wild Jack for a lover;
Though like a road
That men pass over
My body makes no moan
But sings on;
All things remain in God.
                    W.B. Yeats

PROLOGUE

"You can open your eyes now, Hannah!"

The child gazed around the dazzling showroom, a parent clutched in each hand. Suspended between adults, she could afford to slip into dreaminess, to lose herself in rapture to the shimmering constructions that glared back at the toy-department spotlights. It never occurred to her to make sense of it all; she was all eyes.

A shadow loomed toward her, but she made no attempt to differentiate it from the clamor and reflecting surfaces that swarmed beyond. It boomed nearby: her parents would take care of that. She was free to give in to the assault of pure sensation, to drift with its currents, to swim in it.

But her mother's voice turned abruptly formal. "Hannah," Jennifer said, "wake up. The gentleman is speaking to you."

She lurched into panic. What had the man said? Bicycles? She was supposed to be thinking about bicycles! A demanding silence nudged her on all sides. She had no idea what was expected. They had come here because it was time for a two-wheeler, and she had assumed they would provide her with one. Now the crowded floor began to surge and flash and clatter until she dived deep into the back of her privacy. Whenever her parents withdrew and left her to fend for herself, which they seemed to be doing more and more lately, she came here. Inside. Now, safe, she peered out at the world as if she were crouching way in the rear of an empty theatre.

Her parents moved forward; she tripped and would have fallen without their firm grasps. Their lips tightened with annoyance. She winced apologetically, but she couldn't help these bouts of clumsiness, for she was drawn so far into herself that the best she could do was try to steer the body that housed her. She banged into walls and fell down stairs. Her body wasn't trustworthy; it couldn't hang from crossbars by the knees, stand on its head, or climb to the top of a jungle gym. In her mind, in her drawings, she ran free with wild horses over prairies or hunted with wolves, eyes wide and flashing in the light of gypsy campfires, but actually, at recess, she stood in the concrete schoolyard with her arms wrapped around the steel pole of the swing set, waiting for the bell to release her.

To her relief, her parents led her away from the salesman and deposited her closer to what she now recognized as a display of bicycles. Magnificent bicycles! So much better than the squat, battered, cast-off things her playmates rode.

James had urged her to borrow a friend's two-wheeler to practice on before buying a brand-new one, but Hannah was far too shy and proud. Like many precocious only children, she was ill at ease with people her own age. The attention her parents lavished on her made her idiosyncratic, serious, highly imaginative; she found it hard to blend her own fantasies with the more social and conventional impulses of her playmates. On the rare occasions when she lost her bashful self-possession she could become a leader, enticing others into her private dreams, but if she couldn't invent the game, she often couldn't play at all.

Besides, why should she struggle to make her meaning clear to other children when her mother understood everything instantaneously, at least when they were alone? Even James understood, though he did tend to ask for explanations. But explanations came naturally to the Eriksons; the three of them talked together by the hour, describing the texture of their separate days. Often James came home from the bank to find Hannah and Jennifer still sitting at the table over cookies and milk, sharing Hannah's adventures at school, and though at first he would complain that his daughter should be outdoors playing with friends, soon he would shrug, take off his hat, lay down his briefcase, and join them to talk about his own day in the city.

When Hannah refused to learn to ride a bicycle from her neighborhood playmates she sensed tacit support from her mother. Jenny was always just as happy to postpone her withdrawn daughter's adventuring, not only because she enjoyed the child's company, but also because she feared that one day Hannah might steal through the gate, daydreaming as usual, and tumble into the deep lagoon that brooded beyond their backyard. Of course, James had taught her to swim as soon as they moved to this seashore town, but that would be little help if she fell off the dock in the dead of an ice-locked winter. So Jennifer preferred to keep Hannah close, and Hannah was glad to stay.

Now, under her intense scrutiny, the bicycles fell into separate shapes, then two in particular, one red and one aqua, both imposingly large. She glanced up to catch her mother's eye. As far as Hannah knew, she and Jennifer shared almost identical needs and impulses. She depended on her mother for everything, talked to her so frequently about so much that she had formed the habit of talking to herself as well, aloud and silently, and scarcely knew the difference. There wasn't a time when she had not taken for granted that she was her mother's best friend. Now Jennifer was gazing at the blue.

"I think I like the blue one most," Hannah said. "Don't you, Mommy?"

"It's your decision, dear. You're the one who'll be riding it." But there was a note of approval in her soft voice.

There was an answering note of approval in Hannah's eyes as she studied her mother. Hers was by far the youngest, prettiest mother on the block, so graceful and slender, with long hair that curled on her shoulders and shimmered like a glass of ginger ale. In her fuzzy white sweater and skirt, her teetering pumps and shiny stockings, she had attracted admiring glances everywhere they went today.

Men weren't supposed to be pretty, but if they were, James, tall as a Viking, would be. His hair was more golden than Jenny's and straighter; it gleamed like a polished doorknob. Hannah couldn't focus on the rest of him quite as clearly, perhaps because his clothes were the color of tin, but she sensed that wherever he happened to be, he was right. When people saw father and daughter together, they exclaimed at the resemblance, especially the eyes, so large and green. Though James seemed pleased, Hannah was not. She was tired of being called her father's little owl, solemn and speechless; she wanted to look like her mother who was beautiful.

She looked up and saw that, as she had guessed, James was wandering. Annoyed, she tugged at the high hand she held until at last he turned his head and vaguely gazed down at her. "Made up your mind?" he asked.

"No!" Then, because he was still peering down, she relented. She let go of Jenny's hand to point. "I like that red one and the blue one over there best."

"The red one is a boy's bike."

"Oh." She was somewhat befuddled over the difference.

"Take your finger out of your mouth, Hannah," chided Jennifer, reaching over to hold the hand again.

"Why can't I have a boy's?"

After a pause, Jenny answered, "Because it hurts girls more if they fall off the seat onto the crossbar."

"Anyway, Banana," continued James, "you pick the color you like and we'll ask for a smaller girl's version—"

"Why?" Hannah smoldered. He had promised she could have anything she wanted. She dropped her mother's hand and jutted out her arm. "That one," she pronounced. "That big blue one—that's just the one I want."

"It's too large, Hannah; you'll fall off; you need one your own size." But Hannah could see from the glint in his eye that her assertion of will secretly amused and pleased him.

"You said I wouldn't fall off," she insisted. "You said it would come to me naturally. You said I could have whatever I liked best. Well, I like that one—I love that one!" Then she added more reasonably, "I'll grow."

James chuckled, as she had sensed he would. "I hope you'll grow, Banana; I certainly plan on your doing so, at any rate. But that bicycle is large enough to stunt your growth. After all, you want to be able to ride it now, not when you're eighteen."

"I'll never be eighteen," she said with disgust. Then the salesman hovered back into her line of vision and her voice faltered.

He blasted her like a boat horn. "Well, little princess, have we made our decision yet?" She shrank back into herself and grunted inaudibly. Although her parents' irritable rustling unnerved her, she preferred it to exposure to this stranger.

Finally James took over in his most regal manner. "I believe we prefer the blue model fourth from the left, but in a smaller size if possible." Then, to his daughter he added, "Hannah, you might consider those English versions over there with the skinny tires and complex gears; they allow the rider more speed and control."

Staring at her feet, she shook her head.

"Are you positive? The fat tires could prove awfully slow—"

"Hannah," scolded Jennifer, "look up and pay attention. This is your decision. Sometimes you can be impossible to do anything with."

Little though Hannah liked to hear that, it was true. Why didn't people in public just say what they thought and felt as they did at home? She sensed how much her parents changed when they had to perform for outsiders, and the change made her anxious. In her own domain, Hannah had the natural power of anyone, even a child, who can find her own rhythm; yet the closer she came to that rhythm, the harder she found it to march along with the rest of the world. Every act of leaving home became a terror of leaving herself behind.

"Well, sir," the salesman reported after a trip to the storeroom, "I'm afraid that's the only one we have in blue. In the beginner's size there's just orange and yellow."

"It is pretty, isn't it?" Jenny sighed. "You don't even have red in the beginner's?"

The note of compromise made Hannah clench. "No!" she was able to say before the temerity of contradicting a huge stranger made her voice knot.

"It's the same bike, princess," he crooned. "And in yellow it's pretty as a picture. Let me bring it out to show you."

Scorning this attempt to seduce her, she glowered from behind Jennifer's hip and remained silent. She mustn't be taken in only to regret her acquiescence later.

Jenny reached down and prodded. "Hannah?"

"I like the blue one."

"It's too large, honey."

She went even more rigid with determination.

"Maybe," sighed Jenny to her husband, "we should find another store."

James fidgeted. It was Saturday, his day off; he yearned to escape to the health room of his club to work out the cramps of a week's steerage in the bank he had the misfortune to captain; he would settle for his favorite chair and a book. Why Jenny couldn't manage this errand without him he didn't know. And tonight—in a few hours, in fact—they must go to a dinner party, which meant hours of wet and muddled conversation topped by some charred beef at midnight. Not that he meant to complain, for he agreed that a couple was obliged to seek fun together on weekends, but he did dread it. "No," he said, "they have the largest selection here, and whether it's red or purple is irrelevant. Let's make a decision and get this over with. Unless you want to drop me off at home and go on alone—" He looked meaningfully at his wife, who quickly shook her head.

"Then it will have to be one of these, Hannah, unless you prefer to wait and order one in the color you like." James took a long guilty breath, avoiding his women's eyes, and looked around as if he hoped to spy some door or sign that might somehow brush the responsibility for this day off his shoulders. He sighed again, trying to dispel a weariness and impatience greater than the simple boredom of placating a child, as though he were trying to exhale all the aimless dissatisfaction that had become so pervasive he hardly knew he felt it anymore.

And on her next breath Hannah sucked in that same charged air. She was so sensitive to her parents that when they steamed with tensions too familiar to notice, it was she who clouded like a mirror in the shower room, their most vaporous moods condensing on her small, serious face.

"You'll have to make your decision from what you see," James repeated.

"Maybe we should lift you up to the seat and see if you do fit," suggested the salesman, and he reached for her, but Hannah sagged back against her mother's leg. At last James reached brusquely down and swung her up to the white seat, holding her in place while supporting the bicycle with his knee. The sensation was heady and strange. She clutched the handlebars anxiously.

"Look, sweetie, I'm afraid you can't hardly touch." The loathsome grown-up snuffled around her ankle and grabbed one foot.

"I can so touch," she muttered angrily but almost inaudibly to her mother. "Look." She stretched her other leg to its full length and did manage to place her toe against the pedal.

"Yeah, but, princess, can you reach with both feet?" the villain challenged dubiously as he moved back to observe.

Everything depended on this. Vibrating with determination, Hannah succeeded in forcing all but her heels onto the rubber. "You don't want me to outgrow it," she asserted.

"Well, sir, if the little lady is so sure—I guess she is the one that's gonna be riding it after all—" The salesman shrugged.

James frowned, admiring Hannah's stubbornness, impatient to be home, and aware of the mistake. "Well, Jen," he concluded, "she does seem able to reach. Hannah, now, you're sure it feels right to you—?"

Never having sat atop a two-wheeler before, Hannah didn't know what the right feeling was, but her parents' doubt made her all the more emphatic. She was determined not to let the adults' vacillation decide her future by default.

"Hannah," Jenny began in a pleading tone; the resolution of the child's jaw stopped her. "James, perhaps we—" But she trailed off, uncertain what she wanted to say.

"That's settled then; we'll take it as is." James lifted Hannah to the floor, took out his checkbook, and went off to complete the transaction. Hannah and Jennifer stared wordlessly across their new possession. On the way to the car Hannah learned how to walk it, and swelled with pride at the picture she must make. At home she walked it to the garage, parked it with care, and went up to her room to savor her happy dream of mastery and motion.

It didn't happen. That promised miracle of grace and balance did not occur. Hannah discovered that when she was on it she couldn't see it, and all the opulence of size and color made little difference to the rider. She came to dread her nightly lessons with a horror that blighted the entire day. For the first time in her memory, James would not relent; he was determined to teach his daughter to master the expensive toy in the garage. Hannah added a plea for rain to her bedside prayers, but this was to be a spring of drought. Even God, it seemed, wanted her to ride.

Every evening after he had paused over coffee just long enough to spark his forlorn daughter with hope, James slapped his palms on the table in theatrical enthusiasm and suggested the lesson as if he had just thought of it. The dishes rattled, coffee slurped into saucers, and Hannah gazed up in liquid-eyed resignation.

"A great night for a ride!" he would exclaim, "right, Banana? And we feel like a little exercise, don't we?"

She ducked her head. How could someone who loved her deny the reality of her despair?

At that hour on an early summer's evening, all the neighbors who did not yet have their boats in the water grouped on their front porches, sipping coffee, while their children played in shifting, quarrelsome alignments up and down the long curving block. The languid rustling of the lagoon's shifting tides behind them, the ocean sighing farther off, the crickets practicing for the new season, made all the world peaceful and hushed, with only a child's cry or a gull's call to punctuate the stillness. Sprinklers and hoses looped across the grass lent their own swish to the deeper moan of the water beyond.

And then, when Hannah appeared, waves of diverted attention and amusement rippled over the lawns to center on her. She began to stiffen and withdraw. James too was growing distant; she could feel him hardening in his resolve to enact this pantomime of gaiety, to shove her from behind down the length of their twilight Jersey street until she gathered enough speed to sail off on her own, to coast in doomed arcs and loops that would all end, inevitably, at the foot of one or another of the widely spaced streetlights that lit their way. This, it seemed, was to be her summer fate.

She clambered onto the seat. The monstrous toy suspended her at a dizzying height from the tar below. She tried to swallow, blinked her eyes, and strained for the pedals her toes could barely touch.

"All right?" James said. Full of optimism, he explained again the backpedaling necessary to brake, the leaning necessary to steer, the coordination necessary to chart her course. None of it meant anything. By now she was helpless to touch the perimeters of her body from within, much less able to extend beyond herself to guide this foreign contraption of sharp steel. Doomed, she gathered back within until she was almost unconscious with fear. The edges of her vision darkened and fell away until she seemed to look out through a long tube, the wrong end of a telescope, so that the world was dwarfed and distanced. She was safe beyond contact. She heard her father's advice and the neighbors' chortles as if through a diver's suit—out there, while she was within.

Still barking instructions, James began to jog. Hannah tightened everywhere. For a moment, when she sensed the worried approach of Jenny, she shifted hopefully, but then she pulled back, for Jenny never contradicted her husband; at best she meekly complained. She dimly saw her mother's hands play with the dish towel she still held, then try to smooth down the wave of tawny hair that always fell over one eye, but she knew from experience that Jenny's submissive anxiety would only increase James's now guilty insistence on his will. "Jamie, so many people—another night—so hot—not the best way—of course you know best—" And with each cavil floating after them, the remorseless grip on her fender tightened.

As they at last began to gather impetus and fly down the slope, Hannah, despite herself, flinched under the thrashing, gasping and choking right by her ears. Through it all came Jenny's far-off warnings of heart attacks and heat strokes to persuade her that now, along with anguish over her own rapidly advancing crash, she bore responsibility for her father's audible struggle with death. Each wheeze on her neck was her fault. Every second she expected to hear him collapse—splat—on the tar behind her as she continued to ebb helplessly away. Every crack of his sneakers and rasp of his breath seared her heels. She began to sob in simultaneous terror that he would soon let go and let her crash and that he would never let go and so die in his efforts to protect her. The longer he postponed her doom the closer he heaved toward his own. But then the bike tore from his grip and sailed off, leaving him to stare after her in furious tenderness.

Yet even when she heard him drop away and realized that she was on her own, with no balance or guide, still all Hannah's concentration flew back to him, flew back to see that he still survived, so that when he cried out to brake or steer she didn't comprehend the words, only the welcome sound of his voice still calling. Relief mixed with the wind pounding past. She clamped closer to the handlebars in mute confusion and everything hurtled by in a flood of undifferentiated sensation and shadow. She was one clenched fist of terror. The sole point of stability in her lonely ride was the calm, straight, motionless vertical of the streetlamp. It stood in its pool of gentle light and watched, drew her in a soundless gesture across the swiftly narrowing distance, and she surrendered to it. She watched in submission, gathering speed, until in the last seconds it loomed wildly forward and smacked her down. The crash, however painful, was at least a completion, a grim relief. Then, as she recovered her bearings in a tangle of spokes and bleeding joints, the first thing she looked for was her father's guilty but disgusted figure, erect and alive, ready to send her back for another try.

In school, Hannah was disconcerted to find herself the only one who had failed to master a two-wheeler, but only mildly so, for she was accustomed to being found peculiar by other children. She sank more deeply into her incessant drawing. Though she was talented enough to succeed in school despite her inattention, she disliked it; she fantasized that someday a languid illness might rescue her from the classroom and provide her with a tutor all her own. This idea came from her favorite of the books she had inherited from her mother's attic. Joy, a winsome suburban princess with golden curls, was a temporary invalid and thus earned a reprieve from everything that made life arduous. Not only did Joy gain a tutor, she also ran away from home with a kindly band of gypsies, including her special friend, Joe, who was fiery and dark and mysteriously wise. Hannah deeply envied her. She could never quite decipher what it was that made the gypsies so appealing to both Joy and herself, nor why they were so forbidden that, in the end, Joy had to understand that she was not of their kind and return home. But she did know that whatever that free and primitive attraction was, she yearned for it. Joy's meek return to her guardians' lock and key earned from Hannah only contempt; in Joy's place, she was certain, she would have run back to Joe, back to that circle of painted wagons around a campfire where fortune-tellers danced away the nights, forever making their home on the wing. Had the authorities pursued, she and Joe would have flown all the way to California—a place Hannah had recently visited and loved, and which she believed to consist only of woods, cliffs, a wilder surf than the one she knew, and occasional rides on cable cars. There she and Joe would wander and play at will, two friends who felt and thought as one. How could Joy settle for school and pals and social approbation when she had known mystery? Mystery, adventure, and the wilderness!

Then, one afternoon the following summer, when she was dreamy and bored, her few friends having abandoned her for the Girl Scout camp in the Poconos that she had scorned, Hannah wandered up to the attic. There she unearthed her old aquamarine bicycle, brought it downstairs, and wheeled it cautiously out to the street. It was shrunken and faded, but also less intimidating. Now she could sit confidently on the seat with sneakers planted on cement. She could teach herself. It made all the difference. After a few tentative pushes she found she could coast, then pedal, the swoop and swerve; and then, at last, Hannah was able to ride just as her father had promised. Over the next months she cycled up and down the streets of the seaside town until she could sail on land as well as she could swim in the surrounding ocean. But even those were pleasures she continued to seek alone.

PART I

JINX

1

Life had not turned out as Jennifer and James had been led to expect. Everything a man was supposed to do, James had done, and now where was the reward? He felt betrayed. By the time Hannah turned seventeen, he felt desperate. He fought with his wife, but jaggedly and absentmindedly, like an insomniac swatting at a persistent gnat. He felt, dimly, that Jenny wanted him to play Dagwood Bumstead to her Blondie, to be the comic-strip bumpkin of a husband scampering twice a day after the train that would ferry him between the manipulations of a shrewd wife and the asphyxiation of the job. And in her uncertain way perhaps Jenny did want that, or perhaps she was vague and admiring enough to be molded into another scheme if James had been sure of what he wanted, what he was missing, or sure of himself and his feelings, but he was not. He castigated her for refusing to acknowledge any complexity beyond the newsprint squares of Dagwood's world, yet, apart from his thwarted fury on the one hand and his lofty philosophizing on the other, he too failed to discern a world beyond those perpetual lines of neatly drawn boxes. What was there but blank paper? Even as he prostrated himself nightly before the stereo or brooded on the stern of his moored boat, near unconsciousness from alcohol and strain, he was really only casting out into emptiness in hope of hooking another, more habitable, box.

He turned from reading romantic poetry to philosophy and social criticism; locked in the library on weekends, he rewrote the first chapter of the autobiography that would depict a more ingenuous Henry Adams in a less hospitable future. Too confused to reach the second chapter and too much a perfectionist to enjoy expressing his confusion, he would then retreat to his collection of atlases and lose himself for hours in their pastel outlines.

Within the isolation of his home, which began to seem to them all as marooned as a lifeboat lost at sea, he became a fierce critic and nonconformist; beyond the home, however, since he needed even more than most men to be liked, he continued to act the respectable young executive. Had this actually been the simple hypocrisy he claimed, a self-serving tactic, he would not have suffered the terror of fragmentation that daily ripped up and down his spine as if along a perforated line, but in truth, each of his costumes seemed fitting to him as he wore it; only the incessant changing filled him with dread. Adams, Lenin, Dagwood and Augustus Caesar, Nietzsche, Jesus, and the poetry of Housman: all struck deep chords in James's psyche, but together they made a muddle.

He often sensed what was wanted of him before he could define it and complied too easily, needing the applause; then later he pondered his actions, doubted them. He had always been unusually capable, suave —all his life, friends had looked to him for leadership. Yet gradually he had come to wonder whether he was really as autonomous as they believed, or only better able to oil and spin the exercise wheel of his cage. He wished to be decisive, unhesitatingly virtuous, his father's sort of man. Instead, when he tried to rest, shrill voices preached clashing definitions of virtue. Knowledgeable, persuasive, he impressed others and himself as a man of reason: he fought to lock those wilder voices in the attic. But they banged on the floor: his head throbbed: his dreams jolted him awake. Such a man, having willy-nilly met the troupe of performers and motley of scripts that animate him, is doomed to a period of considerable upheaval. James's crisis intensified with the deaths of the alcoholic mother who had resented his talents and of the commanding father who left him and his more unstable (and less talented) brothers controlling interest in a small Philadelphia bank, which tempted them every day to dramatize old rivalries in new ways. When, after the war, in what had then seemed the natural course of things, James had left the orderly world of ships for family, bank and city, joining his wife and new baby in a cramped apartment, he broke out in a severe rash on his genitals, which he diagnosed as scabies and scoured with disinfectant.

The strain was brutal. He had incipient ulcers, too many automobile accidents, a shaky marriage, a dependence on bourbon, nervous tics, a temper that appalled him, migraines, erratic bowels, first one and eventually two unhappy children—indeed, the full litany of modern ailments. The very familiarity obscured the problem. If he was badly off, well, many of his friends had only half their stomachs, two or three unhappy families, hangovers so cruel they could only brag about them. In fact, more than a few of his friends were dead. A member of his club had hanged himself at a medical convention; another, after a stroke, sat perpetually in the corner in a leather chair that had once belonged to Benjamin Franklin.

Hannah adored him. Night after night she absorbed or argued delightedly with his views on everything from communism to religion to sexuality. She eagerly looked forward to reading his book, confident it would explain himself, the world, and her place in it. It confused her, however, that whenever she imitated his radical voice, he shifted to the skeptical tone of the man of the world. And when he lost his grip on both voices—when he could muster neither the romantic truth-seeker nor the detached conservative, but instead broke down into a fierce and tormented man of thirty-nine, even a desperate child—she was devastated. His moods tore her violently from admiration to anguished empathy to a self-defensive loathing. She fought to separate herself, but she felt bound to him as tightly as a witch to the stake, and burning.

She couldn't trust fully in anything. She couldn't get a grip on anything. She couldn't afford to relax or trust. No one would take hold for her. She had faith in nothing. She stiffened. She was perpetually on her guard.

Despite, or because of, their closeness, Hannah and James battled frequently. There were times when the sight of one could drive the other to a paroxysm of nerves. When James was upset and drinking, Hannah would turn sullen. For weeks he would try to ignore the accusation in her eyes, but little by little it would erode what patience he still had. Finally one night he would arrive home very late, hulking through the door with his back bent as though literally shrugging off his wife's unspoken denunciation. Miserable and trapped, his face disfigured by alcohol and tension, his mouth drawn meanly down, his eyelids at half-mast, he would take his place at the head of the table. The cold dinner had been waiting for hours, since one of Jennifer's few unshakable convictions was that happy families always eat together. Stomachs clenched, the women brought in the last of the dishes and sat. Because the signs of incipient rage on her father's face were as clear as the Coast Guard weather flags at the far end of the lagoon, Hannah forced herself to be scrupulously polite, but she couldn't conceal her disdain. She answered every perfunctory query in a clipped tone that shivered with distaste, so, when James's resentment at last fired forth, the detonation was far out of proportion to Hannah's crime, since only her manner was at fault.

"What did I do?" she asked indignantly. "I didn't say a thing—!"

"Now dear," Jenny began, attempting to soothe him, "she didn't really say any—"

But James pounded the table until the knives clattered off the plates and the steak bones bounced. Jennifer fell nervously silent, telling herself that parents should never divide loyalties in front of the children.

"Shut your impertinent mouth when I speak to you!" he snapped, clobbering the table again. Little Kate, eight years Hannah's junior, shrank back in her chair as her milk spilled over. All three females quaked. James's eyes fermented with wrath; he snarled again, visibly shaking. Vengeance erupted beyond his control. He said that Hannah was selfish, greedy and cruel, that she tormented her helpless mother and sister, that she made the home unbearable for everyone else, that she was cold and uncaring, that she was beyond salvation—but far worse than his words was his tone, simultaneously so icy and yet so inflamed, so virulent and spiteful, that it seemed to deny that any vestiges of affection had ever existed or could again. Jenny quailed helplessly before it, afraid that everything that made their lives tolerable would drown under this disgorging malice. It horrified her to see him like this, the man she loved for his patience and wisdom. She prayed that Hannah would submit and retreat, would do anything to end it all as quickly as possible.

But Hannah went rigid with hurt and fury, her head high, and stared contemptuously at the wall ahead. As the attack continued, she sighed elaborately, shrugged, flared her nostrils, pursed her lips, and spat inaudible sarcasms until finally there was a pause.

"Did you ever stop to consider," she struggled to say in a clear voice, "that you might be the one who makes life miserable for the rest of us?"

Again he raged that she wasn't worth the time and money they spent on her. At the next pause, Jennifer hastily leaned toward Hannah and ordered her to go to her room, but when she rose and began to stalk to the stairs, James followed, swearing, throwing silverware and plates at the floor, and when she wheeled and held her ground, her revolt only maddened him the more. He castigated her arrogance, her disloyalty, her coldness. She shook with intimidation, pain, and an anger that seemed as vast and frightening as the ocean around them.

"You're supposed to be my father!" she wept. "You're supposed to take care of me. And look what you do—just look at yourself! I don't care if you drink yourself to death, I don't care if you kill yourself, just leave me alone!"

James raised his fists and lunged for her, calling her a slut, a bitch, a selfish whore, any epithet that came to mind. "You don't give a good goddamn for any human being but yourself!" he bellowed. "You're a greedy pig so swollen with your own self-importance you think the rest of the world is one big sty for you to wallow in." His face contorted with loathing and he began to stagger about and snuffle in gross imitation. "Oink oink! Any more garbage? Any more garbage for me?" He thrust out his fist as if to ram it down her throat and she flinched back instinctively, horrified. "I'll stuff you with garbage until you burst, you worthless pile of slop—" He spat his disgust at the carpet, then flapped a hand dismissively and turned to leave.

But Hannah felt that the only way she could survive was somehow to strike back with equal cruelty. Ashamed of having shown her fear, she desperately pulled herself together enough to speak, furious at her voice for trembling. "If I'm so bad," she managed to say, "did you ever stop to think why? Did you ever think it might be because I have a weakling and a drunk for a father? Did you ever think it might be because I'm afraid to come home at night because—" Her voice wobbled and broke. She shuddered with fierce need to hold herself unyielding, impermeable, composed. She would not fall apart. She would not let his words inside; she would never give in; she would never let go. "You're a failure!" she yelled, "a failure as a father and as a person, and I don't care if you—"

He leaped forward and threw her against the wall.

She bounced off the fireplace, her heart thundering. These abrupt gestures of suppressed violence terrified her; she felt like a rabbit in a dog's jaw. But no one would defend her but herself, and if she let him shred her pride, no one else would put her back together.

He wheeled around with his arms dramatically extended, his expression anguished and murderous at once. "You don't care what you say," he pleaded, "you don't care how much you hurt people. I don't think you're capable of love or a shred of loyalty. It's unnatural." He shook his head hopelessly.

Their battles seemed to last for hours. They ripped and clawed until their passions ground them down to bloody pulp. And through it all, Jennifer cowered nearby, weeping, begging them to stop. In the end, father and daughter staggered into a mute and heartbroken embrace, driven near collapse by each other and themselves, numbly apologetic for this fury that periodically stung one of them like a sniper's bullet and rebounded to rip viciously into the other. More than forgiving, they were battered enough in that moment simply to accept one another entirely and without question.

Yet each retained an unreasonable annoyance with Jennifer, who stood so meekly beside them, having dared to rise from her chair only when the conflict had passed. Now, as soon as she saw them hug, Jenny sighed and beamed. As if she heard music swelling in the background as the credits began to move up over the screen, she would now be able to forget that such raw aggression had ever occurred or that, since nothing was resolved, it would occur again. She shut her eyes wearily and rubbed her temples. "Oh," she breathed once James had limped down the hall to nurse his wounds in private. "Oh my goodness, Banana, look at the time!"

Blank as a robot, Hannah stared at the clock. It meant nothing.

"You must have homework to do—didn't you say you had a Latin exam tomorrow? Oh well, I always say it's better to get the sleep you need than to study one last page."

Hannah turned slowly to look at her, and immediately Jennifer began to bustle around the large room, emptying ashtrays into one another, plumping pillows, gathering newspapers, straightening the footstool Hannah had knocked over when James pushed her. The orange glow in the fireplace guttered into the disintegrating logs, its periodic snaps startling the sleeping dog. Every morning before his family was up, James built a new fire to drive back the wind that lashed in from the bay to turn the walls to its own dank temperature. Hannah watched the flame's reflection on the back of her mother's blouse. By now she had sunk into a depression so deep and still that she could hardly imagine what would happen when she got to her room.

"Better get going, honey," Jennifer sang with her back turned. She emphatically shook out the afghan and refolded it over the back of the couch. "No sense brooding; it's all over. A good night's sleep and by tomorrow you'll hardly know it happened."

With great effort, Hannah located words. "You'll forget, Mother; I won't." Then, with an almost scientific curiosity, she asked mildly, "Tell me, do you really think my Latin exam is important right now?"

Vexed, Jennifer first turned to confront her obstinate daughter, then looked away and nervously drew the curtains shut against the gloom. She heard the lagoon's perpetual slap at the dock. She disliked these formal curtains, she thought again, but James's mother had custom-made them for the house when she lived here, and it would be improvident to replace them until they wore out a little more.

"Really, Mother, I want to know," Hannah insisted in the same monotone. "Do you think I can just run upstairs to concentrate on my vocabulary lists—do you think that's important?"

"Well, it will be tomorrow, won't it? Life goes on, Hannah; this isn't the end of the world. You know perfectly well that your father didn't mean what he said. He's having business problems again, his brothers—well, the same old story. And he apologized. Many parents, you know, would never apologize to their children no matter how wrong they had been. Mine wouldn't have."

Hannah studied her unemotionally, then finally said: "He didn't mean the words, no, but he did mean the feelings. He went crazy. He's driving me crazy. We're all going crazy."

"Honestly, Hannah, I wish you wouldn't be so melodramatic!" Then, instantly sorry for her tone, Jenny forced herself to confront her daughter's white, impassive face. She looked almost hopefully for signs of adolescent grief or confusion, but found none. This iron self-containment always intimidated her. She drew back. Her own mouth trembled.

"Families quarrel," she said pleadingly. "Arguments clear the air; they're necessary. We'll all feel better for it in the morning." Her instinct was to touch, but she suppressed it, for Hannah sometimes brushed her off like lint. Besides, she didn't know how to pat someone who was that reserved, that regal. Yet why did Hannah just keep watching, then, as if she were waiting for something, expecting something? Jenny knew she had no answers to give. She wiped her face with the corner of the apron she had been wearing when the argument flared up, automatically went to untie it, then remembered that the dishes still remained to be done and felt almost relieved. She moved efficiently toward the kitchen, and as she passed Hannah she cheerfully went to hug her, but Hannah flinched and drew back, then turned with composure and stalked toward the stairs. Jenny watched her helplessly.

Hannah had sunk past tears. She felt like an inflated doll that must walk with great care in order not to lose any more air through the leak in her side. She knew she was moving haltingly, unnaturally, but she couldn't control her body; she could only think of reaching the safety of the third floor where no one could see her clumsiness. Then a footstool leaned over to trip her, and she sagged.

"Don't you ever watch where you're going?" Ashamed, Jenny pressed her palms to her temples. "I'm sorry; I'm tired too, but I don't know why you insist on dramatizing everything so."

This was a frequent refrain. On the one hand Hannah was cold, on the other hand melodramatic. She took a deep breath to reply, but found she hadn't the energy. Perhaps her mother was right. After all, even though she felt as if she were sprawled on the floor in hysteria, she was actually observing herself and the scene as coolly as a movie director coordinating his cast from a crane; it was true that she rarely made an uncalculated move. Perhaps, like a director, she invented the emotions that seemed to swirl around her—and in that case, why couldn't she bring her drama under control?

She went to her room, shut the door, and sat on the edge of the bed, too stupefied to undress, too roiled to sleep, too pained to concentrate on anything but the television that she turned on very low when the sounds of Jenny's preparations for bed had faded. It soothed: a placid voice murmuring banalities in an undemanding tone. It deflected the silence. She prayed for sleep to overcome her, but it didn't. How could she be so entirely drained, so empty, and yet be unable to sleep? In time the national anthem played, the screen shuddered, went blank, and emitted a piercing beep. She automatically lurched to her feet and clicked it off, then pulled off her clothes and methodically set her hair in twenty-two wire curlers. Setting her hair lent her a meager sense of order. Tomorrow her eyes would be as conspicuously white and swollen as boiled eggs, so it was important that the other details of her appearance be normal.

Still strangely reluctant to give herself over to dreams, she arranged her crown of bristles on the pillow. Tomorrow at breakfast, she vowed, she would be perfectly haughty and dignified: they would never guess how much power they had to hurt her. All day she would be poised and cool. In public, in school, she would hold herself firmly together. If not—? She couldn't imagine an alternative. She would be proud and composed; she would observe everything, including herself, and understand everything, because then nothing could touch her. Her only remaining problem, then, was her recalcitrant self. Why couldn't she shrug off these moods of self-disgust and loneliness? Why didn't she have the willpower to dispel the gloom and paralysis that made her head throb so viciously by afternoon that she had submitted to the family doctor's latest enthusiasm, hypnosis, in hopes of relief? Why was she unable to give herself freely to any activity but her fantasies?

2

The following night, at an hour even later than his usual late one, James again entered a house rigid with suspense. To allay her own nervousness, Jenny had already drunk too much, and to demonstrate her uncondemning attitude to her husband, she now drank even more. Quarreling lashed out at the table and continued to erupt throughout the evening until James finally and furiously locked himself in his room, having threatened divorce, broken a glass tabletop, and intimidated his family into tears. The women huddled together. The wind thrashed the neighbors' trees and slapped the lagoon until it rumbled and simmered. Only the occasional flash of solitary headlights speeding down the hushed street relieved the blackness of an overcast night in a resort town that was nearly vacant in the winter. Everyone moved on tiptoe and conversed in the low tones of imminent catastrophe. If James growled a surly command to his wife or hulked into the kitchen to pour another drink, his children hid by the stairs. His bleak animosity and Jennifer's submissive panic, her haste to do anything at all to placate him, filled their daughters with dire suspense. In hopes of prompting him to sleep, as well as to obscure to neighbors and to herself what was happening, Jenny switched off most of the lamps. The girls skittered and quivered in the dusk, their nerves too exposed to pay attention to anything but the grave rumblings in the bowels of the house. Surely this time, they prayed, surely after all this, something would have to change.

When James finally did give in this way to his unexplained, unadmitted turbulence, he became the very incarnation of it. This was a purge, a letting go, and he willfully discarded all the normal inhibitions of his everyday, civilized demeanor. He gave in with a vengeance. Like a skilled actor turning into Mr. Hyde before the eyes of his audience, he let the rage mold him to its own shape. The liquor flushed and subtly distended his face and slackened his features; his mouth dropped into a rancorous sneer; creases deepened like gouges from his bloodshot eyes to his chin. He pawed open his collar, rolled up his sleeves and yanked off his belt. Often, in fact, with an innate sense of drama, he consciously dressed the part he was playing, vindictively choosing a costume he never wore otherwise; a black shirt hanging out over dirty pants smeared with fish gore, and a heavy tooled belt meant to support the holster for his pistols.

At last persuaded that her husband slept, Jenny, sobered, went up shakily to Hannah's room, whispered her name at the door like a conspirator, and was admitted. There the two women spent most of the remaining night, commiserating, analyzing, falling silent now and then to assess ominous noises below. Long after midnight, as Jenny left to get some sleep herself, Hannah said wearily that she felt as if they were all entangled in a web of snarled fishing lines, so that each time one person tried to break free he threatened to strangle all the rest.

They parted at the top of the stairs in mutual determination, with Jenny finally persuaded that she must follow through on whatever plan they had last concocted. But when she tiptoed down the hall and tentatively tried her own door, she found it open, and inside she found her husband quietly smoking in the dark. She trembled with indecision, prepared to flee, but his manner was calm, and his voice, when he spoke, was warm and assured. He held out his hand and asked her to come take it. She perched forlornly on the foot of his bed, irresolute. He stubbed out his cigarette and pulled her up to him, to eye level, took her hands in his, and said quite gently that she must know he loved her more than he could hope to say. Quite carefully he explained that he was not apologizing for the things he had said earlier, which he still believed, but he was apologizing for the way he had said them, and for the effect his anger had on her. Jennifer, however, remembered little of what he had said; she had heard only the threat and aversion in his tone, and so now it was enough that he retracted that. He didn't despise her; he still loved her; the problems they had were outside again, external, and tomorrow they could face them together. He protectively tucked the sheet around her and began to massage her back, and she sighed like a tree resettling after a storm. Melting relief obscured her doubts and washed away all need to think of past or future. In deep gratitude she closed her eyes and began to dream, while he lay awake and stroked her tenderly.

* * *

In the morning she awakened tangled in the blankets which he pulled loose each night and wrapped around his body like a life jacket. Sharing the same cathartic sweat, the same tired oxygen, the same incipient hangover, and the same profound determination to salvage at least one another from the wreckage of their plans, they made love with affectionate intensity.

"We're connected in ways too strong for us to break, even when we think we want to, which we don't really, and never really will," James whispered into the curve of her neck. "Whatever happens, we'll always have each other. They can't destroy that."

For a long time they lay very still, holding on tightly to one another and their mood, then slowly each drifted into separate anticipation of separate days. Reassured and serene, Jenny listened for the girls and planned her family's breakfast: something bountiful and traditional. They had gone off to school too often with nothing but juice and a mustard-colored vitamin pill to see them through the day. Winter sun streamed onto the crumpled sheets. She felt her husband's heartbeat under her breasts. He began to talk, to explain countless things that he had said last night, that he felt now, that he would feel tomorrow, making it all reasonable and cogent. She didn't quite listen, for by now she was concentrating on her routine, but she understood that he meant that now he had thought through all the confusion that had been eroding their lives, and so, henceforth, all would be different. Naturally she believed him; she trusted him with her life. If the sun stayed out today, she should start loosening the earth in the garden or by spring it would be impossible. She sang to herself in the shower and put on her prettiest robe. Her unset hair fell like waves of foxtail around her face. When James squeezed by her to shave, he pinched her bottom appreciatively, and she grinned.

Her headache passed like distant thunder and left her free and clear. She tied on her apron and took out three frying pans, for bacon, eggs, and potatoes, and happily bustled around her gleaming kitchen, getting the day going. Soon the food was sizzling, the coffee burbling, the toast popping up of its own accord. No more of this cold cereal and frozen concentrate, she vowed, slicing grapefruit; no wonder everyone had been so tired lately. From now on everything would go according to plan. She stirred the eggs with a wooden spoon, added a little more cream, and watched hungrily as the thick liquids slowly whirlpooled into a meal.

By the time Hannah came down, the stove, percolator, toaster and Jenny, all radiated the warmest of greetings. In the background James's electric razor buzzed. Hannah stood by the sink, taking it all in. How nice she looked, Jenny thought fondly. Her posture was virtually regal, which was so rare and attractive for a tall girl. She beamed and paid her compliment aloud.

"What's wrong with you?" Hannah asked stonily.

"Why nothing!" Jenny cried in shock. "Everything's fine."

"What about last night? Did you get any sleep? Where is he?"

"Your father? In the bathroom. He's fine; that's all over. He apologized when I came to bed. He's thought it all out and realized that he has to learn to leave his business problems at the office—he's thinking about renting a room at the club where he can escape and take a nap if he needs it—" She avoided Hannah's incredulous stare and poked the potatoes with a spatula. "Well, we can discuss it when you get home from school, but this time some very practical changes are going to be made, believe me."

"But what about everything we said last night, about how we have to change the way we react to him whether he changes or not—did you think any more about all we planned?"

Jenny flinched, feeling ever more inadequate. The truth was that, when left to her own devices, Jenny did not think in the sense that Hannah meant. She fretted incessantly over her problems, but she did not think them through. She felt she did not know how, that she was not as bright as her verbal husband and daughter, that her talents lay in other areas. (Her own rigidly genteel parents had restricted their conversation to mocking observations of the habits of their friends, and had Jenny ever sought to inject a more speculative note, they would have turned to mock at her. Once, when she had begun to flounder academically in the transition from a small grammar school to an impersonally mammoth high school, her father had, with uncharacteristic gentleness, shared with her his own philosophy, consisting of two poignant words: bluff it.)

"No, dear," she apologized, "I haven't had time to think. I was exhausted and fell dead asleep, and then this morning—well, everything seemed less urgent, with the sun out and all—don't you feel that?" Receiving no response but a relentless gaze, she added more maternally: "I do wonder if we don't make a mistake discussing things so late at night when we're tired and upset. Things seem so much less dramatic the next day." She smiled with crisp optimism, buttered one batch of toast and began another.

"Oh Christ!" hissed her child in a voice too low for her father to overhear.

The headache which Jenny had warded off now renewed its throb at the back of her neck. Her forehead and hands, already damp from the stove, began to sweat. What on earth did everyone expect from her, what was it they thought she could do? Life just keeps going on, that's all; it's just another day. Last night we quarreled, this morning we made up; it happens in every home on this peninsula; it's natural. So why was her daughter in front of the window, casting the entire kitchen into shade? The side of Jenny's mouth twitched. Did she have to walk out on her husband at 7:00 A.M. to make her daughter happy? She began to bustle with even greater efficiency, stabbed a fork at the bacon, and forced herself to hum cheerfully.

"Better hurry, dear, you'll be late for school," she sang with aggressive good will, trying by her tone to say: I love you far too much to ever glare at you as accusingly as you're glaring at me.

"I didn't sleep at all. I'm too exhausted to go to school. I feel sick."

Jenny's pulse fluttered. Why, every time Hannah was tired or upset, did she claim to be sick, and why did she announce it as though it were the signal for her mother to do something? She had missed almost a week of school this month alone. Competing guilts vied for Jenny's allegiance: it was her job to see that her child performed successfully in school; it was also her job to protect her if she were truly ill—Oh, why didn't this serious girl ever just go off and do what daughters do? The last thing Jenny needed today was a glum teen-ager following her around the house hounding her with questions. That thought made her feel even guiltier, however, and she sighed and bit her thumb. Again she could only think to squeeze out cheer and hope it would prove contagious. "Don't be silly, Banana, it's a beautiful day. You'll feel splendid once you're outside. Besides, you have a doctor's appointment this afternoon."

"I'm so dizzy I can hardly stand up."

"Well, you look very pretty. You're all dressed already—" Her earnest smile withered in her daughter's shadow and the headache rapped out another warning. "No, Hannah," she almost cried, "you've been absent too much already!"

Suddenly James blocked the doorway. "What's this?" he inquired ominously.

"Oh, Hannah's not feeling well again and wants to stay home," Jenny reported after an uncertain pause. She fumbled with the bacon; it was starting to burn; she hurriedly ripped off a piece of paper towel. Without daring to look at either of them, she sensed her daughter's contemptuous shrug and her husband's impatience.

James heard the shrill note in Jennifer's voice and saw the tension in her shoulders, the same tension he had worked so hard to ease away last night. He placed his hand on her waist and turned sharply to his sulky child. "Hannah, this is getting to be a morning refrain and it's got to stop," he said crisply. "Stop badgering your mother. You are going to school, today and every day."

Jenny sighed and lifted the bacon out of the furious grease, her pleasure in her fulsome, traditional breakfast rapidly diminishing. Parents should, after all, present a united front and if, as James accused, she had been coming between father and daughter, this was the way to mend the gap: not to take sides, to let him handle it. And anyway, he could deal with Hannah so much better than she could. Left to herself, she would have succumbed, ultimately, to such an imperious demand. Now she relaxed a little. It was just another morning.

The day proved as peaceful and bright as Jenny had hoped from her pillow. By keeping busy, by darting here and there and attacking every chore with zest, she sweated out her memories with her headache. By the time she picked up Hannah at school her mood was as sunny as the afternoon, and without thinking about it, she expected her daughter's to be the same. But Hannah heaved into the car like a duck with a broken wing and answered Jenny's gay questions in morose monosyllables. She was no more capable of maintaining a grudge than was her mother, but these glum depressions had much the same effect.

Jennifer gave up attempts at conversation and lost herself to her driving. At that hour, once they had passed over the bridges to the mainland, there was little traffic. It was the kind of early April afternoon that, without promising, suggests spring: when the sky is so cold it freezes everything below into a frozen tableau but the sun is so brilliant that colors are warm and welcoming. No wind anywhere disturbed the stillness. Sky and sea were a dazzling blue with speckles of whitecap and cloud, and even the long black jetties that the towns drafted to protect their beaches from the ocean's incessant greed were somehow gay and, to Jenny, accepting. Not sympathetic, she thought, but accepting. The smooth ride along the water soothed and relieved her, so that soon she had no thoughts at all but a drifting well-being, and since Hannah was distantly quiet, she assumed the landscape had wrought a similar calm in her.

She even rather enjoyed her wait in the doctor's anteroom. She eavesdropped on conversations, added a few rows to her afghan, and answered the nurse's questions about an ailing garden at home. The doctor, she was certain, would make Hannah feel better. She began to tell herself that this evening James would come home early as promised, and they would have time for pre-dinner cocktails in the study and perhaps even take a walk together on the beach, hand in hand—but she found that the least consideration of his homecoming made her stomach palpitate, so she tucked that out of mind and instead planned to have spinach instead of broccoli with the lamb chops.

"Okay, you might as well open your eyes now, Hannah," she heard the doctor conclude, and she imagined him tucking the old-fashioned gold watch that had served as magic wand back into his shirt pocket. A minute later the door opened and Hannah, rolling down her sleeve, walked over to the receptionist to arrange another appointment.

Her daughter's grave good manners made Jenny proud. Tall, poised, her thick earth-red hair belying the patrician bones and demeanor, she seemed older than a teen-ager, awkward in a way that was not adolescent, as if she were too sophisticated an actress to be cast in a juvenile role. She wondered why Hannah worried so much about her appearance, comparing herself so invidiously to Jenny, who was, admittedly, conventionally prettier, but less striking. Appearance is no more than a useful tool, Jenny mused with the disinterest of someone who had never had to worry about her own, and Hannah was certainly attractive enough to accomplish whatever was necessary. True, she was neither fashionable nor beautiful, but fashion is slavish and beauty promiscuous, drawing people equally and unselectively and thus only confusing the possessor. The most fortunate woman is one who looks like what she is. And that, of course, was Hannah's problem. Her appearance would mature with the rest of her; she wasn't finished yet. But how to explain that to such an impatient girl?

She tucked her skeins of wool and needles into her bag and got up to hand Hannah her coat. Adolescence was such a difficult stage, she philosophized to herself, with unbearable moods coming and going for no reason at all, and it must be all the harder for a child as sensitive and searching as Hannah, who must feel things of which her more ordinary mother had no experience or comprehension.

Reassured, then, that she had done her duty in ferrying her troubled offspring to an expert, Jenny settled comfortably into the car, her mind happily elsewhere, and was enjoying a rare complacency until she had to admit that those were indeed tears etching their way down the neighboring cheek. She couldn't help wincing with annoyance, and Hannah instantly, characteristically, sensed the annoyance and went rigid with resentment. A sudden conviction of complete inadequacy brought tears to Jenny's eyes as well. What was it they all wanted from her, what on earth was it they so painfully needed? All she could think to do was ignore the tears and crackling silence in hopes they might just ebb away.

"I'm not going back," Hannah announced.

"Why not, dear? Did the iron shot hurt worse than usual today?"

"The shot! Do you think I care about a stupid pain in my arm? I'm not going back because that man is a fatuous baboon—swaying that brass watch. I know what's causing my headaches: it's all the tension at home. And every time I try to tell him about it he gets nervous and says we should all be understanding because Daddy's having a rough time. Daddy's having a rough time—so the nice man gives Daddy six different prescriptions for sedatives, and then, lo and behold, Daddy has a worse time. I know he's having a rough time, for God's sake, and I understand it all too well for my own good—better than that pill-pushing idiot does, that's for sure. You'd think he was Daddy's lawyer instead of his doctor—!"

Jenny squirmed, again assaulted by conflicting guilts. It would be just like Hannah to blurt out her low opinion of James's doctor at the dinner table. "Well, Hanny," she said slowly, "we don't have too much right to complain, after all, because he is your father's doctor. James went to him first, and I truthfully don't think he expected all of us to follow—"

"That's what you say every time and every time I answer that, since I loathe the man and since Daddy wants to hoard him all to himself, the obvious solution is for me to switch to someone right back home in General's Bay, where you wouldn't even have to drive me."

"I just don't know of anyone there who's as good—" Jennifer's hands grew slick on the wheel. It was so much easier simply to keep doing what you had done before. She didn't know how to find a new doctor.

When they moved, it seemed so simple to follow her husband's lead, and it was simpler to weather his annoyance than to find someone else she could trust with her children. She certainly didn't want responsibility for delivering them into the hands of a crank. "Anyway, though, honey," she sighed, "how did the hypnosis go?"

"Horribly. First of all, he doesn't like me, and I know it. He thinks I'm arrogant and spoiled. He's only willing to put up with me because he needs a guinea pig. But he can't get me to go from an initial dreamy state into a real trance, so he's starting to get impatient. He says it's because I don't fully trust him and won't let go of my self-control—which is absolutely right, I don't and I won't. I'm not about to lose control for one second to some pop-eyed Svengali waving his watch at me, some dunce of a GP who tells me I shouldn't try to read Freud because I'm too young to understand him, by which he means too young to read about sex, and then turns around and says I shouldn't let my father upset me so much because he's just more sensitive and emotional than the rest of us! Christ." To Jennifer's horror, Hannah began to sob, abruptly and harshly, her knuckles white as she dug her fingers into her knees. "Oh shit," she gasped. "Fuck him, I hate him."

Jenny almost braked the car, so intense was her revulsion at the language and the hysteria and her own helplessness in the face of the pain behind them. "Hannah," she blurted, "stop it; stop this melodrama right now; you're driving yourself crazy with it." It was so unfair, she thought miserably, when soon she must begin the long anxious wait for her husband, for which she needed all her strength. Did they think she was a bottomless reservoir? What was it they thought she could do? "Do you think you're the only one I have to worry about?" she asked plaintively.

"I know perfectly well you have other things to worry about, Mother," Hannah snapped back, her face flushed with anger. "That's the point. I'd like you to stop worrying and—oh, damn it, I've said it a hundred times, what's the use—?" She subsided into silent weeping.

To Jenny this seemed appallingly contrived. It had to be. "Get hold of yourself, please," she ordered, her eyes fastened to the road, but Hannah continued to sob, quietly but helplessly. It was obviously incumbent on her mother to say something, but no words at all came to mind, and meanwhile her child's cruel tears rasped her nerves. James would know what to say, she thought guiltily, anyone else would know what to say, and no one else would feel this defensive wrath. What he had said last night must be true: underneath her constant display of solicitude she must be cold, cold and selfish and stupid, a failure as a wife, a mother, and even as a woman.

"Hannah," she said stiffly, "I do realize you're upset. Your father and I agree that you're in too many activities at school. You come home so overtired at night you look like the wrath of God, I swear." They all did. What did the world do to them out there that they all dragged home in tatters, even little Kate? She held up her hand as Hannah went to burst in. "I know last night was wearing, but your father is trying, he really is, and he needs the support of his family more than ever. I just can't think what it is you want from me that makes you behave like this day after day until I—"

"All right, Mother," Hannah interrupted in a suddenly cool monotone reminiscent of James's business voice. "I'll tell you one thing I want, and I'll explain it so even you can grasp it." As if in imitation, she raised her hand to prevent interruption. "Let me finish. It's bad enough that Daddy is drunk or vicious every other night because he hates the life he leads, but it's worse now that you've decided to join him. You were so far gone last night you could hardly talk. Do you realize the pot of boiling water you dropped missed my leg by an inch?—or do you even remember dropping it? Katie is confused out of her wits; she's coming to me to be put to bed." Her voice quavered, but she took a deep breath. "And with every slug of bourbon you dash into the bedroom to add another pin or necklace until you end up looking like—I know Daddy's been back on that tangent about your being cold, but you must know that's to make up for his own—Anyway, I can't stand it." She turned her head miserably and looked out the window.

Jennifer pulled over to the side of the road, though they were only a few blocks from home. When her eyes cleared, she turned to look at her daughter, and the sight of that trembling back filled her with shame. Still, she wasn't sure how to make contact with such a bitterly straight spine. She tentatively touched one shoulder, then, when she felt it shudder like a hurt animal, instinctively pulled Hannah into her arms. With abrupt clarity, as though headlights had switched on in a fog, Jennifer realized that for months she had been trying to keep her husband company in despair by joining him there. When both had finished crying, they simply held one another, mute with pain and powerless love.

3

Hannah jerked awake with a gasp in her mother's demanding grip. "Come down and help me," said Jenny calmly but urgently. "Hurry up, put on your robe."

"What is it?" Hannah asked groggily, her body shivering with excitement and interrupted sleep.

"Just put something on and come downstairs."

Hannah trotted blindly along in her mother's wake to the bathroom, where she stood looking disconcertedly at Jenny's back and listened for sounds of James. Then she saw him. He lay naked on the cold blue tiles, curled around the base of the toilet like a fist around a glass, his head hidden from view. He and the toilet were very white; Jenny was a scrupulous housekeeper. The morning sun filtering through the frosted window made a rectangle around his shoulders. The colorful pills scattered around him sparkled prettily, individually, like the pure dots of primary tones in a pointillist painting. As the sunbeam shifted, the pills and the pieces of broken cup made a bright stained-glass frame. The dog, Matty, shoved past Hannah to snuffle the familiar body curiously.

"Is he dead?" she asked.

"No, I can hear his heart and I found his pulse and he's still breathing. He's cold to the touch, though, and very stiff. I can't move him alone, that's why I woke you up."

"Oh." Hannah couldn't quite grasp the situation. "Uh, I—where do you want to move him to? I mean, don't you think we'd better get him to a hospital?"

"First," Jenny said flatly, "let's get him to the bed."

"You don't think we should call a doctor?"

"We don't know how many he took. I mean, since there are this many pills lying around, it's obvious he didn't take a whole bottle of anything—didn't do it on purpose, in other words. He probably just passed out while he was in here. He was up with insomnia all night—he must have lost track. . . ."

"Oh. But still, if he took enough to pass out on his feet, couldn't that still be dangerous—?" Hannah didn't know what she was supposed to feel, or what she did feel. For an instant, not from anger but from impatience, she had distinctly hoped he was dead; surely things had been moving to a climax, surely this was not just another senseless event in the senseless narrative of her adolescence.

"Help me get him to the bedroom," Jenny said again.

Hannah gingerly approached the body. She looked up for instructions, didn't get any, and grasped the knee joints and pulled, first gently, then as hard as she could in concert with her mother. Nothing budged. He was wedged in the corner and snagged around the porcelain base. The comatose skin was cold, unresilient, and retained the marks of her fingers like a soft plaster cast.

Eventually they were able to free the outstretched arms and head, and when, on their last yank, the entire body bounced backward an inch, they straightened up, panting with accomplishment. The icy tiles had long ago numbed Hannah's feet. She wondered about the temperature of her father's skin, whether rigor mortis moved in gradually, as life ebbed, or whether it politely waited for death to extend the invitation.

"Okay," commanded Jenny, businesslike. "Now I'll try to lift his legs and you take his arms."

His upside down face was the color of frost on frozen meat. When she heaved up his shoulders, his eyes rolled back and opened, puffy and spiked with blood, and his skull separated from his jaw. Inch by inch they worked the heavy, inert mass through the narrow door, tripping over the dog, who thought it was a game and barked when they swore at him. When Hannah had at last jockeyed the shoulders into the hall, she paused to catch her breath, looked up, and was lost in the sleepy blue of her little sister's eyes.

"Is he dead?" Kate asked as she stood there in the doorway, her pajamas on inside out, and groggily rubbed her face.

"No," said Jenny, "just sick. Move back, please."

Working like tugboats with a massive liner, they were able to prod, nudge and yank him most of the way, and with Kate steering his head, which kept obstinately catching on the thick rug, they finally worked him next to the bed. The large master bedroom caught the morning light, and today, even diluted through a few tenacious clouds, pale bars of sunshine streamed between the open blinds. The white curtains swayed slightly in the breeze.

As Hannah's hands grew damp, James's skin began to feel as slippery as wet rubber, as slippery as the bathing-capped heads she used to dunk under the bright opal surface of the fresh-water pool at the Yacht Club; and when she stood up to regain her balance, her vision reeled, and she saw James fall languidly away, tumbling through depths of blue-green water, turning slow-motion somersaults and pirouettes down into the stillness of the underside of water, undulating gracefully, falling, continuously falling, to settle at last, unprotesting, on the iridescent bottom. She sat abruptly on the edge of the bed, and when she brought her hands down from her eyes, was surprised to find them even damper.

"Come on," Jennifer said impatiently. "Let's get him up there. Katie, you too."

"I don't want to touch him."

"Don't be silly."

All three dutifully placed their hands on James's body, and Matty, enthusiastically following their lead, scraped at him with his paw. "Once again," commanded Jenny. "Hannah, get your palms farther under his shoulders, and Katie, you lift his waist this time. All hands in position? Okay, one—two—threeee—!"

To a chorus of groans, the body lunged onto the bed. The rescuers sagged with exhaustion. Clouds moved outside, and the light suddenly exploded against the glass and blinded Hannah until she cupped her palms over her eyes.

"Katie, go draw the curtains, please," said Jenny softly. "I suppose the whole world can see in. I don't know. It seems like maybe he just passed out, like he has before. I don't know. What do you think, Katie?"

"I think you should send him away."

"I don't know—" Jenny's voice trailed off and she disappeared momentarily, then returned with a washcloth, which she folded over his forehead. They all stood over him and watched.

The breeze softly puffed the curtains, and the sun, now strained through the squares of white fabric, shifted back and forth with them, tracing evanescent patterns on James's skin.

"I'll call the doctor and see what he thinks." Jennifer disappeared again, leaving the sisters to keep watch.

"Is he going to die?" asked Kate.

"I don't know."

"Do you want him to?"

When Jenny returned, she was blinking very quickly. "He's sending the rescue squad; he'll meet us at the hospital." She moved toward the closet, hesitated, went to her bureau instead, then clasped her hands and turned to Hannah. "I'm supposed to take a sample of each pill with me. Hannah, will you please put two of each kind in a bottle? Kate, there's no need for you to stay here now. Why don't you go to your room and read until I get home?"

"You mean you're going to leave us?!" Emotion for the first time raised Kate's voice and clenched her fists.

Jennifer's face tightened. "I must go to the hospital to sign papers—"

"I want to go with you!"

"Katie, you can't. I'm sorry, I don't like this any better than you do—"

Katie looked at her wordlessly, then crawled up on the other bed, pulled a blanket to her chin, and watched. Hannah watched her.

"Hannah," said Jennifer tensely, "did you hear what I said about the pills?"

When Hannah walked back to the bathroom, she almost stepped on the pieces of broken glass, and, thinking of barefoot Katie brushing her teeth or Matthew's curious nose, she began to drop the shards, one by one, into the yellow wicker basket. Staring at her hand, she noted with interest a welling drop of blood, and only then realized that she was squeezing the fragments of glass. She felt no sensation; the cold tiles had numbed and anesthetized her.

Concentrating more closely, then, and taking care not to kneel on any hidden splinters, she examined the pills and chose the most perfect specimen of each color and shape to line up on the white toilet seat. Apparently James had broken into Kate's old bottles of vitamins, left from her various allergies, and had probably thrown them on the floor in disgust—translucent eggs of green and yellow, long crimson capsules and orange spheres. Some had bled onto the moist tiles and left a rainbow, which she mopped up with a tissue. She was so hypnotized by this rapt cooperation of hand and eye that she heard the siren for a long time before registering it, and even then the fact that it did not wail past and fade into the distance as sirens do, but instead, screamed to her door and stopped, horrified her. Matthew burst into raucous protest and hurtled from one end of the house to the other.

She dropped her sixteen pills into one of the empty bottles, like miniature Easter eggs in a glass basket, and ran back to the bedroom to slip the container into her mother's pocketbook. Jennifer returned almost at once with two boys, a stretcher, and a disgruntled dog snorting closely in their tracks. Hannah recognized one of the faces as that of a recent graduate from her high school, though she didn't know his name. Without thinking about it, she had assumed that the town's professional rescuers would be old men, retired from business like so many seashore citizens, whose impersonal faces would be seasoned by a half-century of similar experiences, disinterested, benign, wise. Her nameless schoolmate blinked curiously at her but said nothing, then, with his partner, assessed the logistics of moving her father.

"Boy," muttered the other, "the doors on these old houses are pretty narrow and he's pretty big. Make sure you strap him in tight; we're probably gonna have to tilt him around a little."

The team heaved him onto the stretcher, blanketed and strapped him down, grimly took their positions, and lurched forward. By the front hall they were sailing smoothly, led by the graceful back of Jenny, with Hannah, Kate and Matty bringing up the rear, dry-eyed mourners at a ceremony still pending the decision of the corpse.

That night, as Hannah dried the dinner dishes, she watched the dip and sway of the close-branched trees that lined the side of the neighboring house. Poplars, but they had a longer name. Lombardy Poplars, she thought; James would have known. He had explained that they were doomed, each one, for they sent down a taproot much too long for this shallow island soil, and in the next few years they would hit salt water, suck it up unknowingly, and strangle. The sea encouraged transient things, plants that could scratch enough from the surface of the land to blossom quickly, trees that were content to spread across the ground and leave ambitious heights and depths to others.

But for the time being the poplars were oblivious to their fate: a long column of narrow stalks swinging softly with the breezes from the bay. Through the window that her mother had opened to free the steam, Hannah heard them whisper and rustle, bowing back and forth, first toward the sea, then to the land, then back to the sea, and then, when the wind briefly rested, straightening in proud perpendicular to the sky. Together with the pale side of the empty house they bordered, they formed a nave that ran from lawn to lagoon, a nave Hannah had often wandered in search of mewing kittens dropped by independent cats. The faint light from the kitchen, diffused through darkness, touched the white-gray undersides of the damp leaves which were rolling over continuously in the restive air.

Jenny paused as she wiped the last suds from the sink with her towel, and stared meditatively out the windows. The cries of the flocking gulls began to sharpen, resounding over the water, wild keening and harsh croaks: they called to their gathering kin, night hunting.

"Oh," Jenny breathed, "listen! The shiners must be up, the blues must be jumping! And look, the stars are coming out; it must be a full moon. Come on, let's go out and see—!"

Summoning the child, the two women descended to the ground floor, switched on the outdoor lights, took off their shoes, and, hushed with expectation, moved barefoot out along the creaking, salt-corroded surface of the dock. The smell of retreating rain hovered in the air and stars flickered faintly in the heavy sky. The boards underfoot were sticky and slick with rising water. The tide was so high that the sudden flip of a leaping fish sent a wash of foam against their ankles, and they seemed to be standing in the center of the sea.

In the pool of man-made light, the lagoon was as deep and murky green as a liquid forest; close to the surface hundreds of mullet and minnows hung suspended, stunned by the elements and moon-like globe of the lamp, so mesmerized that, when Katie knelt to scoop them up in her hand, they fled only at the touch of her warm fingers. The magic combination of flood tide and full moon, still masked by haze, rendered them indifferent to the hurried schools that usually insured their safety and identity, left them splintered, vulnerable, but oblivious, as if, in the final analysis, ecstasy erased all care, all self.

And swiftly up from underneath came the ravenous snapper-blues, jaws wide with hunger, so that out beyond the edges of lamplight, between black expanses of sky and lagoon, flashed arching spheres of silver, blazing momentarily, churning air and water. The lunges of the great blues came too fast to be more than gleams of brilliance and spinning water, but the shiners, bolting awake at the last moment, shimmered in a glistening fountain as they scattered up and away, and tingled like struck crystal when at last they slapped back into dangerous water again.

Far out in the darkness the fish seemed like streams of newly liberated mercury fleeing the touch of flesh—but flesh came down to meet them as white spheres hurtled from the sky to pluck out the sea creatures with dry claws and carry them back again, up. Despite the danger the blues continued to soar in the whipped water, their scales colorlessly bright, and Hannah imagined they must yearn to see just once with their own eyes the universe that, heretofore, had been no more than a reflection. Until now their lives had been lived at the bottom-most point of the world, but tonight they danced, hurtled, sliced into the air, while cawing gulls, red-eyed with excess, dipped and fell again, and, in the intoxication of mystery and death, sea seemed to meet sky and birds joined the blues in a duet of perfect comprehension: one's tranced death fed another life, and more—bliss.

At last, as they sailed and cavorted, the full circle of the moon emerged to paint fish and fowl the color of itself. Hannah felt she was what they were; she was the land and sky and frozen reflection of the moon. The sea.

"Oh, look, the rain's blown over," said Jennifer, laying a hand on the shoulders of each of her daughters. "Look, the moon's coming out. That means summer can't be far behind."

In the morning, Jenny drove James to a country retreat for the battered affluent, and returned from the trip—exhausted, having been the target of his wrath for hours—to find him on the telephone. The next day she drove back and brought him home again, calmer now in his rage. He reentered his house in taut control and resumed his reign as husband and father, man of reason. Life went on as always.

4

James's too-deep dive into oblivion was never mentioned, never remembered except alone, in dreams. Awakening in a hospital bed he could not leave without his wife's signature had lacerated his pride: he blamed Jenny for turning a private bender into a public humiliation. As always, she chose guilt over conflict and trembled so violently when her daughters mentioned the incident that they too fell silent, confused. It had not been important, she assured them and herself: they made too much of such things.

Hannah became precociously introspective, observant, analytical of the life around her. Intensely curious, she ransacked books of all varieties, movies, magazines, television, anything that might help to explain the underlying despair in her family. Unable to trust the good times that did alternate with the bad, unable to believe that sunny days would last an hour because her parents so desperately insisted they would last through the night, she felt like Cassandra dragged to a prom. She lectured James on the pitfalls of the Protestant Ethic and countless other theories she had gleaned from his library. He agreed with all her generalities and none of her suggestions.

"You and I cannot change the world," he would explain, "and we can't be hermits in the United States of America in 1960. Not that I haven't come about as close as I can. We left Philadelphia, took you out of that fine old Quaker academy and sunk more gold than I care to count in weatherproofing this old summer house, all so I could get as far away as possible from your 'Protestant Ethic.' Also to get your mother out of suburbia, by the way, where she was going batty too, in her quiet fashion. Get her worked up enough, you know, and our Jenny just might start her own revolution, but she knew damn well she didn't want to spend her life being the 'Daughter' of one. And we both had such happy memories of General's Bay—the sun in summer, the quiet in the winter. We figured it was worth the commute. After all, we met in that damned yacht club across the water, two suntanned teen-agers who believed in God and our parents' wisdom and making the world safe for democracy a second time—in togetherness, families. Ah, what well-mannered youngsters we were, what innocents!"

"Yeah," said Hannah unromantically, "the American dream. How angry you must have been when you woke up."

"No, not angry," he said with surprise, for James, the smasher of glass tabletops, the dramatist who clamped murderous hands at his daughters' throats and threatened his wife with upraised fists, claimed to be a man entirely of reason, singularly lacking the emotion of anger. "Not angry; what would be the use of that? No, I had always seen it for what it was, seen my parents for what they were, but I tried to rise above that, to transcend it. When that proved too difficult in the crowded suburbs, we came back here: the ocean seemed an appropriate place for new beginnings. That's why we let my brothers take all that damn furniture after Mother's funeral, you know. We didn't want some mausoleum full of antiques so valuable we'd have to have the police patrol the street if we went away overnight, the way she did."

James had a repertoire of stories, private myths of a kind, which he recited whenever he heard an internal cue, not to inform his listeners—usually family members who knew the words by heart—but to remind himself of the molds in which he sought to pour his life. Some of the stories were borrowed from the past—the Battle of Thermopylae, the conquests of the Khans—others were sifted from his own past. Sometimes he recited Edgar Allan Poe. He spoke fluently and well, stirring an atmosphere rich with whatever emotions he wished to evoke but not analyze, and Hannah imagined him in an earlier world carrying his ballads from campfire to campfire, mesmerizing strangers with their histories.

"So," he went on, "here you are, with your own room, your own bathroom, your own study, even your own telephone, all so you can get away from even your parents if you're of such a mind—but you know as well as I do what's behind that. Money. The money I go back to Philadelphia every day to make, the money your great-grandfather founded the bank to make in the first place. Talk about your Protestant Ethic! Too bad your great-great-grandfather didn't suffer a bit more from it: then he might have hung on to a fraction of his fortune and we'd all be pretty well fixed. You and I could abandon society altogether and revert to a blissful state of nature in Pango Pango, assured of all the pineapples we could want. No, the freedom to be yourself is something you'll always have to look for at home, I'm afraid. I make sacrifices daily that make my teeth grind at night, literally, and I force myself to be hypocritical and conventional in a thousand disagreeable ways, precisely to enable me to afford this pleasant haven by the ocean where I and my three sensitive dependents can lead our own lives in our own way, in privacy. That's not to mention the fact that my brothers would sink the leaky old family treasury in a month if I were ever rat enough to desert it. Do you think you and I could close our eyes to the sight of your cousins and dignified aunts sinking under the waves for the third time? Well, eventually you'll have to learn to conform outwardly and settle for being your own man—or I should say, your own woman—inside."

"But it doesn't work," Hannah blurted. Then, seeing the look on his face, she hastily added, "I mean, it isn't fair. It isn't fair that we should be trapped just because your brothers are incompetent. You could sell your shares in the bank to that other interest that's always trying to buy you out, and then the Erikson clan wouldn't have the power anymore to sink itself, or to sink you. Or us." Hannah was well acquainted with the subtleties on both sides of this debate, but she could always be stirred to argue her own position again with ardor, for she had no doubt where justice lay.

"But then the family business would no longer be a family business. The main puppet string that supports my flailing brothers would be snapped . . . and you and I would have to leave Philadelphia, city of our birth. . . ."

"We have left Philadelphia!"

"No, we have only made a tactical retreat in order to remain. All the gentlemen at the Club continue to respect me as a responsible young man of fine old family who holds a fine old bank together, and they do not have to know that you and I read Marx at home."

"Then you should have opened a bank in California, like Howard," Hannah glumly concluded, referring to a schoolmate of James's who now ran a growing establishment in the shrinking woods around Carmel, where the Eriksons had long ago spent a happy vacation.

"It's hard to 'open' banks these days. And I don't think I would be happy as an innkeeper. Nor, for that matter, was that what Harold intended to be when he set sail for Hollywood to become the American Olivier. Nor is he all that happy even now, having shed first his childhood sweetheart and then her sexy supplanter, and meanwhile bred flocks of children whom he knows mostly as out-of-date snapshots in his wallet—all of whom he must support at great cost. Alimony, you know, has severely altered his attitude toward that hotel which he founded as a lark, a hostel for fellow wayward spirits. Would you like that? For yourself, for me?"

"Not that exactly, no," she admitted reluctantly. "But at least he did try, at least he began to explore. What we have here doesn't work for me either."

"It gets easier as you get older. In one way we did you a disservice bringing you here to a small town, almost literally an island. Jenny and I are grateful to be outsiders, but it's harder on you. When you get to college, you'll meet more interesting people your own age."

Hannah sincerely hoped so. Meanwhile she fantasized. Her childhood dreaminess was transformed into an intense sexual fantasy life, or rather, romantic fantasy life, since it was the characters and situations that made her flesh and emotions tremble. From movies and bad novels she stole the inspiration for hundreds of diverting plots, but whether they took place on Arabian sands or in Greenwich Village, they all contained one essential theme: always there was a cocky and fearless man, something of a rebel himself but a successful one, who would acknowledge with a knowing grin his immediate recognition that she was anything but the cool librarian for whom others mistook her. Perfectly sure of himself and of her, oblivious to her protests, he would strip off the unflattering glasses, hairnets, brogans or whatever, draw a quick intake of breath at the sight of her revealed loveliness, and seduce her there in the library stacks. Or on the sand dunes or the Hollywood set or plantation terrace. Actually, Hannah would willingly strip off the glasses and brogans herself if she could find someone who even then would see what lay underneath—and show it to her. In fact, she did not wear glasses, and she spent even more than the usual adolescent hours leafing through movie and fashion magazines, to the astonishment of her friends, who looked to her to set the example of the rebellious intellectual. She sat by the hour in front of the mirror in hopes of finding just the hairstyle or cosmetic trick that would bring the recognition for which she ached.

But alas, in real life she was not popular, not with boys her own age. Disregarding James's advice, she was outspoken at school, flaunting her contempt for traditional wisdom like a pirate's banner. She declared herself an atheist and refused to read the Bible, declared herself a socialist and refused to salute the flag, remained seated during pep rallies, silent during cheers, and enthusiastically defended homosexuality, Negroes, Communists, condemned prisoners, and any other unpopular cause. With most adults, she was bright, talented, and almost reflexively polite enough to get away with it. And since she had earned a sufficiently imposing reputation from the aptitude tests she waded through every season, as well as from her erratic but impressive efforts in anything that caught her interest, even those teachers who disliked her were chary of penalizing her lest it reflect badly on them. To most of her classmates, however, she was an unwelcome shock, a pretty and self-possessed girl from the right corner of the right side of the tracks who was openly scornful of everything they took for granted. She didn't even know how profoundly she distressed them. When the astonishing rumors starring herself in apparently lurid Technicolor drifted back to her, they flattered as much as unsettled her.

She had had very few dates and those few had been disagreeable. She had accepted them largely to be able to say to herself later that she was not a girl who had never been out at all. Unlike many of her girlfriends, who seemed to have certain rules that they applied democratically to virtually all males, Hannah shuddered at the approach of those she found unappealing. And she found almost all the boys she knew unappealing. It was not their appearances, exactly, that repelled her; it was their depressingly obvious distrust of their own sexuality and of the girls who provoked it. And it was equally obvious how they felt about the formerly nice girls who had provoked and then capitulated to that sexuality. They sneered and flinched and ogled with the same fascination that used to lure Hannah to the window on hot summer mornings when half-naked men came to her part of town to collect the trash.

Of course there were exceptions. The confident way the smartest boy in her class manipulated his slide rule occasionally provoked her interest, but apparently the only chemistry that interested him was inorganic. There was another who was even more unhappy than she, a bright and talented boy who flunked all his subjects, whom only a splotchy complexion kept from being handsome, and she liked to daydream about their being rebels together, she an artist, he a musician, making love in deserted beach homes—perhaps it would clear up his acne. But from his snarls whenever she mentioned Kerouac or Marx or Freud she had to conclude that he was anti-intellectual in earnest. He squinted at her as though she wore a three-piece suit and monocle and might at any moment chase him around the classroom with a yardstick in her hand. He went steady with a nice girl who worked hard at reforming him, whose heart he periodically broke when he dropped her to dally with what he called a pig.

And for all the time James spent in lengthy conversations with Hannah, it was a woman like Jennifer whom he had married, and Hannah believed she had nothing in common with her feminine, compliant mother. When James was weary of philosophy books and debates on nature and society with his daughter, it was Jenny, gracious and gay, whom he sought for rest and an intimacy deeper than words. The seemingly great disparity between her own temperament and her mother's—which Jenny, in her modest and uncertain way, praised and exaggerated—greatly troubled Hannah. She queried James endlessly on the nature of his affections, but he only smiled and claimed that no one could account for such things. As a kind of instant Rorschach test, Hannah often asked people to name their favorite movie stars. James's was Marilyn Monroe.

"Why," Hannah pleaded, desperate for clues.

"Well, it's difficult to verbalize these things," James mused, not much interested in the subject but interested in Hannah's obsession with it. "You know, she's the kind of woman who makes a man want to hold her on his lap and cuddle her. Like a soft little kitten with a bruised paw. You want to take care of her and protect her."

Greedy to be taken care of and protected, Hannah pressed him for details, but without much success. "Is Mother like that?" she asked. "Does she remind you of Marilyn that way?"

"Your mother?" he laughed. "No, Jenny's like most women, I'm afraid: she'd bite the lap that held her. She reminds me more of that girl from the brickmaking family in town—the one, you know, who married the prince of the gambling casino—"

"Grace Kelly?"

"Yes, John B.'s daughter, that's right. But of course your mother's more frisky than that, thank heaven." He leaned back in his chair, sighed, and reopened his book. Movie-star gossip and girls who marry princes were the kind of thing Jenny read to him over coffee in the mornings: they couldn't hold his interest very long.

"But I gather that in real life Marilyn's nothing like she seems on the screen," Hannah insisted. "They say she can be a real bitch, that she drinks too much, and that she wants to be taken seriously as an actress—that she might even be kind of intelligent." Somehow it seemed acutely important that, behind the camera, Marilyn was not always delicious and submissive, or even amiable. Hannah wondered why she wasn't. How could she be unhappy when there were scores of men around to murmur soft things and stroke her till she purred?

James chuckled. "I daresay you're right. Still, in some of those films she is lovely—don't you think so? You go to more of her movies than I do."

Hannah did think so. Marilyn inspired her, too, to put a protective arm around those tremulous shoulders and offer sage advice. She was sweet and entrancing and as graceful as a child, and Hannah didn't belittle her charm; she envied it.

Other people, often with mixed emotions, described Hannah as very strong, and Hannah, sensing the mixed emotions, resented it. Yet she did have to admit that she exerted a kind of power, could influence her friends, even adults, and the influence troubled her: it made her feel masculine. It made her feel lonely, larger than her classmates, larger than her five feet, eight and a half inches, which, as far as she was concerned, was quite large enough.

She yearned for reassurance that she was lovable and pretty, yet when the compliments came, she couldn't absorb them. She was attractive and intense enough to drive them dangerously near capitulation, but she ignored the flattering signs of their temptation and recognized only her failure to evoke the attention she craved, and thus felt all the more unappealing. When adults told her she was striking, that she had the poise, the rather regal air, of a great ship pulling into port, and that she would become increasingly attractive as she got older, she could hardly keep from wincing. The popular girls her age were tiny, boyish, and cute, childishly adorable in their transports of giggles. At least she didn't hunch like so many tall girls: Jenny often praised her carriage. Yet Jennifer herself was delicate and fluid. Hannah's height, like her owlish eyes, wide shoulders and long limbs, came from her father, as if, in the very act of loving a tall and powerful man, Jenny had betrayed her daughter.

For all her dieting, Hannah couldn't shrink or compress herself. She continued to feel as if she were lashed to a bicycle she couldn't steer, careening down the street to howls of derision. Her behavior, every nuance, she could control, but her body gave her away. Yet, very occasionally, she wondered if, much as she stiffened in fear against it, she did not in fact pray for her body to betray her, to give her away in some mysterious fashion she couldn't even understand, much less bring about. What if her body, to which she had always felt so disconnected, turned out to be her last and most desperate hope? She often thought wryly, that the only difference between herself and the proverbial princess entombed in a castle surrounded by thorns, awaiting the prince both strong enough to rescue her and peculiar enough to want to, was that she was not mercifully asleep. She was wide awake, peering through the tower window, petrified that no prince would be interested.

5

So, like many a princess before her, she sought out a man who traditionally would not have been allowed through the castle gate. She had heard of Jinx Hershey long before she met him. General's Bay, so often in those days excluded from the headline problems of distant cities, was almost proud of Jinx, their only glamorous juvenile delinquent. Of course there were the usual number of bad kids, hell-raisers and incipient criminals from negligible families, but they had no flair; they merely slouched through their trite and timeless destinies. Jinx, however, had belonged to a respected and popular family, until an automobile accident rendered him fatherless in kindergarten and cancer orphaned him just before junior high. In grammar school he began earning his reputation, contriving to be suspended for smoking at least once a term while other boys his age still stuttered in front of grown-ups and saved their money for model airplanes. He fought and stole and, when caught, spat out words he couldn't spell. A nearby aunt dutifully took him in after the final tragedy, but she was as incapable of disciplining him as his mother had been from her sickbed.

Jinx was not entirely vicious, but neither was he merely mischievous. He dropped out of high school after a series of violent but unoriginal acts of revolt. Rumor implicated him in more beatings than he had attended, but not all his victims were deserving. He stole, mostly a variety of cars, trucks and tools that were difficult to conceal in a small town, even after repainting. When a black dared to move five blocks beyond the unofficial demarcation line, Jinx was the first to welcome him with sand in his gas tank and rocks through his windows, but fortunately for Hannah's social conscience, she wasn't told about that until near the end of their brief relationship. When Jinx was nineteen, he robbed the gas station where he worked, and that crime, added to his impressive list of juvenile offenses, at last earned him his first serious tenure in the county jail. He was away just slightly less than a year, and was twenty-one when he came home, four years older than Hannah.

Months before his arrival, Hannah, without realizing it, was waiting. The high school buzzed with news of his exploits in and out of jail, and the openness of his rebellion fascinated her. She listened to all the tales and listened as well to the scandalized but impressed tones in which they were told. He had been home for a week when she finally saw him at a Friday-night basketball game. It had to be the renowned Jinx—who else could radiate much excitement? Who else had a presence riveting enough to deflect attention from the game, even among people who had never seen him before? Wherever he happened to stand, or slouch, the crowd eddied around him. He attracted sycophants like a celebrity. From her safe perch in the bleachers, Hannah watched intently as he postured nonchalantly for his court of pals and admirers.

Even weeks later, when she knew him much better, it was still the way he stood, the way he cocked one hip and squinted sideways at a hostile world, that attracted her. He hooked one thumb in his low-slung waistband as if it were a holster and casually fingered the toothpick between his wary lips. Too restless and self-centered to listen to others for long, he never looked at the person speaking to him. Instead his small blue eyes raked the audience, the players, the teachers at the door, the corners of the gym, as if all his life he had been haunted by some ghostly posse that was slowly closing in. His arrogance and indifference were tantalizing: invariably his audience fought all the harder to catch his interest, and the harder they tried, the more contemptuously he ignored them. In the classic style of delinquents of the late fifties, he wore his light brown hair long and elaborately sculpted up from his forehead and neck in whorls and waves that reminded Hannah of carvings on primitive temples. Fortunately his hair was thick and naturally springy, so he needed no grease to mold it in place. His face was innocuously American, boyish and almost pretty except for a faintly weak chin. He wasn't much taller than Hannah herself, and he was very delicately made and lean, though tautly muscular. Hannah always suspected she outweighed him.

His constant, vague distraction, that air of listening to distant hoofbeats, plus the simmering intensity and violence under the aloof pose, lent him an unmistakable sexuality that recalled the movie stars whom he unconsciously imitated. At a distance it was easy for Hannah to romanticize him. Brando and the petulantly appealing James Dean were favorites of hers; if not the most probing critics, they were at least rebels, outsiders like herself. Jinx's thefts and even his preoccupied bragging about past adventures didn't faze her: she interpreted them as nihilistic sabotage against an all-powerful and cruelly complacent society. She savored the charge of excitement in his criminality, his air of power and control in the face of danger. In fact, she shared it: she often shoplifted for the same reason, although, unlike Jinx, she devised elaborate schemes to insure that she wouldn't be caught. She had no desire at all to adopt the role of the nice girl who brings middle-class redemption to the bad but sexy and victimized boy. On the contrary, she wanted to share his feats, vicariously or in fact, and to stand at his side in the face of an outraged community.

He noticed her at the game. It was mysterious to her that the few males whom she wanted to notice her invariably did. She attributed it to luck; it never occurred to her that her own oblique but electric concentration on him might have been the reason. After the final buzzer, with all her nerves attuned to him, she swept past his crowd as though her jeans were a gown, and from the corner of her eyes she saw him turn to watch. She loitered at the door, consciously performing, and chattered nervously with her art teacher, eliciting an assignment to do more drawings for him over the weekend. The adult was puzzled, trying to decipher her unusual mood. He was her favorite teacher and he taught her favorite subject, and the way he liked, respected and laughed at her all at the same time, pleased Hannah enormously. If she could have pried him away from his pleasant wife and four children, she would have infinitely preferred him to Jinx, but though he flirted with her incautiously in public, he managed to resist her in private. That evening they feinted verbally, entranced with their game and it implications, until Hannah grew aware that she was blocking traffic. Then she remembered Jinx, saw that he still was watching, and left to walk home.

Monday, after school, he walked up to her at the front door as if they had agreed to meet. She concealed her surprise and admired his nerve.

"Your name is Hannah Erikson," he mumbled past his toothpick, running his eyes over her torso.

She pressed her books to her coat. "Yours is Charles Hershey, otherwise known as Jinx."

"How'd you know that?"

"You're infamous."

"Infamous—?"

"Known far and wide across the plains—notorious."

"I heard you was smart." He grinned slowly and not pleasantly.

"I've never learned to hide it, I guess."

"Ain't your blonde mother comin' to get you today in that big black shiny Imperial of hers?"

Hannah was taken aback. Who on earth had described her family car to him? Who noticed cars? She shook her head.

"Is she comin' in the little white Corvette?"

"No, my father takes that to work. How do you know about our cars?"

"You mean I ain't gonna get to see your pretty little mother at all today?"

"No." She was annoyed and a little insulted. "You'll have to settle for me."

"I guess that'll do." He grinned broadly and again flicked his eyes along her body.

He walked her home that day and each day for a week, until he took a job at one of the gas stations he hadn't robbed. Then he purchased an old car and drove her home whenever his hours allowed it. She discovered that cars were in fact the central preoccupation of his existence. Their conversation consisted largely of a lethargic monologue from him about cars: cars he noticed, cars he worked on, the insides of cars; carburetors, pistons, plugs—words she had never really heard before. She listened in placid boredom. Occasionally she asked questions about jail, the people he had met there, or about his past, but he replied so hazily that she could scarcely make sense of his descriptions, then veered right back to cars. Day after day he worked on his own car, while she leaned sleepily back on the grass and watched.

He worked in the driveway of his aunt's house, where he continued to live. That was her second surprise. She had expected him to have a bachelor apartment, a wolf's lair, stark and dimly lit. Instead he slept in a sunny room with polka-dot curtains and a white flounced bedspread. On the wall hung a dime-store painting of two cows and a tree. When she giggled at it, attributing it to his querulous aunt, he shrugged. "It's pretty enough, I guess," he said reprovingly. More from curiosity than generosity, she gave him a pencil drawing she had done of a tussock of razor grass on the beach, a study of grays and whites and precise, delicate lines. He grunted in surprise, said it was an odd thing to draw, and never hung it.

He claimed to like the comfort and the cooking at his aunt's and to need the money, but Hannah gradually realized that he also needed a place and person to belong to, even if that person disapproved of him. Indeed, Jinx respected her all the more for her disapproval. Sometimes he boasted of his badness, sometimes flaunted it, sometimes defended it, but he never contested the label itself; he knew he was bad. In his wallet he carried a snapshot of himself embracing his tiny, brittle aunt under a heavily laden Christmas tree. The incongruity made Hannah laugh and shake her head for days, and she chose to keep that picture over a number of more flattering ones. There stood her romantic delinquent in his jeans and undershirt, the wide belt with the massive buckle, pouting toothpick, ornate hair, pointed boots—there he stood with one obedient arm around a scowling little old lady in a print housedress that came to her ankles. Her frowzy head came to his armpit.

In a few years he would probably turn fleshy and puffed from the beer he drank continuously, and, since he had not gone to a dentist from the time he was too strong to be carried in, his teeth would go. It was his youth, his energy, his seething narcissism that lent him such force: with his buddies he was clearly the leader. But even that, Hannah saw, would dissipate with age and continued defeat. Most of his anger was self-hatred. He bore no conscious grudge against society—to the contrary, his prejudices were conservative and violent. If the Army would have taken him despite his record, he'd have gone with enthusiasm. They, he explained wistfully, would have straightened him out.

Had there been a frontier, Hannah thought as she lay on the lawn studying his boots protruding from the car, maybe he would have directed his rage at nature. If there were whaling ships, he might have imprisoned himself at sea and escaped his impulses that way. If there were a war, he might be a hero.

As it was, he and some of his pals and their girls tooled around in their cars at night and occasionally robbed miscellaneous equipment from building sites or the backyards of small shops. Hannah and the girls stood sentry. She knew what a scandal there would be if she were caught, but she didn't expect to be, and they weren't, although the police did stop them often. They threatened Jinx and he snarled back, as the script dictated. He kept intending to buy a motorcycle and Hannah hoped he would. She could already feel the wind in her hair, the power between her legs, his strong leather back against her chest. But he could never save the money.

She realized how incongruous she was at his side and it delighted her.

The moments she liked him best were when he swaggered into the drugstore to meet her at lunch. He would slink through the door as if a camera were moving in for a close-up, flicking a comb cockily through his hair, sucking casually on his omnipresent toothpick. He and a taller, uglier and more muscular sidekick, Fred, would saunter with self-conscious arrogance down the full length of the counter and pause at her stool. As in a movie, the entire line of heads and all the customers elsewhere would turn to gape in fear and outrage. Hannah's girlfriends would sniff and squirm in an excess of disgust. Hannah, dressed in her classic tweed skirt and matching sweater, with her most aristocratic air, would swing coolly around to greet him, inwardly convulsed with mirth and titillation. He could have screwed her there on the stool if he had wanted.

His buddies thought she was attractive but stuck-up, since she rarely spoke in their presence. Her silence was due to shyness, but she did find them charmless; they were necessary, she realized, for the crowd scenes, but they were no more than interchangeable extras to her. The girls, on the other hand, she liked, and she worked hard and successfully to overcome their suspicion. She made no attempt to emulate them, but she studied them with respectful care and admired their brazenness. They wore cheap black skirts molded to their thighs, colorful sweaters over brassieres that shot out their breasts like torpedoes, black-tinted stockings with silvery runners, and shoes pointed like ice picks at toe and heel. Their hair was a blend of man-made colors, back-combed to great dry bushes. With them Hannah was honest and unpretentious. She complained openly about her family's antics, and that particularly won them, for they were fascinated to hear that her family was as chaotic inside that expensive house as theirs were on the front porches of their apartments. And as soon as they could sympathize with her, they liked her.

Rhonda, a skinny girl whose orange hair hung to her waist in lacquered spikes and whose purple sweater protruded past anyone's, was the girlfriend of Jinx's most frequent companion. It was only Fred's charms, invisible to Hannah, that held Rhonda in General's Bay, or so she often proclaimed between loud snaps of her gum. Her teeth were perfect, large and square. Every day she slathered her face with cosmetics, but it was an attractive face, with a lusty, uninhibited grin. She had good bones—even better than Hannah's—and she moved with an appealing swagger, full of greedy challenge. For over a year and a half she had lived in South Philadelphia with relatives—she had even appeared twice on American Bandstand—and her adventures lent her more self-assurance than her friends could muster. She had met Fred when she had come home to visit her mother and get a tan, and had been hanging around ever since just to be with him. She complained frequently of the boredom of being stuck in such a dump, and repeatedly made Fred promise to take her back to Philly, but perhaps they both sensed that Fred could never shine with such luster under the neon lights of the city. His manly silence, infrequently broken by spasms of boasting, rang to better advantage in South Jersey.

Rhonda sometimes met Hannah by the gym door on the rare afternoons when she had no responsibilities to hold her after the dismissal bell. They strode through town together to Jinx's if the boys were home, or window-shopped, or lingered at the drugstore over Cokes. Rhonda talked at the top of her shrill careless voice; her spiky heels clattered like cleats and her hair bounced in one stiff mass. Hannah enjoyed listening to her chatter while the other students and shoppers gawked.

"You know, I think Jinx must really and truly dig you, 'cause he's never stayed faithful to any girl so long that I can remember, and I knew him pretty well before he went to jail and I went to Philly—not that we ever got together *that* way, you understand. We're not each other's type." She glanced deferentially at Hannah. "Frankly, I think he's kind of shocked at his good luck getting such a classy chick, 'cause let's face it, you ain't exactly the kind of thing he usually hangs around with."

Hannah sighed. "To be honest with you, Rhonda, it sort of bothers me that Jinx treats me like a china doll."

"Well—" Rhonda was a little hesitant; she screwed her face in thought, then plunged on. "Well, he says you're the only broad that ever made him come three times in the backseat of a car just dry-docking."

"Oh." Hannah detected a compliment of massive proportions but couldn't quite translate it. "What's dry-docking?"

"Dry fucking—you know!" Rhonda was first shocked at such ignorance, then embarrassed by her own language. "I mean dry intercourse. When you do it with your clothes on. Like for real, you know, except with your clothes on."

Hannah chuckled. "Oh, you mean to say that has a name? And he ejaculates when we do that?"

"Sure. Can't you tell?"

"Not really, to tell you the truth. Usually my head is rammed into the window handle and I'm so busy trying to keep his hands out of my pants, or at least keep my pants up, that I feel more like a wrestler than like I'm swooning in the arms of love. It's not like in books. I suppose it's different for you." Hannah had stared unblinkingly at a drive-in movie screen one long night while Rhonda and Fred fucked furiously in the back seat and roared with laughter as the whole car shook to their rhythm. Jinx had leaned over occasionally to evaluate their performance and give advice. Of course he had tried to persuade Hannah to take a turn, but seemed favorably impressed when she refused.

Rhonda looked suspicious, then realized that the younger girl spoke respectfully, not accusingly. "Oh hell," she said good-naturedly. "I don't like it all that much. Women don't, I don't think."

Hannah was aghast. This was a girl who had carved Fred's initials in her arm and thigh with a razor blade and stained the cuts with iodine and ink. "I mean, it's not so bad. I like some things—like for instance, when he—uh—sucks my breast, if you'll pardon my language—"

"If you ask me one more time to pardon your language, Rhonda, I'll hit you with my chemistry book. Since when is 'breast' a bad word, anyway?"

Rhonda giggled. "Okay. Well, I like that, you know. And when he puts his finger up there, that's exciting sometimes. But screwing is basically for men. They're the ones who need it—they're the ones that hurt like hell otherwise."

"Hurt—?"

"Yeah, you know, or else it gets all blocked up in there. It's really pretty painful." She glanced sideways at Hannah. "That's why you really should jerk them off at least."

"Jerk them off?" It was becoming comical. Her mother's description of the act in answer to her childhood questions had been considerably more erotic than the pragmatic tone of this teen-ager who rocked the car at least twice a day.

"Yeah, with your hand, you know."

"How?"

"Well, you can imagine—" Rhonda glanced around, then made a rapid motion with her hand as if she were milking a cow. A shopkeeper sunning in his doorway ogled her in amazement. "Like that, on his joint, so he can come. Of course, he does come with you anyway, I forgot. So I guess you're okay."

Hannah sighed with relief. The obligation to masturbate as well as listen to Jinx might have proved too much.

"I mean—I don't really think it's right to make love when you're not married anyway. I honestly don't know why I do it. Cause I'm in love with Fred, I guess, and I want to give myself to him. I always mean not to, and I do go to confession almost once a month, although I'm not what you'd call a devout believer. But then I get overcome and do things I know I shouldn't. Carried away by passion."

"Fred's passion?" asked Hannah dryly.

"Yeah, because I love him so." Rhonda's profession of faith shook with an operatic vibrato of which Hannah hadn't imagined her capable. "But then when I see Mom afterward sometimes I feel so ashamed, cause she suspects, even though I lie fit to bust—I mean burst."

"But do you use any kind of birth control?" To ameliorate her monthly cramps, which had so far been even less responsive than her migraines to cure by hypnosis, the despised family doctor had put Hannah on the recently developed pill. She was now very grateful indeed for that, but she couldn't remember very clearly the literature which she had been given at the time, couldn't ask for more information without arousing his suspicion, and was wondering if she should seek some other method as well just to be certain—should she decide, that is, to "wet-dock" with Jinx.

"Oh no. I mean, I douche sometimes, but basically I leave that kind of thing to Fred. I feel like it spoils the romance for a girl to do anything. And like I said, I never really mean to, so I couldn't bear to admit—I guess I'd feel like a slut—Oh good, the boys are here!"

They turned into Jinx's driveway and found the men, as usual, visible only from the waist down, their top halves having blended, like modern centaurs, with the hood of the car. Fred peered out, snail-fashion, and frowned. His whole head, Hannah thought again, had an unsavory luster. His receding yellow hair could not be coaxed into a pompadour or DA, so he daily attempted to paste it in place with handfuls of oil, but after five minutes it once more jutted out like greasy broom bristles from behind his ears. His cheeks were incongruously full and pink and shiny, and his round eyes bulged over them. Hannah had never known him to be other than sullen and mean, though she thought she brought out the worst in him. Perhaps in reaction to the comparatively deferential way Jinx treated Hannah, Fred was unfailingly vicious to Rhonda when he bothered to notice her at all. She shrugged it off or else protested, with an embarrassed glance at Hannah, that he was never like that when they were alone.

When they reached the garage, Rhonda draped herself invitingly over Fred's indifferent back. Hannah positioned herself near Jinx, who greeted her perfunctorily.

"Freddy, let's go the beach, what do you say?" Rhonda said.

Only silence emerged from the hood. Finally Jinx, more amiable, muttered, "Let's not and say we did." He reached for a larger wrench.

"Oh, come on. Pretty please. Pretty pretty please!"

The suggestion startled Hannah. Although it was a bright day in late spring, hot enough to take off their jackets, and although they were only five or six blocks from the ocean, Hannah could not conceive of the four of them on the sand. She walked her dog there almost every clear evening, jogging along the water's edge, watching Matty rout flock after flock of skittish sandpipers and lazy, waddling gulls. Yet that was an entirely separate world, in her mind, from the one where she met these people.

The men allowed themselves to be talked into it. In summer, when, as they put it, crew-cut college jerks crapped up the place, they rarely deigned to go, but now, after a long dreary winter, even they were drawn by the sun. Hannah, however, was uneasy. Her school skirt was hot on her thighs, her stockings were sticky. Her girdle had rolled down into a suffocating belt, the garters were biting her skin, and her whole pelvis felt chapped and itchy. She was unhappily conscious of how small and childlike Rhonda seemed beside her.

Deciding to sacrifice beauty to comfort, she went upstairs to Jinx's bedroom, politely greeting the scowling aunt on the way, and stripped off the damp girdle and nylons. Her moist slip made her tight skirt cling to her legs, but she felt freer. If only the legs themselves weren't the color of week-old snow, if only they weren't so long and muscular. If only they were as shapely as Jennifer's.

They drove the five blocks, then turned and parked a block away to avoid smirching the car with salt or dirt. On this part of the coast, the beach was shallow, gnawed by the ocean, and the town here was more crowded and obtrusive. In summer it swarmed with noisy families clutching melted food, and with pretty young people who came for the seasonal work and play. Here the boardwalk spanned half the beach and cast it in perpetual gloom. At high tide the water sucked deep grooves around the pilings and eddied into whirlpools that lingered when the tide left. Farther up, the ocean washed straight in and broke and splashed underneath the walk, licking the polished white shoes of tourists with spray. The hollow crash of the waves echoed underfoot.

The four of them walked along the rickety planks that the lifeguards laid every summer and the moving earth redirected every winter. Hannah, who had left her shoes in the car, against Jinx's advice about shells and obscure bugs, hopped off into the dirt and began to run in a long heavy tread toward the sea. For the first time all year the sand was hot enough to warm her feet. Suddenly she was blissful. The sea breeze wiped away her clamminess and combed back her hair. Had she been alone, she would have plunged full speed ahead, but, too self-conscious for that, she settled for hopping about in the foam that clung to the lip of the wet sand. Then, to her surprise, she saw Rhonda sprint past in heedless clumsiness, arms outstretched.

"Oh!" Rhonda moaned, "I forgot how good it feels—ah!" She spun in circles until she lurched down on her bottom; she dug her polished fingernails into the crumbly ground. "Mmmmm—!" Deliriously playful, she stretched out her black-stockinged legs and let her head fall back. The salty wind whipped her hair into something like the orange plastic scrubbies used to scour pots, yet, when the hair swept back from her radiant face, she seemed to Hannah quite beautiful. Eyeliner leaked into the creases of skin at the corners, but from a distance that gave her face an Egyptian cast. She rolled happily down the slope, shrieking with laughter, and stopped just in time; when she got up, the back of her skirt was mottled and evidently cold. She swatted it indifferently, amused. Then, to Hannah's amazement and great admiration, she performed an agile cartwheel. Her tight skirt hampered her, so she yanked it up to her crotch and did a whole series, landing finally in a sprawl, breathless, her pink underpants sandy under her garter belt. Hannah clapped with enthusiasm and envy.

"Jesus X Christ, you really are a pig—you know that, you dumb broad?" Fred's face twisted with more than his usual contempt as he and Jinx picked their way toward them, their boots sinking in the drifts. "Shit, what a stinking mess. Will you just look at yourself?" Ostensibly to wipe off the dirt, he walloped Rhonda on the rump with such force that she staggered. She slowly turned around, her face expressionless, and looked at him. He met her eyes in a kind of intimate loathing.

Jinx, in contrast, favored Hannah with one of his rare approving grunts. She turned in confusion to the ocean and wandered in, watching her feet under the spume until the cold surface sliced her calves. Evidently Jinx admired her decorum, but her decorum was precisely what she had hoped he would fight. She lifted her head and plunged out even deeper, deliberately kicking hard enough to wet the edges of her skirt. Only when her legs grew numb did she wade back to shore, and then, still unwilling to go near Fred, she climbed up onto the jetty and found a perch on a flat dry slab rock. It had sucked in heat all day and she smiled, relishing the warmth as it thawed her legs.

Rhonda was playing in the ripples, ignoring Fred. He and Jinx stood well back on the dry sand and glowered. Now and then they cupped their hands over their eyes and squinted out at the horizon. "Pipe down, cow," Fred muttered, although Rhonda hadn't said a word. Sweat now adhered his hair to his skull like melted gum. He had tugged off his undershirt and his white belly sloped out and over the damp waistband of his pants. Jinx didn't look much happier. He frowned vaguely, then also pulled off his shirt; his skin was very pale with a slight peppering of freckles.

Hannah thought they looked oddly vulnerable half-stripped of their uniforms that way. They couldn't swagger in the loose sand, under the broiling sun. She watched them squirm irritably and wonder what to do next. They were not about to sit in the sand; they swatted themselves whenever the breeze blew it against them. Their exposed skin looked as mealy as cottage cheese. Finally they gestured angrily at Rhonda, blaming their discomfort on her whim, and picked their way squeamishly back to the car.

6

That night, her skin still prickly from the beach, Hannah decided to lose her virginity. Bored as usual, the four of them went to the Canteen, a weekend dance for the local teen-agers. Throughout the week Rhonda had been teaching Hannah a South Philadelphia dance, a combination of the Twist and the Limbo. Rather to her surprise, Hannah found she could do these solitary gyrations fairly well, and after a week's practice, she was able to sway backward from a crouch while making suggestive motions with her hands to great effect.

In the middle of the lackluster Canteen, she and Rhonda gleefully caught one another's eye, then, already grinning in anticipation, began to bend backward and undulate as sensuously as they were able to. They danced beside one another, in front of the men, who stood erect and slightly scornful, like idols receiving an offering. Neither of them could dance or would deign to learn, and their impassivity made the women's movements, in contrast, seem more lewd than in fact they were. All around them adolescents began to gape, stand still, and then move in for a closer look, until finally they formed a circle around the dancers. A heady sense of power swept through Hannah; she loosened and took hold of the music, flexing and rippling as naturally as branches sway in the wind.

Abruptly the circle broke. The assistant manager, a girl who had graduated two years before, barged toward them. The dancers coolly swayed upright and observed her through half-closed eyes.

"Obscene!" she stormed. "And the three of you are way over age! Hannah Erikson, you should be ashamed—how can you lower yourself like this?"

Hannah smiled at the pun. Such public outrage amused more than unsettled her, and she knew the expression on her face was serene.

"Well—well!" The girl was speechless with indignation. "Well, you'll just have to leave, that's all. And you're barred for the evening, Hannah."

"Alas," drawled Hannah. The quartet sauntered out, Hannah splendidly aware of the waves of shock they were leaving behind. The front doors were wide open, music and light blared through onto the grass. The night was warm, pulsing with suggestion. The girls exchanged another conspiratorial glance, and then, bursting with exultant energy, once more swooped into their seductive dance. A crowd gathered again. Spotlighted by the outdoor lamp and the bright doorway, Hannah and Rhonda rapturously swooped, shimmied and gyrated through two more records and well into a third before the furious official discovered them.

Smug under the ensuing tirade, they then left. Hannah could hardly contain her euphoria as she settled back into the car beside Jinx. No one else, however, seemed to share her mood. Fred was even more sullen than usual because he had to appear in court early the next morning for yet another speeding ticket and feared losing his license, so Jinx dropped him off with Rhonda. He and Hannah drove on in silence. Since they had nothing to say to one another, these rare times of solitude were awkward.

Rhonda was wrong, and Hannah knew it. Jinx didn't really like her; in fact, he almost disliked her. But he was attracted enough to treat her politely, since he correctly sensed that any other treatment would drive her away. He resented the power she thus had over him, and he expressed his resentment in a heavy teasing that often became snide: he nicknamed her Annie the Owl and asked her repeatedly if she planned to ever stop growing. She heard the hostility and didn't like it, but she was attracted to him too. He was a sharp relief from her perpetual boredom and restlessness. He was decidedly better than nothing.

She had wanted to sleep with him from the beginning. At least, no matter how suspicious he was of her personality, he was attracted to her sheer femaleness, and his reputation, plus his cool, knowing air, reassured her that he was experienced enough to initiate her. But she knew she could never really trust him, and the deference he paid to her respectability oppressed her. Every time she fought him off he liked her better for it. Besides, with her head rammed into the door handle, her feet on the far window, and him grinding his unzipped pelvis into hers until she was bruised, she was hardly aroused. Her reasons for wanting to go all the way were more ideological and hopeful than sensual—although, alone in her room at night, fingering the bruises on her breasts and thighs, she did become moist with vague yearning. And when she saw Jinx at a distance posturing arrogantly, his eyes half closed with the threat of his own power, she flushed with amorphous response. It was the hope of desire, the promise of ecstasy, that led her on. She had been reading and thinking about it for years. She had made up her mind that if, as even Jennifer agreed, sex was good, then it should be just as good without ministerial blessings, which, being an atheist, she didn't believe in anyway. If it was good with love, it would be almost as good without it; and love, alas, was a long time off—too long to wait for. If sex was good for unmarried men, then it would be good for unmarried women as long as they didn't confuse pleasure with love. She was wary but also determined, and she had no conflicts about morality other than a grim awareness that most of the people around her, including Jinx, subscribed to the nasty conventional one. She was also conscious of a blurred but powerful motive of revenge, a murky feeling that connecting herself to someone like Jinx was a way of disconnecting herself from her father, but she attributed that simply to her need to rebel against the environment that had failed her.

After her exhibitionistic dancing at the Canteen she felt more warmth than usual for Jinx. In fact, she felt warm in general: her face was pleasantly flushed from the strong sun on the beach that afternoon. It had been stirring to sway and shimmy that way while he leaned on one hip and smiled down appreciatively, and it had been fun to startle her classmates.

After they dropped off Fred and Rhonda, Jinx drove aimlessly past the construction sites where they made their nocturnal raids, then drifted toward the nearest patch of ground that served as a local lovers' lane. When he switched off the motor, the sudden quiet was striking. He smoked in silence for a few minutes. Hannah waited. A few yards beyond the car, the bay sloshed at the bulkhead.

Finally he cleared his throat uneasily, almost apologetically. "I think Fred and me are gonna ditch this town for a while," he said.

She paused, then asked, "Ditch?"

"Leave. We gotta get the hell out. We've about had it. The cops are breathing so heavy down our necks we can hardly move. They got a goddamn squad car parked around the clock in front of my house, I swear. Shit! It's driving my aunt crazy, you know? She says she feels like she's harboring a criminal or something, and she's driving me bats." He jerked at the stuck ashtray, then lowered the window and gave his cigarette a practiced flick; it spiraled in a white arc through the darkness. "I wish I could take you with me, you know. Rhonnie might come with Fred, I guess, if he lets her. I dunno. I mean, if you wanted to come it would be sort of cool, only you're not eighteen yet, and your parents would—"

"Yes, they certainly would," she said. "When are you leaving?"

"Shit, I dunno. A couple of days, maybe, a week, something like that."

Hannah felt a mild disappointment but a greater relief. Sneaking out had gotten to be a strain. Her parents were growing suspicious. Graduation was fairly soon, and she had been accepted by every school she had applied to and had already decided on Bennington. The fact that she had a future waiting was gradually becoming real. Jinx already belonged to the past.

"Oh, well, that's too bad," she said calmly. "Where will you go?"

He faced her for the first time. Grateful surprise spread almost audibly over his face. "Up to Philly, first off; we got some friends there. And maybe to Chester—there's a lot of guys there, too. And we're talking about heading out to the Coast." He shrugged. "I'll drop you a postcard, you know, and I'll be back when the heat cools some." He mused a moment. "You going to work next year, or you going to some college?"

The clash of their expectations and their sense of one another struck her again. "College."

"You know where yet?"

"New England."

"Hmmm. Well, I could get up there, too. You can't never tell. I always planned to do some travelin'."

She imagined how jarred she would feel if he were to arrive at Bennington. Not that he would. Getting away geographically was the most constant theme in the conversation of Jinx and his friends—breeze through Chicago, then out to the Coast, down to Mexico, maybe up to Canada—but they never got farther than Philadelphia. When he left, they would lose touch instantly. She relaxed a little in the anticipation of being alone again, and warmed to him. "That would be nice," she said politely.

"Yeah. Why you going all the way up there? I figured maybe you'd go to Trenton, or maybe Penn State if you done real good here, which I heard you did."

She brushed her hair back, uncertain how to explain. "This particular place just appealed to me more. They don't have compulsory chapel or football."

"Oh."

They sat in awkward silence a little longer, contemplating their disparate fates. Then he reached for her.

This time, when he crunched her down onto the ripped plastic seat, she found herself somewhat more responsive than usual. Like Rhonda, she enjoyed having him play with her breasts, though it was the glee of revealing something she had been trained to conceal that thrilled her more than his energetic massage—it was like finally sharing a secret and hearing the confidante gasp in admiration. But when he shoved her bra up against her throat, she felt half-strangled and silly. It had never occurred to her to make suggestions: she assumed he had some innate knowledge of these mysteries to which she, wholly ignorant except for the lyricisms of books, must faithfully submit. When he began fumbling toward her crotch again, however, she realized that he was never going to intuit her wishes. She cleared her throat, wiggled her chin free of his clavicle, and forced herself to address the situation. "I want to, Jinx, but not here."

"What do you mean not here?" he panted.

"I'm terrified the police will catch us. They patrol here all the time—you know that—and it's only a few blocks from my house. And most of them know both of us on sight."

He wheezed for a moment and tried to think, his weight making it difficult for her to breathe. "We'd see their headlights."

"It just makes me too panicky. Isn't there anywhere else?"

"You mean it? You really want to?"

She squirmed irritably. "I think I do."

"My aunt's in Camden visiting a girlfriend—"

"You mean we could have your house?"

"Yeah."

"Why didn't you say so before?"

"I didn't think you would—"

"Well, I would." She dragged herself out from under him to a sitting position and squinted at her watch. "It's not even ten yet. Good." She straightened her underwear, pulled down her sweater, buttoned her coat, and tried to comb her hair with her fingers. She felt much better, cooler, far more self-possessed. But the little spurt of hot excitement that had flashed through her had gone.

When they drove past her house, she had an impulse to spare herself having to go through with this, but she sighed resignedly and looked out through the windshield. If she backed out now, she would only regret her cowardice tomorrow. There was nothing waiting for her at home.

Very separate, they stepped out their individual doors, dutifully clasped hands, and stalked up to the house. Hannah wondered indifferently what neighbors were observing them, already eager to report everything to the aunt. Jinx fumbled with the key, then let her into the dark house. Wordlessly they looked around. He switched on one lamp.

"Want a drink?"

"No thank you."

Hannah stalwartly led the way up the stairs to his bedroom, but then she faltered. What came next? She felt as cold and flat as wet sand at night. Her jaw began to tremble with tension; she clenched it resolutely, impatient with herself. She took off her coat, folded it neatly on a chair, and stared at the frilly bedspread.

"Sure you don't want some Seagram's?"

"You know I don't drink," she said, thinking that if she needed to be anesthetized to enjoy sex, the books had lied.

Finally, to her relief, Jinx abruptly pulled her down on the mattress and began to repeat the tussling that was familiar from the car. She was slightly less self-conscious here, and she tried to ease the plank-like rigidity of her spine, but without much success. She tried to deflect her mind from what was happening so that her body could respond autonomously, naturally. The result was that she seemed to be observing herself from a lofty height, interested but not involved. She assumed that he was too preoccupied with her epidermis and his own jagged fight for oxygen to notice, but he muttered something into her shoulder blade.

"Excuse me?" she asked timidly.

"Relax," he groaned. "You're all stiff."

It seemed to go on for hours. He pummeled various parts of her, bit her in jarring places, and in one flurry of haste, knelt above her to tug down his jeans. Hope flashed in her then, but nothing different happened except the feeling of something stiff and damp against her stockinged thigh. Her clothing was wedged up under her chin and wrapped around her knees, making it impossible to shift position or separate her legs. Between her own constraint and that of the fabric, she seemed to be undergoing a process of mumification. The fact that his genitals were exposed somewhere down there did intrigue her. She wanted to see them, but her view consisted only of his shoulders and the dark ceiling. When it dawned on her that her strongest emotion thus far was boredom, she was furious and determined somehow to take a more active part. She began to thump her hips against his as she had instinctively done on previous nights in the backseat. The pleasant rhythmic motion was somewhat relaxing, like calisthenics, and at least gave her a feeling of participation. She hated sprawling under him as passively as a patient on the operating table. When she began to imitate his grinding motion, his breath quickened.

"You're something!" he muttered.

Encouraged and eager for more hints, she tried to lift her torso even more emphatically and earned more approving grunts. With her body thus independently programmed, her mind was free to drift. She wondered about the time and how she would behave when she got home. When was he going to get around to doing it—or had he already? Impatience mounted along with apprehension. This was like waiting in a dentist's chair, neatly bibbed and fastened, straining to hear the soft slap of the rubber-soled shoes that warned of the approaching novocaine injection; dreading it, yet so eager to have it over with.

"Lie still," he instructed hoarsely.

She complied. He began to tug at the coils of clothing, including the panty girdle that still bound her legs. His difficulties embarrassed her, and she pushed herself up to help, straining awkwardly as she doubled over and writhed in the dark. Finally she was free, and she plopped down again moist with humiliation. He crouched over her lower torso, so that all she saw was a black mass hovering purposefully at the far end of her. Then he lurched forward and there was an insistent pain in a place where she had never before felt any clear sensation at all. That was all she felt—a strong pressure and pain. It was not unbearable, but it was hardly what she had expected. She forced herself to breathe regularly and rolled her eyes up to the ceiling and endured. He repositioned himself and the pressure relented, then increased. How did he know where to push? She couldn't have told him. Desolation began to wash over her. This was futile: she had read that some girls had to go to doctors to have the hymen removed. Gradually she grew almost panicky with disappointment; tears pricked her open eyes and drizzled down her cheeks. It hurt and hurt, but what scared her was that she had no sensation at all of opening, no yielding, no new and unprecedented awareness, only sore discomfort. He seemed to be pressing against a solid wall of flesh. It was not much different, she thought bleakly, from having a cucumber rammed in one's navel.

"Relax," he commanded, breathing hard from the effort.

She was grateful for his persistence and sorry to be so much trouble. His breath rasped like invisible machinery. Then, just as she was preparing to thank him for his patience and admit that they might as well give up and go home, he suddenly collapsed on her with a jolting thud.

"Phew!" he gasped. "Well, that's that. You ain't no virgin anymore."

"You mean it?" Her eyes widened with hope.

"Yeah, sure I mean it."

He performed further motions against her thigh that bewildered her until she felt him shudder, then heaved down beside her. They lay in silence for a time, Hannah lost in immensely relieved and increasingly cheerful wonderment. It was done! All at once she was exultant and very eager to be alone to investigate the new soreness. Was she bleeding? It occurred to her that now she might at last be able to use a Tampax. The whole area burned and winced. But the pain pleased her. She grinned proudly at the familiar ceiling and almost leaped to her feet with the energy that was coursing through her.

"Well, girl," he murmured, "you sure was a virgin after all."

"Didn't you believe I was?"

"Well, I dunno; you seemed so sure of yourself, I wondered. But I ain't wondering now. Sure as hell ain't nobody else gotten in down there 'sides me."

The pride in his voice amused her. She felt no obligation to insure his pleasure, since he placed as high a premium on her innocence as everyone else, but on the other hand, she imagined the act itself must have been as much fun for him as ramming a fist into rock-hard ground in winter, so neither did she begrudge him his triumph.

"How come you decided to sleep with me?"

"You're the first person I've really been attracted to," she said truthfully. "And I thought you probably knew what you were doing—since I certainly don't."

"You'll learn. I wish I could take you with me when we leave." He inserted his warm face between her neck and shoulder, plopped one arm over her, and promptly fell asleep.

She twisted her wrist in the dark until her watch face caught the light. It still wasn't very late. She tried to relax and let the night eddy around her, but she was still full of vigor and elation. The little snorts and bubbles of Jinx's breathing against her skin, the banging of doors somewhere on the block, the rattle of insects, the occasional yelp of a lonely dog or human, all seemed unusually abrupt and startling. She tried to concentrate on the warmth of his flushed skin, to conjure up some sentiment or romance, but she felt very little beyond a diffuse fondness. Somewhere in the house, boards creaked of their own accord and the refrigerator burped and ceased to hum, deepening the silence. At last she allowed herself to look at her watch again.

"Jinx," she whispered. Then more firmly: "Jinx." She wriggled her shoulder.

He sat up like a dazed little boy, rubbing his eyes. His naked and rather thin legs gleamed colorlessly. She had a piercing sense, suddenly, of how frail he really was, and an almost impersonal tenderness stabbed her.

"I hope there isn't any blood on the bedspread," she said dryly, thinking with irony of those pristine flounces.

"Uh," he grunted, still rubbing his face. "I hope not, but I'm always getting myself cut up, so if there is, I'll just tell her I was in some fight or something." His serious concern for his aunt's opinion always disconcerted her. "I guess I oughta take you home. Will I see you tomorrow? I gotta work till seven, but then I could pick you up—?"

"Sure. When does your aunt get home?"

"Sunday." He ducked his head pensively, then blurted: "We could come back here if you wanted." His face brightened with hope.

"Sure. That's what I meant." She raised her eyebrows. The increased solicitude and uncertainty in his voice intrigued her.

It embarrassed her to dress in front of him. She retreated into the bathroom to shimmy into her girdle and pull up her stockings. Then, almost bashfully, she switched on the light. She looked very pale and disheveled, with deep gray shadows under her eyes. But after she combed her hair and rubbed off the mascara that had smeared, she was disappointed that she didn't somehow seem more changed. This was the event that supposedly made her a woman, but she looked the same.

When she came out, he was perched on the edge of the rumpled bed. She couldn't see any stains. Diffidently she sat beside him and regarded his profile. The strangeness of being here with him made her inward and aloof. An unexpected conviction of power wafted through her, a feeling of invulnerability and complete separateness. She wondered if she was capable of deliberate cruelty, and the thought pleased her.

Then he startled her by wheeling abruptly to grab her again. She flinched back instinctively, then composed herself and endured the passionate embrace, opening her eyes to study his white forehead and wavy hair. His eyes were closed as chastely as those of little boys in advertisements for church, and, watching him curiously, she had the same sensation that used to fascinate her when she peeked while the rest of the family were saying grace. He tried to press her back onto the bed, groping at her sweater again.

"No," she said firmly, trying to smile with enough warmth to mitigate her determination. "It's late."

"I'll really see you again tomorrow?"

"Of course."

When they parked in front of her house, he again engulfed her in one clutch, but she was able to open the door while he worked his mouth against hers, and as soon as he took a breath, she darted out.

"Good-bye," she chirped. "See you at seven."

Alone at last, she thought happily, pleased with the bruised throb that pulsed as she moved. The dog was barking welcome in the living room, which probably meant that Jenny was waiting up. At the doorway, Hannah greeted the wagging Matty with prolonged affection while peering over his head at her mother, who sat in the farthermost armchair, dressed in her flowered granny gown, leafing groggily through the week's magazines. Except for the pale circle cast by her reading lamp, the room and the rest of the house were dark and still.

"Hello, dear," Jennifer sleepily whispered, squinting up at her. "Have a good time?"

"Uh huh," nodded Hannah. "We went to the Canteen, then out for hamburgers."

"That sounds nice." In her most characteristic gesture, Jenny vaguely began to straighten the fat pile of newspapers and periodicals on the large footstool by her bare feet. Her hair was rolled into a pink plastic crown around her head, and her pretty face gleamed as she bent over in the lamplight. She smelled, Hannah knew, of washed flannel and cold cream. It was good to see her waiting there, scarcely conscious at this hour, patiently waiting to gather her entire family before going off to sleep. Hannah was tempted to sit on the opposite couch, lean comfortably into the nest of throw pillows, and describe the entire night to Jenny, just as she always told her about every school day as soon as she dumped her books and kicked off her shoes. For one sharp instant she yearned to tumble heedlessly into that cottony lap, to huddle there, to weep, to feel someone's arms around her. But, of course, that was impossible.

"How's Daddy?" she asked instead.

"Oh, he's fine. Things have been so much better since all the changes we made after Easter. We had a nice evening tonight."

Hannah was disappointed. Had James been troublesome, Jenny would be more awake and open, eager to share the details of her own evening, and afterward Hannah might have been able to take her turn. It was curious, Hannah thought, that only pain and conflict could press her mother into awareness. Left alone, she might sleepwalk through decades. And yet, at the same time, the very serenity of that sleepwalking, the fact that Jenny was never vindictive, never even regretful, was perhaps what enabled them all to keep going as they did. Sometimes she seemed a dreamy amnesiac, who kept taking them by the hand and leading them back together, back into touch, time after time, by the power of her sheer, blind, faith.

So Hannah did and said the usual things and once more felt as if she were acting in a movie until she finally headed upstairs. There, alone in her private room, she could at last undress in slow wonder. With a warm washcloth she gently patted the tender flesh that was still mysterious to her, still latent, hidden from her eyes. To her disappointment she found no blood until she probed as deep as possible, and then only a spot. Still, this was the first time she had ever had any real sense of there being anything there amid those folds of rosy skin that had stared opaquely back from so many awkwardly held hand mirrors. She shrugged bemusedly. So that was where it—she—was. Well, though hardly a dramatic moment, or even a proper trauma, it was progress of a sort, she supposed.

Pleased, she wiped off her eyeliner and climbed into bed. Matty heaved up to join her, and she hugged and stroked him with lonely intensity until he moaned in bliss. Tired but not sleepy she gazed through the open windows that lined two of her walls. Up here on the third floor the old structure caught the full sway of the sea winds. Outside, a little below where she lay, the columns of neighboring poplars gently rustled and creaked, swishing their branches against the empty house. The dog groaned with happiness and stretched out to offer his belly. The breeze ballooned the pink curtains along the walls, then inhaled and sucked the fabric back against the wood with a snap. Behind the house the water shifted and cooled the air. Hannah fell asleep gradually, peacefully, and slept dreamlessly into the next afternoon.

7

The following days and nights blended into a mixture of frustration and excitement. She moved through Saturday afternoon in a shiver of expectation, washed her hair, took out her clothes hours beforehand, and walked the dog aimlessly on the beach in hopes that the ocean's eternal restlessness might put her own in proportion. When Jinx picked her up, he surprised her by being alone. They went straight to his house, stiff with mutual shyness. As he walked up to the door in front of her, she admired his languid gait, the wary confidence of his body. The way he cocked his head as he turned to usher her in burned her. She wanted him until the moment when he actually pulled her down to the bed with him, then went cold and hard. And she didn't know why.

She did get some pleasure from his enjoyment of her, his breathy raptures, but she felt like metal cast in the shape of a goddess. He worshiped the form that had been engraved upon her, but within, just beneath the contours, she remained untouched. Even while she undulated rhythmically to accommodate him, she huddled somewhere within herself, waiting in bored patience. Sometimes, as when he grabbed her hungrily and made her eyes widen in pain, she surfaced into pleasure, but soon she fell back again, cool.

He would have been content—in fact, he would have preferred—not actually to have intercourse. He would have been satisfied to thrash about on his aunt's couch for hours. But Hannah was adamant. It was education and adventure she wanted, not this dull slurping and jabbing. So that night and every afternoon that they could manage, and every school night that she could sneak away, whether in the house or in the depths of the Jersey woods, she insisted that he enter her. At least that got it over with. The pain eventually lessened, but intercourse was always uncomfortable, and the worst of it was, all she felt was a dull pressure, nothing more. She was curious and acquiescent, retreating into herself like a guinea pig charting its own sensations, and her chart was largely blank. Not that she blamed Jinx, who had begun to offer a shy tenderness; she assumed he was doing all one could. Nor did she blame herself. She just kept experimenting, taking a rather scientific attitude, assuming that in time something would happen.

He took a wearing time to get to the point of shuddering, splurting against her thigh and going limp, but she had nothing better to do. They had nothing to say, nothing in common until he overpowered them both with his ardor, and they were still awkwardly shy. Afterward, when he was thoroughly spent, they could at least lie comfortably, wrapped together in happy silence, enjoying the curious pleasure of intimacy with a stranger.

They even talked a little then. He told her, under her probing, that his dream was to live someday in a white house, surrounded by a green yard, enclosed by a white picket fence with rosebushes growing over it, and to have a son who would be good in school, respectable, play football even. Maybe he would like to have a gas station of his own if he ever had the patience to keep at something more than a month at a time. None of the ironies escaped Hannah, but sometimes, lying in his muscular arms, she could view that daydream with a certain sensual tolerance. She vaguely envisioned that she would get pregnant and marry him and ride through the twilight on the back of the cycle he couldn't afford, home to a clean bed in a house bathed in the scent of roses. But she knew that she wanted to go to college, and if she did get pregnant, her parents would arrange an abortion.

She liked, too, to explore him. It embarrassed but pleased him that by the car light or the moonlight or a candle brought from his aunt's kitchen, she would sit dazed by his hips and admire the pale foreign symmetry of his body. His penis fascinated her. It was so ludicrous and yet so magical in its metamorphosis, so comically stalwart in her hand. His testicles were amazing. She had expected plums or little moons, not this tender pouch of raw chicken skin. Laughing at herself, she confessed to him that she had dimly expected that he would look just like herself plus his male equipment. The fact that he had no holes, no grooves, no flaps or recesses at all, just clear skin as firm as a cheekbone, was a wonder to her. She smiled shyly and told him that she wished she could take this part of him home with her to scrutinize and puzzle over in private.

She treasured those times, and they grew fond of one another as strangers do who experience some natural phenomenon, like a blizzard, that temporarily disorients them. He lost much of his suspicion of her, at least when they were alone and naked, and he came to tell her that he loved her and wanted to marry her someday far in the future. With careful precision she did not say that she loved him, but she did say that she, too, daydreamed of marriage, and he, who did not understand her at all, was satisfied.

For ten days she was distracted and delightedly nervous when she was apart from him, bored or content when lying at his side. The brief time they spent clothed, upright, or with other people, she viewed as wasted. She spent all her time apart from him calculating how to see him sooner or describing her adventures to her friends.

He quit his job because he was frustrated, vexed, and Fred was eager to leave for the city. But Jinx kept postponing the departure, partly to stay with Hannah, largely because it was his style never to commit himself to any idea, any plan, any action beyond the present. Hannah knew he was afraid to leave; he had lived in General's Bay or in jail all his life, and he could see nothing in the future or in the distance that really drew him. He harbored a strong wish to change, to grow, but he had no idea at all how to go about it. Hannah sensed his thwarted yearnings and terror of failure, how bottled up he was, near to explosion. But his explosions were all either inward and destructive, tearing himself apart, or they provoked outside forces into bottling him up even more effectively—jailing him. He knew he was near to bursting again, that he had to leave the pressure of General's Bay that was closing around him each day, but in his unfocused way he also knew that escape was futile, just a postponement of a fate he sensed and dreaded. And Hannah was relief to him; he found surcease and hopeful rest in moments with her: there was so much about her that embodied the highest reaches of his hopes. If he had been a girl and she a boy, he would have looked to her to marry and rescue him. As it was, his hope was unadmitted but present, a little wince toward an impossible alternative, like a hounded fox who sees a forest full of hiding places across one narrow but unbridgeable chasm. It all combined to hold him in mute stubbornness against Fred's very practical pressure.

His plight saddened Hannah. She realized that he did have a certain force and intelligence that set him apart from his cronies and made him a lonely and poignant leader—a leader who didn't know where to go. But she could see nothing to help him; certainly she had no faith in rosebushes and white picket fences. Even if he could achieve them, they would merely be a harness for his diffuse energy, and she doubted he would be much happier in harness. She hoped he would find a nice girl to marry, the nice girl he dreamed of to submit to him and mother him, but meanwhile his sentimental respect for her was becoming oppressive. She, after all, had looked to him for release. After ten days she began to feel stifled.

Then her parents discovered her web of lies and reacted with outrage and drama, enough drama to revivify her flagging romance. She had lied about her boyfriend's identity, and when they discovered who he was they were appalled. She had cut school two successive afternoons when his aunt was working the noon shift, and had claimed to be at a girlfriend's on innumerable school nights to escape the house.

James was perturbed over the ornate and uncontrite deceptions. Hannah had actually rather enjoyed the acting and the inventiveness it required, and refused to claim to be sorry. She was sorry about the necessity for lying, she said, but surely, if she had told the truth, they would have forbidden her to see Jinx, and she did want to see him. To her it was simple, a battle of wills. James took her for long boat rides and discussed the place of contracts in the human condition, discussed the relation of honor and self-respect to keeping one's word, discussed the historical meaning of trust and truth—then, when she stole out again and was again caught, threatened to imprison her in a boarding school for wayward girls. She said it was a matter of power and respect: she saw that her father had the power, but she didn't respect his right to it, so she had resorted to subterfuge and would do so again. Finally, after a tirade in which he accused her of subhuman deceitfulness, she wept and declaimed that the only safety she had ever known was in Jinx's arms, and somehow, through her tears, it felt true. Jinx became very precious to her then.

James calmed down, as always, and when they were both too exhausted to fight, they discussed it a little. She realized with disappointment and a snort of self-derision that James really didn't care very much about the issue of virginity after all. He shrugged as if to say that he regretted it had come so early, but it wasn't of much importance, just another dashed expectation for him to assimilate. He hugged and patted her as she wept, and murmured that he knew it was hard, then wandered off alone to cope with his own despair.

It was Jenny, for once, who provoked the real conflict. It was Jenny who prodded James until he blazed at Hannah, not for her actions but because she was the source of her mother's frenzy. He didn't really know what he thought of his daughter's adventuring. Probably it was unfortunate, but mostly he wished his wife had not found out. Without warning, Jenny would turn on her daughter with unprecedented ferocity, and Hannah was flabbergasted. She was not, however, chastened.

Again and again Jennifer trailed Hannah even as far as her bedroom to vent her indignation. "A boy like that only goes out with a girl for one reason!" she shrilled, red-faced and beside herself.

Hannah observed her incredulously. She had never seen her mother this furious, not even at James, not even after his surely more cruel and personal betrayals. Why was this incident the sole issue on which Jenny was prepared to make a completely self-righteous stand and for once wield her parenthood?

"You know what he wants and you're probably giving it to him—there's only one thing he could want from a girl like you—"

"Well, I'll tell you, Mother," said Hannah with all the calm she could muster, "there's only one thing I want from him, too—a girl like me is only attracted to a boy like that for one reason."

Jenny visibly paled, then flushed, then took a trembling step nearer her daughter, unable to speak, fists clenched with passion. Hannah drew back, more in disbelief than fear; she didn't really expect her mother to retaliate physically. But to her shock, Jenny suddenly hurtled forward and slapped her across the face, knocking her backward onto the bed. Hannah was too stunned for a moment to do more than stare up, hand to her cheek. To her disgust, tears of hurt and outrage began to trickle over her hand; she tried to choke them back. Jennifer was obviously aghast at her own action too, but not sorry.

With furious dignity, Hannah rose as haughtily as she could and confronted her mother eye to eye. "Well, I'm sorry to see you're going so berserk that you have to resort to violence," she said shakily.

Jenny's whole arm lashed out and belted Hannah again, much harder this time, but this time Hannah didn't budge. She instantly slapped Jenny back.

The two aroused women stared at each other, quivering. Then Jennifer's eyes ran angrily over her daughter's tall night-gowned body and focused on her chest. Before Hannah had time to respond, Jenny ripped open the translucent fabric—and tried to sneer but was too appalled. Hannah's firm breasts were bruised around the nipple and sides. The rose and lavender marks, tender but not bothersome, had acutally pleased Hannah and reminded her of the colors on the under-curves of seashells. She liked to feel them wince under her prim school clothes.

"Never," her mother choked, "never has my husband done anything that ugly to me!" She hissed with repulsion. "Not even my husband, much less—"

"Too bad for you, Mother. You should suggest it to him sometime."

Hannah was able to duck the halfhearted blow, and Jenny crumpled to the bed in momentary paralysis and began to cry. Hannah watched pitilessly.

"Should we get a referee up here, Mother, or is the fistfight over?"

"What did I do wrong—?" Jenny wept. "I did try—I always thought we could talk—"

"For Christ's sake!!—I hereby absolve you of all responsibility for my appetites and my future—do you want it in writing?!" Hannah too coughed and threatened to break down, but a last spasm of self-control saved her pride.

Jennifer left then, but she returned again and again to renew the assault, triggered by some internal combustion that was invisible to her daughter. Such persistence from a woman who ordinarily suppressed memories of far graver crises amazed and upset Hannah, but it only spurred her into greater determination to have her own way. The conflict between the women took weeks to abate.

8

Hannah continued, with renewed excitement, to go out to meet Jinx whenever she saw a chance. She invented a volley of excuses and subterfuges and shamelessly fled, now truly finding her only peace and affection in Jinx's arms. She allowed scenes from *Romeo and Juliet* and *West Side Story* to waft through her imagination as she tumbled half naked in his bed or car or in the sand, and her anticipation of her parents' grief when they found her dead in her lover's arms, more serene than in her tormented life, was keen. She saw her mother's despair as she brushed a strand of seaweed from that soft young cheek, and her father's agony as he turned away from his daughter's eternally open, unaccusing eyes, and she hugged herself with satisfaction.

The headiest times for her were the long forays down alleys and side streets to meet him, or the long journeys back home when she sweated with apprehension at what was coming and pride at what had just been. Even if it was fear, so much compelling emotion was wonderful, a kind of delirium of being alive and beside herself. The tension heightened all other sensations as well, until the whole world moved at the rate of her speeding pulse. It was much like the adventure of shoplifting. After so many morose years of lethargy and tedium, this was ecstasy. The sight of Jinx leaning casually against the concrete wall at the end of the alley, his hips cocked and his eyes intimately cool, was enough to make her collapse in his arms with admiration, relief and lust. But it was a lust of the nerves and the eyes, and she was still helpless to extend it to the rest of herself. Sometimes she suspected that the delicious, breathtaking thrill itself rendered her all the more unresponsive to Jinx's actual presence. The blunt fact of his embrace was necessarily a letdown. She saw that her agitation inspired him to passion, making him gasp compliments and exclamations, but as his lust grew, hers faded. She wanted him with her eyes and nerves, that was all.

Yet the extremes to which she drove herself were seductive and addictive. She cut school with abandon in order to meet him and was far too distracted to care whether anyone doubted her succession of forged notes and faked telephone calls. She would wait in the schoolyard until her mother's car was out of sight, then slink away under the cover of more cars and arriving crowds, appearing too poised and cool to attract suspicion as she charted her route down little-used streets and alleys. Those walks across town on school-day mornings in the spring, when she was deliberately and happily duplicitous, a genteel teen-age girl striding to her waiting lover through the pure blue sunlight, smiling cheerfully at shopkeepers, self-possessed, were the most acutely alive stretches of time she had ever experienced. The exhilaration she felt then was worth anything to her, any risk. Colors vibrated; she was drugged with her own intensity. She understood why spies and thieves might love their work.

If Jinx himself was an anticlimax, he was valuable all the same because without him she would have nothing to whip her into such nervous raptures. Away from him, stewing alone at home on the third floor, pacing out onto the sun porch to see the bay and half the town, she treasured him. He had the power to elicit these feelings in her; he was adventure. He was certainly a release from the monotony and purposelessness of her high-school years, and from the deadened moods of fatigue and fantasy that were her reactions to her father's despair. This rebellion over Jinx gave her the first hours since childhood when both her passions and her mind were intently, dizzyingly, happily engaged. Thanks to him, she could overwhelm herself.

Yet, at the same time, she was glad he was leaving, and every time he postponed his departure, she frowned inwardly. The rest he gave her was sweet but very shallow, and it was more than outweighed by the tension. Her flesh drew closer to the bone; her face was pale, nearly translucent, and the lacework of blood glimmered through under her eyes and cheekbones. Her hair was more lackluster every day. Her eyes, surrounded by deepening shadow, loomed larger and larger in her drained face: they didn't seem to blink. Sleep was impossible. Her heart quickened the moment she turned off the light; her inner eyes flickered and jumped until she would have to stare out her windows into the darkness to comfort herself. She would get up and wander out onto the porch in her sheer gown, the shingled floor rough and cold under her bare feet, hoping to find some company in the dissatisfied breezes that creaked the rusty weather vane to and fro. The dog would follow and sink his wet nose worriedly into her hot palm. Finally, hours later, exhaustion would stun her into some rest, only to be interrupted by the alarm and Jenny's cheerful greeting. She would drag herself out of bed even more worn and tense than the day before.

The conflict with her parents was wearing her down. She sharpened her nerves to the fine point of a pencil, then drove and blunted herself against their unyielding opposition, then ground herself down to another point, each time diminishing. Nothing replenished her energy; only her will kept her going. She burst into inexplicable tears the minute she was alone and had to fight them back in public. She closed doors on her fingers, grew increasingly forgetful of details, and gagged over the meals she had hungered for a minute earlier.

He decided to leave Saturday. Friday afternoon she took a girlfriend home to dinner and had Jenny drive them afterward to the Canteen, explaining that she was going to spend the night at her friend's house. At the dance she spent twenty cautious minutes of outward calm, chattering and twisting with her girlfriends, before she fled back into the cool night air. Summer was coming. Moldering clams and seaweed and brooding storms came to her on the wind and aroused her with familiar need. Dissatisfied girls shouldn't live by the ocean, she told herself.

She wrapped her sweater closer around her thin dress, feeling the wool grow damp, and padded down the driveway of an empty summer house to reach the alley. She felt entirely alone, cut off from everyone, isolated in the starless night and close salty air. She trembled, taut with expectation. In such a mood it was important to keep moving, so she began first to stride, then to run, to fling herself down the concrete path and across the streets. Many of the homes she dashed past were still vacant and locked; others buzzed faintly with family voices. Lamps glowed behind curtains that shifted a little in the wind, making shadows sway on the alley pavement. Some rooms were eerily dark except for a cold blue light, and sounds of television drifted from them. Hannah hurried by softly in her thin summer pumps. When her heart began to thud, she pulled up to a quick walk, then ran again as soon as she could breathe. At last she turned into the alley of one of the main streets, scampered half a block, then, her throat raw from gasping, knocked gently on a back door. It opened at once.

"Did she go?" Hannah whispered, still panting.

"Yeah, she went all right, suitcase and all. Damn thing weighed a ton. You look like you could use a drink."

"No." She stepped in, shivering, and ducked against his firm, upright body. Dress, underwear, skin, hair, eyelashes: everything was damp with sweat and condensed moisture from the saturated air. He pressed her close, mistaking her agitation for regret at his leaving.

"I'll come back and see you for sure," he soothed. "This isn't the end."

It was, though. Hannah groaned inarticulately and thrust herself against him like a demanding cat. She hated these moments of talk, of clothing, of formality, of overhead lights and mutual scrutiny. Not that she was any less separate in bed, sharing his perspiration, but there at least she was alone with her own sensations.

"Not in the kitchen," he chuckled. "C'mon."

They advanced hand in hand to the bedroom and spent a tender night, a mixture of gentle fumbling and prolonged passion on his part. Hannah was curious, interested, and glad to be here rather than elsewhere. Long past midnight they returned to the kitchen to snack. Hannah wrapped herself in a shiny blue and black striped robe of his that was almost too small for her, and Jinx pulled on his jeans. She liked this time best, when they were physically at ease with one another and past the need for preliminary talk. Despite the ceiling light's cold reflection on metal and tile surfaces and the icy touch of the counter top under her thighs, the ritual had some of the warmth of a picnic in the sand. She liked watching him scrounge in the icebox for lettuce, bread, bologna, peanut butter, beer for himself and milk for her. His aunt didn't keep much food on hand. And Hannah, although she was suddenly hungry, forced herself to eat skimpily and daintily, as though it were a tea party. He teased her about her pickiness, but it clearly pleased him, as further evidence of her refinement.

Hannah felt self-conscious in the blunt glare of the overhead bulb. The sleazy robe made her legs seem the color of the packaged bread. When Jinx was not preoccupied with her, he scarcely noticed her—though he no longer teased her suspiciously. On the other hand, she didn't know what other reaction she might have wanted: certainly not conversation. He was considerate and even affectionate in his stifled way. Bemused, she tried inconspicuously to scratch her chapped thigh and noticed that her legs were clamped together and her arms tucked as primly over her lap as if she were wearing white gloves and high heels. She forced herself to sprawl a little, as if she were at home reading, then she sighed and cheered up at the thought that tomorrow he would be gone and she could paste this memory neatly in the past. She would have spent the night with a man, would have munched peanut-butter sandwiches in his kitchen, dressed in his robe, before she was even eighteen. At least she had attained one of her ambitions. She contemplated Jinx as proudly as a hunter contemplates the pheasant he plans to stuff, already anticipating his memory.

Determined to make their last night worth remembering, they didn't fall asleep until shortly before dawn, and they both awakened again after only an hour or two, their skin burning dryly under a sticky glaze of perspiration. Sated with so much impersonal intimacy, she asked him to take her for a ride. He was surprised but glad, obviously as irritated as she was and equally happy to escape the house. Her face was bleached and her madras shirtwaist was still crumpled and moist from last evening's race down the alleys. He was drained too: his eyes bloodshot, his hair faintly oily with fatigue.

The day was going to be hot. The pale haze of early morning, like the beach some weeks before, seemed incongruous against Jinx's belligerent uniform of jeans, undershirt, and black boots: it highlighted his youth and defensiveness; he looked out of place, lost. She took his hand, and smiled as she felt the gaudy ring that his aunt had given him one Christmas and that he had not removed since, even in bed.

"Shit, it's so damp you might as well be in the fucking water," he complained. For all his claims to like boats and fishing, Jinx would not learn to swim and insisted that he loathed the feel of salt water. Occasionally he would visit one of the motels and wade in their chlorine pool. "It'll be good to get away from this shitty town."

Over his shoulder, Hannah noticed his aunt's neighbor, another elderly woman, with a protruding muzzle that made her look as though she had been peering out of holes like a groundhog for years. She glared at them from behind a gauzy kitchen curtain, then hastily drew back when Hannah nodded politely to her.

"There's your neighbor," she mentioned.

"Old bitch. She'll tell my aunt. Good thing I'm leaving, or that old bitch'd be on my neck for days."

"Which old bitch?"

"Both of 'em."

It felt good to sit next to him while he drove. It was the thing he did best, the only thing he did with perfect ease. He sped, but she trusted him. His reflexes were relaxed and concentrated at once, and she admired his casual mastery. The hour was too early for much traffic besides milkmen and a few farmers bringing fresh produce to the markets in town, and after they crossed the long straight bridge that ran over the narrowest joint of the ocean and the patches of marshy grass and opal lakes, they headed inland and had the back country roads to themselves.

Jersey landscape, so stubby and scrawny and flat, satisfied Hannah far more deeply than any panoramic view. This was ground meant for walking, for foraging, for animals of all sorts; it was land that invited all the senses to browse, not just the eyes. The underbrush was almost as tall as the scrub-pine forests, as dense as her own hair and almost the same hues. The gnarled trees that thrive in soil so near the sea joined hands like slow, primitive dancers. The bracken was misty green in the close air, and the forest, massed behind, was darker. At intervals, pools gleamed between stretches of green: narrow rills and rain-sopped puddles glistening behind the brown verticals of trunks.

Abruptly the woodland yielded altogether to acres of swaying tall grass, the flatland grass that is sharp to the touch but soft and undulant as it bows and waves at a distance, ceaselessly imitating the sea. In the gradually lightening air, the meadows vibrated with pale greens and turquoises that faded to topaz as the horizon swept back against the violet sky. Hannah imagined a painting of nothing but flowing, golden, flatly weaving grass against vaporous lavenders, field after field of water and earth and sky. Over it all swung solitary birds—cawing gulls, one white crane, occasional vollies of ducks arched high in their eternal spear. Farther away, high over the forests that retreated into shadow against the light, patient hawks circled. Crows flurried up. A rabbit dashed off the road as the car approached, and Hannah looked around to watch it hop indignantly back into place as the machine sped away.

Despite the soothing passage of the familiar earth, or, in a way, because of it, Hannah began to fidget. This land had nothing to do with Jinx. This was the ground of her family, the roads that took her father every day to Philadelphia, and brought Jennifer to the farms to buy their fresh corn and tomatoes and the jam they ate every morning on their toast. This was homeland, intimate, subliminal. Through many of these streams and islands the Eriksons voyaged like Vikings summer after summer. James knew the channels and depths and inland waterways as intimately as if he had explored and mapped them once himself, centuries ago. This coarse bracken, razor grass, foxtail and pine: these were the tough fibers that bound her to the people she belonged to. These were her connections.

"Do you want to stop for breakfast?"

She looked at her watch. It was still too early to appear at home, so she agreed. The diner was packed with people who would recognize them and note with glee their breakfasting together, so they swung aimlessly around until they found an unfamiliar and rather tawdry luncheonette. Hannah ordered orange juice and milk, her stomach too agitated for food. Jinx ate his pancakes in silence, then leaned back in his chair and lit a cigarette. Hannah instinctively reached for her wallet, but he stopped her sharply. She complied, feeling peculiar. Why should he pay when he had nothing to do with her?

As they passed back over the bridge that spanned the marshes, Hannah grew distinctly more tense, and by the time they crunched into Jinx's driveway, she was alarmed and eager to be gone. She turned to him shyly, wanting to be polite and warm, and asked when he was leaving.

He toyed with the fresh toothpick he had gotten from the lunch counter and said, "Round four-thirty, I guess. Right into the worst traffic, but that's when Fred gets off. He's gonna get himself every last piss-worth of salary. Too bad you can't see us off."

Hannah nodded. They stared ahead clumsily, unattached strangers again. Finally she smiled tenderly, already more tender over his memory than him, and dutifully hugged him. He held her close and longingly, but when he moved to take her back indoors, she shook her head apologetically. She was constricted now with anticipation of her homecoming, quite alone once more. When he released her, she murmured a soft but hasty farewell with one foot already out the door, then wheeled and strode down the alley, not looking back.

It was still unusually early for her to be coming home, so she invented an explanation about her girlfriend's family. The alley was ripe with mingling odors of frying bacon, coffee, garbage simmering in the cans, and the new sun heating the damp cement, but Hannah was too distracted to notice. She was hardening herself for the conflict at home. This time the excitement that plunged back and forth from her temples to her stomach wasn't pleasant. She was exhausted and crumpled. Although she never would have admitted it to her parents, she was glad it was over.

She didn't even see her mother's enormous car until it jolted to a stop beside her. Hannah jumped with shock, and then, when she glimpsed Jenny's set face behind the wheel, laughed wearily. Appropriate movie jargon occurred to her: The jig is up now, kid; this is the end of the road. She climbed resignedly in beside her grim parent, who jerked the car into motion.

"Well well," Hannah said after three blocks of silence. "Fancy meeting you there."

After further silence, in which she was apparently too rigid to speak, Jenny said: "Your private scandal has become public, as your father predicted. Your friend Mr. Hershey's neighbor kindly called this morning as we were enjoying our French toast to ask if we knew that our daughter had spent the night in a house where the owner was absent."

"And here I was assuming this was just an unlucky coincidence. How the hell did she know who I was, anyway? Jinx said she was a bitch—an old parasite sucking on other people's lives like everyone else in this damn town. Shit."

"Please watch your language with me, young lady. As long as you continue to reside in our house and eat the food we provide, I expect you to pretend to be decent. Obviously I cannot influence your behavior when you're with your so-called friends. As for your question, the woman recognized you from your pictures in the paper—all the times in the past when we've had reason to be so proud of you."

Hannah snorted caustically, but waves of unspecific pain were beginning to break through her defenses; she was too tired to protect herself. And the worst of it was her knowledge that, underneath this fury, Jenny was acting. This was all what she thought a good mother should be feeling and saying, and since she so rarely encountered a crisis where the emergency instructions were clear, she was grabbing at this one. This was the opportunity for the beleaguered adults to unite against a common enemy.

Jennifer took an unsteady breath and then pronounced in a strangled voice: "We were willing to have trust in you one more time, and you betrayed it—"

"Yup, Benedict Arnold Erikson, that's me. And you know, the irony of all this is that Jinx is leaving town today, so last night, you know, was our great climactic scene. Curtains up, lights out." She flapped her hand disgustedly, then looked out the window for the rest of the ride.

Jennifer parked the car in the driveway and dropped the keys into her large straw pocketbook. "Jinx really doesn't have anything to do with this anymore. The issue now is your destruction of all the faith and love we've given you."

Hannah turned to her with a look of hopeless exhaustion. "This is June, Mother. Do you by any slim chance remember what transpired here in this ideal home just last April—our own private little Easter pageant?"

"That has nothing to do with this."

Hannah sighed and closed her eyes. Maybe it didn't. Her parents always denied that anything had anything to do with anything else, especially that their problems had anything in the least to do with hers. "Since Daddy tried to commit—"

"He did not! It was not intentional." Jenny scowled. "And if he had, it might be all the more reason for you to have some consideration for his feeling now. And mine. Instead of thinking of nothing but your own selfish desires."

Quietly but angrily, Hannah began to cry, and as she did, she saw her mother's mouth purse with vexation. Stung, she said much more heatedly, "You just tell me, Mother, what have you got to offer me? Where is this wonderful life and wonderful future that I'm supposed to be so grateful for?" Her voice broke again, and she could only extend her hands despairingly.

Jennifer swung contemptuously out of the car. "Get out. The time for all your melodrama is over—our troubles don't give you any excuse for lying and behaving like a tramp."

"I am a tramp!" Hannah said loudly as she slammed her door, triumphantly noting her mother's guarded glance at the neighbors' windows. "And I'm proud to be one—but not the way you mean it."

Then, spent, she trailed Jennifer passively through the gate. They marched single file into the living room past goggle-eyed Kate, who was forbidden to follow. James waited there impassively, his mouth drawn down in the way that meant he now interpreted his daughter's rebellion as yet another of the world's many vindictive blows at himself. Hannah sighed, knowing that for the next few months she would receive personal credit for betraying his innocent goodwill and faith in human nature. She lowered herself into one of the commodious armchairs and closed her eyes.

"Open your eyes!"

She opened them. Despite her resignation, her pulse quickened. No matter how well she thought she had perfected her stoicism, James's sheer size and stentorian voice could always intimidate her.

"Well, do you have anything to say for yourself?"

She looked at him blankly, then chuckled. "Any last words, you mean? Before I'm off to the boarding school for wayward girls? Not really. Well—except maybe that I regret that I have but one life to give for my—ah, but for my what? That's the point, isn't it? I wish I had something to give one more life for—"

James belted the fragile end table with his fist; the lamp teetered wildly. "Go up to your room! Your mother and I will think of a suitable punishment since you cannot even be talked to."

Hannah was relieved; she had expected another vitriolic confrontation, and he was not to be talked to either, not in this mood. He derived a perverse satisfaction from these family scenes, she knew, for they reinforced his sense of betrayal. Every time the world betrayed its promise to him he was outraged, but he never relinquished his claim to the promise.

* * *

Alone in her room, she lay dazed on the bed. She felt too numb to cry. Once she heard footsteps come up the stairs and tried to tense herself for conflict, but then, instead of opening, the door jerked and clicked. They had locked her in! She chuckled helplessly. Where on earth did they think she could go? Through the floorboards she heard their voices swell and buzz. Occasionally she heard yelling, and then her mother's plaintive wail would protest the injustice with which crises forever boomeranged back onto herself.

The afternoon sun thickened into bright gold at her window, dyeing squares of the wooden floor a deep orange, crimson at the edges. The wind rested as it often did at this hour, and waves of heat floated down from the roof that was her ceiling and embraced her in cottony stillness. She felt as if someone had wrapped her up in a plastic bag and twisted wire around the opening. She drifted in and out of a dazed sleep, her eyes half open and sore; her skin itched gummily.

But by the time Jennifer carried dinner upstairs, the prisoner was washed, combed, and watching television. The air had begun to move again, cooling off the room. The row of windows had deepened to a royal blue, and the curtains flapped gracefully, languidly. Not having to eat with the others was a reprieve, not a punishment. Hannah reached calmly for the sandwich, noting that cold cuts signified Jenny's being too upset to cook.

"We have decided," announced her mother coldly, "to punish you by confining you to the house or yard for at least two weeks—except, of course, for school, to which we shall drive you and from which we shall pick you up promptly at three-thirty. Furthermore, you will not be allowed to entertain yourself as you always have in the past: instead you will spend your free time doing a variety of chores which we shall assign. You will not see your friends or even talk to them on the telephone. Have you any questions?" Jenny folded her hands in her aproned lap and sat primly on the other twin bed. Though she had applied fresh lipstick, her face looked worn, and her expression tensed with this unnatural effort to be cruel.

Hannah leaned back and smiled. "In other words, this is to be the walled-in boarding school—"

She broke off as James marched purposefully through the anteroom and into her bedroom wielding a large pair of shears. Not entirely in mockery, she put her hands around her throat. But he ignored her and went over to her bedside table where he efficiently clipped the wire of her princess phone and carried it away with him. Taken aback for a moment, Hannah burst into laughter as soon as she assimilated what had happened, expecting him to fly back to wallop her. But he continued to clomp expressionlessly down the stairs.

Near a kind of placid hysteria, Hannah returned to observing Jennifer. It was clear from her bloodshot eyes and James's stiff back that he was now as much in opposition to his wife as to his daughter. That was predictable, for it was Jenny's instinct to carry all bad news to her man, and it was James's to decapitate the messenger in the royal manner. Hannah cleared her throat and drawled: "Tell me, about this matter of picking me up at three-thirty—what about the yearbook, the literary magazine, the newspaper, the art club, the drama club, and all the other responsibilities that I am being taught to assume?"

"You will just have to get everything done at school, or else tell them that your parents want you home."

Hannah shrugged. Now that the senior play was over and she had basked in her glory, none of the rest meant much to her, not for these last weeks. Indeed, given her reclusive habits, the only striking changes in this new regime would be the assignment of chores and the denial of the phone, and though they did disconcert her, she was determined to show nothing of what she felt.

9

Ironically, and to her jailors' great frustration, the following two weeks of incarceration were among the happiest Hannah could remember. The weather continued to be bright and warm, and she was glad to leave school at an hour when the lagoon was still a jade green flecked with lacy foam, folded in glassy pleats by the gentle land breeze. Ordinarily she would have retired in restless boredom to her room to lose herself in a book, half-resentful of that beckoning radiance on the far side of the walls. But now, under her parents' new discipline, she hurriedly changed into cut-off jeans and an old sweater and reported promptly for duty, maliciously striving to be cheery and enthusiastic, even offering a mock salute. Yet her act was more sincere than not. Since the maid did the housework, the tasks that fell to Hannah were actually pleasant.

The first task was to rake the grass that Jennifer had already mown. Healthy grass was difficult to coax through the searing Augusts in this sandy soil, and most home owners had resorted to flagstone or attractive white pebbles. Jenny used these for the patio areas, but lawns, she believed, should be rich, moist grass; and hers were. Anything that grew from soil—flowers, trees, bushes, weeds and grass—seemed eager to do their best for her. When the sun was hidden, they turned instinctively to her, and to those lovely beings that grew simply and wordlessly from seeds, Jenny was never inaccessible. Hannah often upbraided her for wasting so much time on repetitive labor, but in truth, when she sprawled on a lounge chair by the water and gazed unthinkingly at the greenery and the roses and hydrangeas that enclosed her on three sides, she was grateful. And happy. Jinx simply fizzled and evaporated from her thoughts like the froth on the Cokes she drank to cool herself as she worked.

Raking the grass was mindless work, but she liked stretching out her arms in the hot sun; she liked pulling back, reaching out, pulling back, until she had made small piles of hay all over the wide lawns. She liked leaning her chin on the handle of her rake and gazing out to sea like a figure in an old painting. The sweat that made her clothing stick to the lines of her body seemed to flush out all the strain and turmoil, and when she walked back to the docks and reached lazily down to swab herself with salt water, the way it stung her sunburned skin seemed to cauterize all infections and old wounds.

She liked pruning the rosebushes that swarmed all over the wooden fences; she found that she had a sense of how roses and fences should merge, and she liked stepping forward to clip, clip, then stepping back to view the work as a whole. Jenny couldn't help praising the symmetrical job she did. Showing off, Hannah reached out and drew from her mother the recognition she needed, and Jenny couldn't help opening and giving: that was her way.

Even weeding proved an unexpected satisfaction. In the front yard under the hydrangeas or in the back under the birdbath that James had sculpted from rocks, shell and cement, she crouched in the moist shade and plunged her shovel into the mulchy soil, unearthing slugs, crabgrass, dandelions, snails and pieces of old shells. The digging mesmerized her, and she worked slowly and dreamily, hours passing before she would feel cold on her burnt skin and realize it was getting late. Then she would wander into the game room, her face glowing with sun and peace, carrying the rusty tools and stiff gloves she hadn't used because she liked burying her hands in the earth, and her parents would gape in frustration.

"Hi," she would purr, "anything more to do before dinner?"

How could they hope to remain adamant against her when she came to them so open and ebullient? They were all connected to one another on levels too deep for mood or will to reach. Hannah looked at James, who had come home early to work on the boat, so tall and already deeply bronzed, his bright thinning hair lacing boyishly over his damp forehead, and she felt, for the moment, a peace and rightness in being here with him. He comprehended her, and she him, in ways that obliterated Jinx from memory, that made her wonder how she had ever been inspired to clutch at him as if he were a lifeline and she were drowning. He couldn't even swim.

All that seemed, now, to have nothing to do with her. Her place was here, with people who were woven into the very fabric of her perceptions. When she gazed out at the lagoon from the living room windows, she was always certain that she could read the direction of the tide from the way the surface of the water swept in shallow pleats out toward the mouth of the bay or inward toward the houses. She was always wrong. Those fanning ripples, even when they listed like miniature sails, audibly slapping as they tilted forward, had nothing whatever to do with the flow of the sea. The shallow surface of the water bent obediently to the whim of the breeze that stroked it, but underneath the sea went its own way, indifferent.

All the signs of Hannah's previous exhaustion faded. Her hair sparkled and bloomed with tones of apple and lemon from the sun. Her nose reddened; freckles sprouted. No longer translucent with internal erosion, her skin regained its healthy opacity, cheerfully holding back the world.

The Sunday two weeks after her last rendezvous with Jinx was brilliantly hot; even the shy land breeze had stopped. The Eriksons awakened early, flushed with well-being. James had been home since the middle of the week doing his seasonal chores, which, though he complained about them, actually calmed him like a week's sleep. The lines around his mouth softened and he stopped gasping faintly as he inhaled, a nervous mannerism that frenzied his daughters. Very gradually, his family was settling down around him.

The four of them met in good humor at breakfast, and at everyone's insistence, James made waffles, which they gobbled in unabashed gluttony. Jennifer sat at the other end of the table and beamed with satisfaction. This was the way things should always be. Afterward, the women did the dishes and made the beds. Then Jenny packed an opulent picnic lunch while Hannah went outdoors to help her father lower the dinghy into the water and attach the outboard to its stern. Matthew trotted eagerly down the slippery dock to confront the rowboat; his eyes glazed over with happy panic, his tail swished convulsively, and his tongue lolled in a delirium of expectation.

"Regard our Matty," said James. "He says that if we would only listen, he could tell us exactly what makes for happiness—a lifetime of long walks, fireside snoozes, ball-fetching, boat rides, plenty of grub, and a painless little operation to quell any unseemly urges that might otherwise interfere with the rational life. If only we could literally embody our emotions the way he does. His whole body wags with joy."

To signal his agreement, the setter tossed himself from side to side so violently that his blunt claws had to scramble to hold on to the already-slimy wood. Finally he gave one anguished bark and gazed at them imploringly.

"Okay," Hannah laughed. She climbed down the ladder into the unsteady boat, then turned to summon the dog, who came with a tremendous leap of faith, landing half in her lap and inadvertently scratching pale welts on her tan thighs. She clutched the sides while the dinghy rocked precariously, and finally grabbed Matty and folded him into a sitting position between her knees. He was relieved to have his enthusiasm contained; his eyes rolled blissfully and he panted saliva everywhere. James unfastened the stern line and climbed in after them, and when Hannah had untied the bow, they pushed themselves free of the pilings. With some effort James coaxed the engine into a methodical little putt, and the boat and its passengers cruised slowly through the mouth of the lagoon into the bay.

Immediately the water quickened. James released the motor to the full extent of its minuscule power; the bow tilted up with humble determination; and they were off. A larger craft plunged past them; the dinghy jerked, shuddered and crept forward, coughing through contradictory currents toward the bridge that spanned the borderline between bay and ocean.

Hannah always anticipated the voyage under this bridge with mild excitement—as a child she had been told to shout aloud to hear her echo boom back. The civilized body of bay water merged with its infinitely larger and wilder parent only with great conflict; the water sucked, gurgled, churned in seething undertows and whirlpools, and was the scene of many accidents on turbulent summer evenings. Directly underneath the bridge, between two massive steel supports, within the wide rectangle of perpetual shadow and dankness, the whole tone of the world changed abruptly. The echoing hum of the cars overhead, the clunk-clunk of their wheels hitting crossbars, the loud ring of the vibrating metal and the gush of frenzied water convulsing against it, made an ominous, almost infernal gloom. Hannah clapped her hands to hear the reverberating sound and Matthew began to pant. James had to shout to be heard.

Then, just as abruptly, the crescendo died and they emerged into bright whitecapped water in clear sight of the beach. Everything blazed with warmth and light, and the ocean seemed to be laughing at its display of power back there at the very point where it consented to be domesticated for the use of swimmers and boats.

They chugged along patiently, with James deftly steering into the most amiable currents. Sea and sky were an equally brilliant blue, tufted with bits of foam or cloud, and utterly placid. The setter stretched his nose into a medley of airborne delights that only he could savor. Gulls swooped and croaked, hoping for castoff fish. On the shore, sandpipers skittered along in precise formation. Fishermen in rubber leggings stood at right angles to the opaque water, their fragile lines forming the hypotenuse to their perpetual triangles.

For a time, Hannah and James chattered desultorily, pleased with the day and one another. Then he turned more seriously to his daughter. "You know, you had your mother in quite a tailspin a couple of weeks ago. Me too, for that matter."

Hannah stiffened. It was unfair of him to assert rank during one of these times of simple companionship. "I think I was more her excuse than the cause."

"Perhaps," he said mildly. "Tell me, now that it's all past—your mother tells me he's left town, and I would infer that he's not the type to write letters—now that the frenzy is over, was it worth it?"

Hannah felt both uncomfortable and a little flattered by his tone, which suggested that they were sipping aged brandy and reminiscing over affairs of the heart that had transpired decades ago. "Yes. I liked him, and I hardly ever meet boys who interest me. And he turned out to be quite nice—not at all the monstrous rapist Mother imagined." She glanced up pugnaciously.

"Mm-hm," he agreed, nodding. "I daresay that's true. I suppose your mother did have me persuaded for a while that he was a monster—at any rate, she had my heart pounding like some old Tartar king who thinks his wife and children and most valuable goats are under attack. A man has those feelings, you know—atavistic, I suppose, but very strong—that he must protect his family. Of course, it all becomes more complicated when you feel you must protect your family from themselves."

They sighed philosophically. Hannah trailed her fingers absent-mindedly in the water.

"Don't misunderstand me," James went on. "I admire that quality in your mother that flares up like the proverbial tigress when she thinks her cubs are in danger. It's just that it's getting harder and harder to agree on what constitutes danger. I did speak to our young friend Lloyd in the police department—he's been promoted to detective, by the way—and his description made your Jinx sound like quite a promising criminal for one so young. A parent likes to think that, when his daughter is out of sight, she is also out of danger. And, of course, this is a small town where gossip travels quickly—witness the neighbor lady—"

"Well, what do we care what people in this town think?" Hannah protested indignantly. "It's hypocritical."

Her father shrugged, manipulating the rudder with casual assurance. "We have to respect the foibles and even the hypocrisies of the people we live with. That's the only way the human race can achieve a modicum of peace, I suppose. It's pleasant for your mother to be able to blat with the biddies at the grocery store or for me to blat with old Mr. Kraus at the sporting goods store, without feeling that they know the most succulent details of our private affairs—"

"I can't respect that when it means I have to tailor my behavior to the prejudices of imbeciles!"

James grinned. "Mr. Kraus has his limitations, I grant you, but I don't think he's technically imbecilic."

Hannah couldn't quite squelch her answering smile, but she still was troubled. "Anyway, I don't think that's what really upset Mother. I think it was the sex, pure and simple." Having said it flatly, she thrust out her chin and stared down at her hands.

"Yes, that did upset her. She still shares—emotionally, at least—the standards she was raised with. And you were hardly discreet."

"She snooped in my mail!"

"A bad habit, agreed—I've often raged over it myself—but still, a predictable habit of hers. And once she knew—" He shrugged again. "Don't you think it's best not to force other people, especially those we love, to know what will only disturb and worry them?"

"She's always saying she wants to be my close friend. Well, how can she be my friend if I have to hide my most important feelings from her?"

James cupped his hand and reached down to splash water over his forehead. "That is a difficulty," he said almost sadly. "But in my experience, even close friends don't make a practice of confiding what will predictably confuse and alienate the other. As for the sex, I think Jenny doesn't remember her own youthful hungers—or perhaps she remembers them all too well. She was quite a spirited girl, your mother. As for myself, well, certainly I was no virgin by the end of high school, and neither, consequently, was my girlfriend, who was an eminently nice and respectable person."

"Really?" said Hannah, startled. "I didn't know that."

"Oh, human nature doesn't change." For a minute James seemed lost in agreeable memories. "I think that adolescent romance was probably good for both of us, certainly for me, well worth whatever clumsiness—" Then he sighed regretfully and toyed with an oar handle. "I should add, however, that your mother has always maintained that my old girlfriend was heartbroken when I became engaged, even though she and I had broken up long before I ever met Jenny. Granted, we broke up because I didn't want to get married then—or even when I met Jenny, to tell you the truth, but she was able to change my mind."

"No wonder the other one was jealous, then. Did she have another boyfriend by that time?"

"I believe so. She was always popular, and I like to think she was happy—"

"That's what you always like to think, though."

"I know," he admitted. "Just what your mother says." His expression turned as beseeching as a little boy's. "Don't you like to believe that people you're fond of are happy?"

"Not exactly," Hannah answered firmly, with a faint smile. This was a frequent exchange. "I like them to *be* happy, but if they're not, then I don't think it does any good—in fact, I think it does harm—to pretend that they are."

"Hmmm. Sometimes I think that substituting wishful thinking for reality is a habit of those of us who have overdeveloped senses of responsibility. Anyway, though, if your mother's perceptions were correct, then my young mistress's pain was probably all the greater because of our physical union, a thought that makes me feel bad even to this day. The sex certainly made it harder to disentangle ourselves when it became necessary, and I suspect these things are even more difficult for females; for me, well, the war was coming and all, and my mind was turning to other things. And much as I hate to admit it, our friendship, which I thought would be eternal, like sister and brother, did fizzle the minute I came on the scene with Jenny. Of course, she's happily married now and rich with offspring, so it worked out for the best. Who's to say— Look!" He broke off and pointed over Hannah's shoulder. "Thar she blows off port bow!"

It had taken the better part of an hour to chug around the tip of the coastline, a journey that took only a few minutes in the cabin cruiser. They were heading for a large sandbar that had formed about a quarter mile off this beach the previous summer, too far to be reached from the beach itself without considerable swimming. At high tide it almost disappeared, but at low tide, as at present, the shoal was about the length of a large lot and half the width, and glistened like the pearly underside of an oyster shell. Symmetrical rows of gentle white waves framed it on two sides. Already one other family was picnicking, their children wading in the shallows.

"Good, your mother and Kate are waiting," James said with satisfaction.

They putted in toward the beach until the sand loomed up a foot or two below the hull, whereupon James switched off the motor and tilted up the rudder. Hannah undressed to her bathing suit and slipped overboard to hold the boat steady while he waded ashore. He relieved his family of the picnic basket and helped them clamber into the dinghy, pushed them a little farther out, then hopped in after them and ferried out to the sandy island.

* * *

There they spent an idyllic afternoon in the pattern they had developed late last August when the sandbar had first formed. Matthew spurred thousands upon thousands of birds into flight, chased his ball whenever someone was kind enough to throw it, and begged for his share of the sandwiches. His family sunned, swam, gorged, played catch with his ball while he hurtled good-naturedly between them. They played hopscotch on designs that were compromises from their various childhoods, a game that Jenny, to Hannah's chagrin, invariably won. It was still very early for swimming and the water was snappily cold, but the shallows trapped between small shoals were slightly warmer from the sun. The contrast between the heat reverberating on the unshaded sand and the chill water was exhilarating. The Eriksons dashed from one element to the other, steeping themselves with well-being.

Her family's graceful and handsome gaiety filled Hannah alternately with pride and bewilderment. The fact that at times the four of them could have such sheer fun together perplexed her. On days like this they were so sensitive to one another's least impulses that their moods played like a team of acrobats, so intimately attuned and practiced that they could soar backward, somersaulting, into the air, and land instinctively in welcoming arms. Each was always there to catch or applaud the others, laughing. Occasionally the other family watched them with a kind of generous tribute, sensing the Eriksons' unusual closeness and grace.

James was in his element. Just as he had steered the boat effortlessly through complicated currents, so he directed the outing step by step without needing to concentrate, much less worry. He knew the hours of the tides almost automatically; he read the Coast Guard weather signs as unthinkingly as he read the headlines. He somehow knew the name and habits of every bird, weed, shell and mollusk, and Hannah often asked questions just to make sure that he always knew the answers. When she was with him, she didn't have to know the names or times of anything; she didn't have to watch the weather; she was free to respond intuitively to birds or fish or changing sky without choosing direction or glancing back. Her father stood between her and the unpredictable world and she played safely in his shadow, perfectly happy. Even when she cut her foot on a jagged shell and James examined it, pressed it until it stopped bleeding, and told her to flex it in the salt water, and even while she bit her lip like a child at the sting, she was happy. He had assessed the anger and told her how to cope with it; she was in his hands. Any threat or danger from the outside, he was prepared for. He was the sentry, the guardian of their small tribe, and under the wide awning of his protection, her day was a tranquil and spontaneous dream. She flopped in the sand, floated lazily in the ripples, and laughed and felt as carefree as in the last moments before sleep, when visions come and go independently.

Then, dimly, Hannah noticed James's attention wander. While Jenny still skipped heedlessly down the hopscotch squares and flailed her arms gracefully and Katie followed her along the outer border, James's thoughts drifted. He squinted in unconscious perplexity back at the land, and the nerve over his cheekbone tensed. A passing wince of obscure and bewildered dissatisfaction flickered across his face; and instantly Hannah's stomach tightened and her neck stiffened. For a protracted moment he inhaled, toying with the air in little nervous gasps and then, with a shrug, he brought his attention back to his family.

"My turn?" he asked innocently, though Jenny was in the act of tossing her shell. Then, with strained joviality, he accused his wife's slender foot of having impinged on a line.

The forced note of his non sequiturs, so mild that he was unaware of it, always aroused Hannah's clenched anger. With a sudden violence that shocked the others, she announced that she was bored and stalked off alone. Her family beseeched and remonstrated, but finally they let her go and resumed their game. From a distance Hannah observed them, feeling muddled, hurt, angry. Their gaiety seemed as deceptive as a lotus-blossom peace; she ached to submit, then flinched back in suspicion. She felt not only like an outcast but like a singularly graceless and unappealing one, rendered heavy and clumsy by so much guilty resentment, and all at once she loathed the sun and the laughter and the teasing melody of the waves. Yet, when James finally lost his temper at her sulking and simply commanded her return to the fold, she was relieved.

The Eriksons were at their best out of doors. As the sun dropped, its rays were even hotter against their burnt skin, and they began to move more slowly and stay in one mesmerized position for longer and longer moments at a time, as if the heat were gradually branding them into place. The other family had long ago departed, leaving the Eriksons in quiet privacy with their still-romping dog. But even Matty was more languid now as he chased after casually fleeing birds, his ears and tail undulating in unison. The others watched him absently from where they sat or stood, tracing patterns in the sand, washing, squinting under cupped hands, desultorily gathering up the supplies. Kate methodically demolished the sand castle she had spent most of the day making, for, if she did not, the tide would bury it anyway, and sometimes destruction is half the fun. She plunged into the sandy remains up to her knees and seemed gleeful.

To someone standing on the shore looking out at them, if anyone had been strolling on that empty beach, the four Eriksons and the eternally galloping dog would have been the only verticals and the only life visible on that entire edge of the earth. Slowly their shadows deepened to indigo, and slowly they lengthened across the flat stage of sand to link together the separate figures against the sky. Behind them the horizon took fire and began to burn; the darker sea stretched out to meet and soothe it, wide and still and blue.

The dinghy, which had been pulled up on the beach with its rudder tipped forward like a tail, began to slip loose as the water tempted it from behind, until finally a particularly insistent wave nudged it altogether free of land and Hannah had to swim a few yards out to reclaim it. Then, still quick with energy, she towed her mother, sister and dog through the gathering tide by the bowline, holding on with one hand while she contracted and stretched in a leisurely sidestroke. James swam beside her, and when they could touch bottom again, helped her tug the rowboat the last distance against the stiff recoil of the waves.

She and James wrapped themselves in towels while the rest of the family trouped with their gear back to the car, walking heavily in the drifting sand. Father and daughter waved at the vanishing figures, then climbed back into the rowboat. On the way back they were quiet, comfortable, commenting languidly about the day. The little boat droned steadily around the coast and headed for the bay. The bridge, long and curving, now traced a silver trajectory across the brilliant sky, and the cars gliding across were no more than hints of color that momentarily flashed back at the light.

They docked the boat, carried the oars back to land, and went in to shower. Eventually the entire family met again in the living room, ruddy-faced and sleepy, talcumed, dressed in neatly pressed cottons, shivering a little when the air touched their skin. Following their usual custom, they drove to the mainland to the diner and hungrily gobbled cheeseburgers and rich milk shakes in various flavors which they shared, and then, on impulse, went back to General's Bay, past their house, and on to the boardwalk to one of the theatres that had just opened for the season.

They walked from the still-empty parking lot up the sloping ramp that smelled of damp wood and splintered underfoot. The air blowing in from the ocean was cold and penetrating; they zipped their matching whalers and shivered. Jenny's dress reared and flapped against her bare legs. Their hair bushed and tangled.

For a time they all munched popcorn and contentedly watched the pleasant movie, each person drowsily conscious of his own red skin radiating intense heat. James, however, could rarely lose himself in films, and soon his eyes began to glaze with private thoughts. He began to fidget and breathe irregularly. Hannah, beside him, started to chew the inside of her cheek. Her father wheezed very faintly, as if his chest were tight; he elaborately lit a cigarette, squinting at it as if his actions surprised him, and drew in the smoke in jerking little gasps. Hannah's neck and shoulders clenched; her head began to ache. James stubbed out that cigarette before it was done, but promptly, with much rustling of the pack, withdrew another, which he sniffed supiciously before lighting. He extended the pack to Jenny, who was already smoking; she frowned impatiently and turned back to the screen.

He squirmed in his jacket as though it were plucking at him, frowned blankly ahead, searched his pockets, resettled, then wheezed slightly and repeated the whole series of fidgets. Hannah, though immersed in the story, began to grow distantly lonely, separate, irritable. Her expression turned sullen.

"You want some more popcorn?" James blared like a siren, making the other three jump.

"No!" she hissed with the others.

He obediently lapsed back into silence and tried to resign himself to the movie. An unreasoning melancholy seeped into Hannah's throat from her stomach. Suddenly she found herself yearning toward the suave actor magnified in Technicolor before her, yearning toward the confident romance he offered the heroine. When she got home, she would fantasize about him.

"Ha ha!" bellowed James in his normal speaking voice. "He did that well, didn't he—that look of surprise when she walloped him?" He chuckled appreciatively and glanced at his family for confirmation. They glowered back.

By the time the lights came up again, lines of tension were etched on either side of his mouth, agitating Hannah beyond measure. She hardened against him. When they emerged onto the boardwalk, the night seemed soggy with futility. Once again James tugged his cigarettes from his pocket, then saw that his matches were gone and requested Jenny's lighter, which he struck repeatedly to no effect.

"It's the dampness," remarked Jenny.

Cigarette drooping from his set mouth, James continued to snap the lighter with his thumb, punishing it.

"Wait till we get to the car, honey," Jenny said with a smile meant to be soothing.

"Don't you ever fill these damn things?!" he barked. "Do I have to think of every damn detail around that wretched house of yours?" He abruptly hurled the silvery object in a long arc over the railing into the waiting surf. He ground the offending cigarette into the wet boards, and his face contracted bitterly.

When his arm lifted to throw, Hannah had instinctively flinched and she observed his gesture with frozen distaste. Her pulse began to speed. The four of them, separate, clomped down the ramp. Only Jenny made an attempt to be cheerful, to which everyone else responded icily. Scenes from the movie replayed in Hannah's imagination, soothing and exciting her at the same time, frustrating her, until her mood sharpened to a pitch of misery and restlessness.

When they were settled in the car, James glared indignantly at the steering wheel, then muttered, "Why in God's name do I let you nag me into going out week after week on Sunday nights? I have a train to catch in seven hours while you sleep on forever. Sleep, sleep, sleep—" he droned theatrically. "Sacked out like that damn dog in front of the fire." He gunned the motor until it roared back an answer to his murky rage.

"I'm always up and dressed in time to make your breakfast and see you off," protested Jenny in a small voice, as if this were the first, or even the tenth time she had heard the accusation. James charged the heavy car out of the lot, tires scraping on the gravel, and she turned her head meekly to the window, thinking it best to provoke him no further. Her chin quivered.

Hannah clenched her fist at the injustice, wanting to scream, but instead she said coolly: "It's not her fault that you have insomnia and wander around the house in the dark like a zombie. If you could sleep, you would."

"Suppose you keep your long nose out of our business for once, alright?" he snapped, and before Hannah could defend herself, Jennifer glanced over the seat and shook her head warningly.

The car swerved down the street, lurched into the driveway, and jolted to a standstill, bouncing the girls against the front. "You put it away," he commanded, almost slamming the door on Jennifer as she shifted into the driver's place. He opened the garage door and stalked into the house.

"I have a pounding headache," Hannah mentioned glumly as the three women walked through the gate. The overcast night seemed bleak with renewed winter.

"It's the humidity," said her mother. "And the sunburn. The combination will do it every time." As she unlocked the lower door she smiled and concluded: "Well, despite that little display of pique, we did have a lovely day, didn't we?"

"No," denied both daughters in unison, for they shared the common human impulse to deny the worth of anything that ends badly, or indeed, ends at all.

Hannah circled around the back hallway to avoid her father, who was pouring a drink in the kitchen. The sounds of cracking ice cubes followed her upstairs. She undressed dejectedly, set her hair, and crawled into bed, dreading the coming day.

When she awakened, she was unsure that she had slept at all until she saw from the luminous clock that it was hours past midnight. Then she heard what had awakened her: Matthew's scraping at her door. She rose grumpily to let him in, and when she stood holding the open door, heard the drone of voices, alternately raised and calm, floating up from the living room. The dog butted his moist nose against her thigh; he had retreated here from the adults' warfare. Hannah lingered by the door, undecided whether to advance to listen or retreat to bed, paralyzed, numb. Nothing lasted. Nothing stayed the same.

Finally she dragged herself back to the warmth of her covers, hugging the dog for comfort, and drifted in and out of a shallow rest. It was late, and she and the others were still on the sandbar and the surf was coming up more and more rapidly. The ground was sinking away beneath her feet. But the others were asleep and she couldn't wake them, and she couldn't pull them all to shore alone. The rowboat kept breaking free of the land and floating out and she kept swimming out to drag it back, but there was nowhere to fasten it, and so inevitably it would break free again. She thought frantically that if only she could be certain the shoal would surface again tomorrow, it would be alright, but she could not be certain: she didn't know why it had formed in the first place, and she had to expect that like all the ones before, it would eventually, and with no more apparent reason, vanish. The beauty of the sunset was long past, and night with its cold winds was closing around them. Water broke against her knees, the foam glowing in the blackness. She still had just enough time and flagging energy to make it to shore herself, but what good was escaping alone, what good was crawling up on a vacant beach where nothing was visible but the distant windows of strangers? Yet the water was beginning to lift her; she couldn't keep her footing, and there was nothing to hold on to in that entire landscape where her family had been the only verticals. How could she swim to safety if she wouldn't consent to let go? Then the choice was taken out of her hands. The force of the water took her, and she was alone in the darkness and the undertow, listening to the inscrutable waves breaking around her, and then she was thinking of nothing but trying to hold her head above the outgoing currents, trying to keep from being dragged out deeper, trying to swim toward something which, when she neared it, she recognized as Jinx's face, drowning.

PART II

ARI

10

Hannah had never seen professional dancing before she came to Bennington, much less imagined studying it herself. A few of her childhood friends had sulked off to ballet lessons after school, limp tutus in hand, to have their deportments improved, but the Eriksons considered that tradition archaic and never imposed it on their daughter. When the freshman acting class had been informed last fall that two dance classes a week would be mandatory, Hannah was resentful. "What on earth do calisthenics have to do with art?!" she had complained to her roommate Rachel. It had never occurred to her that acting might involve more than passion and vocal projection; the implication that grace and coordination might also be important unsettled her. For musical comedy, perhaps, but not for *Antigone!* Last year, Hannah's high-school Thespian Club, of which she was president and star, had journeyed by bus to Philadelphia to see that play performed, and the leading lady, so taut with power, dominating the others, had inspired her with admiration and ambition. And never once had Antigone broken into dance.

The class in introductory technique proved even worse than Hannah had feared: it embodied everything unnerving and foreign about her new school. She arrived in jeans and turtleneck, her ordinary garb, assuming the first meeting would consist of introduction and directions. To her shock, most of her classmates came in leotards or tights—not new ones, either; these were patched and faded. Some wore ballet slippers. Hannah had never seen such a uniform outside of pictures and she found it pretentious. The teacher, however, had a very different reaction. She stared at the few pupils in street clothes as if affronted. Then, as though this class were merely picking up from where it had left off sometime in the past, she plunged into a series of exercises and positions that she took for granted everyone would recognize. And almost everyone did. These things were apparently common knowledge.

Common knowledge was a domain from which Hannah was excluded at Bennington. She had chosen a small, serious, progressive girls' college because, from the distance of her small Jersey town, she had dreamed that at such a place, where people read books, painted pictures, and didn't set their hair, where neither football player nor cheerleader marred the landscape, she might be at home—she might meet other rebels and malcontents like herself. She had rejected her high-school counselor's suggestion of Radcliffe because she dimly believed it to be an elite school and therefore conventional. She did not know that Bennington was also an elite school, the pampered prodigal daughter of the seven sisters. She knew only that the catalogue promised an education tailored to her own needs and that in the pictures the students looked like beatniks.

She was utterly unprepared for the discovery that there existed a culture as stolidly middle-class as her own whose young frequently adopted the costumes and rhetoric of Bohemia, a culture that annually stocked Bennington as if it were its private game preserve. A few girls did wander in from the Midwest or thereabouts, looking as dazed as herself, but for the most part the students were urban or urbanely suburban, from boarding schools, private schools that were not Quaker, or public schools so exclusively upper-middle-class they might as well have been private. They brought with them an education vastly superior to Hannah's, not only in sheer breadth and depth of information, but also, more painfully to her, in sophistication. Somewhere there seemed to exist a secret publication that told everyone in this community, teachers and students alike, which were the approved books, paintings, politics, movies, the respectable thoughts to think: a book that listed the hierarchy of all known things. Accustomed to trusting her own eighteen-year-old responses, Hannah made a thousand blunders. Her favorite author was Henry James; her second favorite, Margaret Mitchell. She preferred Renoir to Cezanne and had never heard of Mondrian. Her classmates took for granted a thousand things that to her were foreign. Abstract art, museums, galleries, concerts, opera, ballet, foreign cinema, long hair, pierced ears, black tights, noble causes, picket lines, swearing, psychoanalysis, the names of famous people Hannah had never heard of: all this was part of their everyday world. Everyone seemed to have gone to the same summer camp; for the first week the air was loud with squeals of recognition. Never had Hannah seen so much long dark wavy hair, worn free or in a braid or bun, styles she still associated with grandmothers—quaint grandmothers from old books, not the elegant pair of her own memory.

It was a disappointment to find herself an outsider again, and to be recognized as one on sight. The dance class was populated with the thin, quick, dark-haired girls whom Hannah found most alarming. And the teacher, who could not imagine that girls might exist who had never so much as seen a leotard or heard of a plié, was even more frightening. Hannah's instinct was to join forces and sulk in unison with the few other girls who, judging by their blue jeans and blank faces, shared her plight, but in a community geared to produce romantic rebels, friendliness was considered rather gauche. Convivial gestures generally met rebuffs, and girls with whom Hannah had chatted amiably in classrooms often snubbed her an hour later on the lawn.

It was not until the latter half of the class hour, however, when the teacher lined them all against one of the mirrored walls and began to demonstrate brief series of movements, that Hannah's discomfort thickened to misery. The only ballerina in a department of modern dancers, this teacher was as fragile as a lost eyelash, and to Hannah, just as irritating. She seemed to flutter between blinks across the room so evanescently that Hannah was at a loss to decipher how she had gotten there. Clearly the young dancer's only vanity was her grace. Her features were ordinary, her eyes bloodshot and circled with fatigue, hair dull and snagged back in a knot. Her bare shoulders wore two Band-aids and were so thin that the joints looked sore as bruises. Her bare feet were birdlike. Drooping over the piano she was the drabbest of sparrows.

But when she soared into motion she was as lovely, inimitable, and perfectly weightless in the air as the most golden of hummingbirds; Hannah could have watched her indefinitely, awed and deeply moved. Alas, however, it was physical, not emotional, movement that was expected of Hannah; she was supposed to join in, not observe. Alongside some unfamiliar girl, she would lumber across the room and struggle stiffly to imitate the lyrical gestures of the professional who was lilting back and forth past them, pausing only long enough to scowl at them all.

Hannah resented her. She admired so much dedication and ability, but she disliked the woman for her assumption that a failure to move was a failure to feel. In the teacher's eyes Hannah saw herself reflected as phlegmatic, dull, even malevolent, like some huge garden slug dragging sullenly across the floor. The teacher once actually averted her eyes at the sight, and that tacit judgment stung Hannah with an anguish all the more intense for her suspicion that it might be just.

Rachel and Hannah were a stiff shock to one another. Although they got along, since both were polite and considerate, they viewed one another with amicable suspicion for months. To Rachel, Hannah seemed chilly, removed, reactionary. To Hannah, Rachel seemed the embodiment of Bennington. They had intense though polite arguments which ended in Rachel's calling Hannah a bigot and Hannah's calling her a knee-jerk liberal. Rachel and her friends sat around singing union organizing songs taught them by their mothers and nursery-school teachers, while Hannah thought of unions primarily as one source of her father's periodic headaches.

But the roommates needed one another too intensely to let their debates become serious. There were meals to be eaten together, gatherings to be gone to, classes to be endured. Rachel smoked continuously, trembled at the dark, shivered in breezes, jumbled her possessions in an oblivious clutter, and wanted to be a mathematician. Hannah coughed at smoke, gnashed her teeth at the night-light, opened windows, periodically kicked all Rachel's paraphernalia under her bed, and wanted to be an actress. Still they considered themselves lucky. After all, many of the other girls furnished their rooms like Pakistani brothels, replaced electricity with candles that regularly seared the beaded curtains, eschewed all furniture but mattresses, did Zen exercises at sunup, got drunk, raised Venus flytraps, hated other women, and locked out their roommates for days at a time while they hid boys behind drawn shades and smuggled food in from the dining room as if Bennington were a way station in an underground railroad.

Rachel's body had ambushed her late in adolescence. As a child she had been skinny, long-boned, and rather gawkily graceful on her outsized legs, so, when she burst forth virtually overnight in all the female richness of a thick-petaled magnolia bloom, she felt betrayed, dazzled, proud and embarrassed. The resulting compromise of nature's fruitiness with the childishness that Rachel would not relinquish, proved almost comically appealing. She still carried herself, or rather, hurried herself, with the earnestness of the worried little girl she had been.

Leaning against the windowsill, Hannah would affectionately watch her as she bounced steadily forward across the campus. So, too, watched groups of young men who were loitering on the damp lawn or lounging on the steps in the cool gray light of early spring. With every step that brought her nearer her gaping audience, Rachel would clench her notebook tighter to her chest in a futile attempt to clamp everything still, but alas, knotting every muscle only exaggerated the delirious dance of her body, and there was nothing poor Rachel could do. The expression on her face disclaimed any connection with what was going on below.

She was close to a beauty, or would have been had she wanted to accept that gift and burden. All those sharp angles and verticals had been transformed to elegance, stylishness. The black hair, freed of its pigtails, proved unusually lustrous and thick. The eyes did still pop a trifle, even in contact lenses, and the jaw was a shade too square, but if she had wanted to be "gorgeous" she could easily have brazened out these rather attractive flaws.

But that was not what Rachel wanted to be. Her parents had pampered her in their anxious way until she was sure that the world would continue to find her a lovable little girl. She had grave doubts, however, that she would ever confront the world as a successful adult. Her parents had so shielded her from what they said was a cruelly judgmental society that she had understood from early age that they accepted society's judgments and standards, which was precisely why they found them so cruel. If they reassured her that they would never care how well she did at school, she sensed that her father, who taught philosophy at Queens College, valued intelligence and scholarship second only to artistic genius. They surrounded her with only the best books in case she was seized with a desire to read, but were not surprised when she wasn't. They bought her a piano, classical records, elaborate sets of oil paints, sent her to dance and drawing classes lest she show any spurt of creativity, and then, though they watched tensely, refrained from mentioning all the opportunities left lying in the closet and the corners. Ceaselessly they told her they loved her for herself, not for what she could do, because they despaired of her every doing any better than they believed themselves to have done.

Exceptionally bright, she did very well even in her grueling private schools, but she attributed her good grades to doggedness alone. She was eloquent in private but speechless before any authority. She rarely read for pleasure because it was not pleasurable to muster the appropriate exalted response to the classics she assigned herself, and lesser books were a waste of time. Since she was too guilt-ridden to waste time by amusing herself with paints or sewing or music or any other hobby that, as she put it, she didn't have the talent to justify, she spent a great deal of time simply sitting. Sitting, rocking, listening to her stereo, smoking nervously.

Through the fall, Hannah and Rachel treated one another with the respectful regard of foreigners who lack an interpreter, and each assumed the other was fully at home. It was only toward the end of the Non-Resident Term, the time from January to March when the restless students abandoned their New England cloister to learn-through-doing in the city—which in Rachel's case meant living with her parents in Manhattan and typing for an ad agency, and in Hannah's, rooming at the Barbizon, selling stockings at Sak's, and limping once a week to acting lessons—that they drew very close. On their return to school they moved into a larger room and spent a pleasant week decorating it, surprised to find their tastes and rhythms in perfect accord. By that time neither was aggressively opinionated: their own day-to-day difficulties took precedence over jobless blacks and Russians hungry for our wheat. They wished they had a television and taxied into the nearby town every time its sole theatre changed films.

Hannah smiled and flinched when Rachel banged through the door with her usual clatter of loose loafers, dropping books and disgruntled sighs, then crossed over to her bed where she dumped her papers and pocketbook into the tangle of sheets and tumbled in after them.

"I'm sorry I didn't make my bed," she said defensively, rummaging in her battered but elegant bag for a cigarette. "But I had to get up early for French and I was exhausted. I noticed you slept through your class. And you haven't even begun your painting yet, have you?"

Her friend's nagging made Hannah grin. Rachel was no fonder of school, but she labored under a much heavier obligation to be dutiful, and she worried over Hannah's refusal to worry. Rachel's confidence in people grew in inverse proportion to her intimacy with them—the more she loved and identified with Hannah, the more she extended her own insecurities to her.

"Well," Hannah said, "actually I only cut one class: I did make it to stagecraft. But I imagine Stansky wishes I had cut, since I managed to nail my flat to the floor and it took him twenty minutes to pry it loose."

"Is that where you were at lunch?"

"Uh-huh. We had to clear the stage for the dance concert tonight. Which is where I have to go now, unfortunately—that damned light-crew I signed up for. I want to go back to bed."

"Then why did you volunteer? You always do this to yourself."

"I know, but it seemed like a good idea at the time—see real dancers close up." Hannah flapped her hand theatrically. "After all," she drawled, "zee dahnce is a high art form which I have scarcely experienced. It'll be good for me, like castor oil. Are you going tonight?"

"To the concert?"

"Or the Jazz Improvisation afterward. This is Jazz Weekend, you know. You're expected to participate with your peers, not huddle like a recluse in your unmade bed. You have an obligation to the community."

"Fuck the community."

They laughed together. Rachel stubbed her half-smoked cigarette at the overflowing ashtray and almost immediately reached for another, but when she found it, scowled, obviously contemplating cancer, and instead took a Coke from the supply of bottles, empty and full, that lined their floor and windowsills. She snapped off the lid and sucked at the soda almost angrily, then coughed, put it aside, lit the cigarette she had hidden from herself in her jeans pocket, raked her rich hair behind her ears. And all the while, as she fidgeted and smoldered behind the sweep of hair that loosened from her ear and fell in a veil across her face, she swayed in a kneeling position, keeping time to an obsessive rhythm of her own.

Hannah marveled at the harsh grace with which Rachel choreographed her anxiety. Where Hannah was contained, watchful, reserved, Rachel was forever in motion, swaying when she stood, rocking when she sat, talking to fill up the silence even when she was alone. Hannah envied such expressiveness and sometimes found herself imitating it, rocking aggressively back and forth as if to illustrate that she, too, was all at sea with herself.

"Well, Rake, are you at least going to eat tonight? They're having liver upstairs—so let's indulge in the snack bar." Glancing at the clock she stood up. "How about it? An evening of romance and discovery at the Commons?"

Rachel grunted assent. "I doubt I'll go to the concert, though."

"But I thought you were a devotee!"

"I'm pooped. Besides, I saw Rosalind Witt's company in the city a few years ago and wasn't impressed—that's who's performing, right?"

"Sounds right. But then they all sound alike to me."

"Christ, Erikson, you really are from the backwaters, you know! How did they ever room me with such a hick? You know who Martha Graham is, at least. And the Bolshoi?"

"Never heard of them until you started raving—which is just like you, now that I think of it, raving over the Russians. But I'm not utterly ignorant, you'll be pleased to know; I have heard of the Rockettes. In fact, I saw them once on a Girl Scout trip right before I quit the troop, and I thought the Easter panorama, with all those newly-risen legs, was very touching." She pulled her handbag over one shoulder. "Anyway, I'm late as usual. See you for dinner."

"Good luck. Behave yourself."

"As if I had any choice."

11

Hannah closed the door behind her, conscious of tension squeaking audibly in her abdomen. She had been sincere in saying she wished she could hide in bed, but when she did finally get back to her room at the end of a long and demanding day, she very often couldn't sleep anyway. Right now a horde of obligations were gnawing at her already uneasy mood. Two themes were almost due and a painting was overdue. She had to scour her collection of plays again for yet another dramatic confrontation between two women for her directing project. Last week she had cut the painting class, intending to do the work in the time she would save, but of course she hadn't. She seemed to be cursed these days with a virulent form of inertia: it was so very hard to get going, and once going, so very hard to stop.

Spring was advancing only in the most sullen and grudging way. The day was warm but damp and overcast. As usual, the sun had shown briefly this morning, just long enough to lure everyone from bed. For a misleading hour, bogs of week-old rain had shimmered brightly, and then the light had slithered back behind a cloud and left its admirers to fend for themselves in the dense and sticky air that made Hannah's plugged sinuses ache with every step. The mud squished and sucked under her feet. On the other hand, a panorama of warmth and rebirth and dancing dandelions and twittering robins would have demanded a response in kind, and Hannah didn't have that response to give, not this year. In a way, she welcomed the clouds; they cloaked her and left her alone.

The campus was as isolated as a cloister. She had come to college full of dreams of a new life and, more particularly, new men, and had found parallel rows of white houses stocked with frustrated girls, plus the smaller assortment of frustrated men who taught them. Somewhere these men presumably had families, and rumor reported that now and then they exchanged families or exiled old ones and imported new ones, but the girls never met the actresses in these domestic dramas. As for young men, they were disappointingly few. Bennington girls, handpicked for the precocity and creativity which in the young are so often indistinguishable from neurosis, had a deserved reputation for sexual and verbal ferocity. Most of them were simply far more sophisticated and far more unhappy than the spruce rosy-cheeked boys who dared to venture up from the nearest men's schools. Moreover, many of those males were drawn like tomcats solely by Bennington's pungent reputation, and they came with teeth bared and claws extended, expecting to meet the same. To Hannah they seemed naïve and yet sly, intent on seizing the sex they wanted and leaving the rest of the girl as far behind as possible. She had seen too many girls miscalculate, mistaking attention for affection, someone's hunger for interest; too many had been mauled; she was wary. Besides, such conventional marauders were unappealing.

She enjoyed trotting through the lounge where half the campus sprawled, past the snack-bar counter, and over to the narrow staircase that led to the dressing rooms backstage. Few people other than dance and drama students used these stairs, and Hannah had never quite lost her romantic sense of them rising to something hidden and mysterious. In those dusty prop rooms, dressing rooms, in the carpentry shop where unfinished illusion leaned against the wall, in the closets full of old scenery and costumes, Hannah, in her modest novice's way, could have at least the hope of adventure: here something might happen to involve her at a level deeper than the brain. She was anything but anti-intellectual, but she was also eighteen and hungry, desperate to make some passionate connection beyond her family. She felt she had reached a kind of dead end. In part, of course, she was simply very tired, much more tired than she, impatient with all limitations, understood. Sometimes she felt attenuated close to the snapping point, a taut boat line straining across an ice-locked sea—but even that was perplexing. How did one go about snapping? Where do the pieces fly?

She glanced at a group of girls in leotards. One of them asked if Hannah was here for the tech-crew, and when she nodded, motioned for her to join them. They clustered aimlessly a few more minutes, then the one who seemed in charge read off a list of names, none familiar to Hannah, and divided them into two groups. Hannah's group she delegated to report back to the wings by the light-board where the dance teacher was to give them their instructions.

Hannah was now petrified. Ed, the teacher, had always particularly awed her. She guessed him to be in his early forties, but only from the attractive creases in his ruggedly handsome face; his carriage, though dignified, was more youthful than her own. For all his grace there was nothing delicate about him; in fact, the close proximity of his massive and powerful body, outlined in dark green tights and a striped jersey, made Hannah uneasy. She had trouble keeping her eyes off his perfectly sculpted flanks. Perhaps he, too, was shy, for he never so much as glanced her way, and with the others, his own students, his manner was reserved, though warm. He teased them affectionately, yet his gentleness seemed belied, or at least modified, by the latent power of that body. He struck Hannah as a sun-seared cowboy fresh from the range who had unbuckled his chaps, unstrapped his holster and kicked off his boots to reveal a leotard underneath. Even his politeness reminded her of the cowboy's bashful deference around women, as if he were always conscious of that power that must be suppressed when he reentered civilization.

She slithered onto the high metal stool in front of the light-board and tried to look inconspicuous while the dancers gamboled and frolicked in private camaraderie. They expressed their pleasure in each other's company less through words than through motion, like affectionate cats settling down in front of a heater. All three girls were shorter, thinner and more finely built than Hannah, and infinitely more fluid and graceful. They were all so sleek in their black uniforms, with their dark hair tucked in neat buns and their serious, unpainted faces, that they blended into a chorus as they skipped and flirted around their teacher, and Hannah had difficulty telling them apart. They didn't so much speak as sing, giggle, peal and trill like matched sets of chimes. When Hannah spoke, she winced at the low-pitched solemnity she heard, but was helpless to change a note.

They called their teacher by his first name and seemed on familiar, even intimate terms with him. From her three-legged observation tower, Hannah imagined that these insubstantial, flawless creatures must all be in love with one another. Certainly she couldn't imagine a dancer loving any but his own kind, and, for such lyrical beings, bedding together must be simply an extension of the beautiful motion they wrought in unison every day. Clearly they all adored Ed, and he seemed, though more reservedly, to adore them in return. Was he having an affair with one in particular, Hannah wondered, or perhaps with one of the renowned seniors? She felt so much clumsier and heavier with gravity than usual that she actually gripped the seat of the stool lest she suddenly hulk over and topple at their bare feet.

When Ed finally raised his palms in an exaggerated attitude of seriousness, cleared his throat, and began to explain the infinity of handles and buttons on the light-board, Hannah was completely lost. He plucked all the knobs in various sequences and hastened through a prepared speech, using as illustrations a medley of dance and music terms that were totally foreign to her. Finished with his spiel, he continued to ramble on about details, showing by the casual inflection of his voice that such mechanical teaching bored him. He joked and laughed with his students in a way that excluded a stranger. As he handed out clipboards with mimeographed assignments on them, Hannah was stricken with anxiety. She hadn't understood a word! Their minds must be as quick as their muscles! When it turned out that he had too few clipboards, having calculated only his own dancers, he was apologetic, but she was wildly relieved. He pointed absentmindedly to a section on another girl's sheet and told her to show Hannah about that, then went off, taking one girl with him. The other two huddled together and discussed their assignments, which were still incomprehensible to Hannah.

"We spent two whole classes on this, you see," remarked one over her shoulder; and for the first time, Hannah felt a dribble of comfort. No wonder they had left her behind; she had never even seen the light-board before.

"Here's what you'll do." The girl explained a few of the markings, then went through a sequence with her by rote. "But you won't really understand till you see the performance and hear the music, because you'll have to gauge your timing by that." Feeling doomed, Hannah wrapped her long legs around the cold rungs of her stool and hunched into herself.

The auditorium began to fill with adult dancers, members of the company, going through their warm-up routines. One by one they straggled in, encumbered with small valises or huge pocketbooks, greeted the others, plopped their gear in the corner, stripped off their street clothes, and rather grudgingly began to work out. At the bar or sprawled on the floor they stretched, contracted, loosened sore muscles, and desultorily practiced a few movements. Hannah peered out at them, fascinated. All of them wore colorful assemblages of leotards, leg-warmers, sweat suits, blouses, T shirts, belts, scarves, and even jewelry, reminding her of the weirdly, often garishly inventive ways that parochial school girls find to individualize their drab uniforms. They yelped at, teased and taunted one another fondly or obstreperously, more like a flock of rather crumpled parrots than the swans Hannah had expected. Clearly they were tired. Each of them seemed to nurse a private assortment of bruises, pulls, strains or more rarefied injuries.

Cliques formed and regrouped. Sometimes they criticized one another's exercises, not always good-naturedly. Particularly they united in kidding and harassing a thin, bushy-haired fellow who slumped lazily against the bar and scarcely deigned to move. He laughed with cocky indifference, grimaced at a few of the girls, and bandied back once or twice in a foreign guttural accent. He had deliberately placed himself at a distance from the others, and seemed aloof even when he bothered to notice their sallies. He gazed as reverently into the mirror as a gypsy into a crystal ball.

A very slender black youth with a large head slid dreamily through a series of movements, apparently lost in a private waltz. One of the women beside him was surprisingly portly, apple-like in an imprudent red leotard that matched her cheeks, with white hair that fell to the small of her back. Beside her was a tiny woman with short knotted legs in white tights, a brilliantly patterned scarf around her minuscule waist; her hair hung in thick braids around her pinched, childish face. When she chattered with the others, she shrilled and pointed and whined like a bad-tempered child on a playground, wiping her nose with the back of her hand; yet, even from where Hannah sat, the deepening lines around her eyes and forehead were visible. Hannah yearned to know the story of each. If only she were invisible, free to creep closer and eavesdrop.

When they began to troop up onto the stage, still clamoring, sticking on Band-aids, pulling off warming suits, tugging long hair into metal clamps, straightening Ace bandages, favoring bruised feet, and otherwise attending to their bodies as musicians tend their instruments, Hannah felt more anonymous and comfortable. She wedged her stool farther into the dim corner and gave herself to the spectacle, freed of self-consciousness as long as no one noticed her. It was amusing how flat-footed the dancers were when they walked; their muscular feet slapped and thumped the hollow floor. Many plopped back and forth as heavily as ducks, their knees habitually turning out in opposite directions. Perhaps they were unconsciously testing gravity, or perhaps they were simply glad for once to be free of the onus of being graceful.

Ed returned from backstage, and to Hannah's surprise, most members of the company threw their hands in the air with delight and sprang forward to embrace him or pummel his back. She inferred from their greetings that they knew him well, considered him one of their own, in fact—and then she remembered hearing that many of the teachers still danced professionally over the winter Non-Resident term and during the summers. Rosalind Witt, the choreographer and director, had once taught here herself during lean times. Hannah promptly decided that she had been naïve to think Ed could be in love with one of his students when he also worked in such close proximity to all these attractive professional women. They congregated together and gossiped and caviled like a family of gypsies. Two women hugged Ed warmly, then lingered comfortably in his arms while he joked with the others.

Then, as if he hadn't entirely shed his role as teacher, Ed clapped his hands and waited for silence, and when the clamor failed to diminish even a fraction, stamped his foot good-naturedly and bellowed. The others turned to him in surprise, and he bowed in amused gratitude, then said that he, at least, having been immured in the mountains these many months, needed to rehearse. So his colleagues struggled accommodatingly upstage or toward the wings, while across the stage from Hannah someone began fiddling with a rather scratchy sound system; and at last, after what seemed insurmountable confusion, the informal practice slowly commenced.

To Hannah's delight, Ed proved to be the principal dancer in a duet with the prettiest of the girls. Clearly the theme was romantic. They began moving separately on far sides of the stage, eyes apart, their gestures asymmetrical yet mutually aware. Slowly they circled toward one another, responding more and more directly to the impetus of the music, picking up and repeating each other's motion. Ed was magnetic: the paradox of his heavy, athletic body and his controlled grace had compelling power. The woman curved meltingly around him.

Then the emphasis shifted rather blatantly from romantic to sexual, and the pair began to twist and lunge more emphatically on flat feet. The drum surged forward with a more rapid and pronounced rhythm; the dancers alternately yielded to the insistent pounding, then stiffened and worked deliberately against it, resistant to the alluring beat and to each other. Eventually the tympani began to soften and, as it did, the performers seemed to gain courage and flow forward, reminding Hannah of children scampering deeper into the ocean in the wake of a retreating wave. But even as they flirted tenderly in the shallows, the distant wave was massing for its next resurgence, and when it finally did come flowing back with an even more overwhelming cadence, these children chose to meet it instead of fleeing. As swimmers dive underneath a breaker in hopes of escaping some of its force, the dancers sank submissively to the floor and let the music pound inexorably over them.

Hannah was a little surprised at how graphically erotic the dance became at this point, as Ed hovered over his flushed and supine partner and they undulated and swayed against one another. She was startled, but fascinated and aroused. Undoubtedly from the distance of the audience the impact of the two damp, intertwined bodies and their husky breathing would be considerably more abstract and less sensual. But from here, their intimacy seemed almost embarrassingly personal as they stretched out side by side, alternately extending and contracting. The affection in their eyes was real and visible even from Hannah's cloistered perch. Obviously they had worked together so long and knew one another so well that they could anticipate every nuance of each other's performance. Ed's gestures were straightforward, muscular and precise, while hers lilted and seemed to melt together. She was small and rounded despite her evident strength, with clean brown hair that flipped up around her jawline and bounced as she moved. She was diminutive, voluptuous, powerful and vulnerable all at once; and just as the contrast between Ed's sculptural mass and delicacy intrigued Hannah, so did the contrast between the woman's soft lines and her obvious power. She smiled up at her partner in unabashed pleasure and confidence, a confidence born, in part, of his admiring attention.

Hannah decided sentimentally that they must be past lovers whose bruised affection was being soothed and revivified by this timely duet, and she envied them. Again she felt that life must be simpler for these lucky creatures whose bodies could express spontaneously what words could only at best evoke at a distance. Dancers must experience a complete union, a quality of graceful coming together, that pedestrian animals like herself would never know. Of course, she knew that this duet was rehearsed, and moreover, was choreographed by someone else, but the interplay between the pair was so subtle and finely attuned that much of it must be spontaneous. It was the yearning quality of the embraces, the tenderness bordering on nostalgia, that persuaded her they must share a past relationship that was now both tempting and frightening.

So she was utterly unprepared when all of a sudden one of the dancers who had been loitering upstage began to mock them affectedly.

"Oh, my goodness, Eddie, we are getting rather involved, aren't we? Heavens how forceful! Such oomph—such soul!"

Hannah was too offended even to glance at the intruder. She immediately assumed he must be jealous of their skill, beauty and affection. Thus she was even more taken aback when the two dancers abruptly collapsed on the stage in convulsions of giggles.

"Oh Jesus, Harry," the woman chuckled fondly. "Your possessiveness is showing. You're supposed to dance it not say it, you loon."

He grinned and continued to tease them archly, hand on hip. "I just wanted to remind you, my friends, that this is supposed to be art, not a peep show. Try to keep in mind that this is a college of young ladies. We don't want to look like an import from Forty-second Street, now do we?"

"Bitch!"

The invisible hand at the tape recorder located the place where the duet had broken off, and Ed and the girl resumed their dance, but methodically now, marking their places, all the while laughing and joking back at their compatriot. Forced to acknowledge that none of the dancers found his interruption at all appalling, Hannah inspected the interloper, who had now strolled closer to the performance. He was slender and handsome, with long brown hair that drooped in a curl over one eye. His entire deportment had the preening theatricality so notably absent from Ed's.

"Ooo la la," he sighed as the dancers moved into what was evidently the grand climax. "Gracious sakes alive!"

"Sour grapes, Harold," teased the girl with a smile. "Just because you couldn't handle the role—"

With a mock roar of fury Harry flung himself between the two and cleverly improvised a comical third role that instantly reduced the rehearsal to a wrestling match. The two men finally joined forces to overpower the girl and tickle her until she squealed for mercy, then all three flopped down on their backs and bantered fondly as the music played itself out. Listening to them chatter, Hannah reluctantly had to conclude that it was Ed and Harry who comprised the duet and the woman who was the friendly interloper. Harry giggled contentedly and now and then pushed his forelock back from his eyes to direct his gaze more effectively at Ed, who met the gazes squarely and warmly, though he seemed mildly self-conscious of his nearby students. With the woman, now that the dance was over, Harry was familiar and tart, while Ed was reserved and a little shy.

Neither of Hannah's two comrades at the light-board seemed at all impressed with the relationships unfolding onstage. She sighed at her own naïveté, but still she couldn't help feeling sad that Ed found attractive what seemed to her a caricature of the woman's responsiveness. And she marveled that the girl herself was so utterly relaxed and physically at ease with two men who presumably found her sexually unappealing. Gradually, as Hannah studied the three of them, the woman's hips seemed to spread, to become embarrassingly wide until they threatened to unbalance her whole supple form. Her upper arms seemed too vulnerably soft and plump. The men's bodies were spare and functional, modern, pared down to the bone and muscle essential to their purpose. They were like contemporary furniture, pruned to simple designs of steel and leather, while the woman, in contrast, seemed as quaint as an overstuffed chair, all oddly bedizened with curlicues, knobs and satiny pillows, a curio designed for the attic. As she cuddled there on the floor her breasts toppled slightly toward the arm she was leaning on; they wobbled as she changed position and suddenly seemed to make an extraneous and unsightly bulge under the fabric of her leotard.

* * *

Then all at once a wave of seriousness quivered through the troupe, and they straightened up and came to attention like a class of unruly children on discovering that a teacher has infiltrated their midst. Hannah looked around for the teacher and saw that it must be the rather plain middle-aged lady who was clomping toward the stage in laced-up shoes with high heels, a style Hannah associated with librarians in old movies. Then she realized that the woman walked with a slight limp. The shoes boomed like nailed boots on the resonant auditorium floor. Hannah had expected Rosalind Witt to be a lithe, costumed figure, discernible from the others only by austere shadows around her eyes. This businesslike matron was a surprise. She knew that Witt had been a young dancer in England before the war, and had married an older man, a Polish choreographer who eventually died in a concentration camp, and that his death was the decisive event in her life, the one that turned her from a graceful girl to a serious and competent woman. Her critics claimed that her dances tried to compensate with moral passion what they lacked in artistic subtlety; her admirers believed that few artists had been able to use their medium to grapple with their times as effectively as she. She had remarried but lived apart from her husband. Hannah stared at her hungrily, trying to find traces of such a romantic past in the impassive white face that was presently taking stock of the small, rather warped stage on which the woman stood, but all Hannah saw was efficiency.

Accompanying her, on the far side from Hannah, stood a rather startling-looking man in a black turtleneck to whom Hannah vaguely assigned the role of business manager. Both of them had the bearing of adults dealing with capricious adolescents. They spoke only to each other, making private gestures and frowning slightly as if the dancers vexed them. Witt's companion was clearly foreign, with large, prominent features and an unkempt mass of wiry black hair that he kept absentmindedly combing up with his fingers, then trying to pat down again. Hannah noticed that he kept one hand proprietorially on the choreographer's shoulder, and with the other, when he wasn't toying with his hair, vaguely stroked his chest and face. He brushed his forehead and lower lip with his fingertips as he frowned over the shortcomings of the college stage, and as he pondered, he smoked, exhaling in audible sighs of self-importance. Hannah thought him amusingly theatrical.

When he stepped back a foot to investigate the meager wings, Hannah was startled to see that the lower half of him wore black tights: apparently he was a dancer. She had half-dubbed him a middle-aged producer, but now she saw that he was considerably younger than that, much younger than Rosalind Witt. Then, even more startled, she recognized him as the bushy-haired dancer with the harsh accent whom the others had teased earlier for his lazy refusal to work out. Now, standing next to the director, he assumed a new dignity. He was thinner than his expressively carved head had led her to expect, but he was tautly muscular and moved with the tense sensuality of a wary cat.

12

With Witt's arrival the rehearsal began in earnest, though the chief problem seemed to be adapting the established program to the new arena. Technical details had first priority, so the performers were more concerned with timing and positioning than with expression. Initially, Hannah was too preoccupied with the light-board and cue sheet to focus elsewhere, but after a nervous forty minutes, she realized with considerable relief that she was not going to have very much to do, and even that would be concentrated in one dance near the end. One of the dance students had stationed herself near the stage to act as a prompter, signaling the cues to her teammates, thus relieving Hannah of even the need to be alert. She had only to pull a few levers when the other girl flapped her hand.

The rehearsal frequently halted to allow Witt to make marks on the floor with adhesive tape, to correct the timing or volume of the music, to modify the lighting or to attend to myriad details that Hannah couldn't make sense of. Meanwhile the performers grumbled, massaged bruised joints, and limped desultorily through their paces. Many actually parodied their parts with a kind of fierce snideness, as family members often reserve their worst tempers for each other.

At last, after what seemed like hours of incoherent confusion, Witt stamped her foot and announced that now a serious run-through would commence. They began all over again, but this time fluidly, seriously.

Hannah was entranced. What particularly surprised and fascinated her was the paradox of the dancer who, while no doubt the embodiment of silent and weightless grace from the far side of the proscenium, was in fact, saturated with sweat, wheezing raucously, counting aloud, and cursing to himself in frenzied concentration as he waited in the wings for his reentrance. From where Hannah huddled, the tribes of bare feet thundered on the hollow floor like a hundred tom-toms beating a ragged war-dance. The performers galloped offstage, flinging perspiration to all sides, wheeled around to watch for the next cue, hectically adjusted taped limbs, clawed back drenched hair, and tugged at one another's snagged costumes while gasping reassurances and anxieties. They were sheer physicality, sheer body. Even as they were dancing Hannah could hear the thuds and thumps as they ran and leaped, the labored breathing and desperate counting. It would seem that dancers were not, after all, as free as dust motes in a sunbeam; they had merely learned to persuade others, from a distance, that they were.

They didn't even appear to be healthy and vibrant with the benefits of exercise as she had assumed they would be. Aside from the injuries, many were pale, drawn, apparently strained to the edge of exhaustion. On stage they vibrated energy, but afterward, sagging against the wall by Hannah's stool, heaving to catch their breath, they were as gray and limp as fish out of water. They handled their bodies like instruments, impersonally. When they sagged together for support and comfort, they were as oblivious to the touch of a breast or thigh as they were to a kneecap. They spoke of their parts in the third person, complaining that the ankle was sore again or that the goddamn elbow was stiff, shrugging and making the best of the equipment with the air of a gambler arranging the hand he is dealt.

At the end of each full dance, Witt called the cast together and read them her notes. Hannah's self-consciousness seeped back a little during these pauses. Amid the hubbub of the performances she felt invisible, which delighted her; she felt free then to stare openly at the preoccupied company. Now, however, the silence threatened to make her conspicuous again; and anyway, part of the next performance was going to be her responsibility, so she tucked her legs shyly under her stool and pored over her clipboard. Panic nibbled at her stomach as she tried to plant the correct series of knobs in her memory. She couldn't even let herself consider the horror of making a mistake and bringing all that aggrieved attention down on herself. She hid her chin in the neck of her sweater and let her hair fall protectively around her face. She had closed her eyes and was running through her list of duties when, to her horror, something powerful gripped her wrist and a guttural voice invaded her private world. She gasped, started up frantically, and almost fell off her stool. The clipboard did fall off her lap, which made her jump again and clutch after it wildly.

"No no, don't be frightened; I don't mean to frighten you," she heard through her confusion. Without releasing her trembling forearm, her assailant bent over to rescue the clipboard, and as he did, she thought she felt an odd sensation on her calf. Before she could assimilate that, he loomed above her again, and she saw a startling apparition with disheveled hair and a wide, hungry mouth. As completely stunned as a deer in a poacher's lamp, she blinked at her kidnapped limb and saw two muscular hands strapping an enormous black watch high on her arm. The hands pushed up her sleeve to affix the watch, then slid under the loose fabric to stroke her arm. She started to yank away and almost catapulted the stool over backward; he caught her; and as she was trying to squirm away from the protective hand on her back, she felt a foreign mouth briefly but tenderly caress her wrist. The touch was so intimate and had such drastic repercussions all over her body that she gasped aloud. "Nice," the harsh voice murmured with some amusement. "Lovely." For a flabbergasted moment her entire arm was massaged as if it were being appraised while she tried to collect herself and focus. She tried again to yank away, but his grip on her elbow effectively paralyzed her. Never glancing at her face, he slid the cue sheet back into her lap and gently brushed her thigh with the backs of his fingers. "Sweet," she heard him say into her lap. Then he was gone. The entire assault had transpired in an instant, hardly more than a second or two.

Hannah trembled violently, then wheeled around to stare through the wings after him. She couldn't see anyone who even resembled what she remembered. Had she imagined the whole swift event? Had her loneliness and fantasies at last gotten the best of her? Half afraid she had hallucinated and half afraid she had not, she looked to see if anyone else had witnessed what still reverberated as one of the most acute shocks of her life. To have a stranger treat her so cavalierly, then vanish! But everyone else was bustling about as usual. She swallowed, glancing at the other student assigned to the light-board. That girl gawked with open mouth, then hastily looked away, evidently assuming Hannah to be a person who habitually offered her thigh to strangers. Hannah blushed. She was hot all over and trembling.

Tentatively, as if she were terrified, she peeked at her arm to discover that she did in fact bear the stranger's watch like a manacle. The sleeve of her favorite green turtleneck was scrunched up so far to make room for it that her arm looked naked. Hastily she fumbled with the buckle, unstrapped herself, and modestly tugged down her sleeve; but then it occurred to her that the watch would surely fall out of her lap if she moved, and that flustered her all the more. It did not occur to her just to let the thing break as an act of revenge. How on earth could she get rid of it? She wanted to delegate it to someone else, but obviously that would be foolish. Besides, the lights had dimmed for the last dance and a respectful hush had fallen: her voice would blare like a siren. He might as well have glued it to her. Her forehead sprang a light wash of sweat and her hands began to burn as if the leather were branding her. For a second she felt almost hysterical, as if she had been catapulted into a nightmare. Then she realized that, indeed, the absurd situation reminded her of those dreams and fairy tales wherein the heroine is helpless to escape from something both attractive and deadly—a plunging stallion or a pair of beautiful shoes that will never stop dancing. She managed a weak chuckle, very primly buckled the offensive object all the way down on her wrist, and pulled her sleeve over it. That was better. Then she wiped her damp forehead and swore under her breath when she felt the cold buckle scrape her skin.

She was distracted, finally, by the bustle coming from the far end of the very front of the stage, the edge that curved out into the auditorium even when the curtains were closed. Apparently the climactic number would soon begin there. Rosalind Witt and her peculiar-looking friend stood in that corner in a spotlight, conferring with the technical director. For the first time, Hannah could see her clearly. She had taken off her tweed suit jacket and, in a pink blouse with gauzy sleeves and a tight bodice, looked more slender and less stolid. A flowered scarf made her small waist look curiously vulnerable, Hannah thought, as if the girlish indentation were somehow a weakness that she was ill advised to expose. Her brown hair was a little frowzy and streaked with gray, but now that it had worked loose from her bun and fizzed around her head, it looked softer. Her expression was serious at the moment and tired, and her mouth was unnaturally thin, as if she habitually sucked in her lips to shield them. But on the whole her face was pleasant. Hannah liked her. She suggested courage and intelligence.

Suddenly Witt frowned and pulled a pencil out of her hair to jab at the dancers wandering around the stage, who promptly hastened into position. She muttered something to the propman, who in turn came over to Hannah's corner and instructed their team leader that, although this segment would ordinarily unfold with the curtains closed, they should leave them open for now in order to see what the lights were doing.

No music started this time. Instead, after a prolonged beat of silence, the prompter turned and gave the first signal, and Hannah slowly pulled the lever that slowly threw both the audience and the stage into darkness. Even the dancers reflexively lowered their voices, and a hush fell, as at the coming of twilight. Then the other student just as gradually raised the beam of the spotlight, which centered, Hannah saw, on that same bushy-haired foreigner. Then it dawned on her that the foreigner, Witt's compatriot, must be the person who had handcuffed her with his watch. He had seemed massive, but now she saw again that he was lithe and not especially tall.

He was poised alone in the beam of light, leaning slightly toward the middle of the audience and swaying as slowly and suggestively as a conductor's wand. At once, with the sheer concentration of his posture and gaze, he cast a spell—and then broke it just as abruptly by plopping back to his heels and muttering something to the sound man. A second later, just as easily, he tilted forward and seemed to grow, to stretch with the force of his quick, flexible body toward the far dark corner of the long room. People in the wings strained toward him as if to hear, though he hadn't made another sound. His very silence was resonant.

He tilted his face up into the light. It was a disturbing face, and the exaggerated chiaroscuro of the theatre made it almost shocking, atavistic. The jutting bones seemed too stark, as in primitive sculpture, and his cloud of hair virtually sizzled with the energy of his will. It was tangled and so dark that, like the background of old paintings, it absorbed shadows and thrust forward everything the spotlight touched. Hannah felt that she had never seen another real person like him but that she had seen his face a thousand times before in old engravings, old pictures: an ageless nomad whom the sun and sand and hot, abrasive desert wind had worn down to nerve and spirit and bone.

Suddenly he was speaking, but his voice seemed to have come out of nowhere. At first, spoken in his guttural accent, the words were unfamiliar but evocative: Hannah guessed he was incanting some mysterious text, and the passion in his harsh voice enthralled her. Then she grinned and had to suppress a giggle both of relief and a curious disappointment. She had recognized his mysterious text: it was nothing more than the first verses of Genesis, the same old rhetoric that had opened a wearisome number of school days and meetings and even television programs. The triteness of the script broke her trance the way a snap of a light switch transforms a monster in a child's room back to the same old bureau. But only for a second.

Before she could even chart the change, some subtle alteration in his delivery reclaimed her attention and belief; almost against her will she was again obscurely moved and fascinated. All at once his voice began to lift and lilt. He began to chant, not to the audience but straight into the power of the wind that daily seared his flesh and carved his torso to muscle and shadow. It dawned on Hannah that now he truly was speaking in another language, one she couldn't identify at all until she realized that, of course, it must be Hebrew. Like an incantation from their forgotten past his voice rose in waves and fell on the listeners; it lifted and absorbed them, ebbed away to leave them alone and lost, then billowed up again to take hold and carry them even further backward. Something weird and luring seemed to pull them all back into their memories, into a familiar darkness, to hypnotize them with some ineffable magic.

When Hannah sensed he must be nearing the end, her self-possession began to seep back a little and she sighed. But then, without pause, he rose again, in body and pitch, and extended out to the empty room and the darkening windows at the rear. He spread his arms and opened like a curtain and began to sing, to keen, to wail, still in that same ancient tongue. His voice mesmerized his audience, even the dancers who had heard it a dozen times before, and carried them beyond themselves; and he, too, seemed beyond himself, lost in a rapture of lament and sheer, impersonal joy: willfully lost, given over to ecstasy and to song. He offered himself, and them as well, to something far beyond their knowledge or control. Hannah soared helplessly in shocked belief, sensing abstractedly that at this moment she was remembering and comprehending something for the first time, something of tremendous importance, something she could never again forget.

* * *

Then it was over. The spotlight vanished and the uncanny dancer disappeared into the wings. A flat voice informed them that this was when the curtain would open during the actual performance, and with that as a cue, the rest of the company, who had all along been posed in formation on the stage, began to slap their feet very softly in unison on the floor. The prompter gestured, and Hannah and the third girl slowly raised the stage lights in an effect of gradual dawning. For the next twenty minutes Hannah was wholly preoccupied with her chores. From what she could glean between lighting changes she gathered that this, the climactic selection on the program, was a passionate dance about beginnings and life and suffering, starting, evidently, in pre-history, and working its way to the present. Judging from the awful screeches and groans and bangs, its view of history was unrelievedly gloomy. Finally she could tell from a crescendo of loud marching and the repetition of a German word that they must reached the twentieth century. Her duties were over by that time, and she was able to relax more fully than she had since early morning and just watch. From close up the effect was more chaotic than profound, just a group of sweaty young people dashing about and stopping every now and then to bang a limb wildly on the stage. It was exciting as any frenzied crowd is exciting, but not much more.

She tried to recapture the exaltation she had felt, that quick apprehension of perfect oneness and perfect song, but it had vanished entirely; now she could hardly remember the outlines of what she had vowed never again to forget. The mystery had drawn back like the tide and the residue it left behind was dead. A little sadly, she supposed that the flicker of ecstasy had been a theatrical trick, a coincidence of mood and effect. The feeling had been real enough, of course, but its very reality had deluded her about its causes. Hannah Erikson from South Jersey was certainly no nomad exploring an unending landscape for the source of the wind that had sculpted her; and neither, for that matter, was that crude actor who had unnerved her by copping a quick feel. He was just a trained magician with a time-tested script, performing in a spotlight she herself had helped to aim.

Nonetheless she searched for him among the dancers. She saw two or three Jewish males with prominent features and curly hair, and when she had decided which one he was, she snorted at her own credulity. Now that the spotlight was off she saw that his haunches were leaden, his shoulders too narrow and his feet too wide, making his movement a little reminiscent of a kangaroo. How on earth had she allowed a kangaroo to intimidate her that way? Why, for that matter, had she allowed anyone to manhandle her that way, as if she had dozed off into a submissive trance? The indignity! As the music climaxed she wryly unfastened the watch that curled around her pale wrist and held it ostentatiously between thumb and forefinger as he and the others came lumbering off the stage. But he hopped obliviously past her, complaining about the tape recorder in an unmistakably New York accent, and she realized that the kangaroo wasn't the same man at all. For some reason that made her oddly nervous. Eventually the stage cleared, however, and all the noise retreated to the dressing rooms, leaving the three students to straighten up in silence.

Then suddenly he and another man strode swiftly by. She stammered foolishly and thrust out the watch, furiously conscious that her hand was shivering. He turned blankly, then smiled, thanked her, and vanished. The abruptness left Hannah inexplicably crestfallen, which only made her the more furious.

Her crew helped clear the stage for the night's program and conferred again with the man in charge of technical matters. Hannah's presence wasn't necessary, but she wanted an excuse to hang around until the last voice had safely gone from backstage, for although there was an alternate staircase to the ground floor, she wanted to walk through the dressing rooms. Their air of latent purpose even, or especially, when they were empty, somehow eased the loneliness that threatened to catch in her own throat at this hour.

But tonight they let her down. She combed her hair and was glad to be alone again, but she also felt increasingly forlorn. The dead quiet seemed full of the music of that proverbial party that is always somewhere else, wherever other, happier, people are. She looked well, however, as she often did when tension drew her tight. Her hair was full and heavy, like drooping branches of autumn leaves. It had been a peculiar afternoon; she and Rachel could laugh about it after dinner. She tucked her pocketbook under her arm in a businesslike way and began to march to the door. Then she paused, thought it over, and prudently elected to use the main staircase after all. The last thing she wanted was to run into that man at the snack bar.

13

At the landing at the bottom of the stairs, Hannah paused again to stare glumly through the wire-reinforced windows of the Commons door. It looked gray and dim out there; a draft through a crack licked her blue jeans. Out of habit, she turned to walk through the lounge to the post office to see if by any miracle she had gotten a surprise in the late mail, for mail was the only novelty to look forward to these days, and she and Rachel mapped virtually every errand to lead them past their boxes. But with her hand on the knob, it occurred to her that she might run into that stranger in the lounge—a lot of noise was coming from there even for a Saturday night, which meant visitors. She noticed with sharp annoyance that her pulse had quickened. This was humiliating and absurd! No stranger, no animalistic stranger, was going to frighten her out of her normal routine on her own turf. Besides, he hadn't even noticed her when he retrieved the watch, and probably wouldn't recognize her, or even care to, away from the theatre. And if he did, she would snub him just as she would any man who whistled in the street.

Stiff with hauteur, she pushed open the heavy door and walked into the extremely crowded, noisy and smoky room. To her alarm, she saw him immediately. He was sitting in a cluster of armchairs near the center fireplace, apparently absorbed in a chess game with some of the campus leaders and celebrities, male and female. She would have to pass quite close to him, but safely camouflaged in a bustle of other girls, and anyway, he was very preoccupied. He never even looked up from the board.

Without visible hesitation and, she hoped, without visible interest, she gripped her shoulder bag and strode airily in their direction, her eyes fixed on the door. As in a bad dream he rose casually to his feet, still answering what his friends were saying, and blocked her path. She gaped at him. It was impossible to snub someone who wasn't even looking at her. She went to slip by on the right and he blocked her. She blushed. This was ridiculous—she certainly wasn't going to wrestle with him! Acknowledging a bad joke, she smiled weakly, then nodded, briskly said excuse me, composed a serious expression, and tried to take a step forward, but he blocked her. Some of his companions were looking at her curiously, and one was reminding him that it was his move on the chessboard. Hannah was mortified. There was no way for her to handle this with dignity, since he wasn't even paying attention to her except to block her path. Every time she shifted her weight he shifted position. She refused to explode in frustrated squeals like a teenager. At last it occurred to her to backtrack. She waited until he was laughing at someone's remark, then lifted her head aloofly and turned around, but a crowd was at her back and before she could move he had her pinned against the back of a couch, worse off than before. She could escape only by literally plunging against him, assuming he would yield even then, which was an assumption she didn't dare risk. He instructed someone where to make his next chess move, and then, suddenly, turned all his attention onto Hannah.

His arrogant but amused gaze and the full thrust of his intensity worked like a drug to isolate the pair of them, instantly, within a circle he seemed to inscribe. He looked so utterly foreign. His quick white face and dark eyes were so different from anything she had encountered before. It seemed as if she didn't have the language to cope with him: she couldn't place him, or herself in relation to him. She jerked backward as though she were about to be abducted by a sheik in the middle of her New England girls' school lounge, then snorted angrily at her celluloid reflexes, smiled with what she hoped was sophistication, and tried again to edge along the couch.

"No no," he said emphatically. "No! you are please to stay. I want to meet you. You are the pretty little girl who is sitting so shyly on the chair upstairs, yes?"

Hardly the description she would have given. She was trying to summon the properly regal answer when to her shock he gripped her by the shoulders and precipitated her backward around the couch and into it. Then he sat beside her and took her hand. She was too stunned to speak. If she hadn't moved when he pushed, she would have sprawled topsy-turvy onto the floor. Finally she recovered enough composure to snatch back her hand, but there was nothing she could do about the leg plastered against her own, and when she tried to rise a palm came down very firmly on her thigh. There was no way she could escape without making a scene. By this time she was thoroughly nonplussed and, for want of anything better to do, on the verge of laughing. Laughing incredulously.

"There," he said with satisfaction. "I hope you forgive me that my manners are bad, but my English is also bad, so I cannot meet you as I like better. You see? What is your name, pretty little girl?"

She told him.

"Hannah, good." He introduced her to all of his companions, who nodded with the scrupulous politeness that people accord someone who has just done something bizarre in public, then went back to their contest, clearly annoyed at the interruption. He reclaimed her hand, and when she went to withdraw it, simply held on. "My name is Ari," he said. "Right now I must finish this match, but I am losing, you see, and so I need a good-luck charm because I cannot afford to lose. My rival has his wife, which is unfair. So you must stay here and bring me luck because I'm a visitor to your college and you are my hostess. Then we will go to dinner. Alright? You will stay here and not make me have to hold you?"

Without waiting for an answer but with his leg wedged firmly against hers, he turned back to his game. Hannah blinked and began to emerge from the tranced circle he had drawn. She felt like a fool, but she was also fascinated. No one had ever imposed his will so straightforwardly on her before, not even her parents, and she couldn't help admiring someone who went about satisfying his impulses so bluntly, especially since she didn't consider herself an easy person to overwhelm. He was like a child, grabbing her as though she were a rattle, and it fascinated her to be wanted and obtained so simply, on sight. She shook her head wryly. To have been baptized a pretty little girl and a good-luck charm in the same hour! She took stock of her situation and realized that she had fallen instinctively into her demurest pose, knees tucked together and hands folded primly on her lap.

She recognized nearly all these people but was on speaking terms with only one, who was ignoring her. This was the elite clique on campus, composed mostly of the men, older than the other students, who came here on fellowships in the arts, plus the various females they allowed to hang around them. The informal leaders were a married couple, both doing advanced work in music. Their house off campus lent them prestige and social advantages. Together they had an air of studied coolness that intimidated Hannah. It was the husband who was doing battle with Ari over the chessboard. His colorless hair, almost as wiry as Ari's, had receded to the very back of his freckled skull, where it crested up like a turkey's tail. One plump arm hung limply around his bony wife, who had protruding front teeth, a shrill voice and a flaccid ponytail, but also had a husband, talent, and exuded such tart self-assurance that, in a girls' school, she was a natural leader. At first she shot a series of derisive glances at Hannah, then dismissed her.

Hannah wondered how Ari had ingratiated himself so quickly with the college luminaries, but gradually she realized that the situation was in fact the reverse: he was the coveted one, and status accrued to the married couple simply because they knew him. Also, there were quite a few unclaimed girls in the clique, which explained many of the resentful glances she was receiving. It dawned on Hannah that she had been forcibly cast in the role of girlfriend-of-the-leader, and the thought amused her enormously.

Meanwhile her escort continued to chatter to his hosts about people and events she had never heard of, and about the game, which, since James preferred bridge, Hannah did not know how to play. Actually she was surprised that Ari could play chess; she associated it with gentlemen's clubs and after-dinner brandies. She was even more surprised when she gathered from the conversation that despite what he had said, he was winning.

After a while she began to feel silly. He seemed to have forgotten her presence; he had even turned in his seat until she had a better view of his back than his face. In a sudden jolt of self-consciousness she decided that he hadn't really expected her to stay there as meekly as if he had molded her in clay; it had been a sophisticated joke for the delectation of his friends, and now he had dispensed with the butt of it, and the only one who didn't know that was herself. The student wife again assessed her coolly, then turned and laughed to someone else. Hannah felt herself blushing again and made up her mind to exit with as much self-possession as possible. She assumed a composed expression, and without moving her head, looked around for the quickest route.

Instantly he had both hands on her waist, holding her down. "You must not leave me," he said gently, as if to a child. "You see, I am winning since you sit down. Be patient. Soon it is time to eat."

So she was patient. It would be less trouble to wait than to fight for her freedom. The bell would ring in a quarter hour. Poor Rachel, though; she was probably starved, and they would have to wait until after dinner, when the snack bar reopened, to eat.

Now Ari paid her attention of a peculiar sort, and each time he did, she jumped. As he pondered his moves he absentmindedly reached behind him to stroke the inside of her knee as he might have rubbed a rabbit's foot in his pocket or petted a loyal cocker spaniel. She shook her head wryly, and as she did, imagined two tawny ears flapping. But in truth she found his familiarity more diverting than troubling: she knew perfectly well she was no cocker spaniel. Besides, her knee was nicely warm and alert.

Twelve long minutes passed while she sat placidly, wondering at herself. And when the bell finally did ring, she jumped apprehensively despite her best attempts at dignity. The whole crowded roomful of people rose to their feet except Ari, who held her leg down with one hand while collecting his ten dollars in gambling fees with the other. He grinned and chortled once or twice in unabashed triumph. His victory in a battle of wits still struck Hannah as incongruous with the primitive quality he radiated, the primitive quality that was pressing her into the couch.

The student wife slung her crocheted bag over her shoulder, jammed her thumb in her jeans pocket, and waited. The group milled behind her, also waiting. She had enviably thin hips, Hannah thought, and an enviably confident slouch.

"Come on, Ari, you competitive son of a bitch," she said finally in her nasal voice. "Time to eat."

Her husband slung his arm around her neck and seconded the command. "Yeah, if we can't steal your money at least we can poison you with our food. C'mon, man, stop gloating and let's get a move on; there's a crowd tonight."

"Ah, my friends, you go ahead without me, and I follow you in a minute. My friend Hannah and I have not yet had a chance to talk."

The wife frowned. "Well, bring your friend; you can talk upstairs. Otherwise we might not get a seat."

"You save me a seat, yes? I follow right after you in a minute."

"Look, man," said the husband, "we'll wait for you over there by the stairs. But hurry it up, okay?"

"No, you go up. You save me a place." Ari's tone was completely amiable, yet adamant. A curious mixture of accommodation, charm and dominance, Hannah thought. She wondered how well they knew him.

The husband shrugged, but the wife sucked on her teeth in pique and her receding chin jerked to one side. Ari smiled genially and put his arm around Hannah. She jumped and the couple sniffed. Their group was beginning to trail away, so they turned reluctantly to follow, the wife adding over shoulder with maternally raised eyebrows that she would see him again soon.

Hannah immediately came to life. "Oh look, you go on with your friends because I hadn't planned to eat upstairs anyway—"

"But now you will change your plans to be polite to a guest." His eyes sparkled and his smile was just as adamant.

Hannah suddenly felt like a fluttering ingenue in a bad play. "But no, I—the food's just terrible."

"Oh, too bad. But I've already paid for a ticket, so I think I eat there, and then come down and have another hamburger. Besides, you must eat somewhere, yes? It is necessary." He ran his eyes so appreciatively over her body that she now felt like a pedigreed, blue-ribbon spaniel, pampered by an ambitious trainer.

"Oh, I'll eat," she said firmly. "At the snack bar. You see, I always eat with my roommate, and she won't know what happened to me. I can't just desert her."

"You are loyal. That's good, I like that. But of course she must join us."

"Not a chance."

"The grill, anyway, is closed, so either she can join us, or afterward you can meet her here. You both must wait either way, yes?"

"Yes," she sighed. Then she sparked with hope. "Why don't you go on upstairs with your friends and save me a place while I call her?"

"No. I want for us to eat alone. I tell them I join them because they want me to, to get rid of them. You see?"

She saw. She scuttled to the nearest campus phone. Alone in the dorm—everyone else having gone to dinner—Rachel answered promptly.

"Hi, Rache?" Hannah's voice sounded a trifle weak to herself. "Uh, listen, it's hard to explain, but I seem to be going to accompany this dancer to dinner—it's the take-a-dancer-to-dinner-program, you know. Anyway, so I'll meet you in the room afterward and we'll go to the snack bar. Okay?"

Rachel was silent for a moment. "You sound strange. I thought you hated liver."

"I do. I'm not going to eat up there, just play hostess. As for strange, well, this is a very strange dancer. I'll describe him when I see you."

"Don't hurry back because of me. I fell sick again; I doubt I'll eat. I had toast a while ago."

Rachel sounded lonely and sulky, and her tone stabbed Hannah with guilt. "You're welcome to come meet the strange dancer—" she offered quite sincerely.

"No."

"Well, okay. See you in about an hour, then."

She hung up and felt a trifle more composed. After all, her best friend was only a sprint away. She could afford to indulge the dancer for an hour.

They marched upstairs together to the familiar clatter of heavy china banging steel, the edgy voices of hungry girls who saw one another all day but still had to force conversation as they waited, and the irritable exclamations of the waitresses. The latter were mostly scholarship students who were expected to perform this service for a pittance. They chafed at the injustice and at the hospital-green uniforms, which they often wore right over their jeans. Hannah knew that she and Ari were very conspicuous as they made their late entrance and very annoying to the waitresses who had already fanned out to the dining rooms to count customers and deliver beverages.

"You're too late," snapped the Matron as Hannah started to lead Ari to what she hoped would be the least-populated room. "Orders have already been taken."

Relieved, Hannah promptly turned back to the stairs. The Matron, a formidably stocky woman with a perpetually overheated face, was not to be trifled with; she was perhaps the only true authority on campus. Ari, however, seemed to interpret her steely glare as a show of favorable interest. He walked easily up to her and began, as far as Hannah could tell from her refuge by the banister, to pass the time of day. Within a few seconds the woman's ruddy face was even pinker with an embarrassed but delighted blush. Behind her wire-rimmed spectacles her tired eyes batted happily.

"Alright," Hannah heard her say with unconvincing sternness, "since you're a visitor. But your friend should have known better. Right here, then, where you won't confuse things too badly." She pointed to the nearest of the two large tables in the anteroom itself, where people ordinarily didn't sit at dinner for fear of tripping the irascible green squadron.

Hannah didn't dare move forward until Ari gestured to her. The Matron ignored her, favored Ari with another unpersuasive reprimand, and began to bustle off to the kitchen. As she went, Ari paid a low but audible compliment to her legs, ostensibly directed to Hannah. And indeed, on inspection, the legs under the long charcoal uniform did prove to be slim and shapely. The flustered woman snorted as she pushed through the swinging doors, but her hand flew nervously up to pat her clump of lacquered gray curls.

"Fantastic," said Hannah, raising her empty water glass in a mock toast. Her tribute was sincere. He had not condescended to the woman, nor did he in any way smirk once she was out of sight. He had simply found qualities to praise in a hefty female in her sixties whom most of the students treated as an object, and had apparently made her feel attractive. "That was nice."

Ari shifted his omnivorous gaze from the platoons of waitresses back to Hannah with some interest. "You don't mind?"

"Of course not. Why should I?"

"You should not, but some do." He continued to study her reflectively.

"What's your whole name?" she finally asked for want of anything better. His blunt scrutiny unnerved her, especially since she couldn't guess what he was thinking. It was not her epidermis he was evaluating this time.

"My whole name is Eli Arieli, but in this country I tell people Ari, from Arieli."

"Why? Why not Eli?"

"Here Ari sounds more romantic, yes? From *Exodus*—Paul Newman. Eli is too much the butcher or the man who works at the tailor's. My uncle is the famous cellist, the one here in New York. You have heard of him?"

Hannah had never heard of any cellists that she remembered, but she grinned at his honesty, and he went back to his survey of the tray-bearing waitresses. He stretched in his chair with the ease of a cat molding a pillow to its shape, and began to flirt with each sulky green girl who stomped by. His energy and arrogance amazed Hannah. Either his eyes dwelled unmistakably on some point of interest, or, worse, he saluted the girl's virtues aloud. As one student joggled by, clearly making a conscious effort to hold her full tray away from her fuller breasts, he asked Hannah if she had ever seen a lovelier body. Hannah gasped. The waitress staggered in shock and almost dropped her tray, whereupon Ari sprang up gallantly to help her balance it. She almost staggered again, croaked in horror, and huffed off.

Hannah was flabbergasted, but she was not embarrassed, since she did not in the least identify herself with him, although the females glaring at her clearly did. It occurred to her that his raw flattery was a form of aggression—he knocked the girls literally off balance with his appreciation in order to help them up, or farther down, again—yet for some reason it didn't offend her. She wondered why. Perhaps because there was genuine pleasure in his ogling, and no hostility that she could see, and no leer. Everything he thought he purred or chortled aloud.

With their own waitress he was at first simply warm and friendly, but then, when she responded with the condescension that was characteristic of Bennington girls dealing with males, he did wield his flirtation as a weapon. She was forced to bob around him a great deal in the process of serving, and as she did, Ari openly appraised her while ostensibly speaking with elaborate deference. Yet everything he said was favorable, and it was all such an obvious caricature and done with such zest, that Hannah continued to be amused, even exhilarated. Unlike the usual covert strategies, this seemed to invite an equally blunt response. She expected the other girl simply to laugh at him, which would instantly make him laugh with her—indeed, he was clearly laughing inwardly—but she only froze stiffer with humiliation and wrath.

Then all at once, with the air of discarding a pleasant diversion, he turned back to Hannah, and again she was impressed with the intensity, and hence the impact, of his concentration. He queried her about a great many things he could not have the least real curiosity about—her birthplace, her major in school—and as she answered, shy again, he studied her. Clearly it was his scrutiny, not her words, that was yielding the information he wanted. It made her uneasy. An observer herself, she was not at all accustomed to being observed, especially when she couldn't control or even guess what was being seen.

"Where is it you're from exactly?" she asked in self-defense.

"Tel Aviv. Israel," he said with some surprise.

"Oh, then that was Hebrew you were speaking during the rehearsal?"

"Of course. And you liked my performance? It was very powerful, very moving, yes?"

She nodded, amused. Every performer was gluttonous for praise but few pursued it so shamelessly. "Yes, I really did find it powerful. I thought it was the most effective part of that dance."

"You are right; you make a good critic. Actually, you see, I am an actor more than dancer. Miss Witt, Rosalind—I call her Rosie—she discovered me in Tel Aviv and brings me here as her protégé. It's a good chance for me to see the United States, so I come. By now there is not much I can learn from her anymore, but I teach for her and sometimes she makes a part for me, like tonight. It makes the rest of the company jealous that she puts my talent above theirs even though I am not a dancer, but there are some things they cannot do because they are too wooden—not their bodies, their emotions. They think only about their technique, dancing technique, instead of the feeling, you know what I mean? The soul of the dance, that must come first. Rosie is a very emotional choreographer. The passion is more important than whether the extension is so perfect. You saw me at the end of the second dance, right before intermission, when I dance alone?"

Hannah confessed that she had not, or hadn't identified him. He was disgruntled but went on nonetheless to explain why only he could have handled that solo so dramatically.

When the main course finally came, he broke off his monologue to stretch expansively, sigh with satisfaction, and hand a serving spoon to Hannah. She handed it back with thanks, explaining that she didn't like liver.

"In my country," he said smugly, "the women serve the men."

"You're kidding!"

He shook his head gravely. "It's very bad manners for them to eat first."

She howled. "And I suppose they give you peeled grapes and sweetmeats for dessert?"

"Peeled grapes? If we want them that way, certainly, but for myself, I like the skins on. I'm very good to my women."

"Ah, how benevolent of you! And how fortunate for your wife. Or wives. Actually I suppose you have quite a few already, there must be such a demand—"

He couldn't quite suppress a smile. "You have us confused with the Arabs, I think. Come, the food is getting cold." He plunked the spoon in front of her.

Hannah stared helplessly at it. "You mean you honestly expect me to feed you? Is this part of a program to teach uppity American women the joys of femininity? Sayonara and D. H. Lawrence and all that?"

"Yes. American women really want to be dominated, I think."

"Do you? I'm not sure this is being dominated, exactly. I feel more like I've been promoted to your mother. But if you insist—" She plunged the spoon into the mashed potatoes and proffered it vaguely toward his mouth.

"No no!" He was grinning but also somewhat serious. "Maybe you find it easier if I give you my plate."

Now she had both dishes stacked in front of her. "Oh," she said solemnly, "now I get the idea. I pray Sahib will spare me the forty lashes for my clumsiness." She obediently plopped the glutinous potatoes onto the plate, followed by a splat of green beans and a plank of liver. "Shall I butter your bread?"

"No," he said, looking dubiously at the food. "I do that myself. But you can polish my sneakers as I am eating."

It struck her that because he was foreign, and from a country she knew nothing about beyond having read *Exodus* in junior high, she couldn't guess anything about his background, point of view, education, even his intelligence. Was he as bizarre in Tel Aviv as here? And she must be similarly opaque to him; certainly she wasn't intimidating him. Yet it didn't bother her that he could not appreciate her depths as an individual; she could take care of that herself. He did seem to be perceiving a great deal about the kind of female she apparently was, at least in relation to him, and that fascinated her. Although, she thought cautiously, perhaps it fascinated her the way a snake fascinates a sparrow.

"You must eat," he admonished through a full mouth, punctuating with his fork.

"I loathe liver and the rest looks putrid." She nibbled a piece of the cottony bread and drank her milk, too tense to be hungry.

"Liver is very good for you—for your body."

"So my mother tells me, but ugh."

By the time he had wolfed down two platefuls of food he had inspired one of three reactions from the flock of passing waitresses: either a blush or a grin or a snort of rage, or some combination of the three. Yet even those who snorted often seemed to sway one aproned hip toward him as they stalked by. Despite his crudeness, or because of it, he clearly had a powerful and well-practiced magnetism.

Watching him, Hannah felt curiously invisible; a kind of heady freedom made her almost dizzy for a moment. She could be anyone, enact anyone. She could go through the actions of a pretty, timid and compliant little girl, and meanwhile chuckle at herself from the audience.

And it pleased her that he seemed to be chuckling too, though not precisely from the same perspective. She was free to play with her situation, to experiment. She felt as if she were a child again, as if she were going backward temporarily to pick up something she had lost on the way.

But he unnerved her by immediately reaching over to stroke her head. "You have pretty hair, lovely hair," he murmured. The assurance in his touch made her tremble. He traced his fingertips over her brow and then over her eyes, so that she had to close them. How odd to be explored that way, as if he could see her better through touch. "Lovely eyes," he said.

He ate three desserts, including Hannah's. The cherry pie looked good, but her stomach had curdled. The other diners began to pass by their table on the way downstairs, and Ari leaned back contentedly, sipping his coffee, and watched them. He called out cheerfully to the prettiest girls, who blinked back and raised a tentative hand as they tried to decide if they knew this handsome male who had greeted them so warmly. Actually he did seem to know a surprising number of people by name, including Hannah's acting teacher, who for some reason looked uneasy at seeing her beside Ari.

"You are in his class?" Ari asked when the man had passed them.

"Yes. Do you know him?"

"From the city—we take the same class once and know the same people. He is very crazy, very neurotic, not a good actor. He is—what do you call it?—a closet fairy."

"Really." She tried to draw him out on the subject, but he refused to pursue it. He interrupted to wave to more people, the group he had stood up, for whose benefit he now created a long-distance call and an exaggerated version of the Matron's restrictions, leaving them with the impression, but not the promise, that he would look them up as soon as the dance concert was over. At last he crumpled his napkin, drained his cup, and sighed with deep satisfaction. "Ready?" he asked.

Hannah raised her eyebrows. Ready for what? "Yes, I'm through." She looked at her watch. "And the snack bar will be opening in a minute. I'm off to meet Rachel."

"Good, I come with you. I like to see your room; it tells me something about you."

"You can't still be hungry!"

"No no, I just come with you while you eat. Rachel, is she pretty?"

"More than pretty: I'd say she's gorgeous. But I can tell you now she won't eat with the two of us."

"Why not?"

"She just won't. She's shy and stubborn; and your—shall we say, idiosyncratic—brand of charm won't appeal to her. And she has a stomachache."

"So, we shall see, yes? I ask her very nicely, and if still she won't come, then you can give me a tour of your college, okay?"

Hannah sighed and nodded her head. By this time it was clear that curiosity, if nothing else, had gotten the better of her. "There's nothing to see, though, but trees and fake colonial buildings."

"So you can show me the trees. In New York there are not enough."

14

It was considerably warmer outdoors than she had expected, and drier underfoot. For the first time in recent memory, stars were visible.

"You are a tall girl," he commented. "Yes?"

"Yes," she said, and blood flooded her cheeks so hotly that she was grateful for the cover of night. She hadn't felt at all cumbersome walking beside him until that instant. Now she felt like the beanstalk peering down at Jack. "About five foot nine."

To her discomfiture, he turned to study her as they walked. "But not very tall; not taller than I am, and I am not a tall man. It bothers you, being tall?"

"Well," she said lightly, "it is one of the classic maladies of adolescence."

"But it still bothers you now," he pressed, "and you are not in adolescence."

"Oh, well, I'm not so very far from it. Actually, I suspect the problem isn't so much the height per se, but rather that I use it as a kind of psychological scapegoat. That is, when I feel insecure about something, I blame it on being tall—I feel even taller."

"Do you feel tall now?"

She laughed. "Gargantuan."

"You should not. Height is very good in a woman, elegant. And you are very pretty, you know; very sexy, womanly." He stopped, turned her to him, and then amazed her by taking her face in his hands and scrutinizing it. "What's the matter? You think that you are not feminine because you are tall?"

To Hannah's horror, tears began to tremble in both her eyes and when she tried to say something bright to deflect him, her voice nearly broke. She went rigid with confusion. She never did this—never lost her composure, least of all with strangers.

"Ah, you are foolish," he said softly. "Such a lovely girl, and you don't even know it. Say it—say that you are pretty."

"God, no!" she gasped, ducking away from him and continuing down the path. She felt pink, distracted, discomfited, and hoped that the dusk was concealing it from his relentless gaze.

"Now look," she said as they entered the living room. "You sit here and flirt with whomever comes through. I'll go ask Rachel if she wants to eat with us. Okay? Lots of pretty girls will come by to entertain you, so just make yourself at home—"

She wheeled and fled down the hall. The breathlessness in her voice unnerved her. All her life she had drawn assurance from her belief that while she could see everyone, no one could see her. And now here was this stranger interpreting the lines of her face like a palm reader.

She plunged into the haven of her room and flopped onto the bed, laughing with relief.

Rachel sat scowling by her stereo, smoking and listening to Sinatra. "Well, hi," she said. "What happened? You had to eat with some of Witt's company?"

"Not exactly." She plumped the pillow behind her and leaned back, beginning to calm down. "What a weird day. Actually, I got more or less picked up, or ambushed, by this incredible person, this actor, or so he claims. More like a highwayman, if you ask me. He's an Israeli—"

Rachel grunted disapprovingly.

"What's wrong with that? You trusted Israelis with all those innocent little trees you planted by mail—"

"Yeah, well in principle I'm for them, I guess, but in person they tend to be domineering and crude. And unbelievably conceited."

"Really? Well, that fits this one to a T." Now that she was back in her own room with a friend, Ari seemed comical again, a nuisance. "He's very peculiar. But look, the problem is that I can't get rid of him. He's determined to meet you and eat dinner with us. You'll find him interesting in a bizarre kind of way, and it won't last long. He has to get back for rehearsal—"

"I'm not hungry. You go without me." Rachel's cheeks took on a violet cast.

"Listen, it's nothing like that. I don't want to be alone with him. You know I'd tell you—"

"No, I'm not being tactful, I'm just not hungry, and I don't feel like putting up with a weird Israeli. I've been feeling sick all day, honest."

"You're sure?"

"Positive."

Reluctantly, Hannah got up again and took a step toward the door. "I'm not hungry either, so I guess I'll take him on a guided tour of beautiful Bennington. You want to come for a walk?—good for what ails you—oh, how do I get myself into these things?"

"You're trapped," Rachel teased, "and there's no help coming from this quarter, believe me. Do you want me to get you something from the snack bar if your concert runs late?"

"Yeah, get me some chocolate bars and a Coke. But you'll see me before then—at least I hope you will!" The prospect of relaxing later over Cokes with Rachel was suddenly very sweet, very soothing. Hannah leaned against the doorjamb for a moment and looked at her friend affectionately, then withdrew to consult the mirror before venturing forth. Like many lonely people, she sometimes thought of her private self as a separate voice, almost a friend. Brushing her hair, she met her eyes in the glass and seemed to be keeping herself company.

Then she thought of how appalled Rachel would have been had she consented to meet Ari, and smiled. The primitive sexuality, the frank egotism that tantalized her would have outraged her roommate. Not that she would have blamed Rachel: truly Ari was outrageous.

Feeling better, Hannah headed back to the room to deposit her comb and brush. From the quality of silence she heard behind the half-open door she guessed something was up, but even that didn't prepare her for the sight of Ari standing rapt over Rachel, holding one of her arms aloft and gazing worshipfully at what hung exposed underneath. "Lovely," he breathed with the awe of a mountain climber surveying the view from the top. "Magnificent." Apparently he had converted an introductory handshake into a tour of inspection.

Hannah's smothered exclamation of horror and hilarity released her friend from her shocked trance. Rachel yanked back her arm, flung it behind her, then thought the better of that and whipped it in front, all the while shooting a furious interrogatory glare at Hannah, who avoided it by diving for her bureau drawer; she crammed the brush in and hastily backtracked to the door. Ari, however, did not take the hint. He continued to beam at Rachel, who dug into the mattress like a gopher.

"Ah," he sighed. "Don't hide! You must never hide!"

Rachel glowered. "You claim you're an actor—have you ever acted in anything real, or just bedrooms—?"

In answer, Ari embarked on a description of the sad state of the arts, lack of Federal funding, rampant theatrical unemployment, and his particular woes as a foreigner, speaking as if Rachel's question had sprung from a deep personal interest in his fate. Then he launched into evaluations of all the famous teachers with whom he had studied in New York and their laudatory comments about him. Hannah was impressed at the names he mentioned, but didn't know what to believe. Rachel was thunderstruck. She kept gaping at Hannah for some confirmation that her new friend retained any sanity whatever, but since Hannah couldn't vouch for that, she shrugged and looked away.

Then with that same abrupt shift of attention, Ari broke off his monologue and again concentrated on Hannah. He smiled in a way that intimated that, although his admiration for Rachel and his boasting had been perfectly sincere, he had dramatized them only for their private fun.

"Come, we must take our walk now," he said as if she had been holding them up. "You have a sweater to take. It will be colder out."

Hannah stammered something about not feeling the cold.

"Honestly, Erickson!" snapped Rachel with real annoyance and real concern. "You've taken complete leave of your senses. He is right about that much—it's cold out. Take the sweater."

Hannah meekly fetched a cardigan, which Ari insisted on carrying for her. She noticed his clothes for the first time: khaki pants and a ragged brown sweater. Apparently his narcissism was not sartorially inclined.

He paid another of his elaborate farewells to Rachel while she gazed over his shoulder at Hannah with an expression of helpless worry, as one might watch Ophelia flutter toward the pond. Disturbed by her friend's anxiety, Hannah walked into the hall and waited. When Ari rejoined her, he took her hand, began to walk, then stopped and gave her another of those assessing stares. He seemed able to concentrate on her like a spotlight, and if, like a spotlight, he illuminated some aspects, he also blinded her.

As they neared the back door, Hannah was beginning to look forward to walking with him in the spring night outside, but at that moment the girl whom she considered the prettiest in the dorm, who reminded her of Jenny, came skittering into the house with two of her friends, blocking their path. Hannah nodded and said a perfunctory hello, but Ari was not so easily satisfied. As the girls clustered past he exclaimed his admiration and began to flirt. Startled, they laughed and answered his questions, and looked curiously at his hand holding Hannah's. Then they looked curiously at Hannah. She merely stepped backward, let go of his hand, and said nothing. For the first time his promiscuity offended her.

"You've just got to be here for Jazz Weekend, right?" asked the pretty one in her enthusiastic way. "Somehow you don't look like a college boy!"

Ari ignored her question and concentrated on the ornate silver earrings that shimmered in the light as she talked. "Very nice," he said, fingering them, and from there his hand found its way to her neck.

"Hey," she squealed, hopping backward, carefully not looking at Hannah.

"There's going to be a dance in the living room in about three minutes," drawled one of her friends. "If you want to touch the personnel, you might try asking them to dance instead of pawing them in the halls."

"Magnificent! You will all dance with me?"

Though his question was clearly addressed to the first girl, the other snorted. "Well, it's a free campus; I guess we'll dance with pretty much anyone." The one who had not said anything yet glanced at Hannah with a look of puzzled superiority. Hannah bristled. She took another step backward to indicate that he was free game as far as she was concerned.

"Are you with the dance troupe?" The girl's yellow hair gleamed under the ceiling bulb.

"Yes. And are you coming to see me dance tonight?"

"Sure!" Even the two more dubious girls nodded their heads and some of the condescension left their postures, for everyone admired dancers.

"And your dance—you have a band?"

The pretty one shrugged deprecatingly. "Oh no, just the record player in there. I mean, it's very informal."

"In where? In the living room?" Ari walked to the doorway and peered in as if he expected to see a silent party just awaiting his signal to begin.

"Well, you can't start without the records," the pretty girl laughed and, taking the pile from the other girls' arms, led him into the main room, her friends following.

So much for that, Hannah thought. Humiliation and the simple pain of rejection washed over her. She had seen him beckon for her to follow, but had no intention of obeying. She was, however, dangerously near tears, so she pushed through the outer door into the night. She might as well take her walk alone.

As he had predicted, it was chillier as well as darker, but not really cold: spring had definitely arrived. And he still had her sweater—damn! She rubbed her upper arms and strode toward the low stone wall that divided the college from fields, forests, and the poorest section of the neighboring town.

From a distance, in daylight, the wilderness beyond this wall seemed to plummet into a deep valley that finally rose again miles away in majestic hills that spread eternally onward, as if the campus were a flat green podium surveying a vast panorama of famous New England landscape: a sparkling whitewashed community of the mind overseeing nature. This was the view photographed for countless brochures and postcards. It was, however, an optical illusion. Close up, the wall became a makeshift line of boulders, unevenly spaced, that arbitrarily divided scrubby grass on one side from scrubby grass on the other. The vast valley turned out to be a modest, though broad, slope. The eternal expanse of green became pebbly earth mottled with tough weeds and the twisted gestures of dead sticks still clinging to living roots.

Yet Hannah still experienced a small thrill whenever she stepped over the wall into unpruned territory. She often walked there when she was lonely and restless: the landscape would seem as deserted as her mood and its gritty tenacity would soothe and absorb her. It seemed the naural place to head tonight. And this truly was a lovely night, which only heightened her melancholy. Deep blue-green dusk enveloped the quad, melting all lines and shapes into one elusive medley of green and gray and ink-black forms. All clear sense of distance and familiarity was obscured. The center lawn was silent and empty, but from the dormitories bordering it came the faint light and music of beginning celebration.

Behind her the dormitory door burst open and emitted a brief squirt of song and partying before it banged shut again. Her walk slowed. She remembered that she would have to report back for the concert soon.

When she heard rapid footsteps behind her, she assumed it was some cheerful couple darting by to cast her in their shadow, so when Ari arrived panting to take her hand, her nerves jangled. It hadn't occurred to her that he might come.

"Why did you go away? I tell you to come with me back there—you didn't see? I almost couldn't find you in the dark."

"I—" She was lost for words. "I didn't want to go to the party—and you obviously did."

His disapproval was almost palpable. Even in the dark he could transmit his moods by sheer energy. Her dismay annoyed her: she had to stifle an impulse to apologize.

"You must not be possessive," he said.

"I wasn't! I don't like those girls and I don't like their parties. And I never like competitive sports. So I left. I did not expect you to follow."

"Sure you did."

"No," she said, "I really didn't. I assumed you'd stay and dance."

"But you knew I want to be with you instead of your friends—"

"No. They're all very pretty and there are three of them. And you hardly know me."

"You are a silly girl. I just wanted to dance with you." Though his words chided, his tone became very gentle. He stopped to help her into her sweater, then put his arm around her and quickened his pace. "Where are we going?"

"I don't know, really. When I thought I had left you behind, I was going to an old cemetery beyond that wall, but if you want a tour of the campus—"

"No, we go where you are going." He held her closer. "Did you really think I desert you?"

"Sure."

As they clambered over the rocks, Hannah felt released, exhilarated. She had always liked to believe that she was not afraid of the dark, but in truth, her cinematic imagination rendered her more vulnerable to its perils than most people. Vision, moreover, was her primary sense, the mode of defense she most counted on. But she also had a certain courage and, more important, a stubborn conviction that she was brave. She hoisted her pride and plunged forward, trembling. All her life she had walked Matty on the beach on moonless nights when she couldn't see more than a yard or two ahead and the sand drifts gleamed eerily and shadows leaped forward like ghosts. She was always frightened, but also proud and resolute. She liked the wilderness of the beach and of her mood, and she liked exploring them both for something she could apparently find only when her eyes were shut.

Now she led Ari down the uneven hill that folded over to the far left of the field. The crumbly ground slid under their feet. Once it gave way altogether and they found themselves sitting on the incline. At last, peering to all sides, she led him into the long-retired graveyard, her favorite place for being alone. Its silence had intimidated her the first time she forced herself to sit here late at night, wide-eyed with insomnia, but eventually she learned to relax and open herself to its gentle mood. The cracked headstones were blurred and hoary in the moonlight, reminding her of the sand dunes she had left behind, though in General's Bay there were no actual cemeteries, for land by the sea is too shallow to hold corpses for long.

Hannah wondered why she had led Ari here, though he seemed happy enough. Certainly they were not going to hold hands and exclaim like Victorian lovers over the picturesque inscriptions that it was now too dark to read. He was apparently lost in musing of his own. She turned to suggest taking him elsewhere, but before she could close her mouth she was eased abruptly but expertly into such a startlingly intimate embrace that she gasped, first into the air, then somewhere into him as he lowered her to the ground. Of course she had expected that he would kiss her, and that she would let him, but she had in no way foreseen this fluid surrender to the suddenly overwhelming gravity of the earth. The earth, on the other hand, proved damp and chilly. They both got up a little awkwardly and laughed at their predicament, but inwardly Hannah was thunderstruck. He had seemed somehow to touch all of her with all of him so that she could find no opportunity to, as the newspaper advisors put it, draw the line. There hadn't been the orderly parade of moves she had come to expect. He had been like a sponge absorbing her, and Hannah had never realized she could melt to water.

When he solicitously brushed her off, then drew her against him again, she was alarmed at her vanishing control over the situation and herself. He took for granted everything she had been trained to dole out like blue ribbons and brass cups. Fortunately, the soggy ground itself could be trusted to exert a modicum of control, so the main worry swirling in her wide-open eyes was what he would think. What kind of girl would he take her for if she let things go on like this? Her clothing was hanging at odd angles, magically liberated from all buttons, snaps and zippers. His dexterity was a marvel. Was he labeling her, literally, a pushover, his respect diminishing as his ardor grew?

Suddenly she was standing under her own power again with a chance to catch her breath. She was grateful and growing calmer until she realized that he was scouting the area for some kind of shelter. When she saw his eyes alight on three metal grave markers imbedded in a row, long enough to accommodate at least their torsos, she squinted frantically at her watch.

"Oh, it must be late!" she said.

He scrutinized her in that same amused way that so discomfited her, then lit a match and looked at his own watch. "Very late," he said sadly.

She moved closer to see. He had to report a full hour earlier than she did, she knew, and it was hardly more than half an hour before she was due. "Oh dear, I've really held you up, I'm afraid!" She imagined him purged from the company; Miss Witt seemed so strict.

He chuckled and put his arms around her in light affection that soon gave way to something more serious. This time, however, he released her as abruptly as he had first caught her to him, apparently surprised at his own momentum, and when he did, she fell indecorously backward on boneless legs, and he had to steady her, which she found mortifying. Her head was still clear and upright, but everything underneath had gone soggy, like spaghetti noodles lowered halfway into a pot of boiling water. She held on to his shoulder and tried to relocate her muscles.

"But you are amazing!" he exclaimed.

That hardly reassured her. It sounded like a tribute he might pay an impressive natural phenomenon, the Grand Canyon or Old Faithful. And she knew that neither a crevasse nor a geyser was a suitable or attractive image for a young woman. She had failed again to be demure, delicate or feminine, although, ironically, she had never in her life felt more passive. She blinked in confusion.

"What is it—what's wrong? You are troubled."

She found herself inarticulate.

"But you are so sweet." He petted her in a way she did find reassuring, then said, "You are coming to the cast party after the performance, yes? I meet you there and we be together."

"No, I didn't even know there was one. I haven't been invited."

"But I know you are welcome to come, surely."

"I don't. Anyway, I wouldn't know anyone. I'd be much too shy."

"Your friends by the light-board—?"

"I don't even know their names."

He sighed. "Unfortunately, I cannot take you."

She didn't say anything, didn't even wonder anything, although she was disappointed. She was prepared to accept him, too, as a natural phenomenon. "You are good not to ask why. It's hard to explain."

"Oh."

He pondered. "So, this is what we do. I have to go to the party, but I leave as early as I can, and then I meet you. Around midnight, I think. I come to your room at midnight. You will wait?"

"Yes." The refrain, "I come to your room at midnight," echoed in her ear like a line from the *Highwayman*, her favorite of the long poems James used to recite to her from memory on Sunday mornings when she came to her parents' bed. But she doubted Ari would come to her room at midnight. The party would be fun; pretty dance majors would be there. She wouldn't blame him for electing to stay.

"Good. Now I must hurry, except not yet." He began to stamp maniacally around on the grass.

Bewildered, she watched him march in circles for a moment, then asked what on earth he was doing.

"Idiot," he said tenderly. "What do you think?"

"I—I don't. . . ."

"Here." He appropriated her hand and tucked it between his legs.

She stifled an impulse to leap backward. "Oh!"

"You see? But take your hand away or it never goes down. How can I go back to that college of nice young ladies like this? How can I go to rehearsal and put on tights?"

"I see."

"Yes, a problem. Silly, at my age. That's why I say you are amazing. Imagine, we just are standing here, after all. My pants are even zipped. I feel like a teen-ager."

An odd variety of compliment she attracted, Hannah thought. Rather like a celebrity's testimonial to a brand of aspirin—guaranteed effective in seconds! She had always known, of course, that some brands were packaged more alluringly than others, but she had believed all to be equal in the dark.

She hastily zipped her own pants and straightened her sweater, but to her embarrassment, had to ask him to fasten her bra. She had never learned to do it behind her back.

"But you are such a little girl," he said, amused, as he fumbled with the hooks. "I think I do it best in the other direction. There." He combed her hair with his fingers, which were tempted to descend, then thought better of it; chided himself, jumped backward and resumed stamping. "Look," he finally pleaded. "My problem is hopeless with you here. I tell you, if you will lend me your sweater I can disguise myself until it goes away or I find a bathroom. Okay?"

She had never been asked to confer on such tactics before, but his pragmatic approach made it difficult to be shy. She handed him the cardigan and, at his request, described the location of the men's rooms.

He took her hand and they helped one another up the hill, then strolled slowly toward the Commons, Ari steering them into pockets of darkness. When they came near the lights of the buildings, he playfully stepped back and tucked her ahead as a shield, walking in single file, but quickly jumped beside her again and lamented that he had only exacerbated his dilemma.

When they were parallel to her dormitory, Hannah smiled and went to turn away. "Listen," he added, not relinquishing her hand. "Maybe after all you find a way to come to the party on your own. It will be nice to be there together."

"I doubt it, actually. You'd be the only person I'd know to speak to."

"But once you are there I can be with you. Perhaps I can find another way to get you there."

"Alright." She unfastened her hand and headed back to her house. The plans seemed overly complicated, but she didn't want to question him: he was much too exotic for her to have any expectations. It was true that, if she were to appear at the party, probably no one would notice her, but she did not trust Ari enough to place herself in a situation where she might be in any way dependent on him. She didn't trust him at all.

15

In her room she found she had time only to comb her hair, wave at Rachel, and flee to the theatre. There she found chaos. One of the students on the sound crew was sick in the infirmary, so Hannah's partner would have to help out across the stage for most of the concert, and Hannah would have to learn most of her assignment. She saw very little of the dancing and a great deal of the prompter's tense face. Ari's incantation had come and gone before she had time to remember it. Her duties were more like painting by numbers than participating in the creation of art or beauty—for all she knew she could have been working the lights for a trained-dog act.

She performed well, however, and earned a compliment from Ed, which pleased her. Only then, as she heard the audience filing out, did she relax enough to think about herself again. She trotted onstage with the others after the curtain had gone up, ostensibly to help dismantle the few props but actually because she saw Ari milling there with Ed, Rosalind Witt and some others, and wanted to show off a bit, perhaps to have him take her hand. He did not so much as smile perfunctorily at her, however. She moved a footstool into the wings and when she turned around again, he was gone. She blinked at the space where he had been, bewildered, then shrugged and helped drag a papier-mâché tree into the storage room, concluding dejectedly that that, simply, was that. Obviously he was not trying to infiltrate her into the party. The possibility that he might have a relationship with someone in the company did occur to her, but she had watched carefully and seen him pay no special attention to anyone. Still, it was hard to tell with theatre people: they were all so effusive. Wanting to be fair, she waited until the dressing rooms and stage were perfectly quiet except for the footsteps of the girls cleaning up in the backwash. Apparently her fellow crew members had not been invited either. She was very glad she hadn't tried to go alone. And then even they began to trickle off, and Hannah slung her sturdy bag over her shoulder and followed.

* * *

At least it had been a diverting evening, she thought as she walked down the hall to her room. And it was already after eleven and she was sleepy for once, so by twelve-thirty, when she would know for sure that he wasn't coming, she could simply turn in, which would do her good.

She stretched out heavily on the bed and stared at the wall, wondering where Rachel was. She felt too depleted to do anything but wait; she tucked her comforter over her perpetually cold feet. Then, as the minutes dribbled by, she had to admit she was nowhere near as placid and resigned as she wished to be. Her stomach was gradually clenching into an apprehensive fist. Her head was light; tension came sizzling up through her body in waves; and at every thirty-second interval she couldn't help glancing at the clock.

Finally Rachel clomped in, gave her a skeptical look, took two chocolate bars out of her pocketbook, tossed them to Hannah, and settled back on her own bed.

"Hi," said Hannah. "How do you feel?"

Rachel frowned gravely, looked very adult, then suddenly picked up her pillow and hurled it at Hannah. "How could you?! Have you gone entirely mad? Neurotic is one thing—but stark insanity is something else again!"

Hannah laughed and tucked the pillow behind her. "I know," she groaned. "But I kind of—well, he sort of fascinated me. Forces beyond my control and all that."

"I'll admit he's very handsome."

"Really?" Handsome to Hannah connoted conventional and distinguished, regular features and smooth hair, which didn't especially appeal to her. What did appeal to her in Ari, more than his appearance, was his powerful, even primitive energy. She realized that the reason she had failed to recognize him was that she didn't precisely see him—she experienced him, felt him in fragments like a storm.

"Yes, very handsome in a—you should forgive my mentioning it, Hannah Wasp Erikson—a very semitic way. But he's also a maniac and a pervert on top of that."

"Oh, I know!" Hannah groveled playfully, face in hands, and laughed. "You're right, you're right. But really you're just jealous because I have someone from the old country—"

"It's the new country, you ass. However"—Rachel's tone was arch; she held one forefinger in the air in the attitude of a professor—"I assume that's the last you've seen of him, so we can munch our candy and smoke our—my—cigarette and head to bed like good little girls, right?"

"Well, probably. There is a possiblity, however, that I could have a midnight date. A slim possibility."

Silence. Then Rachel said, still fondly but more pointedly, "And just exactly what constitutes a midnight date in the middle of the fucking woods, may I ask? You're going to the Savoy Oak Tree, perhaps?"

"More likely the jazz improvisation at the Carriage Barn. But I'm sure the contingency won't arise. He has to go to the cast party first, and I imagine something—someone—will distract him there."

Rachel lit a cigarette and exhaled at length. "So why isn't he taking you to this party?"

Hannah smiled. "You know who you sound like, don't you, Ravish?"

"Shut up. There are times when you need a mother, even mine. Answer the question. What's he got, two dates?"

"Probably." She summarized the events in the cemetery and Ari's cryptic explanation as best she could, and let it hang. She glanced anxiously at the clock from time to time while Rachel glanced anxiously at her.

Finally Hannah lurched to her feet, walked over to the closet and inspected it as grimly as General Custer calculating his arsenal. She stripped off her jeans, hung them neatly on the hook, and folded her sweater into the drawer. If Rachel had not been glowering at her from the opposite bed, she probably would have stood on a chair in front of the mirror above the bureau to confront, yet again, her recalcitrant and very foreign body. But as it was, she shrank a little into the closet. Tonight she needed something familiar and simple, nothing to add to the constriction she already felt. At last she pulled on her reliable black stretch pants in which she felt almost as invisible as in jeans. After more deliberation she added her favorite top, a white silk overblouse, which had added sentimental value because she and a friend had shoplifted it shortly before graduation as something to remember one another by when they got to college. She slipped her feet into insubstantial black pumps and glanced involuntarily at Rachel. Once Hannah had confessed her irrational sense that loafers made her taller than other shoes, and Rachel had teased her about it ever since.

Now she said as if on cue: "It's wet out. You'll get those skimpy flats covered with mud and your feet will freeze."

"I know, but I feel freer in them. As if I could run away."

"Well, why don't you save yourself the trouble and just not go, then?" Rachel looked at her seriously, then tactfully searched under her blanket for her nightgown.

Hannah tried to laugh off the question. "Well," she said, raising an arm dramatically. "Zis is somet'ing I muzt do!"

"Why?"

Hannah moved off into the corner by her bureau, fingered her comb, then leaned against the wall and contemplated her friend, conscious that she couldn't really explain. Rachel had simply never felt what she felt now. "Well, he intrigues me—and I guess I feel we should meet challenges when they come."

"You sound like Davy Crockett or something, for God's sake. Hannah, you could get hurt!" Affection and worry passed over Rachel's face, and so did an incomprehension that, had she not loved Hannah, would have turned to disgust. Why couldn't Hannah just open her eyes and see what was obvious?

Hannah sighed and rubbed her face. "Well, no sense arguing about it, because I'm sure he won't come."

"But if he does come, you'll go?"

"Yes."

Finally Rachel blurted her underlying concern. "Well, you're not going to sleep with him, are you?"

That was a question it had taken courage to ask, and Hannah could see that Rachel expected her to be angry, but she wasn't. She just didn't know the answer. "Well, I want to, so if I don't, it'll be out of caution."

"Oh, Hannah, why?" Rachel's cry was angry, fearful, and sincerely curious all at once.

Hannah grinned. "Some of it, I'm afraid, is just chemical; hard to describe if you haven't felt it, like describing a color."

"What if you never see him again?"

Hannah folded her arms and looked at them. "I know. I don't want to feel I've been used. But why shouldn't I have a pleasurable night for its own sake, same as he would? I don't believe pleasure is a sin. It's not as if I would realistically expect to see him again. I mean, New York is hardly dating distance. Maybe what it all comes down to is his attitude."

"I just don't understand what could be worth that risk—letting someone like that take advantage of you—!"

Hannah closed the discussion by turning to the mirror to stroke on mascara. She didn't want to emphasize their disagreement, because if by some chance he did come, it would be all the harder to leave the room on a note of adamant disapproval. Rachel, after all, was the only person in the community, in the whole state and region, in fact, whom she fully trusted and loved. If she had to choose, of course she would choose Rachel, but she didn't want to choose.

She had circles under her eyes, she noticed, which blended with the green shadow she had impulsively brushed on and made her look intense and haunted. But alas, that was the only visible chink in her armor: the rest of her, as usual, looked cool and sanguine. Tension pared her down, refined her, made her seem all the more serene, healthy and wise.

The wind flapped the shades and curtains. She felt increasingly edgy. Every small noise startled her. She was glad when Rachel closed the windows before tucking herself into bed as a good example, but within a few minutes she found the silence worse. She might not hear him if he was out there, and she didn't want to be ambushed without warning. The front door seemed to open and shut continually to the accompaniment of male voices. This was agony and senseless to boot, since he wasn't coming. The glassy darkness tormented her until finally she reopened a window.

She sat on her bed across from it and tried to concentrate on a book, but the wind was deliberately taunting her, sighing, huffing, rifling through their papers and blowing even the memory of peace from the clean, white, usually orderly room until she wanted to scream back. At last she decided to surrender and close the glass again, and got as far as putting down her book when she remembered the torturesome silence and changed her mind. It was easier to yield to the cruelty of distant music, passing footsteps, intimate laughter and soft conversation than to cut herself off entirely.

When the large clock above the Commons at last chimed midnight, Hannah closed her eyes in glum relief. Ten minutes later she began to breathe normally, though sadly. In ten more minutes, Rachel reached for a Coke, signaling with a sympathetic shrug that the crisis had passed. Hannah promised herself that in another twenty-five minutes she would lock the doors and windows and take off her makeup and clothes.

She told herself that, after all, he hardly seemed able to remember his own name from one hour to the next, much less hers. Like an overstimulated child at an amusement park—like Hannah herself, long ago, on the boardwalk with her parents—he lived without sense of sequence, of reasonable progression, of passing time and passing scenes and changing faces. Gobbling cotton candy, frozen custard, apples on the stick and saltwater taffy, grabbing at popcorn and Kewpie dolls and brass rings and gold, he lurched enraptured from merry-go-round to Ferris wheel to crack-the-whip and back to the carrousel with no memory, or regret, that he had ever been there before. Nothing began or ended. Flux was all. Of course it wasn't safe to depend on someone like that, not if you were grown-up and had no parents to watch over you. Every year-round resident in the resort town knew that the roller coaster had at least one bad breakdown a year—many summers a cart would fly straight off the tracks and deposit its passengers on the rocks below. Often a single child bounced up and over to drop like a lost teddy bear into the waiting ocean. But in a month the machinery would be repaired, the tourists and their memories gone back to the suburbs to be replaced by fresh sunburns and full wallets, and all the fun would begin again. Year-round residents never set foot on that famous metal ski slope over ivory surf; they never let young children go to that carnival alone. How could Hannah have let herself be attracted by all that shoddy glamour like any credulous summer visitor? She was no longer a child to close her eyes to the inevitable ending of things.

The cymbal-crash of the struck screen shocked her like an alarm clock. She looked to see a face swimming in the darkness outside.

"Hi, I am here. I tap before, but you are dreaming. Where is your friend?" The spectral oval peered from side to side. Rachel clutched her blankets up to her chin and hissed at Hannah.

"Wait there, I'll come out!" Hannah sprang to her feet, pulled down the shade, picked up her pocketbook and put it down again, and gave a last pat to her hair. Then she turned to contemplate her cowering roommate. Rachel had put down her book. She stared up darkly from her pillow, twisting her black hair into finger-curls that fell straight again the instant her restless hand lost interest.

"Are you going to sleep?" asked Hannah.

"Yes!"

Hannah walked to the other side of the room and switched on the night-light that Rachel had brought from the city to combat her terror of the dark. Usually Hannah forbade her to use it: to the girl accustomed to the ebony of seaside evenings, it seemed to blaze like a moon. She switched off the last lamp.

"Good-bye," she said softly. Then she slipped a comb in her pocket, fastened her watch, and ran out into the night, leaving her friend to get up and close the window behind her.

16

He slipped her sweater over her shoulders and took her hand.

"I really didn't think you'd come," she gasped. "I thought my sweater would have to find a new home."

"Silly girl," he said in surprise, looking closely at her. "I wanted to see you again. It was hard for me to get away, but I think I am not so late—?"

"No."

"Then come. I want to take you to a special place I have found for us, just for you and me."

He led her back toward the Commons, but this time took her through a small side door, cloaked by trees, which Hannah had noticed before but never used. Inside it was so entirely dark that not even the white of their skin was visible. She guessed that this must be a small alcove that led off in various directions to the post office and business offices. In daytime it was no more than a preface to elsewhere, but at night it was utterly contained and private. Suddenly the great clock on the roof above them bonged the half-hour, and Hannah shivered. This place is like an old church, she thought with building panic. This is how a confessional must seem with its veils and bells and curtains and unseen judgment lurking somewhere within. Her jaw tightened with anxiety. Was he so bent on seducing her and so sure of her compliance that he had brought her straight from her own room and her friend to this black tomb? Beyond the walls she couldn't hear a sound. When he moved to kiss her, she froze with humiliation and fear.

"But what is it? Did I make you angry because I was late? You are so cold."

So tense now that she could hardly move her jaw, too petrified even to cry, she decided to bring the unbearable situation to an end. "I just thought you should know that I am absolutely not going to sleep with you tonight, especially not on this floor," she announced.

"But why do you say that?" he snapped.

"Because it's true." Her chin wobbled dangerously.

"But why do you say it now? Do you think I bring you here and show you this special place just to trick you, to fuck you on this cold floor?"

"Yes," she whispered.

"You are a fool! Do you think I am one of your schoolboys who is so hungry for a piece of ass he try to screw you in the hallway? I have a room, you know, with a bed in it!"

Tears of humiliation trickled quietly down Hannah's hot cheeks. All at once she felt that it might have been very nice to hold him and cuddle in this snug warren after all. He gripped her wrist and pulled her rather rudely back outside. As she was propelled forward, she tried desperately to stop her persistent tears. At least she could creep back home now, she promised herself. Rachel would be proud.

In a slightly calmer but still cold voice he continued to scold her. "How can you be so crude? Do you have no tenderness or sensitivity? American girls are like bulldozers! I don't know why anyone would want to fuck them, but all the time they are thinking everybody does. The man in the library, in the store, in the class, in the restaurant—they think because he smiles at them he wants to fuck them! Who wants to fuck a bulldozer?"

"A mechanic," said Hannah. By now she was shuddering almost audibly at her stupidity in exposing herself to a situation like this.

He reached angrily for her arm and she flinched, which only deepened his scowl. But when he had held her arm severely for a moment, his grip began to relent. Then he looked down at her face and felt her eyes with his fingertips. "But you are crying," he said. "Why are you crying? And your arm is trembling. Have I upset you so much just because I yell a little?" His rough voice was suddenly very kind, very puzzled.

She nodded her head and sniffled, frightened by her incoherence.

"But I only—I yell so often—you must get used to that. I did not understand you were so—so sensitive. But why did you say such an insensitive thing when I am only sharing a special place with you?"

"I just"—she struggled to regain control—"I was just trying—" But her voice cracked and a new wave of tears gulped up from her chest. "Do you have a handkerchief I could borrow, please?"

"Oh yes, you just cry a moment, it is the best thing." Very concerned, he handed her a crumpled hanky.

For all that she was genuinely intimidated by the masculine temper that had broken upon her like a thunderclap, Hannah was still able to observe herself dryly enough to wonder at this uncharacteristic deluge. The part of her that was a sympathetic but independent companion looked down incredulously at the damp little girl who couldn't stop weeping. Finally, with great effort, she pulled herself together enough to clear her throat and test her voice.

"No no," he admonished. "Don't try to hold it back."

To her shock, his advice affected her like some long-awaited, longed-for invitation: she had to clench her muscles and cough as though steeling herself against a powerful, and terrifying, temptation. "No," she gasped quickly, "I'm okay. I'm sorry; I realize I was gauche. I didn't mean to be, it's just that I—" She broke off, wondering how on earth to explain to him. Then, with a resigned grimace, she decided that the whole night had been so bizarre anyway, she might just as well take a chance and try to explain what she had witnessed so often in her dorm—the effect of being screwed and abandoned on the self-esteem of even the strongest girl.

"But why—I don't understand why these boys do as you say."

Though she suspected his innocence was feigned, Hannah tried to explain the double standard and its repercussions. "The awful thing is they think less of a girl they had liked a lot just because she had liked him enough to want him."

He interrupted with an indignant splutter. Yes, he said, he had encountered such malicious, perverted attitudes, and they enraged him! Indeed, he grew enraged all over again, but this time at the injustices perpetrated on innocent girls like Hannah. He then interrupted himself to explain that they were going to go to the jazz improvisation in the music building, which was about a quarter-mile away. Steering her in that direction, he took back his soggy hanky and resumed his diatribe against destructive sexual mores.

Hannah trotted obediently along at his side, considerably calmer now, musing on the irony of his knowing the way to the Carriage Barn better than she. His lecture was hard to follow, since it relied on names and events unfamiliar to her; apparently he took for granted her intimate acquaintance with the drama of his life. Nonetheless, his basic themes were clear and, to Hannah, persuasive. True obscenity, in his opinion, stemmed from repression, not from whatever pleasure two people, or more, could find together. Although he believed monogamy to be unnatural, he did accept a certain kind of fidelity: that is, if he liked a woman enough to share his pleasure with her once, he certainly would want to see her again. Which was not to say, he hastened to add, that a passing embrace in the night couldn't be beautiful too. It all depended on what circumstances allowed. At moments his vehemence struck Hannah as disproportionate, as if it might be more a defense against past accusations than a simple manifesto, and she couldn't help noticing, with both amusement and chagrin, that for all the solicitude that presumably lay behind his monologue, he had successfully wrenched the spotlight back to himself.

More important to her than his rhetoric, however, was the way he walked. She listened only enough to be polite and instead let herself savor the simple sensation of being near him. He moved like an unleashed dog making his daily tour of his territory, perfectly at ease on his own turf, a part of him abstracted in deep meditation, yet another part remaining always alive to the message of passing breezes, of new objects, the texture of the land. He seemed to glide along the ground like an animal accustomed to roaming, comfortable with it and with himself. She thought with amusement that if he were suddenly to lift his leg to a bush, dog-like, she would not be altogether shocked.

The rocky path they were ambling along was indirect and circuitous, taking them past the sculpture studios, past faculty houses, and through two patches of woods. Gradually Hannah was relaxing. The night air felt damp and cool against her flushed face. The young saplings by the roadside seemed to be stretching with satisfaction at having survived another winter, and the rustle of their branches, the fragrance of moldering pine needles, the whole medley of moaning wood and swishing leaves and redolent decay, combined to soothe Hannah like a natural balm. The pinch of sticks and pebbles through the thin soles of her slippers somehow reassured her, reminded her that she was on familiar ground. It felt good to walk through country beside Ari. It felt good to hold his hand and find her long stride merging comfortably with his.

He broke off his monologue mid-sentence to ask how she felt. Much better, she answered, and she smiled tentatively up at him. To her surprise he didn't kiss her; instead he ruffled her hair with his free hand. "But you are such a funny girl," he marveled. "You seem at first so positive of yourself, and yet now you are like a child. Other people tell you this?"

"No," she said with interest. "Not many people think I'm like a child."

"How old are you?"

"Eighteen."

"Eighteen!" He stopped in his tracks.

Hannah smiled. "It's okay, I'm legal."

"But you seem—I thought you were in the oldest class, twenty-one or at least twenty. The girls with you backstage, they look so young!"

"We're all freshmen. I'm just tall."

"No, it's not that. It's the way you look, the way you seem. Much older. Ah, my goodness! So tell me, little teen-ager, how many men have you fucked?"

The word startled her. "Well," she said hesitantly, "one, I suppose."

"Oh." He nodded his head as if her reply had answered any number of questions. "Why you say you 'suppose'? He hurt you, like these boys you tell me about?"

"No, not that. I mean, we liked each other and all. It's just that I wouldn't say we exactly—" She trailed off, reluctant to be so direct.

"I understand, you are still a virgin. Being a virgin is not a piece of skin, you know. You can get into bed with a hundred men and still be a virgin. You see?"

Embarrassed, she nodded.

"You must not be shy to talk about these things; they are natural." Clearly he wasn't shy. He soliloquized briefly on the causes, diagnosis, treatment and cure of virginity. "So," he concluded, "someday you let me show you what I mean, yes?"

"But not tonight," she said hastily. How had the conversation veered back in this direction after his sensitive appreciation of her difficulties just a few minutes before? Fortunately they were nearing the music building. The sound of the concert was already wafting through the trees. "How old are you, by the way?" she asked chiefly to change the subject.

"Twenty-six. Maybe you let me show you tonight. We just talk and I show you what I mean. Wait and see. You can trust me, you know."

Twenty-six was an unknown quantity; neither thirty, which was middle-aged, nor really young, either. Hannah had already been five when Jennifer was twenty-six, four when James was. She had clear memories of his thirtieth birthday party.

The Carriage Barn was a square modern structure, somewhat isolated from the rest of the campus. One of Hannah's dance classes met here weekly, but that was the only room she could locate, especially at night, when bulbs overhead turned stairways and halls into a shadowy maze. Ari, however, with a sure instinct for direction that she was already coming to rely on, led her unhesitatingly to the less formal auditorium.

This room, usually a rehearsal hall, was a large square of tawny wood. The arrangement of folding chairs and a portable platform defined the stage, which was presently occupied by a motley of professional musicians and students happily conspiring to produce an overpowering blast of rhythmical sound. A balcony about six feet wide ran around all four walls, and it was to this that Ari led Hannah. They crept in as quietly as possible, whispering excuses, and picked their way through the mass of bodies to the railing, where they squatted and added their two pairs to the fringe of legs that bordered the room like an awning ruffle.

The music was so loud it obliterated any attempt at conversation. Everyone's blood beat to the same primitive pulse. Dazed and drained, Hannah was glad to be sucked in, to feel herself reduced to one more cell in the sway of an irresistible heartbeat. She ceased to think and let herself drift back and forth with the same impulse as every other person in the crowd, neither liking nor disliking the music itself, merely submitting gratefully to its effect. She closed her eyes and let the almost palpable sound waves buoy around her, and soon, sitting very still, she began to float and drift and feel her tension melt into a drowsy warmth. Suddenly, though, she caught herself listing so far to one side that she brushed against her neighbor, and then, jerking timidly away, she rebounded into Ari on the other side. To her annoyance, he didn't seem to notice. Afraid of being mesmerized, she opened her eyes to find out what he was doing, and saw that he was busily calculating the impression he was making on the people near them. She continued to study him languidly, so sensitized by the music that she could almost feel the delicate rises at the corners of his wide mouth. The tip of her tongue seemed to taste the hungry shadows under his cheekbones. She wished she could stroke his face as she would a sensuous sculpture, letting her fingers follow the arch of his nose to the hollow where his dark eyes shifted impatiently. She wanted to touch his body, too, which had relaxed in the manner of an alert cat, all the tension alive in his eyes and spirit. She wanted to slide her hand under the soft sleeve of his sweater and feel the taut density of his arms. She wanted to press against his loose clothing and his hard slender frame simultaneously, relishing the contrast.

He, however, seemed utterly distracted, and his restlessness finally began to annoy her. Her mood was so intense it seemed impossible he wouldn't soon absorb it from the charged air between them. She wanted to spend the night here with him, both of them carried away by the impersonal force of the music, clinging together like children in a storm. Much later there was to be a party and social dancing and then they might cuddle and sway in dreamy romance. Here she wanted to share with him how loose and sensual she felt and his attention was everywhere but on herself! Finally she made an effort to follow his gaze. To her shock she realized that he was staring down at a large segment of the dance company, including Ed, who were seated below and staring back even more openly. Indeed, they were even staring at her! And discussing her. Why on earth were they so interested? Surely it wasn't unusual for a member of the company to pick up a girl for the evening in such a well-stocked preserve.

"I thought their party would go on for hours more," she heard Ari say angrily. "Damn them!" He turned abruptly and signaled her to rise. Startled and quite disappointed, Hannah followed him from the balcony back into the empty corridors. "I don't like everyone to know everything I do," he muttered by way of explanation.

The night air dissipated some of her calm, and apprehension again nibbled at her stomach. The concert had postponed all further decisions —decisions that she would now, doubtless, be faced with. Her mood was very strange, divided, drawing her so close to Ari at moments that she actually brushed against him as they walked, yet leaving her very distant inwardly, absorbed in her own solitude. She was grateful that he remained silent, and she was not in the least curious about his thoughts, which were clearly elsewhere. He strode rather purposefully down the dark path, occasionally squeezing her hand in a kind of tacit apology or reminder. She felt outside herself, disoriented. Somewhere deep within, her perceptions seemed dazed and foggy, yet at the same time her outer senses were unnaturally keen and agitated. She couldn't quite take herself in hand. Her balance swayed as gently as a sailboat moored in a harbor, anticipating the coming change in the tide. Yet it wasn't really the stranger at her side to whom she was so inexplicably in thrall; rather it was to herself, this unaccountable new self. Even the meadows and thickets they had passed an hour before seemed transformed to foreign lands by the humid and windy night.

With the abrupt shift of attention she was coming to recognize as characteristic, Ari halted, drew her against him, brushed her damp hair from her forehead, and walked on more slowly, still holding her beside him. Her body made no protest whatever, yet even as she shifted her gait to accommodate his, she envisioned herself breaking free and sprinting off into the empty woods and fields between there and her room as clearly as if her shadow had gone on without her. Soon, she promised herself soothingly, soon she would make the decision, leave him, and be alone again. In a few minutes they would near the lawn and there she would say good-night—the words would somehow come to her through this fog—and in a few minutes more she would be tiptoeing back into her safe cloister, trying not to awaken a slumbering Rachel.

But he, or this new aspect of herself, led her past the dormitories, across the wide lawn, and although she glanced back over her shoulder with open mouth, she made no audible demurrer. A heavy, resigned sadness seemed to anchor her to her body. She was somehow too sad, too tired and too sad to struggle any longer. Senseless tears welled in her eyes and spilled quietly over. She had lost all comprehension of the moods that were rushing through her like flood waters, and she made no attempt to fight them back. He led her silently past the Commons, past the far row of houses, past the last lit building, and into a field she rarely explored. Briars bit the bare arches of her feet, but she didn't bother to watch where she walked. Thorns clawed at her trailing arm, but she didn't bother to lift it. In fact she almost welcomed the slight pain and abrasion of the branches: they seemed determined to catch her and draw her down into the damp soil, into their roots and slugs, and she hoped they would succeed. She hoped they were stronger than whatever tugged her inexorably forward with him. Insects sounded their single note on all sides. The wind keened. Her hair was wet to the touch, and strands which she didn't bother to brush back blew across her eyes. Once she tripped on a small hummock and her knees threatened to give way completely; Ari caught her with no expression of surprise. She stared almost yearningly at the place where she would have landed: the ground still cold from the winter, the moribund weeds. Gluey leaf mold stuck to her ankles. Waving milkweed, topaz under the moon, seemed to laugh as it bowed her past. Only the pressure of Ari's arm kept her moving.

She saw a massive black presence emerging from the mist and only then realized that he was taking her to yet another renovated mansion, this one kept as a dormitory for bachelor faculty, a few male students, and occasional lecturers and visitors. It was the only residence on campus barred to the women. She trembled wildly, as if awakening, and finally announced her intention of leaving, but even as she spoke she followed the hand he held. He smiled and murmured reassurances and stroked her just as she had so often soothed her nervous dog, and continued to lead her to the far wall. She hazily remembered saying to Rachel, or thinking to say to Rachel, that she felt doomed, and the thought made her giggle.

"What's funny?" he whispered, but without waiting for an answer he pressed her against the cold stone. He caressed and petted her as if he were trying to paste her to the building, and finally she understood that, indeed, he did want to do precisely that, for he had to sneak past the watchman to open a window for her, and feared she might bolt in his absence. Perhaps she would. She was curious to see. He kissed her again, made a series of promises worthy of a Victorian gentleman to his betrothed, and slipped away. She hoped she would run, but she didn't. She leaned against the gelid rock just as he had left her and ran her palms back and forth as though she could absorb the old mansion's icy dampness like a sponge. She was already so cold her teeth would be chattering if she weren't stiffening her jaw.

A hoarse whisper made her heart jerk before she recognized his face floating at the window. He could only push it up halfway before it stuck and emitted terrible creaks, and clambering awkwardly through such a narrow crack on her way to a tryst struck Hannah as so wonderfully comic that she had to push her fist into her belly to hold back the laughter. Such unladylike gymnastics made her feel cumbrously tall, a steeple imitating a willow wand. She tiptoed down the hall, unable to see a thing, choking with the mirth she was trying to swallow.

"How are you?" he asked.

"Fine," she answered agreeably, wondering what he meant.

The tiny room was absolutely dark; she couldn't even see the bed until he propelled her backward onto it and fell gently on top of her. Apparently he was not going to make even a pretense of keeping his chivalrous promises. He softly swung the door shut with his sneaker.

More hilarity at the absurd situation and her uncharacteristic self-deception bubbled up in her. She couldn't put up much of a struggle now even if she wanted to, since any loud noise might alert the watchman, and she would rather be screwed than expelled. The hushed arguments she offered were so farcical that even she had to grin. Finally she gave up and let him fumble with her clothing. What was she so afraid of? After all, she was an old hand at illicit sex, and a bed was more comfortable than a backseat. Anyway, it was only her body that lay trembling with laughter on the mattress; her real self was quite safely detached, smiling knowingly down at the silly but commonplace scene. She pictured her real self perched smugly on the ceiling with arms crossed, and laughed out loud. What had she to fear from this stranger gnawing at her buttons? She winked down at herself and laughed again.

Surprised, Ari at first laughed with her, then let go of her zipper to brush back her hair and look at her. He moved up a few inches, leaned on his elbows, and studied her even more closely. Embarrassed, she tried to duck away, but he caught her wrists and pinned them behind her head, holding her torso immobile with his own weight so that she could hardly move, much less struggle away from his inspection. She noted with clinical interest that he was much stronger than she would have guessed—she was quite a strong girl, yet he could hold both her arms with one hand. Much too dignified to fight a losing battle, she lay perfectly impassive except for the ironic smile in her eyes. Did he really think he had to rape her? It occurred to her that he could probably kill her if he wanted and all the while she would be so concerned not to disturb the watchman that she would not fight back until it was too late. The thought rather bitterly amused her; she tried to choke down her giggle but found she couldn't manage it in this position. In fact, she couldn't manage to control herself at all, and to her surprise a violent shiver ran through her from head to toe and made her gasp.

"But you are terrified," he whispered. "You are not laughing; you are terrified." With infinite gentleness he again took her face in his palms. "And you are cold all over—even your hands are like ice. Why don't you tell me you are so afraid?" Instantly, to her acute dismay, Hannah burst into tears. God, she thought desperately, if it only takes one tender word to put me in this state, it's a good thing people don't usually go around being tender. Her instinctive reaction was to pull away from him and curl back into herself, but he wouldn't let her move, and when she tried to cover her face he again took her hands and pinned them to her side. "No no," he said firmly. "Cry. Don't try to stop, just cry."

Once again his words affected her like an invitation she must have been yearning for, unbeknownst even to herself, and she began to weep quietly but uncontrollably as she hadn't done even on the day her parents had locked her in her room. When he saw she had stopped fighting, he cradled her protectively and pressed her to him, as if by immobilizing her body he helped free the violence of her emotions.

Minutes later she gasped to a halt and found herself lying damply in a patient embrace. All at once she felt so entirely blissful that she deliberately squeezed out another sob, but apparently he sensed that the force of her storm was over and he shifted to one elbow in order to look at her again. She was grateful for the dark; her face by now must resemble a withered apple. She had never felt more strange or more happy. Was it this she had chased down all those forbidden alleys? Exhausted, depleted and content, she lay in his arms and admired his extraordinary intuition. Now she supposed she would be allowed to go home intact after all.

But then to her alarm, he gently finished the undressing he had begun a quarter hour before. Though she was far too confused to protest, she flinched inwardly with horror. Surely after that pitiful breakdown he couldn't intend going through with it! But when she flipped like a landed fish, he only finished his unwrapping more determinedly. When he had completely stripped her, he hopped up for a moment to spread the blankets over her and shed his own clothing; then, flashing in a sliver of moonlight like a ghost, he sliced into bed beside her.

"Now we must get you warm," he murmured, beginning an insistent but languorous massage that at first made her feel self-conscious but gradually relaxed her until she was too torpid to move. Had it been left to her to decide, she probably would have gone home even at that point, but clearly he was not about to leave it to her, and in a resigned way she was grateful. She dimly sensed that, although her inexplicable grief and his answering tenderness had been delicious, still there might be something more, something long promised, and tomorrow she might regret it if tonight she missed her chance to see the experience through. So, like a brave patient, she wanted to have the operation, to get everything over with at once. She steeled herself for revelation.

But, contrary to her expectations, when he ceased warming her, he did not immediately go to work. Unlike Jinx, he did not plunge obliviously into his usual routine, his diagram of steps, and leave her there on the pillow waiting for sensation to strike. Instead, to her great distress, he chose that moment to begin talking to her, talking about things she had never imagined it necessary to discuss with a man. Inch by inch he scrupulously explored her body, and after every probe and adjustment he stopped to lift his head, watch her, question her, and listen. The process mortified Hannah, who kept praying he would turn to his own pleasure and let her escape back into herself. Yet at the same time, in an acutely painful and unprecedented way, it pleased her, for never since early childhood had anyone paid her so much sustained and solicitous attention, and never since early childhood had someone else been both able and eager to take responsibility for her happiness. She quivered in an agony of confusion and fascination, always close to tears. Again she was grateful for the dark; her cheeks felt in a perpetual hot blush of bewilderment.

"I thought the proper technique was for the woman to sink into a foggy dreamworld where she hardly knows what's happening," she finally dared suggest with a faint smile. Her voice sounded tremulous and not like her own.

He grinned and pinched her in a place she had never thought to treat other than reverently. When she went to yelp, more from shock than hurt, he playfully covered her mouth with his palm and gestured that she mustn't make a sound.

"Blackmail," she hissed.

Then he turned more serious and asked rather sensibly how she expected him to know what she liked if he never asked. "Someone has explained to you backwards," he said. "It's when you do know everything that is happening, that's when you can sink into this foggy dreamworld you speak about. How can I get to know you if I never let you talk to me?"

The answer, of course, was that she had never expected him to know her. She had been willing to let him do anything he liked with her except know her, and it had been precisely the threat that he might be both arrogant and intuitive enough to slither through her defenses that had made her so afraid. She understood that now, but now it was too late. Every time her detached self tried to clamber back to her observation post on the ceiling, he instinctively unseated her with yet another question. Not only would he not take silence for an answer, he equally rejected the whole assortment of modest grunts and suggestive moans she sought to hide behind. He was nothing if not explicit, and she thought to herself at some point that his command of English was noticeably more subtle and extensive on this subject than any other. Like a determined census taker, he waited with pencil poised at the entrance to her private dwelling and took stock of every secret. At first there was not, in truth, a great deal to take stock of, but that didn't seem to faze him. His confidence took her breath away. Now and then he would lean back beside her on the pillow and, with the air of a fine craftsman taking a well-earned break, chat for a while about other things. Once he lit a cigarette and she concluded that the strange affair must finally be over, but when she summoned the courage to ask, he chuckled and assured her it had hardly begun. At some juncture when her benumbed mind was trying to make sense of what her abandoned body was reporting, he asked if he smelled of the onions he had eaten earlier on his hamburgers.

In fact he did, but she had theretofore politely put aside all such issues as bad breath. She tried to deflect his question with an appreciative sigh, but he continued to hound her until she muttered that, yes, he did.

"Ah, I was afraid so; I can taste it. If only I meet you in time, I not eat them, but this afternoon I think to myself for once I can eat all the bad-smelling things I want. You are only lucky they had no garlic, yes?" While he continued to apologize without the slightest intonation of shame, she shriveled with a mixture of keen embarrassment and equally keen admiration for his insouciance. How could they be discussing onions while she sprawled naked and sweaty under the relentless, if approving, gaze of a stranger? "But how can I know what you are thinking if I don't ask you?" he repeated. "How can I know you?"

"I didn't expect you to know me," she said frankly. She had expected this to be entirely an exercise in getting to know herself, having little to do with him beyond the necessary element of attraction. And surely, she consoled herself, it was not she with whom he was becoming so intimate. She was not ingenuous, tentative, childlike, abnormally sensitive, and always on the verge of tears. That was the only weapon her observer self could hold out against him—the certainty that this pale, trembling, damp, rather sweet little creature on the sheet bore no resemblance to herself.

And all along he continued to tell her how beautiful she was, how lovely, how delightful, how adorable, how wonderful to see and to touch and to be with, and under the pressure of the flattery that he wielded like a sculptor's tools she felt herself, at least for the moment, take the shape of his vision. No doubt he said such things to every woman, but his tone was so persuasive that she concluded that his real secret of success must lie in his meaning the compliments while he said them. And the more he reassured her that the wilder she was the lovelier she was, the wilder she was able to become. She lost all idea of what was happening or what was to happen next; she simply followed his touch as trustingly as a blind child. She was so wet and radiant with heat now that it was hard to remember she had ever been cold, and someone seemed to have bathed her slippery skin and hair in scented oil. His questions, which came more slowly and softly now, grew more difficult to answer, not because she was shy any longer, but because under such an assault of new sensation colors swam before her eyes and feelings which she was helpless to identify ran along her nerves. And she was so tired she came close to weeping again each time he insisted on pleasing her somewhere or some way else. Finally she half began to struggle, almost incoherent with exhaustion and feeling and swimming sensation, and he once more pinned her arms over her head and held her down while he moved his hand between her legs until she cried out in something close to anguish and he had to smother her with his chest to keep her from being heard.

They both laughed then and it broke her trance a little. She wondered what time it could be. She had no idea at all, no more than if she had been drugged. He gave a great sigh and snuggled down at her side, and she assumed it must be over. There hadn't been the pain she remembered from before, or maybe there had been and she simply hadn't noticed. But when she asked, he chuckled and again assured her that they had not even begun. She was almost frightened; surely she couldn't withstand much more. But by now she also trusted him. He seemed to know more about her needs—this kind of need—than she, and tonight she was grateful to abdicate control.

Now, at last, he eased himself into the passage he had so patiently prepared, and she instantly realized how naïve she had been to think it could have occurred without her knowledge. He asked her gently if it hurt, and she said no, although it did. She was now, for the first time, more interested in him than in herself. His face had suddenly grown serious and intense, and she understood how he must have been holding himself back in the last hours and why he had sometimes begun to talk about something inconsequential just when it seemed to her he had been the most absorbed. He started to ask something and then broke off, gasped, and closed his eyes, and his features assumed a severity Hannah had never seen before. He asked again if it hurt and she had to admit that she felt mostly soreness, but rather than retreating he pushed forward, and as he did he flinched and gasped again, and she trembled watching him and seemed to loosen somewhere in her center where she never had before. She thought his face was beautiful, but beautiful in a way that made her ache more than it gave her joy, and she was studying his face when he moved forward again. She winced from a spasm of pain and then, suddenly, moaned aloud as she experienced a touch, a pressure almost in her belly, unlike anything she had ever known. Something had invaded the core of her body and split her in half like fruit. Involuntarily her eyes widened and her head fell backward in shock, and her first reaction would have been shame, but somehow he was there even before her self-consciousness, taking her face in his hands and murmuring that she had never looked so pure as when she looked like that. She could only gape at him in almost comical surprise, and he smiled very gently.

"It still hurts now?" he whispered.

"Yes, but—it hurts but—there's something else, too. I don't—I can't describe it—" She broke off helplessly.

"I know," he said.

He began again to move, slowly and tenderly, and her mouth opened in a silent exclamation of pain, astonishment, and wonder; then she saw his attention abruptly leave her, go inward, and he grimaced almost in despair, and she heard herself answer with a shuddering sigh that reverberated in every muscle, and at last she gave in completely. Then, at his leisure, he explored the inside and the outside of her body with all the rapt absorption small boys bring to assembling model airplanes, and like an airplane she felt herself come very slowly together, take shape, and begin, very tentatively, to fly. This new and mysterious place within her was far too tender to allow great passion, but she felt another kind of passion simply at the realization of being first more full and then more empty then she had ever imagined possible. After an unknown passage of time, which felt like a lifetime to Hannah—a languid lifetime in a slow southern climate full of strange perceptions and unsuspected revelations —even the pain began to ease, and she was conscious only that every organ in her body seemed to rock to the same steady rhythm. Too awestruck to be shy she sought Ari's eyes in an ecstasy of gratitude, and when he saw her face, he wrenched backward so brutally that she feared she had somehow hurt him, until he collapsed beside her and she understood that it was, finally, over.

After many minutes of silence, when she assumed he must be sleeping, he sighed rather complacently and propped himself up on one elbow in order to watch her. Dawn must be coming, she realized, for she could see his expression, which was both affectionate and teasing, more clearly now than just a little while ago. "Well—?" he said with a broad, almost mocking grin. "I told you I show you, yes?"

"Yes," she smiled, happily granting him the right to be smug. "You told me so." Then, more seriously, she added, "I—I just never knew. I mean, I simply felt something altogether new. I didn't even anticipate it was there. I didn't know I existed there."

He looked benign to the point of sanctimoniousness, which amused her, and then turned very solemn. "But, little Hannah, you must be careful now not to fall in love with me. You only get hurt if you do, and I am afraid you will because you are so young. If I know when I meet you you are only eighteen—" He shrugged. "But for my sake I am glad I did not. What do you think—are you in love with me already, do you think?"

"Oh no," she blurted. Then, hardly wanting to be crass at such a time, she tried to make amends. "I mean, I like you, and I'm overwhelmed still by all that's happened, and I—"

"I know. But you must not fall in love with me now, do you see?"

"Yes. I mean no, I won't."

"You promise? You see, all my women say they will not, and then in the end they always do." He looked mournful, contemplating all the disappointment strewn in his wake.

"I promise." She hesitated. "And I'm not exactly one of 'your women'—"

"No," he agreed, cuddling her fondly. "You are more my little child-woman, I think. And that makes me all the more not want to hurt you."

At that moment she felt very sure of the promise she had just made so confidently. He was still a stranger, albeit a rather miraculous one. And just now it was her own freshly discovered self she was infatuated with, not the discoverer. Indeed, she was suddenly eager to be alone to sift through and assimilate all that had happened to and within her.

He brushed her damp hair back from her still unfocused eyes. "I will see you again, lovely child-woman?"

Her chest trembled; she hoped he hadn't felt it. Until he posed the question she hadn't permitted herself even to entertain it, much less ask. "How?" she said noncommittally.

He looked pensive. "You can come see me in the city," he suggested finally. "I think it is impossible, me coming back here. You will come?"

"Yes," she said slowly, "if you want me to."

"I never ask if I don't want you. But you will have to come very soon because in a few weeks I am going back to Tel Aviv. You can come soon, do you think?"

"Yes."

He stroked her belly. "But what about school? You are in school here, aren't you?"

She grinned. "More or less, now and then. But it's a progressive school, after all, and I would certainly consider you a bona fide learning experience. Maybe I can write you up. Would you like to be a term paper?" She turned to look seriously at him. "I'll come."

"Good." He leaned over and lingeringly kissed the area he had been stroking. "Ah, I wish it was not so late," he breathed. "You taste so sweet—" Hannah, however, was grateful for the warning gray light at the window, despite her nerves' having quickened so obediently to his touch. She was so exhausted and bruised that her skin seemed to throb, and besides, she wanted to be alone. When he sat up abruptly and assumed a more businesslike tone, she was relieved. "Okay," he said. "I call you sometime tomorrow before I leave if I can, and maybe we see each other again. You like that?"

"Yes," she said doubtfully. "But it will be harder to sneak in here in daylight—"

He shook his head. "I won't have time to fuck anyway. We take a walk in the woods. I don't always have to see you just in bed. It will be nice to take a walk together in the daytime."

"If I can walk."

He chuckled, scrounged on the floor for his pants, and finally extracted a match cover and pencil from the pockets. "Tell me your telephone number and address."

"Hannah Erickson—" she began, but he instantly covered her mouth with his hand. "Imbecile," he scolded. "I know your name. You think I forget it after tonight? Just your telephone."

She repeated the numbers, and as she did she felt grateful. Not that she really expected to see him again—but he was kind to say he wanted to. She knew there would be a thousand distractions once he got back to the city, and she knew he wasn't the sort of person who stays at one task for long, not even one that pleases him. Indeed, even now he had begun to chatter frenziedly about the chores and appointments he had to tend to before he departed for home. All at once he was very distracted, bemoaning the late hour and the time he had to get up the next morning —or rather, that morning—and consequently she withdrew again and felt awkward. Finally he tugged on his pants and scampered off like a character in a farce to check on the night watchman, returning to report that the man was soundly asleep. This time he opened his own window and looked dubiously at the rosebush underneath. "I think maybe we go back to the hall again—"

"No, this is okay," she assured him, as eager to be gone as he apparently was to launch her. He helped her climb out and get her footing, then she turned to go.

"Wait!" he whispered, catching her hand. "Not so fast. Don't you even say good-bye to me?" Then he shook his head wryly as she disentangled her pants leg from a thorn. "This is silly, you know, climbing in and out windows. You'd think we are teen-agers."

"Well I—"

"I know, you are one; don't remind me." With a self-pitying grumble he scowled and clambered out of the window to stand beside her. He held her eyes for a protracted moment until she grew self-conscious and tried to look away, and then he caught her face and turned it back to his. She felt herself blush again and hoped he couldn't see. But then he released her face to stroke her impishly between the legs. "Mine now," he murmured.

"No." She laughed with surprise. "Mine! Mine more than ever after tonight."

He inspected his trophy. "But then you will give it to me, yes? Give it to me for tonight?"

"Oh, well, just for tonight, sure. You can claim full title for the hours from midnight till now."

"You like being with me, little one?" he asked seriously.

Her eyes danced with amusement and she looked ironically at the place where his hand still was tucked. With great ceremony she removed it, held it between her own, and kissed it in the continental manner. "Yes!" she said with a mock salute.

He was delighted. "But you promise not to fall in love with me if I see you in New York—?"

"I promise."

"All right. Then kiss me good-bye until then."

When he released her, she dashed off into the meadow without looking back. It was still so dark that, when she had run until she was out of breath, she could hardly discern the house over her shoulder. Safely invisible, then, she stood still and savored the damp, electric air. All at once she began to spin in delirious circles, laughing aloud, her arms outstretched, and didn't stop until she tripped into a hill and found herself abruptly sitting down. She got up, shaking her head with wonderment. She seemed to have plunged so far into exhaustion that she had come out the other side, ready to run a mile. How she would ache tomorrow! She ran for another quick spurt, then slowed to her usual long stride. She was so sore that with each step some part of her flesh winced. She felt as bruised and torn as a fat peach ripped back to the pit. But the pain was sweet, the rawness between her soaked thighs was sweet, not because they reminded her of Ari, though he was sweet to remember, but because they were hers. Every time her foot met the earth her body announced its presence. Even her breasts protested against the material that bound them. Her belly was a cantaloupe with the seeds scooped out: hollow, fruity and wet. Though she realized it was silly, she couldn't help resenting the few other people she saw at this hour, especially the couples. Surely this night belonged to her alone! Surely her experience was unique.

She even resented the fact that she had only to ask one of the watchmen to secure a key to her dorm, for it would have added to the adventure had she been forced to climb through a window or even spend the rest of the night in the woods. But this was a permissive institution. The expression on the old man's face made it all the harder to keep believing that her experience was unique.

At least no one else was awake in the dorm. She took off her shoes, padded softly to the bathroom, and almost reverently peeled off her sticky clothes. It occurred to her that if she were the proper kind of teen-ager she would vow here and now never to wash them again. As it was, however, she dropped everything into the hamper she shared with Rachel. Rather to her disappointment, there was no trace of blood. Nor, for that matter, was there much blood in her face; she looked as though she had been to a funeral.

The shower was bliss: the steamy water sought out and soothed every bruised nook and cranny. An overwhelming sleepiness hit her so suddenly she almost staggered, but once she recovered her balance it was wonderful to sway back and forth, feeling that she alone was awake in the dark and quiet night. As she gingerly patted herself with a folded washcloth she imagined herself a princess laved with rose water after her night with the king. Surely in a minute pretty maidens would wrap her in chiffon and place fur mats wherever she chose to stroll. Instead, however, she hopped as quickly as possible over the frozen tiles to her slippers and terry-cloth robe, and rubbed her wet hair with a gray towel she had neglected to return to the laundry service that week. In the hall she stood for a moment and listened to the quiet. The insects had yielded to a choir of birds. If only she could prolong this mood, this perfect solitude. As she slipped her flushed and tender body between the cool sheets, she noticed that the window pane had faded from black to a translucent lavender, and already shadows skittered like sanderlings across the floor.

17

She awakened to the peremptory footsteps of Rachel bringing English muffins and juice. For a moment she considered pretending to be asleep, then gave up, shoved a pillow behind her back, and struggled to a sitting position. Her head reeled groggily. It was close to noon and the room was bright and hot.

She munched her muffin and lied to Rachel. It was the first time she had told anything but the full truth to her friend. She sensed that Rachel knew the truth anyway, but for once in her life she felt unable to talk about what had happened. Indeed, she was unable to think about it clearly. She felt light-headed with fatigue and surprisingly gummy all over, and she was reluctant to stand because of an awkward suspicion that warm liquid might sluice precipitously down her thighs. She was far too tumultuous and dreamy to pull herself together and decide what she should feel. All the hunger and determination, even the anxiety of last night were gone. In their place was only a muddle, and Hannah tolerated muddle badly. Right now she wanted to feel proud, impregnable, and indifferent to all she could not control—such as the phone that she could not make ring no matter how hard she concentrated. Yet she had been listening for it even before she had fully awakened. She wanted to believe that last night had been enough in itself, but every time one of the house phones rang, she started. It wasn't that she needed to see him again in order to justify last night—the night had been wonderful—but she knew it had revealed more mysteries than it had resolved, and thus with the full force of her passion to understand herself, she yearned to see Ari again. Yet the yearning rendered her nearly defenseless, so she resented it almost as powerfully as she felt it. All she understood now was that she couldn't face the sympathy she would see on Rachel's face when they both knew he had failed to return.

Rachel suggested they follow their Sunday routine of walking a couple of miles to the nearest outpost of the nearest town to lunch in the only restaurant and purchase enough newspapers and magazines to wile away the afternoon, and Hannah agreed. By now the dance company must be long gone: the most destructive thing she could do would be to wait around here all day. She washed her face, pulled on jeans and a blouse and sweater, and pronounced herself ready to go.

The sun was so warm and steady it seemed to seep into Hannah's bones and ease away the stiffness. Last night's winds had mellowed to a soft spring breeze. Both girls peeled off their sweaters, rolled up their sleeves, unbuttoned their collars and tugged back their hair to feel closer to the splendid day. They walked along the same path that had taken Hannah back and forth to the concert twelve hours before, and she waited for some sensation of melancholy or nostalgia, but none came.

As always, the owner of the small, dusty newsstand, which he preferred to call a cigar store, glowered at the pair of students as though they were squaws who had wandered off their reservation. And as always, they felt irritated and awkward as they browsed through the magazines, sensing that he and his dour pals were examining every nuance of their manners and appearance. Finally, when each had gathered an armload of diversion, they suffered his impatience at the large bills they paid with and escaped with relief back into the sunshine. Next they strolled to the luncheonette and ordered their customary buns and hot chocolate, which today they carried back outdoors to the wide wooden steps where they squatted and picnicked like tourists. The heat of the sun-drenched boards spread through Hannah's hips and the backs of her thighs. She groaned contentedly and sagged back against the railing. The warm air turned them damp with perspiration which the breeze promptly evaporated. When they had eaten the last of the cakes and drained their cardboard mugs, Hannah stayed behind to guard the loot while Rachel crossed Main Street to the grocery store and returned with a bag of apples and raisins and nuts.

They commented, not for the first time, on how this small New England town, so calm under the lofty elms and oaks, the hub of so many narrow dirt roads that headed back to scrubby woodland or uneven rows of shabby houses, seemed to be a setting out of a picturebook past. It was so peaceful, with only the swish of the high old branches or the chug of an occasional car to break the quiet; it was so empty. The girls came here every Sunday, yet were no more a part of it than if they were driving through for the first time, taking photographs through closed windows.

"And if we were really part of it," Hannah said, "we wouldn't find it so serene and picturesque; we'd know it too well."

"Speaking of knowing things well," Rachel tentatively began, "I was talking to some of the dance majors in the snack bar today, and it turned out that some of them know Ari, or at least know about him."

"Really?" Hannah asked with interest. "What did they say?"

"Well, apparently one of them has this actress friend who's been in love with him for years. According to her, he's a bona fide, right-out-of-the-textbooks, Don Juan, and a gigolo to boot, or at least a part-time one." Rachel kept her voice tactfully light and peered obliquely at her friend to see if she looked upset, but Hannah only smiled to indicate that the information jibed with her own impressions, so Rachel went on. "She says that he treats her friend abominably even though he claims she's the only woman he's ever loved. She told some story about this girl inviting him to the opening of a play she was in—it really meant a lot to her, her parents were there and all that—and Ari picked some fight with one of the ushers over his seat and started swearing and shouting and finally hit the guy, until in the end they had to throw him out. The worst of it is, this is one of those poverty-stricken little places where the ticket takers and ushers and so forth are actually the actors in the play, and

Ari had bruised this one so badly it ruined his performance. The girl was mortified."

Hannah laughed, and Rachel, after looking at her curiously for a second, joined in. "The poor girl," Hannah sympathized, shaking her head. "I'm sure it wasn't funny to her. But he's so obviously crazy; she must have known that."

"Jesus, Hannala, you really do pick yourself dillies, you know!" Rachel relaxed, dropped her apple core into a bag, and lit a cigarette. "First a juvenile delinquent, now this. What's left?"

"I always thought Malcolm X was kind of sexy."

"Perfect." Rachel sighed. "I should add that my informant also says that he's having an affair with Rosalind Witt, which I imagine is the reason he couldn't take you to the cast party. She found him on one of her Israeli tours and brought him here, and her other dancers loathe him because he's got her wrapped around his little finger and lets her make a fool of herself over him—that's what they were all gossiping about when I met them. She even consults him about decisions in her work."

For the first time, Hannah looked surprised, though more diverted than dismayed. She admired the choreographer and was rather proud to have shared her man for a night. "Well," she breathed, "that does explain a lot. He called her Rosie. I should have guessed it, but the older woman thing—I mean, she must be well over forty. And she's supposed to be so brilliant and strong. I wonder what she sees in him."

"I rather wonder that myself," Rachel said dryly. "I thought you might have a better idea than I would."

Hannah smiled to herself. "Probably," she said, "it has something to do with his calling her Rosie; I'll bet no one else does. Poor lady, she must get tired of being so brilliant and strong." She leaned down from the porch to pluck a few blades of grass growing in the shade, and wound them around her knuckle, then bent her finger to hear them snap.

"He could call me anything he damn well pleased and I'd still think he was a maniac," said Rachel with some heat.

"He is a maniac—but mania can have its charm."

"Anyway, I gather you're lucky you didn't have time to get hooked. Evidently he's lethal. It's beyond me, but you must be right; a lot of other women find insanity charming too. His specialty, they say, is getting everyone he sleeps with to fall in love with him, and he sleeps with everyone."

"I rather suspected that, since he kept warning me not to fall in love with him. I reassured him there was no danger."

"Were you telling the truth?"

Hannah looked at her in surprise. "Sure!"

"It's just that I've never seen you act before like you did last night when he was around. Sort of half-hypnotized. Half laughing at yourself, I know, but half-hypnotized, too."

Hannah blushed. "I wouldn't claim I couldn't be infatuated with him. Fascinated. But that's not love; at least, not to me. To me, love means, more than anything else, respect. Respect and trust. I liked him, but how could I ever respect him? Much less trust him. The main reason I love you, for example, is that I respect your perceptions, the way you see the world. Not to mention the fact that I'd trust you with my soul, if I believed in souls." Her cheeks grew even hotter and she looked at the ground: it was hard for her to use the word love to a friend.

"I agree that's how it should be. But sex somehow always seems to screw things up. Maybe that's why I avoid it." Rachel shrugged and tucked the remaining apples into her handbag. "Anyway, bubula, it's probably a good thing you won't be put to the test, don't you think?"

"Well," Hannah said lightly as she rose and dusted off her pants. "You know I've always tested well. What's one more SAT?"

After dinner, the roommates sprawled on the floor in front of their shared desk, Rachel rocking back and forth to a ballet score she loved, Hannah leafing through her sketchbook in hopes of finding inspiration. Instead she was finding herself both agitated and sleepy, the perverse combination that was becoming her characteristic mood. Head very drowsy but heart so alarmed it would ricochet her off the pillow if she tried to lie down. "If God must see fit to curse me with high blood pressure at the age of eighteen," she complained, "at least he could give me the nervous energy that's supposed to come with it."

"Cheer up," Rachel drawled over the music. "A little grogginess is better than constipation and nightmares. Take it from one who knows them all."

Hannah glanced at the pile of finished canvases in the corner. Sometimes they heartened her, but tonight they only intimidated: they were good; there should be more. "Who needs a canvas conscience?" she asked aloud.

"Well, you could work on your French instead—"

"Fuckez-vous you."

Drawings had always come to her like dreams, but these days she had insomnia. Tonight, however, Hannah didn't want to think about that. Tonight, in fact, she was having trouble thinking about anything. To her disgust, her wandering attention was still fixed on the silent phone. Furious with herself, she knotted her hair behind her head, snatched up her books, and stalked off to an empty classroom to study.

But there she only found herself listening to every unexpected sound, every creak, every distant swish of wind through the forest. Helplessly she began to count each passing footstep. There was nothing she could do: for all her control over her outward behavior, she had never been able to control the whims of her mind. After a futile hour, she sighed, reassembled her books, and set off to find Rachel again.

Soon it would be late enough to justify thinking of bed. The clover-studded grass was wet with the humid night; liquid seeped in through her shoes and made her shiver. The hills beyond the wall were shrouded in mist. She found Rachel sitting morosely on her bed leafing through the afternoon's well-thumbed magazines, eager to accept Hannah's suggestion that they visit the snack bar once more before it closed.

When they walked outside again, it was drizzling. Rachel handed Hannah one of the books she had intended to drop in the library night-slot, and they scampered to the Commons using philosophy as an umbrella. They camped in one of the large window seats and listened to the rain. Hannah tried to sit on her feet to thaw them. They spread butter on their muffins and peeled the cellophane off their oatmeal cookies with a care close to reverence, for food assumed a ritualistic importance in this small school in the country where most of the students were hungry for something else they couldn't name. When they finished, they gazed in exaggerated but genuine sorrow at the scraped plates.

In unison they threw their weight against the double doors, again held the books over their heads, and scuttled back through the storm, across the squelchy gravel path and into the anteroom of their dorm. "Phew," they gasped together, shaking their arms with distaste. Then Rachel cried, "Oh, look at your face!"

Hannah put a worried hand to her cheek and brought it down stained a watery red. She blinked at it disbelievingly: nothing hurt; she felt intact.

"No, it's not blood," laughed her friend. "It's dye from my book. I guess that wasn't such a hot idea after all."

They frowned disapprovingly at nature and scuffled off to their bathroom to hang their clothes and leave their muddy shoes to dry. Hannah showered to get warm and fled into her bed.

"I notice you're sleeping on top of the covers again," said Rachel chidingly from beneath her own.

"Last night I forgot, but tonight it's more important than ever to get back into routine." Recently Hannah was finding it almost impossible to get out of bed in the mornings, and somehow being buried in crumpled white sheets bright with afternoon sun made it worse, made her feel like a soft slug pressed between the fat white palms of a gardener. So she had taken to sleeping on top of her cool green bedspread with an old quilt from home pulled over her for warmth, and that way the moment she rolled off the mattress the room was in order. The day was under control.

She switched off her reading lamp, turned over and closed her eyes. Immediately she knew she wouldn't be able to sleep. The instant she had dimmed the footlights of the outer world the stage lights of her imagination blazed up. But she didn't want to think tonight. She tried to repeat the kings and queens of England backwards, but to no avail. For a quarter hour she listened hopefully to Rachel's thrashing across the room. Finally she whispered, "Are you asleep?"

"No."

"Me neither."

Each turned resignedly on her back and lay with her head on the pillow and her eyes open to the sightless room. They began to talk then in the way that happened only on nights like this when they were both tired but sleepless, their bodies inert but their minds buzzing with the accrued vexation of the day. Their confidences seemed to flow forth as effortlessly as their almost expressionless voices. Memories and desires poured unguardedly out into the drone of the rain and the creak of surrounding trees listing under the weight of water and departing winter. It was not that they spoke to the night rather than to each other, for neither would have shared her reveries so trustingly with anyone else, but they opened up to the night within one another, within themselves. It was these nighttime revelations that bound them so closely even in the day, even when they irritated and frustrated each other. In these hours they seemed to experience one another at a level almost below identity. The girls were too similar to meet one another's most painful needs, yet that very similarity met another need of equal strength: the lonely hunger to feel the warmth of another person in the same dark and uncertain plight. Sometimes it seemed as if their very litany of woe, their helplessness, must invoke the god of justice in whom neither had believed for years. They were young and not yet free of the illusion that the world could not be so blatantly unfair. Surely, if they could just show some authority their impressive wounds, they would receive a doctor's note of excuse from future trials—at least they would be given time to make up what they had missed.

Hannah was good at dramatizing the events at home calculated to make an audience gasp with sympathy, yet she sensed vaguely that it was not so much what her parents had done as the reasons they had done it that constituted the real threat to herself. It was her absorption of their fears, her loyal and loving and childish wish to dwell in the same world as they, that could affect her future. When her father lunged angrily at her, it was not so much the lunging that filled her with dread, for she knew he loved her, but her shocked glimpse of all it must take to make him so angry, he who would give his life to protect her from anyone else. What was it about the world that made her parents so afraid?

Rachel spoke aloud in a hypnotized toneless voice that merged with the rain in the trees. "I had a dream last night that made me wake up crying," she began. "You were gone. It was about my father. On his last visit, when I think he came less to see me than to escape my mother and the city, he kept telling me how lucky I am to be here, how he would give any decade of his life just to be able to leave his overheated classroom and come here to the quiet woods to rest and read and think. With his vanishing eyesight, you know, it was sheer self-destruction for him to become a scholar—but that's another story you've heard before. He'd love to do nothing else in the day or night but read, not even teach or write, just sit in his study and read and look up at his ferns now and then. Maybe he'd like to hear Mother and me talking in the next room, but I think he'd like to stay in that study forever. But of course he destroys his eyes with each word, and soon the pain makes his temples swell so that his whole forehead pounds. You can see it. It's an agony for the two of us to watch. So he talks of taking a job in the administration—my mother wants him to and so does the Dean—he does half the work already without the pay—but he can't make up his mind. He's been pondering the question aloud at dinner for the last ten years. So of course you can see why he tells me I'm foolish to say I'm lonely and lost up here. He says that's the human condition, and I suppose he's right. When I think of my parents I realize how lucky I should feel, at least in a way. I mean, I do have my whole future before me. Such as it is.

"In the dream I was in a hospital in the Alps with a nineteenth-century panoramic view. You were there too, in the same room, only we were separated by a transparent partition. The room was all one huge floor and we could see all the other patients stretched out in their beds up and down the length of it. Every surface was shiny white. There were huge glass windows everywhere: even the doors and walls, though locked, were glass. We were all calm and resigned. We had trust in the doctors. We knew we were fortunate to have families wealthy enough to purchase these beds overlooking the lavish view. All we hoped was that someday we might be well enough to leave the hospital to go outdoors. We never did see anyone walking out there on those magnificent slopes, however, not even the doctors: I suppose they were too busy tending us inside.

"Then it was night. The windows were dead black, and since all the walls were windows, we seemed surrounded by darkness. The only sound was the sizzle of fluorescent tubes. I was in a clean bed with neatly folded blue blankets and sterile pressed sheets next to my skin, but I was chilled because I was sitting up from the covers to read, and I was naked. All at once I heard a terrible rattling, a clanking of iron coming down the hall, and I was petrified for I was the only one awake. To my horror I saw a pitiful old man weighed down with rusted heavy chains. The chains had rubbed open sores all over his papery skin so that the rotting material of his clothes was crusted with pus and blood and in places seemed to have dried right into his flesh. Each time he drew in a breath the chains jangled. Oh, Hannah, I was petrified and overcome with guilt! I knew he wanted a bed in this perfect hospital, but he was far too poor and old to afford it. I wanted to give him my place, though I knew that was impossible, and prayed the same time I would die before he could murder me. His bloodshot eyes were fixed on my exposed breasts: I felt as though they were trying to suck me dry. Then he began to moan and beg for help in the most pitiful, ghastly, threatening way. I didn't know how to help him. I began to thrash around to escape, but I found that my hips and legs were bound by the blankets that stretched over me as tight as a straitjacket and folded me into their perfect hospital corners. I couldn't see anything beyond the black walls, and, though the partitions around my bed were glass, he blocked the only exit through them. I began to scream, although he begged me not to. He kept whispering that I was young and strong. But couldn't he see that I was sick too and in a hospital: why had he come to me and not to the proper authorities? So I shouted and shouted and as they came to take him away I woke up."

Both girls were silent a few minutes, then Hannah began: "Sometimes in the afternoon when he had been drinking indoors my father would call me in to explain that he had worked at a job he despised for twelve or fifteen or seventeen years—whatever my age was at that time—in order to buy that large and powerful boat sitting unused and unwanted in the dock. We would go to the window together to look out at the cruiser in the back which, he would then explain, he could no longer enjoy. He could no longer enjoy anything. He had nothing to look forward to. He only kept working and kept struggling against the deadness within him to keep his children clothed and fed. I would nod and feel that I understood. After all, I had consulted a thousand books to try and understand his case. Then, for some reason, the sun burning red and blue designs on our rugs would make my head swim. I would spring up and dash to the garden to tell my mother that my father needed help. But she would ask: did I really think he could be feeling so dead inside with all that yelling and carousing he had done the night before? And I would have to admit that my father never said he needed help, he only claimed that he alone among us dared see the world for what it really is. That's when I used to think that even when you're finally ready to give up and submit at last to fate—you can't. There is no fate to submit to, there's only the following day. There is no way short of death to avoid the following day, and fate is whatever you happen to do, or not do, when that day comes. There is no avoiding the responsibility."

After a pause, Rachel spoke: "My mother is so different from yours. From her psychiatrist she understands us perfectly. It's just that she can't bear to be alone, she can't ride in elevators or take buses or look out high windows. She fears animals, night, traffic, too much or too little wind, small places, large places, airplanes, distance, inexpensive food, dirt, all kinds of things. Sometimes I had to stay home from school to baby-sit her, to take her to the doctor's, or bring her home, or sit beside her as she gripped the arms of her chair and stared at magazines. Yet she sees me more clearly than anyone and understands all the ramifications of her effect on me. I like and love and resent her so much that sometimes I'm terribly afraid that I am her, doomed to be her. I had a dream once that I was lying in a bathtub filling to the brim with steamy love. I was as hot and helpless as a baby. My veins had been mistakenly left open just like the tap, and the love in me spilt out to merge with the love around me. It was gushing out to stain the bathroom red. I was awash in overflowing love, spilling to the floor and down the hall and away, leaving myself behind in the tub, my skin all puckered and cold. I told my mother my dream and she wept."

Rachel sat up, her face visible to Hannah only as a lowering silhouette against a light cloud that must be the pillow. Then she broke their mutual trance by reaching for the silver monogrammed cigarette lighter her mother had given her. She pushed it reflectively, and her face went momentarily alight with flickering oranges and reds. In the tiny lamp of her cigarette the ruffles of her white gown reminded Hannah of the foam on the ripples at night when the sea is alive with phosphorous. They continued talking for another hour or two, wondering uneasily about husbands and children they might someday have or not have, vowing that the one who married first would never desert the other. They joked and laughed and threw pillows at one another to ward off the feeling that their futures were as unknowable as a lottery. Finally they agreed to sleep and actually did remain silent for twenty minutes before admitting failure. Rachel lit another cigarette and Hannah, knowing it was foolish, opened a Coke to share. The window had a silver sheen by the time the girls ran out of things to say, and the birds were warbling again in full chorus by the time Hannah was able to stop listening.

18

The next morning she shot upright and out of bed in a panicky haste to stop the awful pounding at the door. Some storm trooper on the other side was hollering her name like a threat. She clutched it open and hung groggily on the knob as a dimly familiar girl scowled at her with the scorn day-people reserve for night-people. "Phone call upstairs for Hannah Erikson," she announced like a recording.

Only Jennifer called at this hour. Something must be wrong at home. Hannah's nerves jangled. Had James done something? She pulled on the fleecy yellow robe she had bought the previous summer with magazine visions of college girls dancing in her head, stumbled up the winding flight of wide stairs, down a narrow hall, and plunged into the small wooden closet that served as phone booth. She forced herself to take a deep breath, propped her bare feet against the door, her elbow on her knee, and her head on her hand. "Hello?" she said glumly.

An operator crackled, then a strange voice came out of a tunnel. "Hello, is that you? Hannah? This is Eli Arieli. I am sorry I could not call you yesterday, but I never was alone, and then last night I dial and nothing happens. Hello, are you there?"

"The switchboard closes early on Sunday nights," she said.

"Ah yes. But all day I think of you. I wish we could take our walk. I think how sweet you were the other night. It was lovely, yes? You thought of me too?"

"Yes, I did." Hannah searched wildly for something more to say. She couldn't make sense of the fact that he was on the telephone. Somehow she couldn't associate him with machinery. "I just woke up," she managed. "Are you in a pay phone?"

"No, I am home in bed wishing you are here beside me." She heard a muffled voice in the background and Ari's hand go over the receiver. Why couldn't she comprehend that he like everyone else had a telephone in the apartment where he lived? Had she pictured him in a tent? Then for the first time she assimilated the fact that he had called after all. They would never get to go for the walk, but at least he had called. Chivalry was not altogether dead. She put both feet on the ground and leaned forward with her arms on the metal shelf.

"Listen, lovely little girl, there is a problem. You see, my first thought is that right away you must come to the city to visit me. But the problem is that in just about two weeks I leave for Israel. My two years here are almost over—what a shame we do not meet earlier! And in these last days I will be so busy packing and saying good-bye to friends that I am afraid you will feel lonely here—that I neglect you. You are the kind—I would want to pay you such special attention, you are so young and sweet, but there will be no time. I never wish to hurt you."

Hannah tried hastily to unravel the message in all that. Caution bade her say a gracious but quick good-bye, yet she also thought the regret and concern in his voice might be genuine. "Well," she said tentatively. "Uh, is the problem just that you'll be gone a lot and don't want to neglect me, or is it also that you'll be so busy that having a guest right now would naturally be a nuisance?"

He paused, but when he spoke his tone again seemed warm and sincere. "No no, you can never be a nuisance, I think. It would be delightful to have you as a guest, as you say; it's just I am afraid you be lonely. You are so sensitive—"

"Oh." She spoke very hesitantly. "Well, if it's just that you would be out a lot, I mean, I really don't need to be entertained every second. I can amuse myself indefinitely and I have friends in the city and so forth. As long as you would be coming home eventually. To sleep."

"Ah!" he said enthusiastically. "Then perhaps you can stay with a friend. Then we can go out for the night and I can spend all of it with you; this is what I am hoping! I can tell from your voice that you are afraid I am making excuses, but this is not true. I like you very much." He took a deep breath. "You see, the problem is that some of the old friends I must say good-bye to are women."

"Oh yes, I realize that," she said bravely. "But my friends aren't the kind I could stay with, not for these purposes." She paused to think. "They have parents," she added elliptically. "The real question is whether you just want to go out to visit your other friends, or whether you want to bring them home. And whether you plan to spend most of your nights—late nights—at home. What I mean is, I really wouldn't mind being left in your place alone, but I *would* mind being turned out on the street for a few hours while you entertained someone else."

"No no, I never turn you out! You might get lost, or I'd be afraid you might get rescued by somebody else. You I never turn out." He stopped, sighed, then asked her to excuse him while he got a cigarette. When he came back, he said eagerly: "I think it over and decide this. You can have the apartment to yourself and I can manage to be home nights to be with you. My only—I am just afraid you will be hurt more than you say. I never wish to make you cry."

"I won't cry," she promised firmly. Then she laughed. "At least not about that. I don't know about other things—I seem to cry a lot around you."

"That's good. It shows you respond to me."

"That must be it."

"But you must come soon because soon I am really busy packing and then I leave—"

"Well," she said uncertainly, "how long do you think I should stay?"

"Two, three days, however long you want—we know better when you are here. It's best to leave it open, I think."

"Okay. Let's see, today is Monday—how about Wednesday afternoon? Our Easter vacation is coming up and that makes it easier for me."

"Wednesday is fine. Only one other thing, little one. I am afraid you come because you think you are in love with me. Or that you fall in love with me while you are here. This you must not do."

"I agree. I'd be a fool to come like this if I were in love with you or planning to be in love with you. But I would like to see you again."

He gave her elaborate directions to his apartment which she transferred to a note pad without really hearing them. All matters of geography were vague to her.

After hanging up, she sat in the booth for a few minutes gazing at the smeared glass in the door. She had negotiated an elaborate contract, but what had she committed herself to? Yet it seemed only fair that he should have the freedom to go on with his own plans and his own life, however peculiar. She had no wish to possess or alter him. In fact, she had few expectations at all, only a desire to experience him again. The nights, after all, were what she wanted; days she could manage by herself.

She retraced her way down the hall and grand staircase more slowly, absentmindedly buttoning her robe and noting the cool dusty texture of the wood under her bare feet. Her hand automatically followed the railing, but for once she forgot to watch where she was going.

In the bedroom the morning sun poured airlessly through the closed glass, glistening on the white walls, white desk top, white curtains, and the white sheets of Rachel's tangled bed until Hannah's head reeled. The brilliance of the motionless light and the dry heat from the burbling radiator stunned her like a parking lot in a heat wave when every car sizzles in wavering air and the yellow clay burns through summer shoes and a deep breath brings more exhaust fumes than oxygen; she reached out a hand to steady herself against the wall. All at once she yearned for the green shadows at home, for the translucent depths of cool water and the sticky sap on the underside of Mimosa roots. She wanted to sit in the shade of a rock jetty and run her fingertips over the barnacles and the slick sea growth. Instead she hastily crossed the room to open the window and draw down the shade.

"Who was that on the phone, for God's sakes?" muttered a sleepy voice from beneath the neighboring mound of blankets. "Your parents?"

"No, it was him, believe it or not. Ari."

There was a muffled exclamation and then a matted black scalp and two dark eyes protruded into the sunshine. "You're kidding!"

"I'm beginning to think I dreamed it." Hannah summarized the conversation, including the contract she had helped to draft, and said she would thus be leaving early for her vacation.

Rachel shook her head anxiously. "Well, you know I think you're raving mad. You wild women from the Jersey swamps never fail to astonish us New Yorkers. But I'll be damned if I'll stay here alone; I'll sneak out with you." She grunted and eased herself out of bed with the care of a sailboat sliding down the ramp to water. She immediately located her loafers, for she claimed it made her ill to walk barefoot on the scruffy communal floor. "And you know, of course, bubula, that you can always come to me, anytime. I'll tie my mother to the refrigerator so she won't cross-examine you—although with you she'd be all sympathy and wisdom anyway; it's only if her own daughter gave her sacred gift to a nice Israeli boy that she'd turn Medea." Hannah grinned. The morning Rachel was an amusing sight. The lush torrent of hair, the heavy breasts undulating under the childish cotton gown, the slim shadows of her dark-haired thighs, the pouting mouth and eyes, all contrasted comically with the clomp and scuffle of her penny-loafers as she launched morosely to the bathroom, head lowered, too tired to do more than drag her long legs behind.

Alone, Hannah stretched lazily, then finally eased up and walked to the closet for a fresh pair of jeans. Squinting in the mirror, she decided she looked a little like a solemn owl, tired from the strain of keeping watch all night.

19

Anticipation shook Hannah awake before the alarm. She and Rachel spent the hours before their last class packing and dressing. They wriggled into girdles, hunted for slips in the backs of their drawers, and carefully pulled nylons over freshly shaven legs. After much deliberation, Hannah pulled from the closet a sleeveless camel turtleneck and matching skirt; she held up the jacket, debating, then with great relief, decided against it. She had loathed getting dressed up even as a child, and the girdles, garters, stockings, high heels, hair spray and tight skirts that came with maturity only made it worse. And the final result never pleased her: instead of feeling as sleek and poised as Jenny and Rachel always looked, she felt clumsy and pinched. Today Rachel wore an expensive gray sheath borrowed from her mother's closet, one cut to civilize rather than flatter her lavish figure, and to Hannah's envious eyes, she seemed sophisticated, elegant, and altogether grown up.

In their class they irritated the teacher by clanking their bracelets on the table every time they wrote in their notebooks. Hannah played with her rings. Rachel twisted strands of hair against her artificially blushed cheek.

When the bell finally rang, they rose with great dignity, gathered their books, clomped decorously to the door in their stylish shoes, then turned and crazily giggled in the sheer exultation of freedom. They ran awkwardly to their room, trying to avoid the mud and gravel for the sake of their heels, dropped their papers, picked up their suitcases, and teetered to the front driveway to meet the taxi—which came tooling along ten minutes later with the nonchalance characteristic of the local citizens. The girls tumbled in after their heavy bags.

At the small bus station they wobbled out and dragged their luggage across the soft ground to the narrow platform to wait. This rural terminal acted as a decompression chamber between the isolated, introspective campus and the world beyond. Even the open driveway and the small group of fellow travelers were as great a shock to the girls as daylight and street noise to a long-secluded invalid. Beside them, a paunchy businessman in a shiny suit twirled his jeweled tie tack with one hand while grasping his overnight bag like a life preserver with the other. "You can just imagine the skinny wife with six kids at home," Hannah whispered. "Anemia, a solitary drinker."

A harassed woman, who could have been that wife but was apparently alone, tried futilely to curb two unruly children whose Sunday clothes were already yellow with the packed clay underfoot. A nervous but perky older woman with blue hair smoothed a brightly patterned scarf into the collar of her coat and beamed at the children with the approval expected of her age and sex. Their only response was to knock dust onto her shoes, which, after tushing good-naturedly at their mother's reprimands, she discretely brushed off. A very young couple emerged from a taxi with mounds of luggage lashed to the roof. The husband, apparently dressed in his father's suit and hat, commanded his wife to wait while he oversaw the unloading, and she meekly retreated, her jacket crusty with gruel from the hiccupping baby she carried, her paper corsage pulled askew.

Hannah felt obscurely relieved when a large black Cadillac swung up to deposit two pleasant middle-aged couples, then swung away again. None of this group carried suitcases. They spoke of meeting someone. Hannah wondered curiously who lived in this town, where they all went and returned from, what jobs they had, and what their memories were like.

The girls exchanged glances with the same thought. It had been so long since they had seen real people: old people, married couples, children, housewives, businessmen, cabdrivers, anyone besides girls like themselves and the homogeneous men who taught them. Sometimes it seemed as though their parents were so helpless to form, aid or educate their offspring after a certain age, so helpless to guide their entry into any stable and predictable world, that they had no choice but to plunk them down in this curious country limbo and hope for the best. The college operated as a kind of packaging house to which fruit from all over the country was to be shipped, slowly ripened, sorted, and eventually shipped out again to supermarkets from coast to coast.

The afternoon sun on the unshaded yard was hot. The girls had slipped off their coats, but still they felt increasingly uncomfortable. Their girdles had rolled down into tightening rubber cords around their damp waists. After months of soft clothes, flat feet and careless hair, their pretty disciplines of narrow skirts, hidden hairpins and heels raised decoratively from the ground made them shift position in an uneasy mixture of pride and irritation. A pleasant gust of air made them pat their hair protectively. A careless step on a pebble made a muscular leg wobble.

Then a shiver of preparation rippled through the crowd. Far down the flat stretch of black macadam, a silvery tube slowly shimmered into focus. Hannah shook her head, chagrined: no matter how often she took this bus, she unfailingly watched for it in the wrong direction.

By the time the girls fell into their seats they were flushed with the effort of managing their unwieldy suitcases down the aisle and up into the rack overhead. The first hour's ride from the valley to the nearest city, where they would transfer to another bus, was an unpleasant one, especially for Hannah, who still retained traces of her childhood motion sickness. The hypnotic rise and fall of the hills made her stomach queasy, and the clouds of cigarette smoke billowing around her nervous companion didn't help. Glad as they were to be leaving the college, this journey from the rough and beautiful countryside into the grimy towns that pitted the land like blackheads, did have a quality of defeat. Who could be happy to watch pellucid sky over whitewashed villages fade into a haze of grit? Some lingering vestige of Calvinism had denied these upstate cities even the bright neon glamour that usually paints at least a thin coat of excitement over basic urban textures of concrete and litter. The perfume of meadows yielded to gasoline and Hannah's head reeled. "It must be easy to keep them down on the farm after they've seen Albany," she said.

They clambered off that bus, suitcases bumping clumsily against their calves, and made their way through the hollowly buzzing terminal to the next. Rachel slept and Hannah leafed through their newest horde of magazines. Then, when the former blinked awake, they talked, lulled into an almost nocturnal solitude by the bus's lazy sway, the close seat, the rhythmic hum of the vibrating wheels below. Miles of forest swam by.

After a few peaceful hours, however, buildings began to flash by more frequently between the trees, until gradually trees yielded altogether to whole minutes of continuous storefronts and bustling crowds on curbs. Soon the stores grew taller and the crowds grew larger. The wracked cough of congealing traffic shattered the interior stillness of the bus. Bloodshot lights winked at intersections and the bus began to jerk, stop, lurch, crank into gear, jerk, and stop again. Eventually the only surviving trees were a column of naked stalks with metal spikes for branches. Hannah's stomach tightened and the whirr in her head meshed with the whirr of the wheels on the tar beneath her legs. She stopped talking and began to swallow more deliberately.

The bus joined swift tribes of cars and trucks wheeling across concrete bridges, speeding and diving and swerving in vast figure eights until, suddenly, New York emerged whole-born on the far side. Finally, the bus dipped again and swept underground.

Passengers dived for their bags, squirmed into the coats wadded behind them, lurched upright to clutch at overhead suitcases, and sat on the edges of their seats, ready to bolt. Some staggered forward in the still-moving vehicle, grabbing seat backs for support. Everyone ignored the bored caveats of the driver.

Rachel led the way to the taxi that would first deposit her friend, then carry herself up the far side of the city to her parents' home. Hannah was by now sick with tension; her jaw seemed clamped to the pounding top of her skull. The city was gloomy with oncoming night. Hard-faced strangers pushed one another in a race to their separate homes as if unknown dangers awaited stragglers. The cold lights blinking on above lent spectral shadows to their set faces. Neon solicitations flashed luridly. Traffic squawked and rattled and hissed. It was a brutal shock to a sensibility fresh from the country and it jolted through Hannah. Dread screwed every nerve tight.

"You'll call me as soon as you get a chance—?" Rachel said.

Hannah nodded. She fumbled through her small address book, lifting dry finger to dry tongue.

The taxi poked its way uptown into the West Forties, an area Rachel knew very little and Hannah not at all. Suddenly the city seemed alarmingly dark and empty. Motley clumps of people stood on the corners, but the blocks in between were barren and dim. Hannah's lungs felt stiff. Together they found the number: a worn brown building indistinguishable in the dusk from its neighbors stretching into oblivion on either side. Hannah hurriedly clambered out with her suitcase and stationed it on the curb, then turned to contemplate Rachel through the open window, her own face perfectly neutral with conflicting emotions. Rachel's mobile expression signaled anxiety, concern, anger and love. She felt, Hannah knew, as helpless as a mother sending an eager son to a war she didn't believe in.

"I'll call you sometime tomorrow," Hannah said, raising a hand. The cab belched, slowly turned in the almost empty street, and drove off. Abruptly Hannah was alone. She took a deep breath, hoisted her bag and walked toward the inky entrance of her destination. She heaved her weight against the large door, battered in with her awkward burden, and confronted the row of mailboxes. She squinted; the light was so dim she could barely make out the numbers. On her first skimming she didn't find his name, so the second time she read them through more carefully. She didn't find it then either. On the third reading she held her breath. Neither Ari's name nor his number was there. Leaving her suitcase she dashed out to make sure she had the right street-number and almost moaned when she saw that she did. She forced herself to walk calmly back and read the list one more time. No.

A telephone. Struggling with her saliva and recalcitrant throat, she dragged her bag back through the heavy door, bruising her shin in the process, and stood beside it while she battled the moisture threatening to cloud her vision and stared toward the farther but brighter corner. All she could see for certain were two bars and an ominous masculine crowd. But she had no choice—somewhere there must be groceries, drugstores. Taxis. She could walk out into the street, hail a cab, and be home in time to watch the late movie and sleep in her own bed. But she steeled herself against the temptation, clenched the leather handle that still bore Jenny's maiden initials in gilt, and strode deliberately toward the faintly humming, glowing crowd.

She braved the inspection of whiskey old men in shapeless jackets by aiming her eyes unflinchingly ahead. Suddenly she was very conscious of the expensive green coat she had bought last January to wear to her birthday celebration with her parents. The gold owl with jade eyes pinned to the collar seemed to attract every beam of light and reflect it back. Her alligator shoes clattered with every step. At the corner she stopped to look around, but instantly a male voice asked if she knew the time, so she turned sharply and kept walking, her throat constricting with misery. Trapped between the necessity of getting her bearings and the necessity of moving forward at a good clip with her gaze straight ahead, she was concentrating so hard on appearing serene that she nearly missed the drugstore as she passed it. She plunged in, oblivious to the stares and insinuations from the counter, and at the back, to her inexpressible relief, found an old-fashioned wooden booth. She kicked in her suitcase, sagged into the seat, and closed the door. The night was warm, her coat heavy, and under the added assault of panic, she was drenched with sweat. Trembling, she dialed Ari's number. After ten rings she hung up, waiting for the bing of her coin in the cup, and dialed again. After twelve rings she hung up again. Finally she couldn't hold back tears. She found a wadded tissue in her pocket and dabbed her eyes and nose, feeling as if the light bulb overhead that had gone on when the door shut must be placing her on exhibit. When her vision cleared, she looked up Rachel's number in her book, stared blankly at it, wondered exactly how far she was from Port Authority, and hopelessly decided to try one last time. On the fifth ring he answered with a very irritable grunt.

"Hello, this is Hannah," she said in the numb tones of an operator. "I'm at the corner of your block, but I can't find the apartment. I found the building, but I can't find your name on the buzzers or the mailboxes."

"But I explain to you the other day it is in the back of that street, behind it." His voice was cold with annoyance.

"Oh," she said uncomprehendingly.

"You still don't understand?"

"No—" Her monosyllable quavered and she bit off the rest of her sentence. She wanted to say she was going home.

Perhaps sensing that the paralysis of her voice was more than confused directions might warrant, he relented and told her to return to the front door, he would meet her there.

She thanked him politely and hung up. Now the options were closed: she was far too well-mannered to think of leaving him on the stoop. She made her way to the street in a daze, then halted in terror that she had left her wallet in the phone booth. A glance in her pocketbook reassured her. And she had her suitcase and her gloves. She plodded back in her heavy coat through the gauntlet of faded men whose faces seemed ridged like the skin of reptiles under the harsh streetlights.

The center of the block of dilapidated buildings was now even darker and colder. She was trying to focus on peeling numbers oscillating in the dusk when a door burst open and a guttural foreign voice ordered her to enter. As she approached, a shadowy figure grabbed her suitcase and lunged down an ammonia-rich hall that ran behind the main stairs. She hadn't noticed it before. He led her to a door and then, to her surprise, ushered her through it into the open air again. She seemed to be standing in, of all things, a species of garden—a backyard still holding its own against the filthy stone looming over it from every side.

The vague stranger in front stopped suddenly and put down her suitcase; she almost walked into him. She stared at the battered valise as a wandering American stares at a Coca-Cola sign, simply because the name, at least, is in his native tongue.

"I'm sorry to be impatient before. I think maybe I hurt your feelings —yes?"

She stared blankly at him. She wished she could tell him not to expect prompt responses from an organism as complex as the human body. Sound, after all, took eons just to shiver its way down the maze of ringing halls in her ear. She wanted to close her eyes, but instead continued to gaze up at him, unblinking.

"Yes, I hurt your feelings. I am truly sorry. I was trying to take a nap, you see, and I didn't want to answer the phone—it keeps ringing— all day it is ringing. And I didn't want to talk to anybody. I am waiting especially for you, but I expect you to knock on the door, you see? And I am tired. Lately I can't sleep, I am jittery. You ever have that—insomnia? No, you are too young; you don't know yet. Before I was annoyed at being waked up, but now that I see you I am so glad you come. Very very glad."

While he spoke, Hannah abstractedly studied the curious garden there in the groin of the city. It must have been a long time since anyone had deliberately buried seeds here, but more humble plants, gritty weeds and wildflowers, somehow managed to shove aside bricks and chunks of cement block to form their own careless patterns of khaki-green. A mossy clothesline sagged from one rusted pole to another. Broken bottles and tin cans caught the faraway lamplight and gleamed frostily. It was all a kind of forgotten ruin, Hannah realized. These were the battered souvenirs of a past too recently gone to be commemorated by more than cracked rocks, corroded poles, and a rotting rope sliding gradually back toward earth.

A warm hand between her legs jolted her out of her revery. She leaped backward, but Ari caught her before she tripped.

"Ah, I have hurt your feelings. I forget how vulnerable you are. But I make it up to you—come."

He marched decisively toward the building directly opposite the one they had come through. Hannah went to follow, but her shoe caught in one of the old pieces of flagstone that evidently had once made a decorative path across the garden. She bent down to ease her heel back into her pump and saw that the stones had grown so cracked from years of neglect that the trail they made was more hazardous than the bare ground, so she tried to find her own way through the weeds, though by now she could hardly see. Ari stepped back politely to let her enter first, and when she turned around to help him with her suitcase, she glimpsed her own reflection swimming in the wire-reinforced window of the closing door. As usual, although her neck muscles ached with tension and her shoulders were as taut as bridge girders, her face looked perfectly calm and self-possessed, the disinterested expression of a stranger. She sighed and glanced up as though to chart her way by the stars, but all she saw was a dusty ceiling bulb. Perhaps she would go home even now, she mused, if she didn't know in advance that she would only have to leave again; she might as well start here as anywhere. She vaguely wondered how long she would be searching out her dim reflection in the clouded windows of strange doors.

She followed him up flight after flight of poorly lighted stairs, until at last he turned into a hall, opened another door, and deposited her suitcase inside. She walked numbly in and began to inspect her new quarters, but before her tired eyes could focus, Ari kicked the door shut and propelled her across the room, toppled her down onto a low mattress, fell on top of her, and reached over her head to snap off the only light. Hands yanked at the girdle that by now had bitten deeply into the sore skin around her waist. He tugged impatiently and muttered that it wasn't good for her to wear these things.

Stunned, relieved, embarrassed, nervous, stiff, she submitted to his haste and watched one stocking rip as he peeled them off in a single motion with her girdle and shoes. While he fumbled with her skirt, she wriggled awkwardly out of her coat and nudged it to the floor, then tried to raise her hips to make things easier for him. Next he aimed for her sweater; she twisted into a sitting position to accommodate him. With her arms in the air, lost in the wool and the straps of her slip, blind against the soft fabric, Hannah desperately wished she were a child again in her mother's practiced grip: surely that was the only other time she had ever been undressed with such businesslike speed. But this new person fighting with her clothes was a stranger, stripped even of charm by her deadly fatigue. At the same time, she realized she would rather lie here in the wreckage of her costume and submit mindlessly to his force, than have to sit in a chair somewhere trying to make conversation. Perhaps he understood that. Under the battering of his impersonal assault some of her stiffness eased away. Finally she was naked except for her jewelry. She lay back, cold and motionless.

To her surprise, he then stood up and instructed her to unfasten him. She kneeled forward and complied, teeth chattering, hoping they would soon get under the covers. She was working as assiduously as a schoolgirl on his belt buckle when he moaned weirdly, ripped the job from her hands, and swooped hungrily down on top of her. Suddenly she felt as helpless as a mouse in the talons of an enormous, devouring bird that had zoomed out of the night from nowhere: eyes burned strangely above her; great wings buffeted everywhere; she was blind in a blanket of feathers, falling, rolling, at the mercy of rapacious mouth and claws. Coarse brown quills smothered her. She was dry and mute, stunned. Gradually she realized that the rough wing against her nose was his shoulder in the sweater he still wore, and the claw in her side was the buckle tangled in the sheet. She grew increasingly sore and tried to distract herself from the pain by watching him grimace and listening to the curious sounds he made, until at last, to her great relief, he collapsed beside her, gasping and wracked. Rather tentatively she touched his shoulder in a gesture meant to be consoling, for he seemed in frightful pain, but he immediately murmured a series of heartfelt compliments, cuddled her against him as she used to cuddle her teddy bear, and fell instantly dead with sleep.

Though she felt wide awake, Hannah lay still for a while, not wanting to disturb him. The tension had drained from her: she felt even more exhausted than before, but relaxed. When she thought he was too inert to notice, she carefully extricated herself from his embrace and slowly made her way through the dark room until she found the bathroom, directly adjacent to the front door. With the door safely shut behind her, she switched on the light and confronted herself across the sink. Deep moats of purple outlined her eyes; her cheeks were feverish. She found a washcloth in the tub and very diffidently patted her tender crotch. When she lowered herself onto the toilet, the parting of the bruised skin felt as though bandages were being peeled from new scars. The hot zing of urine burned sharply. She washed again, then splashed water on her face. Leaving her face dripping, she rummaged in the jumbled medicine cabinet for aspirin and swallowed three. She had expected to find an impressive array of women's toiletry in the cabinet but saw only a bottle of pink nail polish and a compact. Then she borrowed a comb and began to untangle her hair. A curly black strand attached itself to her cheek, and when she quickly brushed it away, it stuck to her fingers. Annoyed, she rubbed it off onto his towel. At last she sighed. She was beginning to feel like her own person again.

She left the bathroom light on but half-closed the door to mute it: she wanted to see where she was. Stretching, she tiptoed rather painfully back into the room. The low bed in the far corner, she saw, was simply a mattress on a wooden platform raised from the floor by cement blocks. A small orange crate served as night table, holding the phone, clock and lamp; over that was the sole window. On the same long wall as the bed, to Hannah's immediate left, was the kitchenette, divided from the rest of the room by a counter running parallel to the foot of the mattress. A great mass of pans and dishes were in the sink. The opposite long wall held a low brick and board bookcase, a battered phonograph, and a wooden chair. To her right was a bureau.

She limped over to the window and looked out, but all she saw was the side of another building. She rescued her coat from the floor and draped it over her suitcase; then, too chilled to explore any farther, she stepped quietly over him onto the bed and tried to wrap herself in the rough army-surplus blanket. At first she was as reluctant to touch the stranger's naked body as she was the icy wall, but after a moment she was forced to wriggle closer for warmth. He radiated heat like a campfire. She pushed herself up to peer at the luminous clock and saw to her surprise that it was already close to eight. Very little streetlight found its way through the forest of buildings into this room, and not much sound, either. It was dark and quiet and she was nowhere at all, alone with someone she didn't know and trusted only on faith. Trembling with fatigue and the aftermath of anxiety, she laid her head on the pillow and thought fitfully of home.

20

She awakened to find Ari lying on his back, smoking. She sat up dizzily. "Ah, little one, you are awake. I sleep very well; I think you are better for me than a pill. Now I feel fine, I am very grateful." He stubbed out his cigarette, propped a pillow against the wall, and pulled himself lazily up to it. "Maybe I should keep you in my medicine drawer, yes, for insomnia? Now you tell me, what do we do next? You are hungry? What kind of food do you like? I am starving. What do you like to cook? Do you want to go to the movies?"

Hannah glanced at the watch on her wrist, couldn't make out the hands, and squinted at the clock. It was disconcerting to awaken a few hours before she usually went to bed. She looked at him and, for the first time, smiled. "I'm still too disoriented to know if I'm hungry, but generally I'm not picky about food. I like all the kinds I've had. I can't cook anything to speak of, beyond heating up hot dogs. I adore all movies."

"Can't cook! Ah, American women are so blonde and lovely and useless." He grinned approvingly. "That doesn't matter, I am a wonderful cook. You can wash the dishes, then, if I cook for you—yes, that is fair? You are cold?"

"No more than usual."

"But you shouldn't wrap yourself up in that blanket like this. Are you afraid to let me see you? I love to see you, you are so lovely, such a woman and little girl all at once." He appraised her from his pillow, then casually pulled down the cover in which she had swathed herself like a mummy. "Here, come lie against me, I warm you. When you are cold, you should not hide in a blanket; you should come warm yourself against me. I am always hot like a heater, I never get cold. Someone tells me it is because I have high metabolism and always am full of nervous energy. Here, tuck your feet under my legs—brrr!—I make them hot." He massaged them vigorously. "Like ice. You like Greek food?"

"I've never had it." She felt very naked, but it was true that his touch was more effective than the spread. She nestled closer.

"Why can't you cook?"

"I don't know. I guess—" She broke off and laughed as he gave up massaging her, pulled her between his legs and wrapped all his limbs around her, then pulled a blanket across their laps.

"Now I can't see you, but I can touch you, which I like even better. Your mother, she can cook? Why doesn't she teach you?" He nuzzled her neck.

"She never made me learn any of that stuff. She never learned herself until she got married—but anyway, I guess she never assumed I'd grow up to do the things she does, to be like her."

"So who are you like, then, your grandmother?"

"God, I hope not! She was an alcoholic autocrat—and I'm sure she couldn't cook, only order other people to. My father's mother, that is; I never met the other one."

"So who? I can see you're not so much like your father." He gently cupped her breasts. "The family cat, yes?"

"The family cat is a dog."

He grinned. "No, you are not a dog. So I tell you what you are like then. You are like an owl with your big green eyes. A hungry owl, I think. A hungry owl who gets lost and can't make dinner. I see you need to be taken care of, yes? A pretty princess who needs me to wake her in the morning and tuck her back in bed again at night."

He switched on the lamps and they dressed together. He helped her with all the rapt delight of a child with a new doll, and his enthusiasm both flattered and perplexed her, for he must have played this game so very many times. In the bathroom she sat in her underwear on the edge of the tub and watched with fascination as he dabbed his face with foam, lathering it as generously as Jenny used to spread icing across a naked cake. She reached out a shy finger to scoop up some of the snowy stuff and had it halfway to her mouth before he laughingly grabbed her hand—as she had known he would. James shaved only once a day, and then with an electric buzz that mixed with the morning smell of coffee and the rustle of crunch of Katie's cereal.

Her mood was lifting: she liked this easy absorption in commonplace things. She liked his simple good spirits, his deft efficiency with objects. For all his nervous restlessness, he never made a graceless motion. He chattered continuously as he moved about, musing over his everyday activities, worrying, justifying himself, denouncing people whom he never bothered to describe. Little of what he said made sense to her: he made no attempt to clarify and she made none to sort it out. He seemed to talk as another person might hum or chew his nails or crack his knuckles, and the English words in his novel syntax, foreign inflection, and rough voice, harmonized into a kind of abstract music that Hannah enjoyed. She could intuit the flow of his moods and random associations without needing to understand his sentences. He didn't like to make sentences. He didn't want to take hold, take over, shape, organize, or abstract from his experience; he wanted to be like seaweed, taking the shape of the currents that carry it. Of course he liked to dominate, but only in the sense of wanting things to go his way: he didn't want to understand; he didn't want to see beyond himself; he didn't want to see himself; he didn't want to see. He wanted to fly. He wanted to fly as a bat flies, alert with the radar of its own quick instincts, blind, careless, spontaneous, without a thought. Hannah liked the sure intuition with which he guided her into his world when he wished to, gently and firmly. She liked the grace of his least gesture. In fact, she decided, she liked him.

As he shaved, she reached out and touched his buttocks, which were like knots in a slim tree trunk, hard and round. When he had dried his face, he began to brush his hair with a formidable grimace, trying vainly to smooth the wiry recalcitrant clumps, but the best he could manage was to squash it momentarily into a mat that sprang back into a cloud the instant he moved his head. Hannah was glad. That crown of wild wool seemed to her a kind of warning, a rough, wind-whipped flag that announced his true colors to anyone willing to see.

She stared glumly at her skirt and stockings on the floor, then with intense relief, folded them neatly into her suitcase and took out her jeans. While he pored over the movie page of the paper, she sat pensively on the chair and watched him, quite prepared to follow his lead, and when he had come to a decision, she picked up her jacket and followed him down the three flights of stairs into the garden of shattered glass and persistent weed. It was cooler. The air was crisp and heady. She took a deep, exhilarated breath. He held her hand, squeezed it, and asked if she was glad she had come. She was.

They paused at the same corner where she had been so miserable a few hours ago, but now his presence shielded her from the eyes of the gray men. She was so oblivious, so happily following him, that he had to stop her on the curb or she might have plunged heedlessly into the brilliant milky way of orbiting headlights. He laughed at her carelessness and playfully caged her in his arms, as if fearing she might momentarily fly into the meteoric traffic and be lost.

"So, crazy one, are you in love with me yet?" His tone was teasing, but he waited for the answer.

Hannah was amused. "No, you needn't worry; not yet. I'll let you know if I think there's imminent danger."

"So tell me—" The light changed and he led her across the dark space between armies of blazing automobiles. "So tell me this, have you ever fucked at once with two people, two men—I forget what they call it—"

"A *ménage à trois?* No, you know perfectly well I haven't." His question took her by surprise and she began to withdraw.

"Maybe you like that more than you know." He proceeded to describe the advantages objectively and graphically, as a salesman might compare the virtues of various products. "I like it best with two women," he concluded, "but it is very exhausting that way for me."

"I can well imagine," she said dryly. "It must be a real trial."

"But seriously, I think you like having two men fuck you like I show you tonight, yes? Twice as much pleasure. If you want to try it, I have a friend—many friends, in fact. We can see what one you think you like best."

She realized that he was testing her in some fashion, and indirectly fending her off. Underneath the oily solicitude his questions had a cruel bite. "I think we'll postpone that adventure," she said.

"But soon I am going back to Tel Aviv—we haven't so much time."

"You can always leave me the telephone numbers of your friends." She let go of his hand.

"It shocks you that I call it fucking?" he asked after a pause. "Not 'making love,' or some sweet word like that?"

"A little, I suppose. I'm only used to hearing it as a swear word, and so it always seems to have a slightly hostile ring."

"But it is not making love we do because we are not in love, you see. We don't even know yet if we like each other very much, just that we like each other's bodies. Yes, this is true? We fuck. It is nice, but not love, right?"

"Right."

"So. And there is no other word. I do not like this 'screw,' like a machine, and 'intercourse' sounds like science." He delivered a short lecture on the regrettable Anglo-Saxon linkage of sexuality and profanity.

Hannah had never pondered this shortcoming of the language before, but she decided he was correct. It was not his logic she objected to.

"So, when you get used to the ways I fuck you, you probably get bored with that, and then you like to have two men do it. You get bored with just the same thing and want more adventure. This happens to many people; you want more thrill."

She studied the side of his face for a moment. "No, I won't want more of that kind of thrill," she said slowly. "It's not just what you do, I mean your technique—anyone can learn that from a book. It's something about the way you do what you do, the way you are. The way you 'do it' is inseparable from the way you are. And I like the way you are. I like you." She thought a moment. "In a sense I did choose you, you know, despite the fact that you virtually tackled me on sight. I am attracted to you in particular, and I'm not attracted to many men. I doubt your friends would meet my standards."

He thought that over for a minute, and she wondered what he made of it. Then finally he said, "But it would be even better to have two of me, yes?"

She laughed in genuine delight. "Well, twins would be nifty, but I'm not at all sure I could handle you both." She tried then to explain her sense that three people in bed might face the hazards of three people in any intimate situation: two tend to pair against one. If there wasn't open hostility, aggressive or defensive, then there would almost certainly be its mask: sophisticated good humor and detachment. "No, you're about all I can cope with," she concluded. "And I've never been much for team sports."

He deliberately took back her hand, walked silently for a few minutes, then asked meditatively, "But you think about things, yes? I like that. It's not so common, I think. I like the way you talk—it's different, you know—I can't say how—"

"People have told me all my life I talk like a book. Actually I talk like my father."

"I like it, but I am glad it is you and not a book or your father."

Apparently she had passed his private entrance exam, because he drew her very close and held her with quiet affection as they walked. He ceased to talk and seemed to be musing on some question of his own. But his arm around her shoulders was warm and sentient, and now and then he absentmindedly stroked her neck. It was pleasing to walk intertwined with him through the cool, dark city, pleasing to feel her stride blend comfortably with the swift rhythm of his own.

The restaurant was small, quiet and attractive. There were only two other customers. She and Ari sat toward the rear and smiled at one another over the candle. Until he asked her if she wanted to share a bottle of wine she was almost fully relaxed: only then did the lurch in her stomach tell how frightened she was of alcohol and men combined. She said no but told him to go ahead, then almost gasped with relief when he admitted rather sheepishly that liquor of any sort tended to make him dizzy. He ordered something that he claimed had the flavor of champagne but was really a kind of soft drink, and she asked calmly to taste it, inwardly appalled at her unreasoning fear that he might be trying to dupe her. Reassured by the bland liquid, she then tried to tell him something about her parents.

"But if you are afraid about me drinking," he puzzled, "then why don't you just ask me not to? Why do you tell me to go ahead like you don't care at all? I never could tell from your face that you are nervous."

"I don't know," she said honestly. "It didn't occur to me. I guess I didn't think I had the right to ask you to change your habits."

"But if I ask for wine, you be afraid, yes? And you be quiet in that way you get and go away from me inside. That's how it makes you feel?"

"Yes, that is how I would react."

He studied her in both perplexity and concern. "I think I have to watch you more carefully than I realize. I think instead of telling me what you want, you just wait to see if I do it, and if I do not, you only are quiet and go away. Not just go away inside some time, but go away from me to your friend Rachel."

"You're right," she said with considerable amazement.

"That isn't good, though. You must tell me what you want. How else can I know?" He frowned almost in annoyance.

"But—but you wouldn't want me to try to change you—"

"No, but I don't let you do that. You tell me what you want, then I tell you if I do it. I don't care about drinking wine, so it is silly if you are upset because I am drinking it and I don't even know. You see?"

"Yes," she said meekly. His perception astonished her, and so did the force of his disapproval—clearly he was accustomed to instructing people, at least women. She suspected that for as long as she knew him, he would be simultaneously warning her against dependence and trying to dominate her.

When he explained that the green pasty-looking appetizer was mashed peas, she had to suppress a grimace, but when he taught her to scoop it up on the flat pieces of bread, she found it delicious. Suddenly she was starving. She began to gobble it so rapidly that he laughed and ordered another, which made her blush. When the lamb and vegetables arrived on skewers she literally salivated at the aroma, then sadly tried to conceal her appetite. It was not feminine, she knew, to like to eat. Men liked to tease women with mock forbearance about their birdlike ways. If she ever did get married, she would probably have to eat her real meals in the closet. So she was shocked when he abruptly commanded her to finish, though she promptly cast caution to the winds and complied, and more shocked when he beamed at her empty plate and announced that he hated women who were picky eaters, asked if she wanted more, and without waiting for an answer, signaled the waiter for seconds. This time she truly was full and didn't mind when he ate the bulk of it. He had little in the way of conventional table manners, she saw, but had an innate grace that perfectly sufficed.

The waiter, too, seemed expansively proud that she had consumed so much, and applauded her performance until she blushed again. When he brought the coffee, he complimented her to Ari in a foreign tongue until she reddened even more, and her embarrassment seemed to please them both. She felt like a ruby in a jeweler's showcase, ablaze under the eyes of owner and admirer. Unlike a pretty bauble, however, she offered to pay her share of the check. It seemed unreasonable that Ari, who, judging from his apartment, was as poor as most actors, should automatically support her as though he were her father. But he only looked at her oddly and told her to save her money until they wanted to do something special together. Then at last they reeled to their feet in a satiate daze and headed for the door. The waiter extended his arms and made Ari promise to bring her back to him soon; Ari made flowery pledges; they all laughed; and the couple swung contentedly toward Times Square.

Hannah had never dared walk here before at an hour so close to midnight; she had only been carried through, fascinated, in taxis. Now, when she was so pleasantly soporific with food and the late hour and the aftermath of strain, the whole area seemed impossibly brilliant and alive. She entrusted her body to Ari's care and let her senses step out into the fantastic carnival. Her head swiveled like a radar cone; she tripped on a bump on the pavement and Ari laughingly balanced her. Since they were both movie lovers, each of them had seen the few resuscitated standards the other hadn't, so to Hannah's delight they were forced to keep strolling from marquee to marquee. At last they settled for John Wayne winning the West, Rock Hudson finding God in the tropics, and Don Knotts finding happiness as a fish. While Ari went to buy the tickets, Hannah leaned against the glassed-in poster display and watched the crowd. Everyone seemed masked and anonymous, as carefully costumed in his sleazy way as if this were a perpetual Mardi Gras: a ravishing crowd of perfect strangers. The colorful litter and smeared food underfoot crackled with an invitation to abandon, to the absolute freedom of indifference. No one noticed, no one cared; or even if they did notice, they didn't care: you could run away to join the circus here and never be missed or found.

When Ari took her hand she jumped as if awakened. He looked down at her, puzzled, then pressed against her and kissed her as if to blot out her view of the street, so that around the dark silhouette of his head she saw a penumbra of cold color and sound dancing like a perverse halo. "But you daydream so," he murmured. "I feel that you forget me the second I leave you alone. I think I always have to keep you right beside me or you forget who I am and where you are, yes?"

In the ornately tawdry lobby he headed directly to the candy counter and purchased an enormous bag of tiny Turkish taffies, then led the ecstatic Hannah to the balcony, where, to her amusement, the evenly spaced solitary men seemed considerably more interested in Ari than in herself. They snuggled together, feet on the seatbacks in front, and held up each piece of candy to the scant light to try to discern its flavor before parceling it out. They were just in time to see Rock Hudson's epiphany and reformation, which seemed to involve lepers, a woman, and terrible dangers.

When the fish movie flickered on, Hannah sighed with disappointment and turned back to the candy, and then, finding the bag empty, pinched Ari in protest. He laughed and held her closer. Legs entwined, hands traded into one another's laps, they slid into a warm bath of anonymity, letting the figures on the screen carry on the burden of action and identity for a while. Don Knotts exchanged his identity for a fish's. A wise choice, Hannah thought; she had always wanted to be one. Mermaid, daughter of the sea—as a child she had almost puckered to death bobbing around in those waves hour after hour praying for transformation. The animated passages of the film, when the entire screen swam with dazzling aquamarine, surprised her with their loveliness.

She turned, curious to see Ari's reaction, and found him watching her. He drew her forward, insinuating his subtle hand into her clothing as simply as the fish on screen eased silkenly through the opalescent green and gently explored the dampness beneath the fabric. It seemed natural to Hannah to yield to this diffuse melting and drifting in theatres, for movies had always been the occasions of her most consuming sweeps of desire, though always before the desire had been for what she saw, not what she felt.

The walk home was silent and easy. Hannah liked the sure swing of Ari's torso against hers, the fact that he led her so confidently through the strange pre-dawn streets that seemed to hum with the sound of other people sleeping.

Inside the apartment, she hung her jacket neatly in the closet, then went to the bathroom to brush her teeth. The face in the mirror, she decided, was that of a child still curled unconscious in the backseat during a long drive home, confident that someone would carry her, dreaming, to her bed. She tucked her toothbrush into a flap of her suitcase and slipped off her jeans, entirely conscious of Ari watching from the bed where he lay smoking. As she pulled off her sweater, the damp shaved undersides of her arms seemed shyer than her breasts. She stood there a moment, a little unsure, still dressed in the white cotton underpants she had bought in General's Bay a few months before, and thought this was how a plump new teddy bear must feel as it waits under the tree for someone to wake up and untie its satin bow. She glanced obliquely at Ari and was reassured by the almost grim softening of his wide mouth and the concentrated narrowing of his eyes. Instructing herself that she was quite capable of untying her own satin ribbons, she dropped the rest of her clothing into the case, turned, and walked deliberately to the bed.

He lit a candle on the makeshift table, then rose and went across the room, his gaze still fixed on her, to latch the door and switch off the bathroom light. When he slid beside her, she gave a shuddering sigh of releasing tension and relief. Taking his time, he eased her in and out of various positions with gentle assurance and as he moved over her, he continuously praised her in a kind of litany partially obscured by the closeness of her flesh. Although she was still as sore as a newly toothless gum, she was also unprecedentedly slack, loose-hung, wanting. When her mouth fell open in wonder, and her cheeks went crimson with blood, and her palms flew up to touch his back, he continued to laud her in almost a whispered chant. All her life, Hannah had been haunted by the vision of a woman serene in demeanor, knees clasped as if in prayer, hands joined over her lap, eyes elsewhere, lips enigmatic, her skin as cool and clear and impenetrable as a diamond: the lady whom men would respect. Her greatest fear was that she might repulse the very man who tempted her to lose her self-control, growing dirty in his eyes, like a ministering nurse stained by the wounds of her patient. So when Ari told her that her face was lovely when she let it open like a flower, she was able to leave it to his care. When he murmured approvingly over her small breasts and wide, slender shoulders, she made a gift of them to him. When his rapt hand said her flushed skin was the softest of vestments, she lent it to him to wear. It was not that he filled her with pride, rather that he freed her of the need for that and most other protection, freed her to slide into a darkness where she could bless even the pain for making the fullness more palpable and the emptiness more stark.

When he finally shuddered and nestled down beside her, he asked if she had come, adding that he was sure she must have. Not knowing what he meant, she answered yes, assuming that he must know better than she, for he had been present the whole time except the end, whereas she had been elsewhere. While he lit a cigarette with the flame of the candle, she limped to the bathroom, trying to walk so that no part of her touched another, she was so raw and sore. After she washed and patted herself with talcum, they fell asleep, their turned spines touching.

21

She awakened to a grasp rough with passion, and lay dazed and cold with pain while he thrust back and forth between her offended thighs until she prayed he would snap at the base like a dried-out wishbone. Then he muttered a series of destinations and instructions like a bored priest's hasty liturgy over her inert body, hurriedly dressed and left. Relieved to be alone, she rolled back to her stomach, stretched out gratefully across the empty bed, and slept another hour. Her eyes finally flickered open again with great reluctance. She felt agitated, nervously alive to the few sounds that pierced this far into the center of the block.

To reassure herself that she had not been kidnapped into another world, she reached for the phone by the bed to call Rachel. Fortunately Rachel had a private line, for if her mother, whom Hannah liked enormously, were to hear Hannah's voice so close, she would interrogate her in a kind of maternal reflex, as if all daughters were alike.

"Hi, did I wake you up?" Hannah asked apologetically at the slurred sound of her friend's greeting.

"No, not really, I was just lying here in bed trying to adjust to being home."

"Well, I just wanted to let you know I was alive." She tried to sketch the events of the past evening, conscious that her words were woefully inadequate, that whatever knowledge her flesh and psyche had assimilated still wasn't clear in her mind. But it didn't really matter. Rachel's responses, though affectionate, were still vague and obtuse with the shock of homecoming. Hannah pictured that tiny bedroom with the built-in cabinets and closets, the special shelves for television and stereo, the elegant bedspread hanging on a trapeze on the door, the furry white floor, the framed prints of black and white children singing together, the heavy damask curtains blocking the sounds of the courtyard at the only window, all the clothing from yesterday littered on the floor along with the contents of the suitcase, the boxes of clothing from Bergdorf's and Bendel's that had been brought home for Rachel's approval, and in the middle of the rumpled sheets, a drowsy brunette rubbing her eyes with her fist and trying to disentangle the wire of her princess phone from the pile of velvet throw pillows. Rachel, she knew, had momentarily expected an invasion by a mother no longer able to tolerate the closed door, eager to burst in and scold about the wrinkled clothing and scattered books and carelessly folded bedspread, all of which she would straighten while her daughter scowled. Rachel was forever wondering why her mother dashed in that way four or five times a day to rectify mistakes of the last hours, why her mother questioned her every move as if they were handcuffed together so that the sneeze of one was automatically the wet cheek of the other, and why the nagging, since it was so incessant and predictable, still bothered her so very much. Nonetheless, if this was an aggravating ritual, it was also a deep-seated one, and if the welcoming embrace was stifling, it was also a welcome home. Rachel was a daughter again, and if the atmosphere was overheated, it was also safe, intimate, familiar, and the intrusion of Hannah's report from the disorder of some man's unmade bed was jarring.

Sensing that Rachel had not yet adjusted, Hannah cut short her descriptions, promising to call back later. She hung up, then walked lightly, respectful of her new tenderness, to the refrigerator. Since she could find no clean utensils, she drank milk from the carton and broke off a piece of cheese, which made her feel better. A hot shower felt even better than that. She wiped a circle of steam from the mirror and inspected herself curiously. The word jaded played in her mind, and she happily pictured Simone Signoret slinking around the apartment, growling huskily. She hopped back to the other room and pulled on jeans and a sweater.

In daylight the room seemed much larger because everything in it was so makeshift, fragile or low that the sun had all the space it needed to improvise. She pulled back the curtains and opened the windows; the air was balmy and surprisingly fresh. It proved hard to straighten the bedcovers since the low mattress was wider, but she did her best, using a blue madras throw that enhanced the sunny gold patterns playing on the white walls.

She had carried an ample supply of books with her, but found herself reluctant to return to the familiar, so, with the same impulse that draws other snoopers to medicine cabinets, she walked over to Ari's bookshelves. There were many more books than she would have expected, and most looked well-used. She thought they must be borrowed, for she couldn't imagine Ari sitting in one place long enough to absorb so much print. She noticed a Hebrew to English dictionary, numerous classic and modern plays, including Racine in French, some Freud, Jung and Fromm, some girlie magazines, which she promptly plucked out, and to her surprise, a battered Marquand novel that she thought she hadn't read.

She returned to the sink, stared queasily at the congealing mess of last week's meals, daintily washed one glass, filled it with milk, and returned to the bed. The magazines proved disappointing, the girls were neither as air-brushedly perfect as in *Playboy* nor as lurid as she had hoped, so she picked up the Marquand, plumped up the pillow against the wall behind her, and sank happily into the soft mattress and familiar prose. Time passed slowly but contentedly. She liked the quiet, the warm sun and occasional breeze on her shoulders, the flutter of the drapes and the pink and lavender rainbows they cast on the walls. Now and then she heard the echo of a basketball ringing on concrete, followed by the soft slap of sneakers and the high-pitched yells of boys. A mother's voice called Jimmy six times, then a half hour later called Pete. In the alley under her window, cats discussed the coming night. The mellowing light, shaded blue by its madras frame, gradually left the wall to shift and play a lazy game of solitaire on the matching squares of the bedspread.

Hannah was agreeably conscious of a difference as she sighed, changed position, and read on. Ordinarily, at home or at school, such reminders of other lives drifting in on a warm day would unsettle her, insinuating that this solitude, however pleasant, was an insufficiency on her part, a poor substitute for the promise of spring that quickened her pulse and dampened her thighs and finally would force her up and out, restless, dissatisfied. But today she only stretched, yawned, poured more milk, and returned peacefully to her book. Inevitably the outside world and its challenges would come again through that door, and in the interval she was glad to be spared any necessity to go forth and meet it.

Indeed, such a lazy afternoon was so sweetly drenched with satisfaction, so perfectly self-contained, that when the rattle of a key in the door did at last come, she jumped and her heart plunged. If Ari had heightened her appreciation of privacy, he also had the power to shatter it. When she realized that the demanding rattle was continuing because she had bolted the chain, she ran to unlatch it, then stepped very quickly back into deep retreat, close to tears; she turned to go back to the bed. But Ari, with quick sensitivity to her mood, caught her, drew her close and murmured that he had missed her, and when he asked if she had also missed him and received only a noncommittal grunt in reply, he chuckled. She realized with grudging respect that he soothed her as naturally as a good rider soothes a filly who has shied at a fantasy by the roadside, and began to relax.

He led her back to the bed, drew the curtains, and explored her slowly in the now fading light that cast her clear skin a delicate shade of ivory-blue. She looked down and saw herself melt into his tawniness. Still, when he eased her gently but firmly to the foot of the mattress and instructed her to put her mouth where her hand had been, she went stiff with confusion. She was not so much repulsed as frightened, and frightened less by the act than by his reaction to it. That serenely unapproachable lady who haunted her shook her head warningly. Hannah's only knowledge of this practice was the famous set of numbers that used to cause such smothered hilarity in math classes and football games—an inexplicable hilarity to her, until someone had drawn a picture. She did not want to expose herself to that kind of mirth. She did want to please, and in a deeper sense to pleasure Ari, but not at the cost of his respect. She looked up in open anxiety. But his gentle smile, and his firm grip and firmer instructions, persuaded her to comply.

It felt strange. She warmed to the power she now had to make his head fall back so sharply and his eyes flicker shut, but there was also an undercurrent of fear: how easily he could choke her. She was concentrating only on neither gagging nor hurting him, when he again startled her by drawing her hips to him and locking his face in a place she could only strain to see in tilted hand mirrors. The shock and ecstasy of such unprecedented intimacy made her shudder and flinch wildly back. He held her firm and continued, but this nerve-trembling delight of her skin was so wild, so profoundly different from the sweeping abandon she had felt the previous night, that she flopped like a netted flounder, and her clumsiness only horrified her the more, so that she wrenched away and begged him to stop, and to her acute disappointment he did. He pulled her up and resumed his exploration with his hand, which was far less overwhelming at first but rapidly intensified when he refused to let go. Again her external nerves leaped wildly and seethed with electric shock. This obsession of her skin, not the darkly flowing, all-absorbing experience of before, but this specific agitation of the outside of her, was nearly as excruciating as it was pleasurable. Instead of an irresistible sweep to self-abandon, it threw her back to herself, eyes jolted open, jarringly eager for the end. And when, after a strangled gasp and jerk from her, he sought her hand for immediate release, she was as disconcerted as she was relieved.

She lay there, speechless and unnerved, and he stroked her absently while he smoked. At last he leaped up and commanded her to follow him to the bathroom. He scrubbed out the tub, then turned on the spigots full blast and poured pink powder from a pink box with a clown on the front, until clouds of bubbles climbed so high that Hannah felt she was in an airplane looking down, and, as she had always yearned to do from a plane, she plunged in, chin-deep in foam that rustled, as it grew and died, like the hundred crinolines Jenny used to wear. Ari dove in after her and they played like curious children, giggling, relearning one another's secrets with their toes. Finally, when their mirth had subsided back to smiles, he soared out in a wave of water, instructing Hannah to run more hot, and disappeared into the kitchen.

After many mysterious bangings and hissings, he made a majestic reentrance, still naked, bearing a gold, white and red enameled tray with matching pitcher and cups, which he deposited with a flourish on the side of the tub as he hopped nimbly back in. To her surprise, since she disliked regular coffee, this thick Turkish brew was sweet and good, so when she saw how proud Ari was of his concoction and his impromptu ceremony, she drank it enthusiastically. Even more than the flavor, of course, she relished the faintly sinful luxury of sipping from ornate cups in a steamy tub, her skin flushed and swollen with perspiration, languorously watching Ari do the same. She closed her eyes and leaned back against the cooler tiles in amused wonder that she was here—and after a moment, she realized with interest that she could no longer picture the face she had been gazing at in stupefied contentment an instant before. She opened her eyes and blinked and decided that in a sense she still wasn't seeing him. He was very pale, she made herself note. His hair was lank where sweat pasted it to his skin. He hadn't shaved that morning and his whiskers reminded her of ants on a gray sidewalk. Yet all that observation took an effort of will, and was as irrelevant to her experience of Ari as knowing the gaseous composition of the sun is to lying on the beach. Judging from his agreeable expression, it was the same with him, which was a blessing because her inspection of him had given rise to anxiety about her own water-logged appearance. How comical she must look in this green shower cap!

She mused over this as they drained the pot. Despite the caffein, she was limply relaxed and beginning to yearn for a nap when Ari began to explore her again, first playfully with his foot, then with mounting intensity. He leaned forward and entangled himself in her limbs in a way that nearly drowned her.

"Oh, no," she gasped, "I really can't again. I'm dead tired and terribly sore—"

He looked at her seriously. "You are really in pain?"

"Not agony, but pain, yes."

"You should tell me before; I be gentle. But listen, little one, because this is something I believe very much: two people who like each other—and we like each other a lot by now, yes—?"

"Yes."

"Two people who like each other must never say no when one of them wants to fuck. If they start saying no, it becomes a game between them or a way to punish each other, and soon everything is ruined. Fucking becomes just another way of fighting; it is war instead of pleasure. Horrible!" He shook his head solemnly, dwelling on past horrors. "You see?"

She did see. She remembered all those strategy discussions with one parent about the other. So she allowed him to lift her out and dry her, duly dried him with the same towel, and followed him back to bed. Relaxed beneath him, she moved gradually from comatose goodwill to a soft stir, then an unexpected flush that made her vibrate and catch her breath. "You see," he murmured, "sometimes it is best when you think you are tired."

He got up to shut the window, for the night air had turned cold, and to draw the shade over the black glass, then snuggled back under the covers, thanking her for having made the bed—which surprised her, since she had done it from habit, not for him—and finally turned over into earnest sleep. Hannah baked pleasantly in his body heat and wondered whether to turn on the light and read, but before she could gather herself for any action, the telephone rang. Ari grunted angrily from the pillow and pulled the blanket over his head, but the ringing continued insistently, and finally stopped only to begin again. Apparently the caller knew his habits and was determined.

At last he heaved over, swearing, clicked on the lamp, and answered with a scowling monosyllable. At the same time, he scooped his arm under Hannah and tenderly cupped her near breast in his warm hand. She was amazed that anyone could be in two such different moods at once. She strained to listen, but could hear only blasts of husky female rumbling between his clipped replies.

At last he tried to interrupt, was thwarted, and tried again. "Well, I have been very busy lately," he said twice. "So? You know I end my stay in your rich country soon, so you have to get used to it, yes? Then with the money you save you buy long bananas, hot dogs, Pepsi bottles, let's see, and candles and cucumbers—candles are best I think—to keep you company. You can think of me when you use them. You can close your eyes and say, 'Eli, Eli,' or 'Ari,' if it makes you happier—"

The caller answered with another blast, but Ari's face only grew more frigid with each assault or plea. He reminded Hannah of James answering business calls at home.

"Yes, yes, of course I am still here!" he snapped. "But I am leaving in only a few more days than a week for good, so what do I need for theatre tickets a month from now—you keep your presents, or give them back to your husband: what do I need for so many gold lighters and cuff links—I just give them to my friends!"

How could anyone withstand rejection that vicious? Hannah's inward shrinking was becoming outward when, to her astonishment, Ari leaned over, balancing the receiver on his shoulder, and studied her face curiously. Then, with infinite tenderness, he nuzzled her neck and stroked her breast as he might a kitten. Finally he put the receiver on the bed, where it continued to squawk noisily, and turned to lie half on top of her, keeping his weight on his elbows so he might still see her face. Fascinated, almost mesmerized, Hannah gazed back with perfect composure. What disconcerted her more than his cruelty was the serious affection in his hands and eyes. How could he enlist her in this sadistic ritual and at the same time brush her cheek with a sweetness that was genuine? From the receiver came scratchy, gulpy sounds that she recognized as sobs. She almost winced, but chose not to, and instead met his scrutiny with calm impassivity. He held her face firmly to keep her from glancing away, and stared into her eyes with an intensity frightening in itself, as if he were challenging her to something, asking a question he had never thought to ask before, and she felt her silence committing her to something neither could name. She did not blink. Neither of them breathed.

Then at last he sighed, flopped back on the pillow, and picked up the phone, which by now was emitting only questioning gulps. He listened a while longer before speaking, continued to interrupt the ensuing tirade with even nastier sarcasms, and finally slammed the receiver down. For a full minute he stared grimly ahead, then he reached for a cigarette, and as he did, the black box began to ring again, first fifteen times, then twenty, then eight, until at last it broke off mid-ring and went dead.

He stared at the wall. Hannah absentmindedly traced the trail of his cigarette until it fanned out into the atmosphere, then yawned and began to climb over him to the floor, but he pressed her down beside him. She made pincurls of the still moist hair on his chest. Obviously he was waiting for her to speak, which she was not going to do. She settled into the pillow and waited, curious.

Finally, with no emphasis, he said, "She is older, in her forties, but very beautiful. Beautiful like a profession. There are tiny scars all around the edges of her face. She looks younger than you. Her husband is a doctor, very rich. He give her anything and she give it right back to me." He apparently saw unending spirals behind his half-closed eyes, and added, "Everybody gives anything for something, for somebody, but never together. I mean, they never want the same thing." He looked at her coolly. "It's not that I never like her—when I first meet her I want her very much."

The sudden distance and bitterness in his voice made Hannah wary. She gestured noncommittally and began to say that he wasn't obliged to explain, but his face softened and he stopped her. He stroked her hair pensively, then went to say something, but didn't. Instead he rolled over decisively and fell asleep.

Hannah lay very still and tried to sort out her feelings. It was as though it had been a brutally hot day and someone had sought to cool her flushed face with the flat side of an ice-cold knife, just flexing his wrist enough to let her know the edge was there. Ari's apartment was furnished from the driveway of a lumberyard; he wore old khaki jeans, battered sweaters and T-shirts, and torn sneakers with torn socks. The implications of all that should be clear; any woman who tried to buy him should soon realize it was a very different game they were playing. Any woman who gave him lasting power over herself was a fool. In a sense he probably did love women, in the sense that alcoholics love the taste of wine and gamblers thrill to the sharp slap of the cards. She vowed that the moment she saw the flicker of satiation or indifference in his eyes, she would leave.

And yet her body was aglow in the aftermath of pleasure: warm, loose, as sensuous as a cat in a sunbeam. Sleep began to soften her mood, and she pondered the intractable black hair on the pillow beside her, the sometimes fierce mouth, now soft and vulnerable as a boy's. She wished she could picture just one likely scene from his childhood, but she couldn't: she doubted she had ever seen a single picture of modern Israel. All that came to mind were Bible stories, eternal flights across deserts, ubiquitous enemies, fathers willing to sacrifice sons on mountaintops because some disembodied voice in the thunder told them to. Ari moaned and shifted position, his taut cheeks mobile with dreams that made his forehead furrow. He rubbed his eyes with the back of one hand in a childlike, puzzled gesture that pierced her with tenderness.

Very drowsily, she supposed that he sought from women not friendship, nor security, nor understanding, nor even mothering, but rather some ineffable mystery. In the hidden recesses and caves of their bodies he found promise of something more, something other, a forgotten map in a bottle tossed to sea by children now grown to men and concerned with other things. But always that elusive promise vanished like mercury from his touch, then paused just out of reach, shining with hope, silver and pure. On and on it led him, fleeing with familiarity only to reappear elsewhere in a stranger, and he plunged after it like a half-crazed sailor in search of the piece of earth to match his obscure and fragmented map. If sometimes his belief snapped along with his faith in himself, then it must be understood that his was the despair of a man of single purpose, who, against all evidence, still blindly believed that if only he were true to his part of some covenant made and forgotten generations ago, justice would be done. The very history of his failures must guarantee the rightness of his struggles: so much suffering could not be without purpose; that was the bargain. He must never question, doubt, or look back; he must never try to see beyond himself, beyond his single path. What if there were nothing to see? No end in sight—nothing at all, emptiness? But what was inconceivable: the sheer difficulty and pain must in themselves prove, or even create, the power that would ultimately give him rest. Or else it was all a senseless whirl, a roar of laughter in an echoing cavern in the back of his mind, the brutal vibrations of which occasionally gave him such merciless headaches.

And the women? But all the women he sailed through and past were oblivious to the clues and promises he found in the spaces invisible to them. They felt only his passing reverence, the awed intensity of his exploration and concern. They felt themselves made into temples in his abstracted vision, and they never wished to understand that a man who ravishes them for a temple won't settle for a home.

22

Hannah awakened from a murky dream about trying to swim in a bottle to find Ari at the counter, happily preparing a picnic dinner from the brown bag he had left there earlier when he had burst in on her solitude. He spread an army-surplus blanket on the bed, and, wrapped in more blankets Indian-style, they munched an assortment of delicatessen delights, culminating in three-to-a-package cupcakes that reduced them to friendly squabbling over the division of the third. Between great bites, Ari rambled in his typically aimless fashion, answering a question or two of hers and sliding into lengthy tangents of his own.

Hannah wanted to ask about his parents, but her questions were vague because she had no frame of reference and because she sensed how much he hated being pinned down. Even more vaguely he answered that his father was from Russia, his mother a Sephardic Jew, both very brave and ardent and beautiful, fighting side by side in the war, now bitterly separated. Hannah tried to decipher how old he was when they had parted, how he had felt, with whom he had lived, but it seemed they had all moved back and forth through the years in a cat's cradle of combinations which it bored him to remember. Once he had been a fanatical Zionist, he added, even joining clubs and such, but not now—hence the ham he was so happily eating. He loved bacon. Hannah scarcely knew what a Zionist was; she imagined it must have made a deep impression, but didn't know how to probe. So she asked about the mother again and whether he had any siblings.

"No, just me," he said with a dismissing flap of the hand. "You remind me of this other woman, the only woman in this country I think I really love. The only one who is, you know, a friend and not just for bed. She always asks me about my mother and how I feel about her, or how I used to feel." He shrugged. "But how do I know, or why do I even care? It is all so long ago. I hardly remember before I was fifteen. We were always moving around, very exciting and messed up, you know, hard to keep straight. But I don't try to remember. I don't believe in this past being so important, that it makes you what you are now instead of just deciding to be what you are. Do you?"

"Yes, to some extent I do, I guess."

"I do not. I believe in fate and controlling one's own mind. Like, I am here now in your country, and so I do not like all the time to answer everyone's questions about Israel—I am not a magazine. And anyway, what does that matter? What matters is only where you are and what you feel right now. Right now—" he repeated emphatically, and glanced around as if daring the atmosphere to circle clockwise to future or past while he had his eye on it. "You agree?" he challenged.

"I—of course I think the present moment is important—" There had been so much she was so eager to ask him: she had been waiting only to learn enough to shape her questions properly. Was he saying that in order to be with him she must sacrifice any attempt to know him that did not have his approval in advance? It seemed a curious inversion of her own initial attitude, that she would gladly tell him anything as long as they conversed at arm's length.

"Good. Then you will not always bite me with so many questions like my friend. This friend, this girl, Beth—you probably like her—she says I should go to a psychiatrist to see why I like sex so much, but I think I like it just because it is beautiful." He grinned. "She thinks it is beautiful too, but only when I do it only with her." Then he looked up with more interest. "She says I like women so much because I'm afraid of being a faggot. I don't know why she wants me to change so much if she thinks I'll find out in the end I'm really a faggot, but she says it's true. Do you understand?"

"I understand what she means. A Don Juan complex."

"Yes!" He seemed impressed. "That's the word she uses: Don Juan. Don Eli!" He grinned and thumped his chest comically, a Tarzan of the bedroom. "Do you think I am queer?"

She laughed at the absurdity of being asked that question in this setting. "I'm suspicious of theories of latency. Have you ever slept with a man?"

"Yes," he admitted freely, surprising her. "We were seventeen—we were best friends for years. We love each other in the way of friends, you see, though we each had many girls. We thought we try it together. He went, you know, down on me, which I like alright when I shut my eyes, although it seems strange. Very strange. But then I try to go down on him and I can't. I mean, I make myself do it for a minute because it is only fair, but I hated it. No pleasure, no loveliness, not like with a woman. Yet I loved him. He knew I hate going down on him and it hurt him because he like doing it to me, to give me pleasure. Then he wanted to kiss me, really kiss on the mouth like in making love, and I could not. It hurt him and he cried. I left him and felt awful because the only thing I could do to help him was what I couldn't do."

"Did that break up your friendship?"

"At first, for a week or two, then not so much and we were close again. But in the last few years—well, partly because we are apart. But he still sleeps with men." He looked a little sad, remembering, then brightened. "Still, I go to his wedding and he goes to mine—"

"You're married?!"

He grimaced, regretting having mentioned it. "Not anymore. We are divorced. It's a very boring story, you know, both eighteen, too young. She is very neurotic and I—well, I am not a good husband. Now I have two sons I almost never see, which make me feel bad sometimes. I think she is a good mother, but sometimes I don't know. She loves them. She loves me too, unfortunately. One of our sons was started before we are married and the other after we are divorced. I think it's good for her I am here instead of there. I am not so good for her." Then, to shift back to cheerier topics, he added with a laugh, "At my friend's wedding, right after the ceremony, he goes into another room and fuck with one of the bride's friends and I fuck with the bride on the bed beside them. We do not believe in monogamy, yes? It is not natural. That was the problem with my wife: after we are married, she change her mind. You believe in freedom too?"

Hannah sighed. How could he ever have a sense of who she was, or she of him? "For now, yes. But I suppose I would like to fall in love one day, and then—then I think I'll believe in monogamy."

"But you are never so much in love yet?"

"No."

Munching on a pickle, he began to reminisce about the legions of supposedly monogamous married women he had seduced. Though too close to cartoons for Hannah to sort out fact from embroidery, the tales were vastly entertaining. Once, he claimed, a husband had returned early from a weekend military maneuver to find his wife and Ari stark naked in the kitchen making bacon, lettuce and tomato sandwiches. A great disadvantage to be naked in front of a uniformed man more than twice one's size who has turned bright crimson and is waving a gun in the air!

At last, after scampering six times around the table brandishing a butter knife, clutching a paper napkin to his crotch, and howling to the paralyzed woman to call the police, he desperately tossed mustard in the man's face and sprinted for the bedroom where his clothes were, locking the door behind him. The soldier instantly barricaded him in from the other side and tore outdoors to climb in a window, but as soon as he disappeared into the garage for the ladder, his wife rescued her lover. Ari's last memory was of a lingering embrace with the woman, now wrapped in a plastic tablecloth, then a mad scuttle through a forest of garbage cans to safety.

Then, as if the husband were sniffing dangerously nearby even now, Ari sprang free of his blanket and began to scrounge on the floor after his clothes. "I have a rehearsal tonight of the company," he hastily explained. "You see, we put on a performance as soon as we reach Tel Aviv, so we still have to practice even now. I be gone until maybe ten or eleven." He scribbled a telephone number, which surprised Hannah, and gave her strict instructions to call only in an emergency. "Maybe we go to a movie when I get back, yes?"

She wondered why he was dressing so rapidly, but assumed simply that he was late—to wherever he was going—until he suddenly stopped and walked over to where she still sat cross-legged by the remains of their meal, and studied her face. Only then did it dawn on her that he expected her to be upset, even to make a scene. But she wasn't upset, not at all. She knew he couldn't stay in one place for long. She liked it when he was here, she also liked being in the apartment alone; in fact, the prospect of returning to her book was attractive. Talking to him, or rather, listening to him, was diverting and even fascinating, but not, after all, like talking to Rachel. So she smiled easily up at him.

"I think it is best if you not answer the phone, all right?" he asked tensely.

She nodded amiably and wet her finger with her tongue to pick up the last crumbs of chocolate icing. He continued to scrutinize her dubiously, then finally frowned with a mixture of relief and perplexity, and finished dressing. More calmly now, he fastened his belt, tucked his wallet in his pocket, then meditatively sat down on the bed beside her. He slowly peeled off her blanket, but though he stroked her, he was essentially watching, lost in some reflection of his own. "I wish I do not have to leave you—" he finally said as though he had just realized it. "I wish we have more time. I wish I meet you earlier." He pensively brushed her hair from her forehead.

Then, abruptly energized again, he leaped up and bounded for the door. With hand on the knob, he glanced back. "Oh, listen, little one, I know it's a lot to ask, but I wonder if you do me a favor—the dishes in the sink—? It is impossible for me to cook for us the way it is. It means so much to me if you—but only if you are not too tired. You look tired; try to take a nap." The door closed behind him. Hannah yawned and began to stretch, but before the latch clicked, the door opened again. "You will be here when I get back?" He was smiling, but he waited for her answer.

"Of course," she said, startled. "Where would I go in your blanket at this hour?"

"Yes, stay just like you are for me to come home to—I like that." And he was gone.

Hannah eased contentedly to her feet. It didn't occur to her to wonder if he was really going to a rehearsal. It didn't matter very much, after all: he would return in due time. In the bathroom she twisted her hair into a careless roll, wiped under her eyes to determine how much of the shadow was emotion and how much mascara, and paced naked back to speculate on her suitcase. Much like an actress choosing her costume for the part of a mistress about to do serious housework, she pulled on an old denim skirt, dispensing with underwear, and frowned: why should she dirty a sweater of her own? Impulsively she went to Ari's bureau and chose one of his, a gold pullover with a scooped neck, then went back to the mirror to assess her choice. But so strongly did she feel a sluggish sensuality, a sense of walking barefoot on sun-baked clay, as if she should carry a basket of ripe fruit on her proud head, that she found it hard to focus on what she saw.

So she hung up the towel they had dropped earlier, scrubbed out the tub-line that still drew the measure of their previous play, and drifted back to the bedroom. She put away the food, straightened the bed and whatever clothing she could, then moved curiously to the heap of dishes and pans. Amused at herself for performing so amenably a task she never would have done at home, she awkwardly arranged the sticky debris on the counter board, then filled both sides of the sink with steamy water, one soapy, one clear—this much she remembered from home economics, the only class she had ever failed. The hot wash of water clouding her face was rather pleasant. When both sinks were empty, she washed them in a thick lather of detergent, and in genuine satisfaction watched the swoosh of the foamy whirlpool suck the last bits of color down the now shiny drain. Holding the fetid and dripping bag of garbage well out in front of Ari's sweater, she bore it to the hallway disposal and cautiously dropped it in, listening in awe to the muted roar of the furnace blazing somewhere in the bowels of the building.

She found the dustpan and broom and scraped at the floor with unpracticed tenacity, wondering with amusement why she didn't mind, then sank to the bed and glanced at the clock. He would certainly be later than eleven, so she had plenty of time. She brightened with a novel idea, and in another spurt of energy hunted in the closet for a rag and began to dust. At the bureau she stopped, reflected, then deliberately opened one of the three drawers at the top. As she had guessed, this was Ari's miscellaneous file, cluttered with wrinkled ticket stubs, loose keys, battered wallets, pennies, paper clips, letters and piles of pictures. Again she reflected, then impulsively slipped out the entire drawer and carried it to the bed.

The largest stack of photographs proved to be nothing but duplicates of one portrait of Ari, the kind an actor needs to make his rounds, and the second pile was only smaller reproductions of the first. Unlike most studio poses, this had been taken outdoors in bright sunlight, perhaps in Israel, but despite the unconventional setting, the pose was flattering in the conventional way. Ari looked more smoothly handsome than he really was and less like the compelling creature of activity and unrest whom she found so attractive. As she leafed through them, however, one exception caught her eye: this was probably a Polaroid gone wrong —Ari's face and upper torso emerged hazily from a splotchy pattern of rust—yet she preferred it to the others. The murky smears of ink and the white areas where little had printed seemed to evoke the roughness she liked in Ari's face, the unfinished quality, as if a sculptor had let the grain of the wood dictate the shape of his carving.

Next she extricated a performer's composite sheet of a dark girl in a variety of poses and dance costumes. Her teeth protruded a bit and her nose was too long, but her body, Hannah was forced to acknowledge, was magnificent. Constructed much like Rachel's, it was alive with what Rachel's lacked: a vital sense of what it could do. Hannah buried that one again. After more scrounging she unearthed another studio portrait, this of a very pretty blonde with Alice-in-Wonderland hair falling softly past her shoulders. Her eyes were wide and round, her mouth innocently parted, her bones as delicate as a bird's, yet somehow her expression conveyed an unmistakable hint of mockery, as if in a moment she would snort at the contrived sweetness of the pose. Hannah couldn't help liking her. In a rather spidery hand she had half-printed, half-written underneath: "Shalom! Hail to mita and pita! Love, Beth."

Satisfied she had found all the pictures, Hannah turned to the letters. Two, to her disgust, were in a foreign language; they seemed to be from men. The third was from a girl, hastily and smudgily written, describing in anatomical detail the symptoms of her separation from Ari five months ago in Boston. Though it conveyed the sharp wet discomfort of a lonely girl in a strange city, it paradoxically struck Hannah as impersonal, like a passage in a sex manual. How different it was from her own lengthy letters that read like pages from a journal.

The drawer revealed nothing more, so she carefully replaced the booty and returned the bureau to normal. Edgy, she first sat, then walked to the bathroom, then returned to the bed. She felt alive, energetic, and it was only a little after eleven. Her hand was moving to the phone to call Rachel when a vicious buzz ripped into the room and sent echoing spasms down her spine. For a moment she was stunned into nightmare, then she remembered that apartments in movies sometimes buzzed this way. Wildly she searched the reverberating walls for a clue. By the door she located a small button and pressed it timidly, only to hear the buzz return even more furiously. Frantic, she flew out the door and down the stairs, the maniacal noise still rattling in the room behind her. To her vast relief she found an annoyed Ari at the lower door. When she shyly let him in, he glared at her, then laughed.

"You idiot, why do you run all the way down here? You only press the button for a single second. I don't have time to get in."

"Oh," she said vaguely, certain that the apartment door had closed behind her and locked them both out. "I wasn't sure if that button—if that was the button—I'm sorry—" She turned and scampered anxiously up the stairs, so intent on the burglars she now saw swarming all over the unprotected room that the hand infiltrating her thighs from behind made her jump.

"You have no stockings on—and no pants!" His voice grew increasingly affectionate. "I forget my keys, little one. Did you lock us out?"

"I hope not; I left the door wide open!" She broke into a run.

"Stop going so fast, I can't keep up with you. You feel so sexy, I can't wait to fuck you—you too? You have my sweater on."

"Oh, I'm sorry," she wailed, still unnerved. "I just—"

"No no, don't be silly; you look lovely in it, I like it." He pulled her to a halt just inside the apartment and swung the door shut behind them. "You are so sexy and adorable—you know that? And so clean!" For an odd moment Hannah thought he was complimenting her toilette, then she realized he was gazing happily around the room. "Even the dishes, all put away! And the floor—it shines! Ah, I thank you very much. Really."

"You're welcome."

"How shy you are. I think you don't trust me yet. But you know I never hurt you." He led her cheerily to the bed, dropping her clothes as they moved. "Tell me, have you ever had anyone fuck you in the other hole? You know, the ass?"

Hannah gulped, thoroughly shocked. "I hadn't even known it was a possibility."

"Ah, so I will teach you, yes?"

She was hardly enthusiastic about the prospect, but so far all the surprising ways he had folded and contorted her had proven interesting, so she remained compliant. But a few minutes later, after instructions to relax, applications of Vaseline and considerable squirming, she suddenly squalled like a stepped-upon cat; there had been not only ripping pain but a dreadful sensation of all the natural processes going backwards.

"Wait," he said. "It will feel better soon." He pressed again.

It felt worse. She gritted her teeth, trying to be stoical, finally told him to stop, and when he didn't, she lunged forward and simultaneously shoved him backward off the bed. He caught himself, then chuckled respectfully, "Alright, enough of that." With a sprightly hop he went off to wash. When he returned, she was curled like a garden snake in the corner. "Ah," he sighed, "I frighten you again."

He slid her onto his lap and stroked her soothingly.

"Many women like it, you see," he murmured. "I like it if you just slide your finger in there in me, just a little. Does that shock you?" It did, but she shook her head. "Good," he said. "You will do it for me, yes?"

With an air of getting back to the pleasant business at hand, he lay back, guided her onto his pelvis, and very tentatively began to move. Astraddle, Hannah felt exposed, vulnerable, pierced straight through;

for the first time she realized the strangeness of having someone else inside her body, someone stronger than herself. Her mind wandered around the room and she remembered that Apache youths once impaled themselves on swaying poles to win their manhood, ecstatically awaiting visions as they hung like bleeding lollipops on their narrow sticks. She bent forward to bury her face in his shoulder, for the less her open eyes could see, the more freely the visions came.

Afterward, he held her and licked her damp skin like an affectionate animal. She was exhausted: his inventiveness amazed her, and so did her own newfound agility. He protectively wrapped her in a blanket and got up to get some cheese and two glasses of tomato juice, which he brought back to the bed despite her sincere insistence that she wasn't hungry. After the first bite she ravenously ate it all, laughed at herself, and lazily commanded him to fetch more. Amused, he obeyed with a gallant bow and flourish.

"I saw some pictures of you in your bureau drawer while I was dusting," she said between mouthfuls. "May I please have one?"

"Sure," he said expansively. "I mean, you are welcome to the wallet-size ones. The big ones are expensive and I need them for my work and there are not so many left." Apparently pleased by the request, he sprang up and fetched the entire drawer as she had done earlier. "You look through all of this?" he asked.

"No," she lied. "I just glanced in and saw the picture of you."

"Ah, too bad, you could clean this out for me too—such a mess. You aren't curious to look in?" To her surprise, his tone not only wasn't scolding, it implied that rifling other people's private drawers was natural.

"Yes, I was curious," she replied with dignity. "But of course I wouldn't have gone through it without your permission."

He shrugged. "I don't care about that—you don't need my permission. Here—you want two?" She nodded and he handed her the snapshots, still puzzling as if they held some mystery even for him. He frowned, then brightened with pride. "They are good—yes?"

"Yes, but I also like that mottled brown one, the one where you look so solemn and fierce. Can you spare that too, or is it one of your favorites?"

"This?" he asked incredulously, plucking it out. "You like this—why? It is so ugly, I think. I was going to throw it out. In the others I am much more handsome."

"Too handsome. I prefer your look of—I don't know—wildness, in this other one." His defensive grunt warned her she was making a mistake. He didn't want to be told he was any less smooth and pretty in person than his favorite picture promised. She broke off her analysis. "I'll put the glossy one in my wallet to show off to all my friends and keep the other just for my private delectation, okay?"

Mollified, he nodded and reached back into the drawer. "Did you see this one?" He held up the composite of the dark-haired dancer.

"No," she said, trapped by her lie, and leaned closer to look.

"She is incredible, yes? Ah what a body she has! You think she is beautiful?"

"Not as beautiful as this girl underneath her."

"Beth?" He held up the portrait of the fragile blonde. "No, Maria is much more beautiful than Elizabeth. Beth is not really so lovely as in this picture—it's a nice picture, I agree. Beth means very much to me; she is the girl I mention earlier, the only one I have loved in New York —truly loved, instead of just liking to fuck." He gazed at the picture with respect. His tribute had a slightly practiced ring, as if he had perfected it some time ago, but it also sounded sincere. Hannah felt an unwelcome quiver in the pit of her stomach. On the whole she supposed she was glad he loved a girl she was instinctively drawn to, but at the same time, their intimacy unsettled her.

"This 'mita and pita,' you know what it means?" he asked. "Bed and bread—'hail to bed and bread!' I like that. She is very intelligent. She reads very much. Like you—you read a lot, yes?—all those books in your suitcase? She gives me most of the books I have here. Beth analyzes me. She wants us to get married. But she is not half so beautiful as Maria."

Hail to bed and bread: Hannah wished she had thought of that herself. He wiggled closer and pulled the other half of her blanket around him and over both their heads, creating a makeshift tent. "Maria I did not love, but she loves me very much—too much—very passionately, like a Spanish woman. Her mother is Spanish—not Puerto Rican, real Spanish from Madrid. They live together here and fight all the time; I tell her it is not good to live with her mother, they drive each other crazy. I suppose it is her temperament; she is a dancer. Such a lovely strong body she had—wonderful! Maybe I was in love with her body for a little while. But then after I know her many months she had this big fight with her crazy mother. Terrible. They tear up the whole apartment, I see it. So she wants to come live here with me. I think it is a bad idea, but she cries and begs and makes many promises, and I like her and she needs someone to take care of her, so finally I say yes. We will live together like roommates, I say, both of us living their own life. By that time I am not so much interested in screwing with her anymore, so I think maybe it work out—"

"But why on earth not?" Hannah interrupted with surprise. "Surely you couldn't live in the same apartment as that magnificent body and not sleep with it!"

"Well, sometimes, yes, but mostly because she wants it." He shrugged, then frowned with the effort of explaining. "Once you know somebody a long time, it is not so exciting anymore, and if you do not love them, then it is better to be friends, I think. If you do love each other, then fucking stops being just fucking and turns into making love instead, but that hardly ever happens, and if it doesn't, the fucking just gets boring.

"So anyway, she moved in, but from the start it is terrible. I hope it be like you and me now, except that she knew I don't want her anymore. I guess that's really why she want to move in, she thinks I fall in love with her; and she gets very jealous, more jealous than I ever see before. Every time I go out, even just to rehearsal like tonight, she was spitting questions at me. 'Where were you? Who were you with? Why don't you call?'" His caricature of the girl's anxiety was so bitter that Hannah promptly vowed never to ask him anything. "Ah, it was awful. It make my life a nightmare! At first, you know, I think it be nice to come home to that beautiful body, those long legs, even just to look at. And for her part of the rent she is supposed to keep the apartment neat, since I am so messy, and that I think will make me very happy, because I hate mess even when I make it. But it got terrible, always this anger and these questions, like an insane person. And always she wants to follow me everywhere, to go everywhere I go, which I hate more than anything. Not like you today. It gets on my nerves, so that I am angry all the time too. And then we have also made in the beginning the deal that if I want to bring another woman to the apartment, Maria will go to her mother's or the movies—I even give her the money—"

"How about if she wanted to bring a man home?"

"Fine, same thing, I stay somewhere else. But she never did. And when I do, she go crazy."

"I must admit, that would drive me crazy too."

"I know, little one." He squeezed her under the blanket. "So with you I not make such a deal. You I let stay here all the time just to keep you. But then I not so much like to just be roommates with you, either, I think. Do you like that? We can be just friends, never touch each other?"

She grinned. "No, I suspect that would undermine the basis of our relationship."

"And Maria is the opposite kind of person from you. I believe that if I hurt you, you just walk away, which then hurt me, but her!—every time I come home she screams and tries to hit me and curses; I think I learn how to curse in English from her." He chuckled. "Every afternoon she is still in her nightgown, the same one. She doesn't even comb her hair, or clean the room, and soon it is filthier than when I am alone. She doesn't even take baths—how can she think I want to fuck her then? She stopped going to auditions, although I show her notices from the paper, and even classes. She even starts to get fat, but I don't know how since I only see her eat when I buy food and make her.

"Then one night I come home very late and tired and sick from a big party, and what do you think? As soon as I come in the door she attacks me with that big knife, the one you wash for me tonight."

"Heavens!"

"And she is very strong, from dancing, and tall. She cut through one of my sweaters, so I have to throw it out, and give me a big cut on the arm, and if I not lift my arm, she would cut my face. I have to hit her across the room to finally make her calm down. And then she does not say anything at all, just sits on the edge of the bed like she is dead, doesn't even cry. I packed all her clothes and call her mother to take her home. When her mother gets here, she is crazy too, shouting in Spanish and saying I beat up her daughter, not even seeing the way my arm still bleeds through the towel."

"God!"

"But that isn't all. I don't think in all the confusion to take Maria's key back from her, you see. About a week later I am here in bed with a woman and the door flies open and there is Maria. Before I realize what is happening she grabs one of those big soda bottles from the kitchen and smashes it on the sink and comes after us, and those bottles are very thick, she has the strength of a crazy person. My poor friend jumps up so Maria gets her first—she has to get stitches in her back. And in her feet from the glass she steps on. There was glass and blood everywhere. The poor girl runs naked into the hall screaming; she was terrified—"

"I imagine she was!"

"The next day I had to scrub her footprints off the floor in the hall." He paused and began looking on the orange crate and in his pants pocket for cigarettes.

"Well, don't stop now! What happened—did she murder you?"

He laughed. "She tried. But I knock her against the wall and got the bottle from her, and then she starts to cry. She tried to cut her own arm with a piece of glass, but I stop her in time. By then there are people everywhere in the hall and someone called a policeman. He make Maria and me come with him while someone help my poor friend to a hospital. Later I think they take Maria to a hospital too because I won't press charges on her. You can be sure, though, that the next day I change all my locks! And I begin to worry over who else I give a key to. I think they will throw me out of this apartment, but I never hear a thing." He shrugged, then sighed philosophically. "And such a waste, too, such a lovely body. Spaniards are very passionate in bed, you know."

"No, I didn't. The stereotype is accurate, then?"

He nodded. "Yes. She used to scream very loud and scratch my back until it bleeds. The scratching I don't like, but the screaming is sometimes exciting. When I was a boy, I have an affair with a lady who screams so loud I keep looking over my shoulder to see what monster is in the room. You want some milk?"

She sat quietly sipping milk while Ari regaled her with more descriptions of the carnal eccentricities of interesting characters he had known. She suggested he write Maria up and sent it to the *Reader's Digest,* but then had to explain what she meant. She felt increasingly at ease. She liked listening to his aimless tales and liked the way he touched her as he talked, combing her thick hair with his fingers like a weaver at his loom. The steady rhythm of his voice and hands began to make her drowsy. She glanced at the clock, saw it was hours past midnight, and snuggled against him like a sleepy child eager for just one more story.

"I was going to take you to the movies tonight, little one," he said tenderly. "After all your housecleaning. But then the way you are all naked like that under your skirt make me forget. Do you mind?"

"No," she said softly. "Movies I can always go to by myself."

"Are you falling in love with me, little one?"

"No. But I like being with you."

"And I like very much being with you also. It surprises me how much

I like it. All night we do nothing but fuck and talk and I am not even restless."

He must have a remarkable amount of energy even to think of being restless; she could sleep for a week. Her head dropped to his shoulder and her eyes began to shut. He slipped out of their blanket and walked naked to his phonograph to click on the records already waiting. With calm deliberation, performing a familiar but reverent ceremony, he first turned off all the lamps in the room, and then, while Hannah lay down and half-closed her eyes in the dark, slowly lit a deep crimson candle. The flames swelled, then seemed to sway with the same rhythm as the slow, plangent music. His face above the trapped red fire in his hands was almost translucent; lit from below, his eyes sank into deep shadow framed by jutting bones. Hannah saw her own skin fade to a deep rose in the flickering light. The hair that fell over her vision was the color of burning coals, and Ari smoothed it back as he rested the candle on the table beside the bed. His face was inscrutable as it turned against the light to her.

After a time, Hannah began to feel the same unearthly sensitivity that came over her on hot, still nights when she swam alone and naked. All around her, small ripples quiver; otherwise, the surface is perfectly calm. Her skin is slick with salt. Noiselessly, she swims toward the very center of the lagoon until she is lost in a circle of darkness with only the faint, faraway line of perpetual lanterns tracing the edge. Silence everywhere—except for the low trill of crickets, the throb of a toad, the occasional long splash of a boat automatically pumping bail-water from its hold. Her flesh shudders in sensuous aversion as a jellyfish blindly undulates by in a glow of phosphorous. Her legs weave in and out of a bouyant net of kelp. Suddenly a swarm of minnows arcs into the air, their bellies flashing silver as if a star is raining. Then a larger flash of scales and a bluefish hops into their midst and they scatter in all directions in a quick fountain of reflecting drops. Wild with alarm, they swim under Hannah and tickle her breasts and stomach like a hundred fingertips. Her whole body is a creamy white crescent as she arches and twists in the cool water, dreamy, yet distantly aware of every current, of the continuous brush of water on her skin. When finally she draws herself half up on the wooden steps, the slime of the algae is scented oil. The salt-corroded pilings gently scrape her legs. There she stays and floats, half-drowned in ebony water, immersed in his arms and the music eddying around them. She awakened to feel him slip into her, her thighs as smooth and wet as moss, then drifted back again until her dream of tidal water mixed with the gentle ebb and flow of him in her until the stars descended to meet their reflections and with a shudder of surrender all elements conjoined.

23

Too early the next morning, the alarm clock on the orange-crate jolted Hannah awake. Ari moaned and folded the pillow over his head, so she reached across him to fumble with the button, then slumped back and closed her burning eyes. But some minutes later, Ari lurched upright and lit a cigarette, coughing and groaning with gloom.

"I must go teach a class at Rosa's. I cannot believe it, always on Friday mornings I promise to go to bed sooner on Thursdays." He spluttered like an engine on a cold morning. "How jealous I am of you—you stay here and sleep, little one. Listen, today you must entertain yourself. I first teach, then I must go to the club to work for the afternoon, and then I come back here to change, but tonight I have to go to a party and I can't take you with me. Alright? You will be alright without me?"

"Yes," Hannah mumbled, wishing he would leave so she could get back to sleep. "I'll be fine."

"You have money for dinner? I won't be able to eat with you."

"Yes, I'm fine."

"I wish I don't have to go to this party tonight. I much rather be here with you, truthfully. But it's Rosie's party, so I have to go. It's to say good-bye to her and the whole company will be there and everyone she knows in the whole of the city. It is awful, but she be very unhappy if I don't go. Rosie has a great talent, you know, a genius. I have much respect for her; she teaches me much. But I do a lot for her, too." He pulled on the clothes he had strewn on the floor the night before. "I love her really, but she like to own me, you know, and sometimes she makes me so I can hardly stand to be around her. She gets so upset." He fastened his pants, reached methodically for his sweater, then brightened.

"Ah, little one, instead I wear the sweater you borrow last night. Then you know I am thinking of you all day, even when I'm busy, yes? You like that?"

"Uh huh, that's nice," she murmured from deep under the covers.

"If you are here around five this evening we can see each other before I must leave again. I think we have time to say hello—that be nice, yes?" He glanced down at her limp form and, discerning no response, sat on the bed beside her. "You like to visit me this evening?" he repeated as he tied his sneakers. Hannah groaned assent.

Perplexed, he felt for her breasts under the blanket. "You like to be with me, yes, little Hannah? Are you in love with me—you are angry that I am leaving you?"

She gave a resigned sigh, rolled reluctantly over, and squinted up at him. "I love being with you, I am not in love with you, and I'm not upset; I am sleepy. It would be nice to see you later. If I go out, what should I do about the door? Do you have an extra key?"

"Oh yes, in the drawer with the pictures. If you can't find it, just leave the door unlocked. I have nothing to steal. Good-bye, darling." He bent over to kiss her and impulsively slid his arms under the blanket. Hannah was heavy and dull with fatigue. When he pulled the blanket off she felt like an inert nude in an old painting, an Ingres odalisque, plump and white and lethargic, sodden with opium dreams, asprawl on brocade pillows and spreads amidst trays of moldering sweetmeats. She stretched lazily.

"You are so lovely," he whispered, easing down beside her as he fumbled with his zipper. "I wish I stay with you all day, just fucking all day. You wish that too, darling?"

She nodded politely, still diverted by this sensation of passive luxuriousness, but she knew she could no more spend the whole day in this mood than he could. She had always assumed that those sleekly fat odalisques endured the embraces of their masters as the necessary price for the drugged visions in which they preferred to pass their time. When he hastily yanked down his pants and turned her to her belly, she simply laid her head listlessly on the pillow and enjoyed his warm weight and his pleasure in her until he had finished and, with a muttered oath at the clock, was gone. But to her annoyance her sleep became light and uneasy, and after a time, she arose dizzily.

A patient search unearthed three half-empty shampoo bottles. Choosing the one whose advertisements of pastel maidens reclining in meadows had always appealed to her, she stepped into the shower and let the water pour over her gratefully bowed head. Draped in foam, she grew conscious of feeling altogether opened-up, newly opened, as if her body were a desert tomb unsealed after centuries to become a treasure trove again. She wondered at the change. Just a few years ago she had worried that she might altogether lack that mysterious chamber that was supposed to distinguish her sex: certainly she had felt no sensation but resistance when she probed and failed to locate it with a tube of menstrual cotton. Now she seemed to taste the very atmosphere within as well as without.

Out of the shower, she felt supremely clean and alive. Still wet, she walked back into the other room, her hair dripping small puddles which she traced into designs with her feet. She rose blissfully to her toes, eyes shut, stretching up as far as she could reach, and swung in circles as children do to trance themselves with dizziness and suspend reality for a moment. When she opened her eyes to the reeling room she was pressed damply against the cool plaster wall. As soon as her balance righted itself, she pulled back the curtains to the morning sun. Hungry again, she cut a large slab of cheese and climbed up onto the formica counter that divided the kitchenette from the rest of the room, the highest perch available. Moisture from her hair beaded on the cheese. She watched the sunlight graze the floor she had cleaned. When at last the slippery surface under her thighs began to feel cold, she hopped down and, with the vague sigh of renouncing a rare pleasure, pulled on her jeans. She parted her thick hair and let it hang in damp strands around her face, then outlined her eyes, but she found the process unaccountably dull; her eyes looked huge anyway. She pulled on her suede jacket, found Ari's key in the drawer, and danced in exhilaration down the stairs.

Outside, the day was mild and full of promise. She lingered in the vacant garden, enjoying the odd sound of the city's clamoring all around her like rivers of garbage cans rolling down distant hills. Then she drew in her breath, tunneled through the front building, emerged into the street, and promptly felt a thud on her hip and heard a squeal to her right. The ball bounced on toward the curb with the embarrassed thrower in hasty pursuit, while the would-be catcher stared at her solemnly. A forgiving smile only made him shift focus to the sidewalk. Flocks of children swarmed along the pavement and flocks of balls seemed to swoop over them like inquisitive birds: solid balls, inflated balls, softballs, hardballs, footballs, basketballs, tennis balls. Hannah even saw one striped beach ball aloft for an instant over a parked bicycle across the street. Why weren't city children ever in school? Three little girls obstinately jumped rope during breaks of traffic. Mothers gathered on stoops, coffee mugs in hand, dish towels tucked in the waistbands of their skirts, and chattered happily: chattered less, Hannah imagined, to exchange information, than to harmonize the quick rhythm of their days with the hint of summer sun warming the concrete beneath their legs. Sighing, they cupped their hands and gazed vaguely up at the drone and silver glint of a jet passing over their heads, and as she strode by, Hannah felt their gazes following her too, knew they were noting the straight hair, expensive jacket, worn blue jeans, the unfeminine length of her stride as she rapidly left them behind.

She searched for a street sign and took off again in her brisk loose gait. Walking alone in the city was one of her greatest pleasures. She forgot where she was coming from and where she was going and exulted in the breeze blowing back her clean hair, her healthy reflection in passing windows. She smiled back at the delighted salutes of workmen as they briefly shared her good humor, and snubbed more furtive overtures. It was the swift clear movement that made her eyes glow, the sense of her own power and freedom as she loped from street sign to street sign, choosing her course as she went. She detoured around the Park for a while, past blank doormen, blonde old ladies with rhinestone-collared poodles, matched quartets of slender young men in sunglasses, one brave little girl on a tricycle, and numbers of earnest students with armloads of books, struggling to keep their masses of curly hair from blowing into their contact lenses as they waited for the bus. By the time she wheeled around for home, she had been walking nearly two hours; it was late enough to call Rachel.

After eight rings, Hannah resigned herself to solitude, and was putting down the receiver when her friend's voice caught her. Rachel sounded strange, but Hannah again attributed it to her being home, to her being in a place and mood so different from Hannah's. They chattered and, as always, laughed, but before Hannah could offer her suggestion, Rachel herself broke through the small talk in a suddenly very sober voice.

"Hannah, brace yourself," she said evenly. "I really wish I didn't have to tell you this, but—but my dear mother, it seems, tried to kill herself last night."

Hannah's stomach contracted sharply; sweat sprang out on her forehead. "Oh, Rachel. Oh. Is she alright now—you say she only tried—?"

"Yes, she's fine. She was careful not to do anything too risky. She knew someone would be home in time to rescue her. That, of course, was the point."

"How—where were you?" The impossibility of communicating her rush of feeling through the black plastic in her hand suddenly enraged her. "Oh, Rachel, I wish I could see you!"

"I know, but it helps just to know you're out there. I was at one of my aunt and uncle's at this sort of annual Passover-season reunion they have every year for us cousins—only since the cousins loathe each other and never socialize voluntarily, you know who it's really for. Well, while I was gone, my parents evidently had another episode in their continuous brawl, and my father threatened to leave her, which of course he does at least four times a week, but this time he actually did get through the door. And you know my mother can't be left alone."

Though Rachel's voice was very controlled, she paused to take a long unsteady breath. "So, after an hour or two he started to think about what she might do—needless to say, he had only gone as far as his office, not to Tahiti or any place decisive. He was reading student papers. He assumed she would call a friend, but he thought he'd better check, so he called me to say that she was alone and I should probably leave the party to go stay with her. At least he waited until I had finished eating so I would be sure to have something substantial to vomit."

"Oh, Rachel," Hannah said again, helplessly.

"Well, he's very thoughtful that way. Anyway, I of course completely panicked and called her right away. No answer. I called her closest friend. Also no answer. Then I called my father back. He went right home, and my uncle drove my hysterical aunt and me there, cursing all the way. If you could divorce in-laws, I'm sure he'd have divorced my whole family long ago.

"All I can say is, thank God my father got there first. He had called an ambulance, which naturally took almost an hour to come—don't ever try suicide in this city unless you really want to succeed. But you should have seen the scene while we waited: everybody trying to get this limp body in the slinky Bendel's nightgown to walk, with my aunt crying at top blast and my uncle yelling at her to shut up and make coffee, and me shouting at everybody that maybe we should let her take responsibility for her own actions for once, since that's what she's always lecturing everyone else to do—especially good old me, who she thought would be the one to find her—" Rachel's voice caught and broke. "Oh, Hannah, you should have seen her, she was so white and cold and stiff—of course you know that from your father. She looked so young, you know, the way they say dead people do in books, with all their sins and troubles washed away. At least she looked like that until they got her vomiting, then she looked a hundred years old. You know she's so thin."

"I know, I do know," Hannah said miserably. "Do you want me to come up there? Would I be in the way? Are you alone?"

"Oh, I wish I were alone," Rachel snapped, suddenly angry. "There's nothing I'd rather do than see you right this minute—shit! But we have a swarm of moaning relatives—oh, damn it!" Her voice threatened to break again, and she coughed. Slowly and deliberately she took another breath to steady herself.

"Mother's in the hospital holding court. I've just been there to pay my respects at the shrine. She's all puffed up on pillows surrounded by flowers and her wailing brothers and sisters who, between sobs, scream at my father that he's murdering her. He looks worse than she does at this point. And he just sits there and agrees with every accusation they make.

"The worst of it, in a way, is that my mother typically keeps telling her family to shut up, that she took the pills for emotional blackmail, that it was a terrible, selfish thing to do, that what if it had been me who found her?—what kind of mother could do a thing like that to her kid?—and that she wouldn't blame me if I never forgave her. So of course, I had to forgive her right away. She kicked everyone else out, and after we got hysterical laughing at them, and I told her what the other side of the family was saying behind her back, we had a long mother-daughter talk. She explained how scared she had been as soon as my father slammed the door behind him, how her vision seemed to go all dark and colors came out of the walls at her, and her heart was pounding so hard the whole apartment seemed to shake, and she couldn't breathe and she was afraid she'd suffocate, so that's why she took the first pills. She said that after that she *did* know what she was doing when she went back to take the rest; she even felt melodramatic in a way because she pretty much knew we would find her, but her life seemed so empty and useless that she just couldn't face another ordinary morning even if my father did come back to her—especially if he did. Which she knew he would. And she convinced herself that I was so young I'd find a better way to live than they have, that I'd be better off without her. So what could I do? I told her I loved her and I understood. And the awful thing is I do, I know exactly how she felt. Oh, Hannah—"

"Rachel," said Hannah firmly. "Repeat after me: I am not my mother, I am not my mother, I am not my mother—"

"But I am, I really am, and I should be able to help her—" She stopped, sighed, swallowed, then pleaded: "Oh, I know I'm really not, and that no one can save her but herself and all, and she knows that too. But, Hannah, how are our lives going to be any different? She understands everything about her life. She was talking again about how she romanticized her father and what it did to her vision of my father, and how they should have moved out of New York, and—oh, all the same old stuff. She knows it all, but nothing changes.

"And then there's my father, the world's expert on the Meaning and Function of Conjunctions, or something. Do you know his advice? Today he lectured me on how we all should try to make my mother's life easier when she comes home, so I should make my bed and pick up my clothes so she doesn't have to tire herself out yelling at me—"

Hannah laughed painfully. "Oh, that's wonderful. Your poor tired mother with the full-time maid in the two-bedroom apartment. God, yelling at you is her hobby; it makes her feel useful."

"I know. So when he said that, I got furious and screamed at him that he was really the sick one, he's so repressed, and that he needs her to be crazy so he can feel strong. Which really isn't fair, since he loved her best when she was stronger than he was. Well, I guess I really got to him, because with probably the second truly decisive gesture of his life—the first being that time when he broke the Chinese vase—he actually hit me on the cheek. It hurt, but it also felt almost good, if you know what I mean. But a second later he was crying and apologizing all over the place and so was I, and we hugged each other and everything was right back where it started. Of course, I know he can't leave: he loves us, and we're about the only reason he has to keep going when his life is such agony. The last two days his eyes have looked like peeled plums—every time I see him I hate her so much! He's asleep now in the other room, finally, and I just heard another swarm of relatives arrive. They're plotting to take me out to dinner to get me off his back. I'd give anything to see you instead, but I can't." The passion had fizzled from her voice and left it flat and listless with fatigue. "Will you call me tonight—can you? Maybe I can see you for an hour or so tomorrow—?"

"Yes of course! Ari's going to a party or something tonight, so I'm totally free, and tomorrow I'm all yours if you can manage it."

"How is it going with him, anyway? A great friend I am, I don't even ask you how you are before I pile all this crap on you."

"You're a first-class friend and my personal favorite. Idiot. You did ask and I said fine, which I am."

"Well, nothing like a conversation with me, then, to put a damper on your fun. And it's such a beautiful spring morning out. . . ."

"Yeah, why do parents always try to bump themselves off in the spring, when February would be so much more fitting and considerate? Honestly, Rachel, stop apologizing, you'll inhibit me when it's my turn."

Hannah said good-bye and stared bleakly at the far wall. Suddenly very tired and low, she slipped off her shoes and lay back on the bed, pulling one of the blankets over her. She began to shiver. Her hands and feet were so cold that only a hot bath or sleep would revive them, but she was too tired to bathe again, too tense for sleep. The pleasant day beyond the curtains seemed futile and unreal. She pulled the cover up to her chin and closed her eyes. Pieces of memory flapped like broken film. She groaned and tried to turn over, but her jeans stuck to the sheet and made her feel clumsy and trapped. Her hair was wrapped so tightly around her neck that she sat up to yank it free, then piled all the pillows together and lay back to study the dust patterns on the ceiling. At last, as she was listening uneasily to her own heartbeat, it occurred to her to distract herself by imagining Ari, whom she had completely forgotten in the last hour. Now she pictured him leaning over her, his brown eyes alive with energy and amusement. She saw his wide mouth soften with delight, and despite herself she smiled back wryly. She heard his relentless questions and saw him cock his eyebrows triumphantly at her increasingly inarticulate replies. She felt him forcing her to come to the forefront of herself, immanent, to come even beyond herself under the pressure of his weight and of his warmth.

24

As soon as she awakened, she slipped on her shoes, grabbed her coat and bag, and headed outdoors again, for she knew from experience that only sun and motion could distract the anxiety that her nap had postponed. Anyway, she should forage for her supper—and that thought sparked an impulse that carried her happily across town and all the way back to the Park.

In the undersized, overpriced delicatessen she had frequented during the non-resident term, she bought a roast beef sandwich and two of the mammoth cookies with jam in the center that had been her chief indulgence during those months. She ambled east then, her package, wetly redolent of pickle, tucked under her arm, and browsed in galleries until the dimming light made her glance at her watch.

She would be late for her possible reunion with Ari, she saw, but she was confident he would be later than his estimate. By now, thickening crowds were pouring from buildings, buses and subways to join the main tide surging in contrary currents down the sidewalks and across the jammed and honking streets, and Hannah plunged in happily, picking up speed as she caught the contagious rhythms.

After a considerable distance she swung across town, conscious that the crowds had begun to thin and the light to fade. The endless crosstown blocks soon wearied her, so she turned down an avenue again, an emptier, dirtier one. Streetlights now drew long shadows and sharp highlights; she wondered when they had blinked on overhead. She turned the corner of Ari's street and continued west. Kitchen smells drifted from closed houses: pot roasts and stews, tomato sauces, fat crackling brown in hot ovens, a hint of oregano and garlic, onions, chili. Windows, small and grimy during the day, now expanded with the lamplight that glowed through filmy curtains. Men in blue work clothes talked quietly on the stoops and curbs where their children had played earlier; some leaned against rusted railings or slumped wearily back against the stoop; they all followed Hannah with slow, unsmiling eyes. She walked faster and tried to stiffen her hips to stop their sway, imposing narrow blinders on her vision so she wouldn't intercept one of those blank gazes droning toward her like wasps. Now and then a female voice lilted from inside, and one of the men would lift a hand to his colleagues, glance a last time at Hannah, and turn toward his door. And in the brief moment of his entrance, light, radiant with reflected color, would flash out like a full skirt to draw him in. There in the houses, there where the women were, that's where she would run if the men moved.

As she drew close to the dingy entrance, she began to hope that Ari had not had time to return after all, or that she had missed him. She trotted through the hall of the street-front building, conscious that no one was likely to respond to her screams if something were to spring at her from the dark stairs, the unmarked doors. The hollow tunnel resounded to her rapid footsteps. In the garden, the neat square of sky between the buildings briefly distracted her, but even there her imagination began to people the recessed spaces. She plunged through the door, up the stairs, and arrived panting at the apartment, key poised—but before she could insert it, the door swung open of its own accord. She leaped backward.

"At last you are back. I begin to think you stand me up." Ari stepped aside and she moved dazedly past, dropping her bag on the sink. Her throat was tight with tension. She had persuaded herself that he would not be here, that she would have time to pull herself together again in solitude and silence, and now she ached to erase him from sight like a misspelled word.

She forced herself to turn around, resenting him yet studying his face nervously. "I just went out to get myself some dinner—I had called a friend earlier and—"

"What friend?"

"Rachel, my roommate, the girl you met."

His face was stern. She went to move past him again to take off her coat, but he scooped her to him, running his hands over her taut spine. "Ah," he breathed against her neck. "I want to see you again before I leave. I stop work at the Club especially early, and now you make it very late. But I'm glad you are here for even now. I wish I can stay with you the whole night. Do you know your soft hair is the color of the sand at night—you have seen the desert when the sun is dying?"

"Only the beach." Her voice sounded ludicrously flat.

"But why are you stiff—you are angry with me?"

"No, I—" Why did his mere presence have this power to render her a continual surprise to herself, as if he lent her a stranger's emotional world? An unforeseen tremor rolled through her in a wave and culminated in a ripple of tears. She ducked closer, hiding from his eyes in his arms.

"Never mind," he whispered. "I know how to relax you, yes?" Continuing to murmur steady appreciation, he caressed her with rising interest and pushed her backward to the bed. They tripped, locked together, and both laughed at their ineptitude.

Hannah followed him contentedly, feeling his sweat slide onto hers, their skin adhere, her nostrils filling with a pleasant mixture of fatigue and tobacco, until gradually she went fully limp, unclenching all over like fingers pulling back from a fist. When he asked if she had come, she nodded because she was satisfied, sore, and uncertain what the term meant in practice. A book in her parents' bedroom had compared it to a sneeze.

"Then let me come in your mouth." Startled, she squirmed down into position and followed instructions for a wearisome length of time. How odd, she reflected, that two bodies could be so close, so awkwardly and intimately connected, while two selves remained so separate. Not that she felt resentful, only that she was so very distant from the ecstacy she was bringing about. How could two people whose memories never touched ever learn to love? she wondered. How could two strangers bridge the gap between epidermis and experience? At last, with a frightening jerk and shudder, he released a salty substance which she swallowed as hastily as he had advised, then realized was much more pleasant than he had implied: no different from tears, sweat, or ocean.

She sat back and looked at him, then let him pull her up and press her head affectionately to his shoulder until he fell asleep. Eventually she freed herself from his embrace and padded softly to the bathroom. The undersides of her eyes were almost as dark and almost as green as her irises. She looked pale and bruised and strangely attractive, like lace that has grown thinner and finer with use. She washed, brushed her hair and teeth, and for want of any alternative, returned to bed.

As she was making up her mind to get her book, he groaned elaborately, heaved to a sitting position, rubbed his face with his fists like a sleepy child, peered at the clock, and groaned again. "Oh, damn it!" he muttered. "I have to go. Already I am hours late."

As if to add emphasis, the phone rang. He grimaced, first turned his back to it, then took the receiver grimly. "Hello," he said unenthusiastically. "Yes, I know. I was napping. I am very tired." He sighed lengthily. "No, why do I even want to when I see you tonight? Oh, Rosie, you know I never live with anyone."

Hannah glanced at him in amusement and he grinned back sheepishly, then toppled her against him, protesting with a gesture at her audible gasp as she fell. A raised voice continued to crackle on the other end. Ari sighed, frowned, took back his arm to scratch his thigh, and finally closed his eyes. The voice dipped suddenly and coughed, and his eyes opened.

"Oh, damn it, Rosie, don't cry. I said I be there. Your face will be all red when your guests come. Yes, I know, but I am very tired and if I don't nap, I probably go into another room and fall asleep like last time, and that make you more angry. You know I hate parties; I only come to see you and make you happy. We see each other all day. Well, not the same, but it is better than nothing, yes?" He frowned again in exasperation and rubbed the back of his neck. "If you keep on the phone all night, I never shower and dress and I never get there. Okay? Good-bye, darling."

He dropped the receiver with sufficient force to send it to the floor, and replaced it scowling. "Goddamn it," he muttered at the instrument. Hannah kept respectfully silent, expecting to see him in a fully bad mood for the first time, but instead he turned his head to look at her, stretched, yawned, and reached out to stroke her nearest shoulder. "You are shaking," he said. "You are afraid I talk to you like that someday?"

"Actually, that hadn't occurred to me. I think I'm mostly tired. But I guess anger upsets me even when it's not aimed at me."

"But you are too sensitive; you should not be."

"I know," she said. "I try to control it."

"No, I don't mean that. You cannot help that. I mean you should not feel upset: I am not at all annoyed at you." He stroked her cheek and added, "I don't want you to be afraid of me. I will not hurt you, or anyhow, I don't want to. You please me very much, more than I think you know." He studied her for a moment with an expression she couldn't decipher, then pulled her by the ear. "Come, I have to take a bath. I smell, yes?"

She grinned. "Surely the odor of sanctity."

"What is that?"

"The perfume saints give off as they decompose."

He looked baffled, but took it for a compliment and grinned. "That's because I smell of you, darling. Now you go run the bath for both of us."

She held her hand under the spigot, watched the plunging water turn the pink powder to white bubbles. His rough, guttural accent could sound both unusually harsh and unusually gentle: it made any emotion sound more primitive, closer to the root. Was that peculiar to him, she wondered, or just a common accident of enunciation? When the tub was almost full, she pinned back her hair and climbed in, moaning aloud as the heat both shocked and soothed her. Ari entered with the tray, and deposited it on the side of the tub with a practiced gesture as he sank into the bubbles and intertwined his legs with Hannah's.

"Aaaaah, that is most good, better than good. Mmmmm." He leaned back until his chin was covered and teased her with his toes. "I am never angry with you, little one, because you never try to make me into what you want instead of what I am."

"Maybe that's because I don't know what I want yet," she said.

"No. No, because no one does, not the way you mean it. If they knew that, then they would know I'm not whatever it is. Don't you think that's true?"

"Yes," she laughed. "Complicated but true. But it's easier for me, you see, because right now what I want happens to be you, as you are."

"You see then why it is true that I like you so much. Someday, not now but years from now, I will marry someone like you."

She laughed again.

"No no, I mean it. I will. I like living with you. If not that I am going home, I want you to stay here longer, much longer."

Nonplussed, Hannah blinked and rather primly thanked him.

"Stupid," he teased, stabbing her with his foot so that she jumped and splashed bubbles into the tray. "I don't say it as a compliment to make you feel good. I mean it."

"Then I wish you lived in Brooklyn instead of Israel," she said sincerely. She was quite flattered. Nonetheless, she thought that anyone who married Ari would have the worst of him. It was easy to imagine him fifteen or twenty years older, still very attractive, with his hungry mouth framed by deeper lines and his crisper hair tipped gray. But his wife would have long since become a mother, both to his children and to him, there to welcome him home, carp a little, and send him off on his next adventure. By then he would be disappointed in his work, less successful than he had dreamed, facing the closing of all those possibilities and the narrow opening of necessity. He would have little taste for the quiet pleasures of home and hearth and a driving hunger to prove that he was not whatever he increasingly seemed to be, no matter what that was. Hannah would rather be the endless succession of young girls he seduced at the theatre. More than that, she would rather be married to someone she had yet to meet.

"Here, take the coffee now," he commanded, handing her one of the small cups.

Tonight she liked the hot sugary mixture even better. It seemed to calm the inside of her as the bath had calmed the outside. She regarded Ari with satisfaction.

"I love to just lie here and watch you," he said happily. "You are so lovely—all the parts of you—" He checked them off with his finger, lingering on those he evidently preferred. "Yes, I very much like to have a picture of you like that. You give me one?"

"I don't have one. No one seems interested in the dorm. How about a high-school mug shot—I must have fifty of them."

"No no, it must be a picture just like this. It's silly, pictures that just show the head. The body tells more about the person than a head. You like me to have a picture of you to take out and remember when I am lonely in Tel Aviv, that I can show to my friends when I tell them about this lovely girl I know in New York?"

"No, I most emphatically would not like that!" She sat up in shock.

"Ah, yes, it is even better when you come up like that!"

She slid back under the opaque bubbles to her chin.

"No no, don't go away from me. Like this, I show you." He leaned forward and pulled her up until the waterline covered her nipples. "There, like that, you see, very proper. I don't want pictures of you naked unless you take pleasure from that—I mean, it is not nakedness I want, it's your lovely face, the mood, the expression when you look so— what is a word?—so content like that. Wait here, just like that." He climbed deftly out, careful not to disturb the tableau that he had arranged, and returned almost instantly with his camera.

"I don't like this," she said suspiciously, having again slid to her neck in bubbles.

He chuckled. "You look like a little kid who has to eat her vegetables —what do you call—? Her spinach. I promise not to make it taste so bad. Really, I do not take any pictures you don't want. I mean, I only take your expression. I am a magnificent photographer. I promise you like these pictures." He studied her with an objective frown.

She sighed, unable to stifle a smile. "Alright, do with me what you will." She inched her collarbone from the protective foam and peered down to make certain she was still cloistered. "Hurry up before the bubbles pop."

"You are so silly when you are so lovely." He focused intently on her head, moving so close for so long that she began to laugh. "There, at last, something besides the spinach look!" he crowed. He clicked rapidly a few times from different angles while she blushed and finally shut her eyes in mortification. "Yes, like that, with your eyes closed. You look like one of those old paintings from the Bible with the mother and—"

"—Oh right, Madonna in bubbles! Good Lord." She clasped both hands over her face and sank to knuckle depth.

"Okay, don't drown, I stop." He put the camera out of splashing range, climbed into the tub again and pulled her up fondly. "I feel very bad if you drown now."

He tickled her affectionately, drained his coffee, then settled back against the tub, soaking in a half-sleep. Twice he moaned that he had to go but didn't move. Finally he raised his arms to the ceiling in anguish, bewailed his fate, and reluctantly stood up in the water. "Unfortunately I must make you leave our happy pond because I must shower, but believe me, I much rather be here with you in the bath all night."

"We'd shrivel into raisins." She stepped out onto the crumpled rug and reached for a towel.

"If we turn into raisins, we can eat each other. Anyway, I like to see you like that, all wrinkled up—then we know what both of us look like when we are old, yes? A warning. We do that someday, stay in here until we're all ugly and wrinkled?" He imitated a monstrous prune, puckering his face into bent pleats, and contorted his arms and legs.

"Let's not and say we did."

"No, you're right. We get old soon enough anyway. Instead, we stay in bed all day." With a sigh, he released the drain, drew the shower curtain, and at last turned his attention to the evening ahead.

Hannah toweled herself, shivering pleasantly, darted into the other room and dived into bed. Covered to her nose, she stretched out in every direction, revelling in her languid drowsiness and her anticipation of solitude. By the time Ari followed, he was preoccupied and irritable. He mashed down his wet hair, rapidly pulled on clean underwear, and swore disgustedly at a hole under the arm of the shirt. He put on a light-blue shirt, looked at the cuffs, swore again, rifled impatiently through a small drawer, and finally yanked the whole thing out and upturned it on the bed and floor, where he found a pair of blue-and-gold enameled cuff links. Then, to Hannah's surprise, he scooped the debris back into the drawer and neatly replaced it.

Finally he went to the closet and took out a dark suit with undertones of blue which Hannah immediately liked. Obviously it had been made for him: the pants were snug, the jacket cut to emphasize the narrow lines of his torso. He sighed with a sense of accomplishment at being dressed at last, smiled back at Hannah, then stalked over to the side of the bed and buttoned his fly, which intrigued her, for she had never seen buttons there in lieu of zippers.

"My father ordered this made to me before I came here," he said with no particular pride. "Fits very good, yes?" He took the jacket off again and dumped it on the chair.

"Yes," she agreed. Savoring his dark hair and skin against the sky blue of the shirt, and the way the bright clean material skimmed his chest and nipped in under the flat outlines of his hips, she wished for the first time that she were accompanying him. He sat beside her and handed her the cuff links, which she obligingly fastened.

"You look very elegant," she said. "Very stylish."

He grinned, peeled back her blankets like wrapping paper, and leaned down over her, the drape of his shirt soft against her skin. The contrast of her nakedness against his elegant apparel startled and sharply excited her. Her eyes widened.

"I think you'd better get out while you can," she said softly. "In a few more minutes I might not feel so blasé. I never realized before that people get dressed in order to get undressed." Without intending to, her body rose invitingly against his.

He lowered his full weight onto her in response, the tension gone from his face. "Ah, I want so much to stay here with you."

"I don't see why . . . you'll be getting all those free peanuts and potato chips. . . ."

"It's not potato chips I'm hungry for, you bitch," he said happily. "You're getting pretty sure of yourself, aren't you?" She laughed up at him. "Well, you should be," he added softly. "Try to stay awake for me, or else I wake you up. I try to be home very early." His eyes turned very serious and he held her again, regretfully. He finally rose, but then continued to stand and study her, and she gazed back speculatively, quite relaxed under his scrutiny.

At last he grimaced and slipped on his jacket, adding his keys. "Fix the chain after me," he instructed. "I'll be back as soon as I can."

25

Both groggy and stimulated, Hannah was tempted to turn over and nap, but knew that if she did, she would only jolt awake in an hour or two, pulsing with anxiety and too satiated to sleep again for half the night. And she was hungry. She climbed out of bed to look for Ari's bathrobe. As she was tying it around her, the telephone rang out so jarringly that she jumped, froze, and waited until the imperious summons finally stopped, as if the disappointed woman on the other end could hear her if she moved. Only when she felt alone again and unobserved did she pour a glass of milk and carry her dinner to the bed, where she plumped up a pillow and found her place in the novel. Halfway through the first cookie, she glanced at the clock and saw it was already ten, later than she had imagined. She read for another hour, fighting sleep, then finally allowed herself to dial Rachel's number. Her friend answered glumly, drugged with excess emotion.

"Hi, am I speaking to Ravishing Rachel?" Hannah asked brightly. "Are you surviving?"

"Oh, Hannah dear, thank God it's you!" Then, frantically, she asked, "How are you—are you alright?"

"Sure I am. Don't worry, this emotional illness crap doesn't come in epidemics. I'll warn you if I'm about to go off the deep end. More to the point, how are you?"

Rachel sighed. "Oh, shitty, but not especially shitty. We went to visit my mother again after dinner, and it went better. Right now I'm sitting shiva with the tv. The clan is in the next room screaming at each other. They're not even really mad, it's just habit: see a relative and scream."

"Ah, I wish I were with you, watching the Late Show and eating Schrafft's ice cream. Are you available tomorrow?"

"No, unfortunately. They're carting me off to my uncle's country place so I can get stung by bees and bitten by snakes. They've never managed to digest the fact that I go to school in the middle of the fucking country—they still think the sight of a little grass is going to make me dance with *joie de vivre*. O damn, hold on a minute! Listen, I have to go, Hannah. They're all calling to wish me a last good-bye before I see them again in eight hours. I guess they're afraid to leave me alone for long: like mother, like daughter, you know. . . ."

"Rachel, repeat after me: I am not my mother, I am. . . ."

After fondly saying good-bye, Hannah fetched the remaining cookie and reopened her book, but found herself too agitated to concentrate. She looked aimlessly around the room, saw that she had forgotten to bolt the door and jumped up almost gratefully to do so, but the moment she was back on the bed, her mind began to wander again, nervously, jaggedly. Annoyed, she forced herself to read the next page word by word, then, realizing she had done it by rote, reread it, but an insistent picture of James, drugged into a desperate knot on the bathroom floor, naked, stiff, as white as the surrounding porcelain in the morning sunshine, kept flickering unbidden across the print. A Viking smashed on the rock-lined coast of a too vast and too distant continent. As soon as she realized it was a memory making her so restless, she leaned back and tried to concentrate on that, for, a modern girl, she knew repression was bad hygiene. But, though she tried to recall each detail, and though some details left her eyes wet and fists clenched, no catharsis followed. She could think of nothing she wanted but oblivion, yet, perhaps for that very reason, some part of her obstinately fended oblivion off. If only Ari had a television. A television, even a radio, something that would carry on for her, without her.

When the telephone rang, it jarred her, but she tried to put it out of mind. After continuing for an absurdly long time, however, it began to ring in spastic bursts of three, stopping in between, and seemed determined to sustain that forever. Finally, as it began its fifth attempt, she gave up and answered, and then was both relieved and unnerved to hear Ari's voice.

"Why do you not answer?" he demanded. "I think my finger will fall off from dialing, or that maybe you have run away from me." He pitched his practiced actor's voice low but piercing against a welter of party sounds.

"I'm sorry," she explained. "You said not to answer the phone, and I was afraid you might have that signal arranged with someone else."

His temper dissolved. "Well, from now on, then, three rings is our signal, yours and mine, okay? Are you alright, are you lonely, little princess?"

"No, I'm fine," she said with some surprise.

"You don't sound fine; you sound a little unhappy, I think."

"Oh, well, I had a sort of bad dream, I guess."

"If I am there I make you happy again, yes? Did I wake you up?"

"No, the dream wasn't that kind: I was reading."

"Ah, good. Listen, little one, I call to tell you that unfortunately I will be more late than I thought. This will go on forever and I cannot get away. It is not good, believe me. I probably get drunk, and for me, that is terrible. So I want to tell you not to wait up for me after all. You go to sleep, because I will be home very late. You are upset?"

"No, that's okay," she said unresentfully. "In fact, it's probably just as well, because I really am exhausted, and I don't tend to get much rest when you're around."

He chuckled, pleased. "No, I don't want to waste the time when I am with you. So you sleep now, that's good, and I see you later, or tomorrow morning. You will dream of me?"

"I'll try to arrange it. Assuming I can fall asleep. Do you perhaps have some sleeping pills around, or tranquilizers?"

"No," he said in a worried voice. "For me, if I can't go to sleep, I just make love, and—not even any whiskey, not even wine. Damn, if I am there I just hold you, we make love, but on this phone—maybe we can try to do it this way, you think?—I talk and you lie on the bed and do what I tell you and pretend it is my hands—?"

Hannah grinned. "An obscene caller's delight! No, I'm afraid that might leave me more frustrated than drowsy."

"But you are too young—you make me so much want to be there! I wish you let me make love to you right there: I'm sure I be able to make you relax. But listen, you try to sleep, and I be home as soon as I can without—causing a big noise. And then I hold you all night. In the meantime, you think of me, okay?"

She agreed to do her best, and hung up more cheerful and a little touched. She had assumed he would be late, but not that he would be thoughtful enough to call and tell her so. Now, having said she wasn't lonely, she felt very lonely, lonely for Ari, and rather than dismaying her, that made her almost happy. She wished he were here and even wondered if she should have let him hypnotize her long distance. Or was that just what she had done? Had she at last given in to the swaying watch, one year and a few hundred miles distant from that doctor's office? To her astonishment, this fleeting thought instantly provoked all that her earlier exercise in recall had not: long convulsions of grief burst through her, brutally; she came back to herself only when damp fabric suggested that if she soaked the sheet she would regret it later, and she reached for a tissue. She propped up the pillow and sank against it. Grief? Yes, certainly it was grief that had struck her, but not simply for James. It had never really occurred to her to weep for herself before. A surrender to self-pity, she chided, but the phrase failed to ring true: it was not pity she felt but a grieving wish that the people she loved might have been happy, and in turn have made her happy.

There is a danger, she all at once decided, in thinking of our struggles as psychological problems: the words suggest answers at the back of the book. In her lifetime even Sunday supplements preached psychology: she knew that little girls desire their fathers, resent their mothers, hate as intensely as they love. Since puberty she had dreamed openly of incest and awakened only to feel startled and thoughtful. If she had repressed emotion in the face of her father's dabbling with death, as Rachel was no doubt doing tonight, it had not been a simple passion she could now exhume, label, and place in perspective against an upright, stable society. She had struggled then to contain her shocked understanding that there is no God-given perspective, no redeeming set of values which all good and thoughtful men acknowledge, and she had, with fair success, managed to bear that invasion of distrust until now, when time and added confidence and the ambiguous solicitude of Ari were enabling her to unclench a little without fear of collapse. But that was not to say she had been wrong. She still saw good and thoughtful men everywhere in pain, inflicting pain, howling for salvation but quarreling even over its definition. No, reliving childhood traumas was not likely to unearth a nugget of knowledge valuable enough to buy her freedom from pain, from confusion. On the contrary, if she was ever to earn any freedom at all, it must be through accepting the pain. Despite her grief, the people she loved had not been happy; they had been desperate, too desperate to lend her much security or certainty. Instead they had jarred her awake at an early age and made her conscious. Consciousness is a mixed legacy, but she still thought it better than most. Many of her friends from stable homes had already plunged into muddles deeper and darker than any she had so far sought out: if they still felt secure and certain, they ought not to.

Was Ari her muddle? He made her happy. Not content, not even satisfied. But he reached out over her objections and forced her to accept happiness like a drug that erased consciousness. Her constant fear of pain, her anxiety that the next invasion would be more than she could contain, had always led her to cling to consciousness as a feverish man might burrow in snow, welcoming the cold, the clarity, the bite, even the drifting, the burial. Uneasily, she now realized how one might choose suicide as an ultimate means of control, a final refusal of chaos, as one might stay behind to kill the lights and lock the door of a valued room after the last clamorous visitors had gone. For her, Ari brought light, heat, unlocking.

For himself, though, he was a muddle. Surely he came to her in need of clarity and coolness. He came to her as Jinx had, in fact, and she smiled rather tenderly at this, for she rarely thought of Jinx. The difference, of course, was that Jinx had been too knotted himself to lend her any ease.

James was addicted to alcohol, Ari to sex: for all their differences they were charming, mercurial, and selfish, searching and driven in similar ways, by no means the opposites she had at first assumed. Hannah, however, did not wish to be an addict, not even of ecstasy. Ecstasy killed all doubt, all anxiety. Indeed, it killed thought, self—and not having fully lived as yet, not having become herself, she was not ready to die. Nonetheless, Ari persuaded her that part of living, of joy, was the acceptance of ecstasy and the blankness it brought. To be oneself one must learn to let the self be swept away—and learn to accept its return again, too. Each phase was hard: the mistake was to think one should or could choose one exclusive of the other. It was tempting to daydream of a life centered on Ari's injections of bliss, to picture herself his odalisque, his wife and child, to be all surrender, simplicity—she saw why men ascribe that capacity to women, then envy them. But of course that was only a daydream. Among human beings, only saints shed identity and thrive. If she was truly to use Ari to her own advantage, as he tried to use so many, then it must be by stealing some of his magic, enough that she would not need him anymore. She must learn for herself what he knew, then use it more wisely than he could, for she was stronger.

Oh, but she didn't feel strong as she slumped further down on the pillow. She didn't want to be strong, for strength confers responsibility, and she had had enough of that already. Why shouldn't she close her eyes and make choices as most people did, by default? Passion for Ari would sweep her into declarations of love and a few days of relief. Then his departure would let her wail uninhibitedly that she might have been happy had events only treated her differently. Since in the final analysis life happens to us, why did she strain so to exert her modicum of power, which was more a power to interpret events than to change them? Was this merely one more form of rigidity? Ari's simple vitality was, after all, another kind of power, even if fueled by obsession; perhaps she would ride on that for a while.

Reluctantly, she awakened from a profound sleep to what took shape as a demanding noise at the door. At last it dawned on her that she had left the chain latched from the inside. She staggered up, fumbled with it, and when he was safely in, skittered back to her bed like a groundhog caught in the open before February. From deep in her burrow she squinted at the lamp she had left on and tried to focus on him, then gave up and fell back to sleep. Sometime later she awakened again, feeling guilty in case he had returned early for her sake, and offered an almost inaudible greeting.

After an abnormally long time, he moaned from the bathroom. "Hello, go back to sleep, it's very late. I cannot talk."

Oblivion passed back over her like the shadow of a gull. Later she dimly heard sounds of muffled retching through a closed door, concluded there was nothing she could do, and drifted off again. For a long time she kept coming to awareness just enough to hear that sound in sequence with coughing and running water, and it troubled her. When at last it stopped and she felt the warm pressure of a body wriggling next to her own, she wondered in a muddled way if she should be polite and inquire about his malady; he was, after all, her host. Besides, women were supposed to be maternal and sympathetic, not as indifferent, sleepily indifferent, as she felt. So she struggled against her animal need to go blank and dumb. "Um, how do you feel?"

"Awful," came a dim groan.

"Oh, I'm sorry. Well I hope you at least had a nice time—did you?" The unnaturally cracked voice beside her growled miserably. "Do not start asking questions, please. You have been so good, letting me alone. You must not start nagging me now."

In a stupefied mixture of outrage and amusement, Hannah turned over and went to sleep.

26

The next morning the steady slap and suck of rain in city gutters slowly drew Hannah to consciousness. She felt displaced, empty, tense. The twisted body beside her still reeked of smoke and bile and now of sickly sweat, and its raw and irregular snore pricked her nerves like a broken mattress spring.

She locked herself in the bathroom and thought about her parents, who, she sensed, had dominated her disjointed morning dreams. Today was Saturday, the last day of classes before Easter break; they would expect her home tomorrow; she should find her bus schedule. She hated these preparatory chores; she hated having to organize her coming and going; she hated the initial shock of leaving or arriving anywhere, regardless of whether or not she wished to be there.

Depressed, she prolonged her washing to prolong her seclusion. When she did emerge, she started with surprise as Ari immediately reeled past her, croaking over his shoulder that she would find tomato juice in the cupboard. She obligingly poured two glasses of the tepid red juice and carried them back to the bed, thinking with relief that at least he wasn't feeling amorous. When she tried to make herself comfortable against the pillow she found that she couldn't—she was too jumpy. Noises of diarrhea and much flushing, washing, hawking and gagging floated in from the other room, like a parody of the radio to which Jenny fried the bacon and simmered the morning coffee.

Ari reappeared, pasty and mottled, hobbled to the bed and meekly took the juice, muttering incoherent but heartfelt gratitude. Hannah couldn't help grinning at him: this desperate malaise was so different from his usual air of energetic well-being. He sank down heavily beside her and grimly contemplated his crossed legs.

"Augh," he moaned, sagging back to the pillow. "Could I please have some more juice? I am dying. This must be awful for you—truly I am sorry, but I feel so terrible. And today I must go out to run errands. Oh God. If only I stay home with you last night! I'm sorry we cannot fuck, but I make it up to you tomorrow, or at least the next day, I promise."

"That's alright," she said reassuringly over her shoulder as she poured more juice. "But tomorrow is when I go home."

"No no, not so soon!" he protested with unexpected vigor, sitting upright to take the glass she handed him. "I leave Tuesday after this one, and it is true that for the week before I will be horribly busy doing things I hate, but I thought you stay at least until this Tuesday. You are hardly even here, I hardly see you at all. If only I meet you earlier I make this week free for just you, you see, but right now life is so—so crowded. So, you will stay till Tuesday, yes?" Wrung dry of speech, he collapsed like a wounded cowboy against the wall.

Hannah was shocked, pleased, and hardly able to believe that, now that the novelty of her presence had worn off, he wouldn't prefer to be relieved of the bother she must be, living here in his den like this. She often felt some relief when even her closest friends went away, simply because the demands of their important company disrupted her privacy.

"Well," she said uncertainly. "I guess, if you're really sure you—"

"Idiot." He scowled. "I never say I want you to stay if I don't." He patted her arm weakly but fondly. "You think I am like some big uncle, just nice to you because it is good manners? I want you to stay because I am selfish. People always tell me that, and mostly it is true. You can see I am really not such a nice timid fellow who does not know what he want or cannot get other women. I invite you because I like very much to be with you."

"Okay," she smiled. "I admit, I don't think of you as a nice old uncle."

Regretting the necessity of lying but not doubting it, she called her parents and explained that she planned to stay at school through Monday to finish the work she would only procrastinate at home, and thus would arrive Tuesday night with a clear conscience.

"Alright, dear," Jennifer said, full of warmth. "If you think it's best. But please hurry home—we've been looking forward to your vacation for weeks!"

Hannah hung up with enormous relief, eager again to segregate her life here from the infinitely more complex entanglements at home. Ari, as if sensing her ambivalence, pulled her down on top of him, a rather clammy and odoriferous pillow. She reassured herself that, after all, this mystery they were exploring together, in which he was her guide and she his map, had much to do with the anonymous pit of maleness and femaleness, but little to do with the overarching bridge of identity.

"I must shower. I stink. In fact, I smell myself," he commented, unperturbed. "And then I have to go to a horrible government office to see about my visa and passport. You want to come with me?"

"Not especially," she yawned. "Will you be gone all day?"

"No, I want you to come with me. Afterward we do something together. Have you ever seen the Statue of Liberty or the United Nations or the Empire State Building?"

"I saw the first two many years ago on a Girl Scout trip, before I quit the troop."

"Girl Scout? You mean you were one of those awful little green children who are always in a circle around the Radio City Music Hall?"

"Yup, that was me. It must have been around this time of year, in fact, because we saw the Easter pageant. Do you want the bathroom first?"

"No no, we wash each other. Only you must be very gentle with me and not expect anything at all, because I am dying. We be like each other's mothers, you see, or like a nurse."

She led him by the hand to the shower, and there, like two robins spluttering and ruffling in a birdbath, they splashed and pruned out their fatigue. Even Ari's queasiness molted away like old feathers under the nozzle. Obediently playing the role he had assigned her, she washed him tenderly until, to her surprise, he ejaculated into the cascade, then she hopped out and shivered contentedly as he toweled her.

"Off to the Empire State!" she said, then darted into the next room to pull on her jeans. Although it was no longer raining, a layer of cloud still cut off the buildings, so she slipped into old loafers and pulled her trench coat from the suitcase. "Hey," she called, "can I wear this again?" She showed him the gold sweater she had worn the night she had cleaned the room.

He smiled through his mask of shaving soap and nodded, so she slipped it over her head, feeling both opulently and delicately female as it fell to the tops of her thighs. To heighten the contrast she pushed a wide gold bracelet high on one forearm.

Ari emerged, smooth cheeked but still wan. "Ready?" he asked, and ushered her through the door and out into the garden. They linked hands and waded carefully across the squishy ground.

The street was wet. Puddles, haphazard and shapeless, washed up the grime. People scuttled by quickly, eyes lowered and collars lifted, glowering with distaste at the moisture still thick in the air. It was not so much a spring rain as a throwback to winter.

Ari suddenly caught Hannah's hand. "Look there!" he said.

There in a tawdry show window, radiant in the central spotlight, enthroned in folds of satin, sat a jeweled, crested, silk and velvet-lined, multi-tiered, crown. All around it sprawled earrings, bracelets, necklaces, pendants, rings and pill boxes, some of which draped from inlaid chests and mosaic cases while others dangled from carved plaques or lay in careless handfuls, all shimmering under the hot bulbs.

"Heavens," Hannah said. "Do you suppose it could be real?"

"No, not in a store on a street like this, and yet it is so beautiful, isn't it?"

They studied it admiringly, pointing out particularly intricate combinations of enamel and gold, particularly delicate embellishments of design. Then, at Ari's urging, they walked into the tiny store, a narrow aisle bordering a small counter filled with gaudy costume jewelry, and behind it, a small round man beaming at them.

"Hah! Welcome!" he cried. "Young love, I see! You deserve that crown yourselves, that's what you're thinking, right? You want it for the pretty young lady."

Hannah, as seemed appropriate for the role, blushed. "Well, no, actually, I wouldn't have too much use for a crown. We were just curious about it."

The shopkeeper clasped his plump hands together, his own rings flashing, and beamed at Ari. "You and I, we don't believe that for a minute, do we? We know she deserves a crown, and you came in to get it for her—pamper the ladies while we're young enough to enjoy it, that's the ticket!"

"We just want to know if it's real," Ari explained good-naturedly. "Truthfully, I do not think I can afford it even if it is fake."

"Hah! It's a real crown, yes, and beautiful beyond what words can express, right?"

"Right," his audience chorused politely.

"It is definitely a real crown and I am proud to have it in my window, and delighted when it brings an attractive couple like yourselves in to talk to me." He needlessly smoothed his oily inkstain of vanishing hair and puffed his chest happily.

"No, but be honest," pushed Ari amiably. "It cannot be real or you would not have it there in that window with no bars, yes?"

"The crown is absolutely genuine. The jewels in it, now them you didn't ask about. As it happens, they are excellent imitations, valuable in themselves, you understand, but of course, the original is priceless. You are correct and clever, sir. We would not be able to accommodate the original here. No, that resides in San Francisco under close guard. But this one is equally as beautiful; to the naked eye there is no difference."

With a regal gesture he swept them behind the counter and over to the window where they all stared reverently at the crown. "Now some of those bracelets and necklaces, on the other hand, are quite real—the topazes, the aquamarines, the garnets over there. Lovely, don't you think? Perhaps, sir, you would like one to grace the wrist of the lovely young lady?" Falling in with the game, Ari grinned and shook his head, and the salesman, equally amused, held up a strand of pearls. "In the same price range, perhaps some pearls—like the crown, a flawless copy of a flawless original. A lady can always utilize pearls, don't you agree? She might require them at the opera—thus the term, opera-length—or at the theatre, at church, at afternoon teas. . . ." He acknowledged Hannah's dubious expression with a lift of his eyebrows, and added, "But perhaps you already have some real ones of your own?"

"Actually, I do," she admitted. "And I confess, I don't wear them very often."

"Now that's a mistake! You should wear them with pride with everything from a tailored suit to an evening dress." He eyed Hannah's dungarees. "Though not, I must admit, with that outfit, charming though it is on you." He returned the necklace to its place with a flourish.

"Tell me, you young people, if you will—I don't mean to pry, but such an attractive pair catches the attention—you aren't married yet, are you? That is to say, this is still the first dawning of fresh love, not yet the, uh"—He pursed his heartshaped mouth tactfully—"the, shall we say, cementing—?"

Hannah chuckled. "That's right, we're still pre-cement."

"Ah, but don't misunderstand, I believe in marriage! Marry soon!" he effused earnestly. "Marry young! You know the song? It is very wise: marry young! You may think I am old and sentimental, but I say this from my heart: trust in love, love will carry you through anything, just so long as you are together. And what a perfect couple you make: one, a princess so fair and sweet, the other a prince so dark and handsome—truly out of a fairy tale. A stranger can't help but notice. Now I, my friends, was not so fortunate at your age. . . ."

Ari tactfully interrupted to nudge him back to the story of the original crown. The resulting travelogue bored Hannah, and she drifted aimlessly down the counter, inspecting the wares. It was strange to see Ari talking to an older man—indeed, to any man. She could only imagine him with women, to whom his talents were so finely tailored. Yet his patience with the jeweler impressed her. Clearly the lonely man needed an audience, and Ari obliged for nearly a quarter hour, never threatening to compete. Finally he reached for Hannah's hand, stroked it as he read her watch, made many promises to return, and deftly extricated them, waving regretfully through the window as they paused for one last look at the crown.

They walked in contented silence, hand in hand, and Hannah mused admiringly on Ari's ability to spy a glass crown in a sleazy window and make of it an adventure. She enjoyed taking his spontaneous cues; she enjoyed the spontaneity itself, she who usually scrutinized before she leaped. And for the moment, she enjoyed the role the jeweler had suggested: a pretty young lady strolling with her handsome beau on a genuine, if overcast, spring afternoon.

"You are very good for me to be with, you know," Ari said.

"What do you mean?" she asked after a moment.

"Well, usually I could not do this, just walk along like this holding hands with someone—or alone, either. And usually I never do what we just did, go and talk without annoyance to a silly man."

Hannah was astonished. "But how do I—I mean, you must walk places!"

"Never. I take buses or cabs, and if I must walk, I am nervous, impatient. Always I am running from one place to another, always I cannot just sit still and relax, the way you are the first day when I come home and you are just sitting in the sunbeam reading. Almost never am I relaxed."

"But you seem so loose!"

"That is just in the muscles. Of course I am loose in the body, because I am an actor and a dancer and I learn to control my body, to make it free. I can shake the tension from my body. But I cannot shake my mind that way, my spirit. In my head it is different. That is where I am so—what do you call it?—jumpy?"

Hannah nodded.

"Jumpy, yes, I am nervous in the head. I hate it, I wish I could stop. But I am noticing this, you see, that when I am with you, this is not so true. I am different. This is one reason I don't want for you to leave tomorrow, because with you I am very much slower, calm even. You are so calm. This is very interesting to me, and very good. It make me like just being with you very much, you see? And that is rare for me. You understand what I say?"

"Yes," she said. "What's odd is that you have a similar effect on me: you relax me too, only—"

"I know, but with you it's easier. I just teach you not to be so afraid of me, to trust yourself. I only—" He glanced around and interrupted himself. "Wait a minute; this is where we are going. Come in here with me."

Regretting the end of the conversation, Hannah followed him into what General's Bay called an amusement arcade, a mammoth warehouse chockful of candy and pinball machines, automated games, and booths where, by hitting ducks or bowling pins or pictures of eager women, one might win a teddy bear or pinwheel or gigantic doll. The pavilion at the summer resort boasted merry-go-rounds, Ferris wheels and a conglomeration of lesser rides; this urban paradise was smaller and dingier. Behind a long bar, a man in a white apron sat leafing through a magazine, his head and shoulders framed by giant paintings of hot dogs, cheeseburgers, and bright blonde women, staring adoringly at Cokes, who reminded Hannah of Jenny. At the far end another man in white finished replenishing the stacks of candy bars, then began to swab the circular innards of his cotton candy machine. He glanced up vacantly.

Ari got his bearings, then led the way to a small booth curtained in black velvet, deposited her beside it, and disappeared within, leaving her eye to eye with a one-eyed, pirate-patched gypsy, who sat resplendent on a faded throne, her plastic skin cracked with age and seamed with dirt. Hannah nodded politely, for the gypsy's sister similarly held court in General's Bay. Put a quarter in her palm and out popped the future, simplified for easy reading. The seashore soothsayer was very old—so old, in fact, that someone had amputated her original outstretched hand, constructed for smaller change, and transplanted a newer, pinker model designed to accommodate inflation.

The question, Hannah thought, was whether or not she should allow Ari to teach her not to be afraid of him, when it seemed, in her best judgment, that she had good reason to be. Trusting him and trusting herself were not the same thing. She met the gypsy's blank stare. Sorry, she thought wryly, but what good does it do to learn the future in outline form, when the things we really need to know can't be summarized on a slip of paper, or indeed, in any cogent statement? She glanced at the velvet scrim and wondered what on earth Ari was doing in there.

When he emerged he looked uneasy. "Here," he said glumly, handing her a string of tiny snapshots of his face.

"Not very good," he grunted. "I always take bad pictures except from a professional photographer. My features are too strong, someone tells me. Let's go." He reached to take them back from her.

"Can't I keep one?"

"Why? They are so awful. Besides, I do not do it for fun, I do it for my papers."

"Oh, I didn't realize that. They're not flattering, or really accurate, but in a way I do like them. You look sort of human. Trapped and taken by surprise."

"Horrible. Here, give me these three; you can keep the rest if you want."

They resumed their trek, now through air thick with drizzle. Hannah made one oblique attempt to revive their earlier conversation, but realized from the tone of his answering monosyllable, not only that he was preoccupied with his errands, but also that part of his restlessness was a reluctance to stay on one subject very long. When the moment became the past, he shied away.

Finally he led her into yet another building, this one framed in glass and padded with carpeting so thick it absorbed noise like quicksand. After the elegant silence and reproving doorman, they gulped at the barrage of sound that assaulted them when they pushed diffidently through the next door. A babble of different languages bellowed at full volume made the air vibrate. Ari flinched, led her distractedly to a chair, and vanished into the frenzy.

Hannah sank into herself like a turtle. With drawn and twitching faces, young and old shuffled through sheaves of paper quadruplicated in color, and shoved furiously by one another in a race from desk to desk, partition to partition. She waited miserably for an hour, until she peered up to see that one of the serious dark faces hurtling toward her was Ari's, and even he looked like an angry capon fresh from the shears. "Let's go," he squawked, taking her hand, and they fled.

The silence on the other side of the door was as abrupt as a descent from the raucous poolside to the ringing blue depths of solitude at water's bottom. Ari still trembled with the aftereffects of intense though impersonal humiliation. "I wish someone teach those bastards how to be polite."

She took his hand, which for once was colder than her own, and he leaned against her gratefully as the elevator hissed to the ground. From the hothouse of wax greenery that constituted the lobby, they first heard and then saw the ferocious downpour outside. Rain pummeled the city like a squadron of firehoses turned on riotous crowds.

"Wow," Hannah gasped. "Will you look at that!"

"We wait until it stops a little." Holding hands like the most forlorn of orphans, giggling, they sank into the deep couch which, the doorman's face loudly indicated, had been put there for decoration and, under the cover of their coats and the mute indignation of their uniformed chaperone, cuddled until the storm weakened to a drizzle. As they left, Hannah smiled politely at the guard.

Outside, she was soon clammy under her trench coat. The breeze blew her wet hair into a tangle over her eyes and snagged the rest in soggy knots. Finally she pulled her crumpled beige scarf from her pocket, refolded it with difficulty in the wind, and did her best to claw the sticky hair out of her collar and off her face and tuck it under the chiffon, the ends of which she crossed under her chin and tied at the back of her neck in a tight helmet. Instantly, as if vexed at her attempt to protect herself, the sky again exploded, not in drops or even spears this time, but in ladles full of frothy soup flung down by furious cooks at scurrying roaches, splashing up around her knees and flying into her face with each successive gust of wind. Brown bundled-up people holding bags and briefcases over their heads streaked by into the streets and threaded through columns of vehicles stopped at the light. Water drummed a great war dance on the trunks of all the cars and crested and waved on the sidewalk with audible splats of rage. The gutters rushed and hissed viciously.

"Just cross this street!" Ari shouted over his shoulder into the gale, dragging her behind him. Determined to make the light, he plunged over the curb, and Hannah, snorting and gasping, averting her face from the wind, leaped into a puddle which drenched her foot to the ankle. On the far sidewalk the sole separated from her loafer and began to flap, attached only at the heel and instep, and she could feel the suction drink in and expel water with every step, making a loud squelch each time her foot hit the ground and a squish as it shot out a fountain of ice.

And then, with a heave and shove from Ari, they were in a calm, dry luncheonette. "Wet out there, folks?" someone called. Her chest heaving from the exertion, she sagged laughing against him, and watched them both drip into the center of their own large lake.

"Are you drowned? I'm sorry."

"Don't be silly!"

He peeled off their coats and hung them over a stool, and she sloughed off her scarf and laid it on top. Still shivering from shock and mirth, they sat at one of the semicircular counters, and Ari ordered coffee for himself and hot chocolate for her, then excused himself to go join the line waiting for the pay phone.

Using the plate-glass window for a mirror, Hannah painfully brushed her snarled hair; she disliked attending to herself in public, but saw no rest room. As soon as she had pulled the major knots apart like sticky spaghetti and dried her face with a tissue, she turned gratefully to her cocoa, relieved and composed. The warmth of the cup in her cold hands felt so good she was reluctant to dilute it by drinking.

Ari still stood in line, and she wondered disinterestedly if he was calling a girl. Wet and disheveled, his blue striped jersey clinging to his torso, his hips cocked at the same impatient angle as his wide, frowning mouth, he seemed to her to stand in a shimmering aura of sexuality, like a distant figure on a day so hot the air around him sends undulant waves of sunshine back to the sky. Amused and a little disconcerted at the intensity of her fixation, she glanced elsewhere to deflect it, and found herself locked in the avid gaze of her nearest neighbor, three seats down. A burly man in a lumberjack's striped jacket, he scrutinized her as a beaver might a tree. She hastily looked away, and had she been alone, might have left. Between them seemed to bristle the possibility of his reaching one mammoth arm across the intervening countertop to pluck her like a hapless daisy; and what would she do if he did? She stared raptly at her saucer, acutely conscious of her peripheral vision.

"Got caught in the rain, huh?"

"Yes," she said nervously.

He beamed back. Though his smile resembled a bulldog's snarl, its friendly intention was clear and heartwarming. Still hunching to make herself inconspicuous, she added, "Yes, terrible storm, isn't it?" He grunted amiably, apparently content with such limited intercourse, and returned to his newspaper, but she remained alive to his every shift of position.

When Ari came back to sit beside her and block her view of her admirer, and presumably his of her, she felt better, and when she heard the man drop a dime by his plate and rise, she prepared to relax. But to her horror he walked over to them and jutted his hand out menacingly.

"Here, you kids wanna read the paper?" he said.

"Oh yes, thank you very much," said Ari taking the present. "I have not seen one for days I think."

"Think nothing of it. That's a pretty girlfriend you've got there. You just take good care of her, hear?" He hulked off to pay his check.

"So," said Ari rather proudly, "you make a victory even here, yes? See how irresistible you are; you believe me now? Tell me, little one, are you too wet and cold to make one more stop now that the rain is over?"

"Oh no," she said, postponing her vision of a warm shower. "I'm okay. Where to next?"

"To the office of my old answering service; I must settle the bill. That's where I just call to find out about." He reached for a cigarette from his back pocket, then groaned comically and withdrew the whole wet pack. "Look at that. Is there a machine in here? No, I will have to make do with this. What a day! And when we get home, the first thing I must do is pack my books in cartons, which I have hardly found any yet, and after that—"

"—well, perhaps not the very first thing. . . ." she said in a low voice.

He blinked perplexedly, then slowly grinned. "What do you say?"
"I said: maybe not the very first thing."
"This is a much better idea, I think. You make me very anxious to get home."
She smiled.
"You are such a funny little girl."
The rain had fully stopped and the storm was drifting over. Though she had felt too stiff to hike, Hannah fell into step beside him and soon found that the steady pace loosened her again. She began to feel warm and pleasantly strong, alive with herself, full of herself. Too tired to do anything as strenuous as dance for joy, she nonetheless felt as if she were already dancing, as if their relaxed, swinging gait were a waltz of sorts. A surprising conviction of her own attractiveness and power filled her, yet when she glanced curiously into one of the conveniently mirroring windows that line city streets like a Hollywood boudoir, she saw only a rather wan girl with a scarf flattening her hair. Ari slipped his arm around her waist and followed her gaze.
"You are incredibly sexy, you know, Hannala," he said. "You make it hard to keep my mind on anything else." He stopped and took her by the shoulders, but didn't kiss her as she expected, only inspected her tenderly. She blushed but didn't try to duck her head.

The building was tall and narrow, each office constituting a floor, like a child's wobbly tower of blocks. Ari opened an unmarked door and said something, then came back to sit beside her on a wooden bench. The paint on the anteroom walls, a peach color slowly peeling back to white, lent the cement the blotched appearance of a nervous rash.
A skinny male face peeked suspiciously through the front door and watched them with narrowed eyes, then suddenly yelped Ari's name and bubbled with greetings. Ari, apparently unable to remember the fellow's name but still glad to see him, leaped up to take his hand. They chattered rapidly in actor's shorthand about people and events foreign to Hannah. The stranger, who was appealing in an angular sort of way, entirely failed to recognize not only Hannah's new power of attraction, but even her presence, and Ari had obliviously turned his back. At first she felt piqued and a little depressed, then gradually it dawned on her that the interloper was animatedly flirting with Ari, conveying warm admiration with every lilt of his narrow body while at the same time teasing him archly, as condescending as he was infatuated. He seemed bright,

and the skeptical edge in his voice made Hannah wish it were possible to ask him about Ari, whom he had obviously observed in a much wider variety of situations than she, but he continued to punctuate his indifference to her with sharp jabs of one hipbone as he pivoted to keep her out of sight. What fascinated her most, however, was Ari's reaction. She would have expected him to recoil from such an aggressive assault of charm, perhaps to bristle with male bravado, but instead he wallowed in the flattery and encouraged it while pretending not to understand all the ramifications. His voice softened with friendliness and his eyes brightened. His elaborate innocence was in itself coy.

A woman wielding a sheaf of papers and a pen interrupted to summon Ari, leaving Hannah and the stranger to stare blankly at opposite walls. How thoroughly he could switch off that ardent vivacity, Hannah thought, and how dignified he looked now, rather nondescript and a trifle weary. When his gaze passed by her in its inspection of the other spots on the wall, his mouth pinched with boredom. Her new confidence melted. Through his eyes she saw a picture of herself as soggy, crumpled; Cinderella after midnight, a lumpy and dolorous pumpkin.

When the prince sauntered back, he was joking happily with the bespectacled secretary, whom he had reduced to a flutter of squeals despite the firm frown she tried to impose on her shiny orange mouth. Hannah stood up with relief, curious to see how he would handle the situation. Fully poised, he patted the woman's well-girdled bottom and laughed when she hit him with her clipboard and clomped giggling from the room, then drew Hannah to him, rather ostentatiously placed his hand around her waist, and warmly bade good-bye to the young man, who sat with his long legs crossed, looking up at them cynically. With a knowing sigh and tired nod, he lifted one hand as if it were suddenly very heavy.

"Farewell, dear Ari, I hope Israel does as well by you as we have," he drawled.

Ari shrugged agreeably and guided Hannah out the door. As they trotted down the stairs his hand fell absently from her waist.

"He's a faggot, as you could probably tell," he remarked without rancor after a minute. "But a very nice guy. I couldn't remember his name, that's why I didn't introduce you—Brad, I think, or Barry." He took her hand again. "How are you, little one? You look tired?"

As always, his quick intuition of her mood, when he wished to exercise it, impressed her. "And cold," she admitted. "Mostly cold."

Ari

"Ah, I apologize. But in a little time we be home and I warm you up. And I am starving. On the way back I think we buy some food. Are you hungry?"

She dreaded the long walk home but trotted good-naturedly after him as he plunged down the street, until he motioned her to stand still, and to her surprise, went out to the corner to hail a cab. As she clambered across the backseat, she wondered why it seemed bizarre to be in a taxi with a disheveled young foreigner dressed in torn chinos and sneakers— as if drivers stopped only for men like her father. It seemed unnatural that Ari should so casually give orders to the man behind the wheel, whereas when James took out his wallet to pay, the money seemed superfluous, as if public vehicles would hasten to do his bidding. Ari, fortunately, sensed none of this incongruity; he slumped against the seat and played absentmindedly with her hand as he watched the blocks roll by, as composed as a prince in his carriage.

When they got out, the rain had stopped and the clearing sky was painting itself the color of water in tropical climates. Spring was reinstated. Within and in front of the crowded market, in crates and on rickety tables, fresh vegetables advertised themselves. To Hannah, who had never cooked a meal more complex than hot dogs, they seemed glorious leftovers from an impressionist painting. She was conscious only of ebullient motion, of laughing men, scampering children, and cheerful women bearing armloads of crackling bags, of brilliant light relaying from one moist surface to the next.

When Ari reappeared he was carrying a very large, full bag from which an unwrapped loaf of bread protruded like a candy cane from a Christmas stocking. "Yum," she said greedily.

He shook his head fondly at her gluttony and steered her down the street to a block which she slowly recognized as familiar. The whole neighborhood was so bright and alive that had it not been for the corner bar, she wouldn't have recognized it. Even the dour pretzel vendor nodded at the passers-by. Ari paused at a pedal cart and, with a shift of the bulky shopping bag, purchased two crusty, mustard-laden pretzels. His he virtually inhaled; hers she munched more slowly.

When they turned the corner to their apartment, the activity around them thinned, and in an overflowing of the good spirits of the whole afternoon, Ari paused affectionately, and embraced her. Laughing, they walked three more awkward steps, then clung together again in a sun-drenched longing to touch, amused and breathless at their own intensity.

"You make me feel like I can take you right here in the street," he whispered.

"Well," she joked, "we could have a picnic right here. You could spread your coat on the puddles like Sir Walter Raleigh."

"I really think you would do it. Come here to me."

So compelling was their private desire that the voice that bleated out over their heads made them both jump and look upward in astonishment to a half-open window.

"You make me sick, doing that in a public place! You ought to be ashamed. Don't your parents teach you any manners anymore?"

Ari's response was to kiss Hannah again, this time with a belligerent disregard of their audience, and she complied just as boldly, for the bitterness in the ancient, cracked throat had shocked and repelled her: surely anyone could see that the end of the day was too radiant and their clasp too genuine to have been mere adolescent exhibitionism, calculated to scandalize the grown-ups and make the young feel young. Indeed, it had seemed to her that for a single pure instant the whole world had sun-danced together, one tribe, however briefly. But when Ari let go, she peered up again, high over his shoulder, at the hoary old woman rocking so fiercely at her ringside post, clenched with visible hate. And as she stared at the shrunken and contorted face, she wondered pityingly if the lady, now doomed to be forever old, loathed the coming of spring the way Hannah herself loathed the sun when she was depressed. Did spring seem accusatory, brutally tactless, a coarse reminder of better times? Worse, did it remind her of all she had never done and never seen or felt or been? That scowling, puckered creature, Hannah realized with a sobering jolt, would never shed the cruel mask she now wore or the stiffening joints and brittle bones that caged her: they would humiliate and falsify her for the rest of her life. They had become her without her willing it, without her permission. No one alive, none of the healthy strangers so carelessly replacing her, whom she spied upon every day, would ever see her as she must still think of herself, as she must dream of herself at night when she could still float to music like a pretty girl at a prom and visions seemed real.

For an instant, in the midst of Hannah's rich and piercing gladness, that vast expanse of unmodified blue above them seemed empty even of echoes. An emptiness so close, so pervasive, that it threatened to lift them all like forgotten balloons, up and away and out of sight, hurrying into the thinning atmosphere until at last they would fly so very high that the sheer force of internal pressure would burst each one, alone, into the surrounding nothingness.

27

In the bath, they played together again like children. It was not until they moved back to the bed that the melting pressure of the street embrace returned, less desperate now but more powerful. They were so slippery from their bath and each other that they slid from movement to movement, into and around one another, until their merging bodies became the atmosphere they breathed and swam, the room they saw, the air they tasted, the sheet they lay on. Once Hannah neglected to breathe, and when she remembered at last, the oxygen reverberated through her nerves until she felt it wash her vision backward and away, as if her mind had given her eyes leave to run outdoors and watch the sunset.

"This isn't fucking," Ari hoarsely stated, more to himself than to her. "This is making love."

The tantalizing aroma of food finally nagged her from sleep; she was ravenous. Ari, dressed only in an apron, was again working at the sink, humming in a throaty, guttural language, his back to her. At the sound of her groan, he glanced inquisitively over his shoulder. "Hungry?"

"Starved, thank you. That bow on your bottom is really cute."

"Never insult the cook."

"Oh, Sahib, your wish is my command," she said earnestly. Then, a little guilty about her domestic uselessness, she slid up onto the counter, a better perch from which to applaud his preparations. When he turned around slowly to admire her, however, she suddenly felt shy, much like a sculpture on a pedestal, and the formica was cold under her bottom. His softening expression had just begun to reassure her when, before she realized what he intended, he reached to the bookcase behind him, turned around, and snapped her picture.

"Oh, you creep!" she howled, more astonished than angry. "You promised!"

"But you look so adorable, I cannot resist." He returned shamelessly to their meal. "Besides, if you do not work, you do not eat, yes? That is the American way?"

"Are you implying that posing in the nude is my work?" she laughed. She didn't really mind. Somewhere in a country she would probably never see, a curious reminder of her would endure. "I suppose that now when I become a famous movie star, you'll blackmail me, right?"

"Yes of course, but not for money."

"Oh, you mean you'll just want that? Well, I doubt you'll have to blackmail me for that."

"Promise, darling, even when I am old and fat?" Grinning contentedly, he came to the bed with a broad platter of chicken, potatoes, and vegetables of every kind, plus two precariously balanced bowls of soup, and on a second trip, plates, utensils, salt and pepper, milk, bread, jam and butter.

"Oh yum," she groaned. "When we're both old and fat you can bribe me with food." They spread a blanket to catch crumbs, then feasted heedlessly, far too gluttonous to do more than grunt now and then with rising satisfaction.

"You're a better cook than my mother," Hannah concluded with amusement.

"Yes," he said seriously, "I am very good; I can cook anything." He looked at her smugly, his appetite finally beginning to flag. He gestured with a drumstick. "You see, there will be lots of jobs I can do for you when you are rich and famous."

When at last they had swallowed all they could hold, and even their fingers had stopped sneaking back for more, she rose like a complacent housewife and cleared the bed and lazily washed the few dishes while he lounged against the pillow smoking, watching her.

"You really don't have to do them, you know," he reiterated. "But I am grateful; you are wonderful. You make me want to reward—hey, I never take you to the Empire State Building like I promise this morning!"

"No, I was crushed!"

"I make it up to you; we go to the movies tonight, yes? Where is that paper your admirer gives you in the restaurant?"

They agreed on a remake about a psychopath, starring a British actor they admired, stretched regretfully, and began to dress. Hannah again wore his sweater, which unaccountably pleased her. Her hair was clean and fluffy from its rainwater bath, the color of rich red forest loam after a storm. Ari pulled on a tattered but elegant black sweater that enhanced the gold in his skin. They linked hands, ebullient as children, skipped downstairs, through the garden of rock and glass, and ambled down the quiet streets to the much livelier, brighter neighborhood of the theatres.

Inside, however, the air conditioning was on, and even with her suede jacket Hannah grew steadily stiffer with cold. The dry air filtered through her thin pumps to make her feet first ache, then go numb. Even Ari was chilled, and though they snuggled together, neither was much help to the other. Nor was the film much relief, for the successive jolts of horror Hannah felt as one head after another toppled from its shoulders, only to reappear in hatboxes on the closet shelf, made her own neck tighten uncomfortably. Ari began to make grumpy judgments on the quality of the acting.

The natural air on the other side of the heavy glass doors was an immediate improvement. They stood by the posters a moment, readjusting their coats and their moods. Neither was eager to go straight home. The unpleasant temperature and film had snapped them out of their former somnolence and left them restless and a little tense. Ari, she guessed, would prefer to be alone when in this mood, but she had nowhere to go to oblige him, and anyway, she too needed to release some of this staticky energy.

"I take you to an exciting place where I think you probably never go before," Ari stated, rubbing his hands distractedly. "Theatre people come there—sometimes very famous people, great actors. You will see, you like it."

"Sardi's?" she asked with interest.

"No, but a place like that. Come, I show you." He took off at a brisk clip, taking her hand—less, she suspected, out of affection than to keep her in step. Probably he was not so much sharing one of his haunts as dragging her along.

Perhaps the streets were so empty because all the people were in the restaurant. Ari ushered her through the narrow door into a dense crush of floating limbs, heads, shoulders, smoke, and tinkling glasses held aloft as buried bodies shoved and weaved to invisible destinations. A sprawling cocktail party. Hannah was aghast. She had never seen people packed so tight, not even in the bars at the shore where young people flocked after dinner. Shrieks, liquid chortles, screams of welcome and hoots of laughter drowned out all but the thud of drums and cymbals from a band apparently playing in the background. It was hard to breathe; the air consisted only of smoke and evaporating alcohol.

Although it proved impossible to see the whole of any individual, Hannah quickly inferred from glimpses of flank, breast, back and thigh that she was inappropriately dressed. Metallic fabrics fought with sequins for the spotlight, brocade and velvet slithered past, lace lined with silk undulated suggestively, and clumps of chiffon bounced—even a peacock feather hung rather flaccidly across the room—but denim was nowhere to be seen. Colors were as bright as traffic lights. Hair was piled high or puffed wide in textures stiffer than the dresses, dyed all shades of yellow and black and orange so vivid it would have embarrassed the fruit. The clank of bracelets on wrists shooting above the crowd like antennae of timorous underground creatures, plus the clatter of plates, the zing of the cash register, the tingle of change and the ubiquitous ring of ice against glass, all lent fierce rhythm to the room that infected every pelvis with irresolute jerk and twitch. Light spat out from chrome and crystal and splintered the darkness like buckshot.

Hannah's heart sank; she wanted to go home. Ari dragged her through the swarm by one extended arm and she feared that if she lost her grip on him she would be lost forever. Never had she so intimately crunched against so many hips and bottoms, nor had her breasts swept so many indifferent and anonymous backs.

Finally they landed in a part of the room where red rug was actually visible between torsos. The men, who in the thicker crowd had faded against the blaze of their women, here stood out. All were expensively tailored, so that even the shortest and stoutest possessed shoulders broader than their waists, and many were suntanned; few were as attractive as their women. Some wore diamond rings.

Hannah would have been delighted to sit in a corner and eavesdrop, but Ari bellowed in her ear that he was going to the men's room and would meet her right back here. And then he was gone. Confused, she stood on her tiptoes trying to peer over the roof of heads. Diagonal to where she stood she saw a sign of a lady in a bustle holding a parasol, and though she hated leaving her spot for fear of never finding it again, she thought she had better dare the journey. Operating on radar, she plunged into the seething current of people, and eventually, rather to her surprise, managed to emerge where she had aimed.

The rest room deserved its name, for it was a haven of comparative calm and quiet. Perhaps the reason it was so deserted, however, was that the fluorescent lights and long mirrors were designed to convince women that their escorts must be necrophiles. As Hannah brushed her hair and tried to avert her eyes, she wondered if those apparently flawless and ageless females in the outer room also winced at secret faults, glaring to themselves when they evaluated their appeal under these sizzling tubes. Comparing herself to those paragons of style, she saw only an unwieldy schoolgirl, with a face the shape and color of an aspirin tablet.

She found her spot again with little difficulty, but Ari wasn't there. She thought she had allowed him plenty of time. The scene around her was fascinating, but as each second flickered by she grew more apprehensive, rocking nervously from foot to foot in a gesture borrowed from Rachel. Finally she began to retrace her steps, thinking they might have passed somehow. She wedged her way along, glancing anxiously over her shoulder, feeling more and more unhappy, until she popped out of a particularly cramped pocket of flesh in the place where she expected to see him, but didn't. Now a hammering sort of misery overtook her. She was about to turn around yet again and forge her way back to the original spot, when she heard the faint rasp of his voice somewhere to her left. Scrutinizing the crowd intently, she finally picked him out, his back to her as he chattered earnestly to two intimidatingly gorgeous girls, one white and one black. Gloomy forebodings almost held her back, but she had little choice. She sidled up to them and positioned herself in a way she hoped didn't appear possessive; and apparently she was all too successful, for it wasn't until Ari flamboyantly illustrated some point with his arm and stepped backward onto her toe that he noticed she was there, and then he looked annoyed. He did not take her hand.

"Oh, Hannah," he said quickly, "I would like you to meet my two old friends, Margo here, and Bambi."

Hannah blinked when he called the brown girl Bambi, and wondered if it was a stage name she had chosen herself or if her parents had done it to her. She did have wide, fawn-like eyes and a soft expression, except when she glanced at Ari. Dressed like a sophisticated prom queen in a chaste pink dress with matching lips, nails, shoes and bag, with a single strand of pearls and button earrings, she seemed quintessentially lady-like.

"Honestly, Eli," Margo drawled, "I wouldn't call us 'old friends' at all. First of all, I think that we—at least us girls—are still pretty young"— she flicked one long silver nail at his forehead—"although I guess you are getting a little thin up there, aren't you? As for the friends part, I'm not even sure we like each other. What do you think, Bam?"

"I think I'd like to sit down."

"Good idea. If you'll excuse us, please—?"

Hannah smiled with relief and was about to nod politely, but Ari quickly spread his arms in protest. "No no, we sit together, the four of us, and catch up on the old times!"

Margo glared, jeweled hands on hip. "'Old times' are something I think we'd be better off forgetting, and there aren't going to be any future times, so that doesn't leave us too much in common, does it?"

Though not actually prettier than Bambi, Margo was definitely more compelling. Steak-knife thin, with hungry edges sharpened by black coffee and compulsive dieting, she nonetheless retained jutting breasts, now emphasized by a scoop-necked sheath of gold. She wore her streaked hair in an elaborately casual style Hannah had often admired in movies, the kind that required hours in a salon but appeared to have been shaped by the wind. Her glistening mouth was full and pouty. The effect was not exactly sensual, for she was wound too tight for that; rather she crackled with electric, abrasive sexuality, like a suggestive name in neon. Her very hunger was contagious.

"Ah, Margo," Ari sighed. "You must always make everything so complicated. Come, sit down with us. You haven't even told me what you are doing. Are you working?"

"Shit, have I ever been working? Do you know anyone who's actually working? Of course I have dozens of bright prospects, as usual. How about you, Bam, do you know anyone who's working?"

"No, but I do know someone whose feet hurt."

"Right, that makes two of us. A miserable day of shitting around on that goddamn modeling platform and I stand here making conversation: self-destructive as ever! Mother always said I didn't have a practical bone in my body. Of course, when you analyze it, this set of bones has been practical enough in other unique lil' ol' ways, right, Ari sweetie? Look, you two kids want to be alone together, right? This nice girl doesn't want to sit with us old shrews, do you, honey?"

Mystified by all the undertones of hostility and intimacy, Hannah had felt as invisible as she used to when Jennifer embarked on a lengthy conversation with a neighbor and forgot all about the small daughter grumbling by her hip. Now, taken aback at being addressed, she tried to reply as politely as she would have to the neighbor, but Ari hastily interrupted.

"Ah, we have been alone together all day. Now you will entertain us. Come."

With the disgusted frown of the child who has exhausted all her ploys and is ready to obey, Margo wheeled abruptly around and haughtily led the others to a table. She stopped by the booth, stared dubiously at the corner, then motioned proprietorially at Ari. "I have no intention of getting trapped in there between you and a wall, you bastard—by this time I know better. You get in first."

"This way is best, so I can see you while we talk," Ari muttered to Hannah, and promptly slid into the corner, positioning her across from him. She had dimly hoped tables might be hard to secure in such a crush, but the restaurant did function like the cocktail party it resembled, with most people preferring to stand and drink.

"So, what will we all have?" chortled Ari happily, as complacent as a cat by a fish pond. "My treat!"

Margo, who had been gazing around their corner of the room, turned to him with one penciled eyebrow lifted. "Heavens, no, darling, I wouldn't dream of letting you waste your money on us. I just did a very lucrative spread today, and Bambi signed for a cigarette commercial, the lucky bitch. I mean, we may not be *really* working, but in the meantime, we're pretty well fixed. We'll make it dutch treat."

"No no, I insist. We make this a party, my party!"

Margo tossed back her hair and laughed with the tinkling sound of glass breaking. "Why, is it your birthday? Face it, honey, you can't afford us."

Ari looked at her blankly. "What do you mean—you mean you want to eat dinner too? Eat whatever you want, I bring enough money for that—and I have a check, too, I think." He took out his wallet to make sure, then obligingly held it open for her to view.

"Jesus, are you going to show us you have rubbers in your pocket too?! You always were so suave, darling, you and your elegant sneakers—do you have them on now?" She ducked momentarily under the table. "Oh yes, I should have known." She tapped him playfully on the shoulder and leaned forward until her breasts wobbled over his lap like fruit on a branch.

Ari, riveted on her actions, seemed oblivious to her tone. He ogled the opening of her dress so unabashedly that she turned away in some embarrassment. "Order whatever you want," he reiterated. "We already eat dinner, but you go ahead."

"I never eat," Margo said flatly. "Okay, honey, squander it on us if you want." She shared an incredulous shrug with her friend.

Bambi, evidently bored by the duel across from her, had been inspecting the room, her eyes moving from man to man, then woman to woman. "Look," she said mildly. "There's Lennie Borden. He's casting a big new show—and he's got what's'ername with him, the one with the big ass. Think we can work up the nerve to say hello? I guess he'd think we were crazy; he'd never remember us. Oh, and look over there behind him—" Her voice rose excitedly. "There's Push Jones! Lord, will you get a load of that suit?"

The man she was gazing at with such reverence was one of the short ones with hips so broad that his shoulders, in order to overhang them, threatened to knock down the mirrored pillars that supported the ceiling. The pleasure it gave the two girls to speak these names aloud, especially the nicknames, impressed Hannah. They continued to stare and speculate raptly until Ari casually began to massage Margo's turned back. She swung around to hiss at him: "Christ, you really can't let up for one minute, can you?! You know, Ari, you really are compulsive. You're really sick. You'd better get someone to look into you before it's too late!"

"But I love to be looked into by you," he chirped, unfazed. "You think I am sick because I rub your back? I find this strange. I do it out of friendship; you are always so tense there. And you know sometimes you like it. Ah, here is our waiter. Hello, hello. What will we all have?"

Bambi and Margo requested old-fashioneds, but despite Ari's urging, no food. Giving up with a shrug, he moved his gaze like a conductor's baton to Hannah.

"A Coke, please," she said in a small voice.

"No no, it is late, it is a party! You must have a drink. You will relax, it is Saturday night!"

"I don't drink. I really do want a Coke."

Ari frowned, turned to the waiter who was waiting for him to approve her decision, and ordered both a Coke and a concoction she had never heard of, plus Scotch and a cheeseburger platter for himself. "You will see," he instructed Hannah. "You like what he brings you; it has chocolate and taste like candy."

During these deliberations, Margo had begun directing a flow of gossip to Bambi about names intended to be obscure to their seatmates. Hannah listened passively, thinking that under other circumstances she would have been fascinated by these girls—or rather, these young women. For while it was hard to tell their age under the elaborate makeup and patina of sophistication, Hannah guessed they were in their early thirties or very late twenties, young for people but old for ingenues. Their days of luxuriantly taut skin were just beginning to be numbered. Although she provided not an iota of competition for their stylish glamour, Hannah was eighteen, and she sensed that Margo in particular loathed her for that.

"—I've told her a thousand times she should leave him," Margo rattled animatedly. "Everybody tells her. But she won't listen, so I guess she likes it; I guess that's what she wants. I mean, she's stuck it out for three long years, which is two years longer than any *happy* marriage I know, so they must have something going, God only knows what. He never does a pope's ass worth of work himself, then he beats her black and blue so she can't work, then beats her again for not bringing in any money—Allah save me from artists! I don't know—" She fluttered her taloned hands gracefully but incessantly as she talked, back and forth to the ashtray, to the water glass, inscribing figure eights in the air with her cigarette. Nervously she plucked and parted her lips like a child. "Really, she should go out to the Coast like that other one did, you know, the one with that face like a beanbag but those fantastic thighs. They're more body conscious out there, the face doesn't matter so much, and she's the type, blonde and leggy and all. I really think she could make it. Especially if she left him behind in his fucking garret. Not that her legs are all that great, when you analyze them, but she's got a hell of a lot of them. Great in pants. What was that girl's name, anyway—you remember, the one with the scrunched-up face—Olive or Pickle or something—?"

Throughout Margo's monologue, Ari's attention stuck like a Band-aid to her admirable torso, although now and then he remembered to glance warmly at Hannah, reassuring himself by his own bright smile that she was alright. She, meanwhile, was gradually becoming aware that her nerves were squeezed so tight her head threatened to splurt into the air, which must be why she felt so dizzy. When her Coke came, she had difficulty persuading her Adam's apple to open, even though her mouth felt like dried burlap. Worse, her throat kept constricting when she tried to swallow.

"So," Ari whispered, pointing his finger at her. "Drink your real drink; at least taste it."

She tasted it, and to her displeasure, found it rather good, but she resolutely put the glass down and frowned. "Ugh."

"But it tastes like chocolate!"

She began to protest that she would prefer a genuine milkshake, but saw that he had lost interest anyway. He abruptly but good-humoredly attached himself to a familiar name in Margo's conversation, and interrupted as if he had let them play long enough.

"Yes, how is he anyhow? You are still going with him? You love him?"

Margo sighed elaborately. "No, darling, that was months ago. Now I'm going with a truly marvelous guy, a very successful actor with family money who I really and truly love—for his mind. Unlike most actors, he has one. And he's gorgeous. He's meeting me here later, so you'll get to see him. You'll like him, everyone does. *Très sympathetique,* right, Bam?" Again she drooped toward Ari as though swinging to his tree on a vine. "Tell me, Ari honey," she began, then shot a lethal glance at Hannah and put a finger in her mouth. "I suppose this is tactless, but curiosity—well, I mean, after all, maybe you don't—do you?" She giggled. "What I'm trying to say, sweetie, now that we can discuss it like two civilized people, is, do you still service that incredible harem you used to keep? Well, 'keep' is maybe not the word—'use' might be better. I never could figure out how you did it! I mean, you're not that large or strong, or even especially handsome. Really, you do deserve some kind of medal. And I've got to admit, you have courage, you always did—for example, your having the nerve to come here dressed like that, and on a weekend yet. I mean, it's not even cool enough to pass for a Brando!" She flapped her hand suggestively toward his chinos. "Like, what if somebody important recognized you, not that that's likely—"

Ari caught the hand she was fluttering and airily kissed it. "I don't give a fuck for what you call these important people. And anyway, you know"—he held her eyes seriously—"I am going back to Israel soon."

"Are you really?" she trilled. "You don't say!" She clapped her hands merrily at Bambi. But then, unable quite to sustain the sarcasm, she added: "When?"

"Soon. Hardly a week."

"I suppose all your girlfriends are planning a big good-bye party—?"

"No, we say good-bye in private. I think that is better, yes?"

Hannah took a deep breath in hopes of getting a fresh lungful of smoke instead of the same one she had been inhaling and exhaling for hours. Her attention kept wandering back to her physical difficulties. Not only was a corset steadily tightening around her torso, but the glass in her hand kept shaking loudly enough to interrupt the ringing in her ears. Dispassionately diagnosing her symptoms, she decided that, although the mere fact of Ari's attentions to such an attractive female would have been painful in any case, the venom of this particular ritual made it worse. For all his indifference to them, the barbs aimed at Ari succeeded in troubling her—and the reason for his indifference was no consolation, though it was a lesson. Ari could afford to ignore Margo's jabs, even the ones deftly on target, because in the end he would win. No matter what she thought of him, she wanted him.

Clearly it was time to go. Hannah had known from the beginning that something like this was bound to happen, and she had promised herself that when it did, she would leave. Her cheeks felt hectic and her heart beat into her ribs. If only it weren't night—that made the logistics of her flight so complicated. Her clothes were at his place, along with her money; there were no buses home at this hour; and arriving at Rachel's so long past midnight was going to be a dreadful imposition. Meanwhile she was trapped in this booth by that girl in pink who was going to light yet another cigarette, as if breathing weren't difficult enough already.

Suddenly, like an ice cube shooting out of a clenched fist, she sprang to her feet, her thighs jostling the table. "Excuse me," she blurted at Bambi, ignoring the other two, then suffered an agony of self-consciousness as her seatmate blinked incredulously for minutes before at last comprehending and sliding out, Hannah floundering after her with a great rattle of dishes and silver. A hot wave of mortification blurred her sight so that everything whipped around the corners of her eyes. She had meant to do this with dignity, but now that she had precipitated the crisis, she must see it through.

She extended one arm toward Ari and spoke as coherently as she could manage. "I don't want to disturb you, but if you'll just lend me the key I'll go back and get my things and get a cab to Rachel's. I'm afraid I'll have to leave the door unlocked."

Ari stammered back in complete astonishment. "But what do you mean—you don't want to go—just sit down and—"

"Oh, I don't want you to leave. You just lend me the key so I can get my stuff, since I'd rather not come back tomorrow if I can avoid it." She ignored Margo's flabbergasted stare, noticed that the hand at the end of her still outstretched arm was beginning to curl into a fist, and straightened it.

"I don't—why do you want to go to your friend's?—You did not tell me—"

Ari looked badly confused and Hannah feared he was never going to give her the key, so she lifted her pocketbook to her shoulder in a businesslike gesture and was about to turn to go without it, when, to her further astonishment, Ari thrust out both hands in a fervent signal to make her stand still, and began to lurch toward the aisle so hastily that Margo had to leap from the booth to avoid being clambered over. Dishes rattled again, and Bambi had to rescue a glass as it tipped into her lap.

"No no," Ari said hurriedly, reaching out to hold her in place. "Don't go. Wait here a minute until I—"

"Oh no," she repeated with great determination, trying to freeze the quaver in her voice. "I'm going. I just wanted the key, but if you prefer—"

"I mean I come with you—I leave with you! Just wait for me to pay the check! Please wait here. Will you do that?"

"Now?" she said unbelievingly, confused herself. "But your friends—you mean you're leaving now?"

"Yes!" he snapped, his face an unhappy mixture of impatience and concern. "But I must pay. Just wait for me while I finish here. I cannot just run out."

"No," she said dazedly, aware of the pair of shocked eyes peering up at her, and frightened at the speed of the spasm that was spreading up from her stomach. "I'll wait outside."

"No, I want you to—" He went to take her arms to steady her, but the clatter of china and jewelry had merged with the ringing in her ears to an unmanageable crescendo, and the endlessly refracting lights seemed to be converging entirely on her, making her reel away and plunge toward the door. As she stumbled through the crowd, afraid to apologize to the people she kicked for fear that opening her mouth would release tears, it occurred to her that she was acting like a hysterical girl in a movie—and that was odd, she thought, because she didn't do things like that.

At last she thrust herself between two disconcerted men, threw herself against the door, and emerged, suddenly, into the fresh night air. The heavy doors sighed shut behind her, sealing away the noise, and left her alone in the silence. She began to slow up, realizing she had run halfway down the block. Everything was strange: her pulse hammered, her skin burned, her chest hurt: this wasn't she. Then the realization that he might follow made her flinch warily toward the door, involuntarily back up a few steps, and rub her face nervously. He would be furious. She had made a scene, embarrassed him in front of people he wanted to impress. She had broken their bargain. Well, she would just tell him to return to them, that's all. She hadn't asked him to come. Where was she, she wondered; how far from the apartment? No matter, she would just hail a cab—

Footsteps closing in made her look up wildly just as someone grabbed her from behind. "Wait!" Ari cried. "It's only me! Don't run, it's me. But why are you so upset? You are crying? Don't cry, don't cry, I don't mean to make you cry—"

He crushed her against him and stroked her with passionate tenderness, and as she sobbed helplessly into the rough wool of his coat, she retained just enough detachment to be shocked. She wanted to warn him against this undermining kindness: it was the only tactic she had not armed herself against; it had never occurred to her that he might be gentle. She had no defenses. Profound waves of grief gulped through her, but she knew, even as she dissolved into successive explosions of misery, that it wasn't really this particular night she was crying over. He had hurt her feelings, but not this drastically. This must be some vastly more inclusive, vastly older and more important pain. She would weep forever.

"Hannah," Ari whispered soothingly. "Little one, here, take this." He handed her a handkerchief. She coughed out damp thanks, then collapsed back into his arms. "Calm down, calm down. It wasn't that bad, not really. I am so sorry. But why didn't you say something or even look angry? You look so calm, and then when you jump up like that you terrify me—I think there must be a fire—!"

"I didn't want to take you away from your friends," she explained unsteadily. "I knew I didn't really have any right to, but I just—"

"But they are not really my friends; I hardly even like them. Margo and I just fight when we meet. She is sexy but not—they aren't important to me—did you think they were? You are so silly, such a sensitive little girl. I just think they amuse us for an hour or two, that's all. They're not worth making you sad; we could have left. Next time you must give me some *sign*, you know. I mean, you look so calm sitting there across from me, so peaceful, just like always, the quiet princess, until the second you jump up like that. You give me a heart attack!"

She gurgled between amusement and tears. "I thought you'd be angry if I said I wanted to go—"

He continued to murmur consolingly, hugging her, and she continued to cry with no intention of stopping, dazedly aware that she seemed to have waited for this moment all her life. She felt, as she huddled in the now-rather-soggy cavern of his neck and chest, that this was the most luxurious gift anyone had ever given her: had all her fantasies really been about weeping in some man's arms?

Finally he wiped her cheek and said firmly, "Now you must stop. It's time to stop. Come."

Obediently and a little gratefully, she quivered into silence. She buttoned her jacket and wiped back her hair, noticing a few strangers looking at her curiously. How strange that this should be she! He held her gently next to him as they walked down the block; then, as if judging her strong enough to support herself, dropped his arm and more casually took her hand. Remorse that the rare indulgence of that moment had ended almost brought tears to her eyes again, but she determinedly fought them back, for the other grief had been something altogether different, almost impersonal in its force and depth, and to follow it with a mere spasm of self-pity would demean it. She would, however, have liked to wonder aloud about what had caused her to behave so uncharacteristically, even to be questioned about it, and she regretted that these things held no interest for Ari. As far as he was concerned, the subject had changed; the scene was over. Discussion would have to wait until she saw Rachel. She wondered if someday she would meet a man with whom she could not only behave, but also share.

"Tell me, little one," he said eventually, frowning. "Were you really going to leave me if I do not come after you? At this hour of the night?"

"Yes," she said honestly. "I didn't expect you to come."

He sighed, shaking his head incredulously. "You are such a crazy little girl. You think I let you go—after today?"

"Yes," she said simply.

As they neared their block, Hannah began to anticipate both bed and sleep with sharper and sharper longing, and only the darkness masked the woe on her face when Ari turned abruptly up the Avenue and stopped in front of the bar. "It's early to go back to the apartment," he said restlessly. "I thought we go in there and play on their machines for a while. You like to play the pinballs?"

"No, but I'll come in and watch you," she said compliantly. She ached to be home under the covers, away from strangers and diversion, but Ari's nervousness was so palpable she pitied him. Did he really consider this an early hour to go home? What a haunted life he must lead.

The bartender raised his hand to greet him and covertly inspected Hannah. His friendliness contained a hint of sarcasm, she thought, perhaps because he had watched so many girls wander in on Ari's arm, perhaps because he found the foreigner peculiar, not his kind of man, and wondered what all the women saw in him. Indeed, Hannah herself found it incongruous to be here with him in such a quintessentially American environment, a place where Jinx would have been perfectly at home, munching his toothpick methodically and muttering out of the corner of his mouth. She felt uneasy. The crackling fluorescent lights lent a sallow tinge to the faces of the three men drinking at the bar and a purplish glow to the air around them. The chairs in the restaurant area were already stacked on the tables, their legs spiking the air. The floor was dusty and the walls unadorned except for a bathing-beauty calendar, which Hannah ignored.

Ari ordered beer and Coke and carried the bottles to the pinball tables in the corner. His favorite game proved to be a facsimile of bowling, a matter of sliding a metal disk toward automatic pins, and when he gave up trying to persuade her to join him, he practiced alone until his quarters were gone. Hannah lifted down a chair, drew it near him, and passively waited, thinking about nothing at all until she dimly noticed that the peeling gold Budweiser sign that was spelled backward on their side of the window had unaccountably grown paler; and even then it took her a long time to realize that the sky must be lightening behind it.

Outside, Hannah slumped sleepily against Ari, infiltrating one of her chilly hands into his coat pocket, but he playfully staggered under her weight and yawned emphatically. "I am exhausted," he moaned, "and I think maybe a little drunk."

Once home, she wasted little time in slithering gratefully into bed; her head was dizzy as if she had been in an airplane for hours. When Ari joined her, she did blink awake to move expectantly against him, but to her surprise and disappointment, he stated rather defensively that he was too tired and turned away from her to curl up in sleep. Annoyed, she in turn rolled away from him, but then relented and relaxed so that their limp sides touched. He was feverishly warm. She would never know what anxieties spurred him to slide disk after disk from one end of a machine to the other in a dim corner of an inhospitable bar until he was sufficiently sick with fatigue to go home. Why did restlessness usually make him grasp at others, but tonight turn away? Was she no longer enough of a stranger: had she grown too familiar to act out the characters in his fantasies? For surely, she thought, that is the charm of intimacy between strangers: unknown bodies slide automatically into the costumes of our secret wishes, without requesting our help with the fitting, without jostling our suspended disbelief. Whereas, when we see a truly known face peer awkwardly out of those fantastic garments, we are embarrassed; our childish excitement fizzles at the sight of the vulnerability, the unsentimentalized childishness, of the other. To love another that nakedly requires charity and discipline. She wondered if anyone knew Ari well enough to view his anxieties without romantic costuming. She was certain that he did not, and it was that certainty, more than his ban on questions, that kept her from asking him all she wished to know. For her, the quality that could most easily turn strangers into valued intimates was their own ability to sift and share themselves: her eagerness to see the world through other intelligent, trustworthy eyes made up for the loss of her favorite private costumes.

28

The floor beside her was a brilliant square of yellow-orange and above it dust wafted in the sunstream. Beside her on the bed, Ari quietly munched a chicken leg. Opening her eyes to find someone keeping watch over her was a new sensation.

"Ah!" he said gaily, "at last, sleepyhead! Here." He handed her another drumstick on a napkin and a glass of orange juice.

She looked queasily at the meat. "First thing?" But she nibbled it, then quickly admitted hunger and gobbled. "Hm, more."

"There is more in the refrigerator; I cook a great deal yesterday. Listen, little one, I have to work at the Club this afternoon, and then in the early evening I have a rehearsal with Rosie, so I will not be home until about eight. Tomorrow, though, I promise we spend the whole day together, okay?"

"Uh huh," she muttered past the bone in her mouth.

He extracted the bone, moved it and the napkin to the floor, and pulled her down on top of him, whispering endearments, petting her in steady affection, and in steady affection she responded. She lay with her face bathed in the square of glass-domesticated sun, sensations of succulent chicken, tart juice, salt and pepper merging with the shifting patterns of light, feeling her sleepy skin absorb the warmth of the sun and him, half dreaming that she was a child again on the beach in June when the temperature is gentle, the breeze cool, the ocean cold and the drifts of white sand hot. She lazed in the edges of shallow ripples, the water sharply chill on her reddening skin, the sand combing icicles in the ends of her tangled hair. Her red-checked bathing suit was still swollen with the soporific meal she was waiting to digest, and now and then she glanced covertly toward their yellow-striped umbrella to see if Jenny was threatening to call her back to bake on the blanket until she was as dry, crackly and dusted with gray as the beached seaweed strewn nearby. Ari murmured gentle accolades and absently stroked her until she itched as though sand crabs skittered over her; she twitched her flank and playfully swatted his hand.

He laughed and stretched, glancing at the clock. "Ah," he sighed, "always I am late. Why is it I forever have to be somewhere else, anywhere but where I am? I am tired of running. I am also still hungry, almost as hungry as you"—He nodded with amusement at the chicken Hannah was munching again, having retrieved it from the floor as soon as he had finished—"but I can eat for free at the Club." He told her the name of the Club and the address, asked if she knew where that was, and raised his eyebrows dubiously at her nod. "Well, it's in the phone book, and I give you the number when I call you at your college—you still have that? Good. I be there if you need me, at least until around six, and after that someone will know where I am. Okay, you will be okay? Ah, I hate to leave—"

But he did leave, and she was glad to be alone. She continued to eat until her conscience stopped her, and then, as blissful as a seagull who has swallowed in stages an eel longer and fatter than itself, she sat blank and bemused on her sunny perch, and was roused to flight eventually only by the prodding noise of a distant radio. Showered, dressed and straightened, she read for a few peaceful hours, called Rachel, who didn't answer, then finally decided to go out into the day. She wanted to move.

The morning was brilliant. She emerged into the street to see that the women, of daylight stoops and noisy children, of twilight kitchens and hungry husbands, were today tilting on high heels in giddy flocks, herding their families alongside. They marched through lines of complaining cars and cabs and trucks. They screeched admiringly at one another's plumage, secured their lavishly flowered crests of hats with white-gloved hands, plucked at the dark dresses that clung to tautly girdled hips. Despite the heat, most of them wore or carried black coats, and all wore black shoes so pointed and stilted that, to keep their balance, they had to mince or waddle along. Sweat made their powdered faces shine like bronze busts. They seemed proud, even exalted, as if this were the day the meek would inherit the earth. And everyone seemed to clutch a crumpled smidgen of greenery.

Of course, it must be Palm Sunday, Hannah breathed to herself as she sank down onto the front steps, hoping to be invisible in her jeans. She looked down at her clothes and laughed. She had forgotten it was

Sunday, much less the Sunday that ushers in Easter. How long had it been since she had been to church, since she had toddled down the aisle holding James with one hand, a rather damp New Testament with the other? How long since she had committed feats of memorization with gold starred ribbons for reward?

She wandered aimlessly in the Park, eavesdropped on families, smelled new flowers, and felt happy, so happy that after a long, drifting time she wanted to share the day, and a waiting phone booth once more reminded her of Rachel.

"Ravish!" she said with delight at the sound of her friend's voice. "Hey, I thought you might want to escape Relatives Inc. and come out and play with me. How was your country outing?"

"Oh, Hannah, thank God it's you! The country was awful, but at least it persuaded the clan they've done their duty by me, and at the moment they've all gone out for an early supper. Can you come here? Can I bribe you with pizza?"

"Terrific! I'll be right over. Lock the door to all grown-ups."

Some of Hannah's bright spirits fizzled up and evaporated on the long ride uptown, and on the crosstown trip she began to feel dazed, a little unreal. The fact that in the space of a day she could leave Ari's bed to visit Rachel, and eventually return to Ari's, seemed as disjunctive as a six-hour flight from one side of an unseen continent to the other would have been to her grandparents.

When she emerged at Rachel's stop she heard her name called, turned, saw someone bouncing along behind a flat white box a half block away and fell back into step beside her friend.

"Oh boy, pizza!" she exclaimed happily. "Here, let me carry it for you the rest of the way."

"Keep your greedy hands off," joked Rachel, who appeared tired, but cheerful. "I'll tell you, Hannala, I'm really glad you're here. You don't know how much I need to see a face that's related to me by choice, not guilt."

"That bad?"

"Pretty bad. I mean, everyone's trying so hard to be good for everyone else, and that's so unnatural, it's more of a strain than a help. I can tell Daddy wants to be furious with someone, and he can't be; he's just exhausted. And we all keep telephoning Mother as though she were some sort of oracle. Frankly, I dread the homecoming tomorrow. We've all been grouped around the living room with no lamps on—if we held hands it would look like a seance—and I swear, she's going to seem like a ghost when she finally does walk back into it all. Here we are." She gestured, and they turned into a spiraling pavement that circled between desiccated gardens, playgrounds and homogeneous brick slabs. To Hannah it was always miraculous that Rachel could unerringly find her own slab without checking the numbered signs planted like wooden tulips along their route. She headed for the staircase: both she and her mother had an aversion to elevators.

"But let's not talk about that," Rachel continued. "On and on it goes, and where it stops, nobody knows. A bolero of the nerves. It's you who has the adventures to tell, right?—so tell already! How does a nice WASP from Jersey find happiness in the big city with a lunatic Israeli? Whoops, sorry, a sexy Israeli."

"Lunatic and sexy," Hannah grinned as they found china, napkins, glasses, ice and soda, and carried the paraphernalia on hand-painted Italian trays from Rachel's mother's immaculate kitchen to her immaculate dining nook, where they sat it all down again on imported brocade place mats. "Do you realize how many times we've done this? We've got it down to a ritual."

When Rachel asked again about Ari, Hannah tried to summarize what had happened to her since they had last met, but grudgingly she realized that her experience was of the kind difficult to convey to someone who does not already know what is meant, which Rachel did not. The description of last night's bolt from the restaurant made Rachel gulp with sympathetic horror, but when Hannah tried to express why, in the end, she was glad to have burst into public tears and be, not chided, but consoled—why she was glad of the whole intense experience, though she had no wish to repeat it—Rachel could only fall silent. She had none of Hannah's taste for walking trembling into unknown situations to see what might emerge. This marked the first significant difference between them that could not be ascribed to disparate backgrounds, and while of course they refrained from trying to argue one another to a common point of view, still its existence reminded them of something they would have preferred not to know: that to be more and more particularly oneself is to be less and less securely the same as others, even those one loves. They had long known all about the growing pains of identity crises, but no one had ever warned them that identity, too, has its loneliness.

So, as soon as she tactfully could, Hannah turned the conversation to mutual friends and Rachel's tales of her family, subjects on which they were instinctively more of the same mind. In the living room, curled up in the richly embroidered chairs, they continued to speculate about families and futures until the light faded and Rachel blurred to a violet shadow against the neutral drapes.

Hannah began to fidget: soon she must leave. "Are your relatives due to return tonight?" she asked Rachel, who was submerging into lowering silence.

"They're not supposed to, but they'll find an excuse to drop in anyway, I'm sure," she answered harshly, reaching for a cigarette. She jabbed at the unresponsive lighter and shrugged. "They'll sit around feeling guilty, and then they'll all sob with self-pity because they're always feeling so guilty—shit!" She jabbed again at the lighter, then abruptly hurled it across the room. "I don't know why I even bother to smoke; at least my mother's route is quicker." She scuffled to the stereo to click on the pile of records, then returned to the couch and clenched up into a curl of resentment. Eventually she resorted to a match from the embossed box she jerked from the drawer; she exhaled in a nervous quickening rhythm, plucked tobacco from the tip of her tongue, and jabbed the remaining length of cigarette into the ashtray beside her, which already overflowed onto the table. Deeply abstracted, she began to sway back and forth into the plush pillows in the corner of the sofa, rocking on her long thin arms to the throaty lilt of the old-fashioned songs she forever played.

Hannah stood up sadly. She knew that this mood of her friend's meant the end of all conversation. Any attempt now to contact Rachel would elicit the grumpy yelp of an interrupted sleeper. Rachel's was an aggressive withdrawal, a retreat protected by the spiny tale of a porcupine. Usually it troubled Hannah, but tonight she was almost grateful, for it permitted her to leave with less wrench. She pulled her jacket from the closet crowded with thick coats and heavy plastic bags.

"I'm going now, I guess, Rake," she called over the music. "Good luck with the homecoming."

The dark knot of misery on the couch looked up and momentarily brightened. "Okay, bubula, I'll speak to you tomorrow. Have a nice time or whatever—I'm not sure what's the appropriate phrase, but you know I love you." She blocked off a spasm of emotion and reached for a shaft of hair, which she wrapped around a finger and rubbed against her mouth. Her eyes resumed their careful study of the fabric of the couch.

* * *

As the outer door wheezed shut behind her, Hannah felt a stab of confused pain and relief, dismay and freedom. But in the bright warmth of the bus, her anxiety turned to excitement, to the stimulation of adventure. All at once she felt strong and brave and in control. She swaggered happily down the aisle and lurched into the plastic cup of a seat, hands in her jeans pockets. Even waiting on a darker corner for the crosstown bus didn't chasten her, though she was glad it came quickly.

Safely back in the apartment, she flushed with satisfaction. She rose to her toes and stretched, then draped her clothing over the suitcase and tied Ari's robe around her. According to the clock he could come home any minute, but she expected him to be late. The way her hair crackled as she brushed it pleased her; she preened as complacently as an owl home from its vigil, proud to have once more won its race with the dawn. Somehow she looked changed, she thought: more sharply drawn and self-possessed.

She settled on the bed and picked up her book, but she had scarcely found her place when she heard his key in the lock. Bouncing up, she sprang across the room and unlatched the door, then, smiling to herself, slid demurely aside as he entered. After he fastened the bolt, he stopped to study her, and to her suppressed delight, she saw that he too was struck by some subtle change. Suddenly flustered, she began to turn, but he caught her waist and held her steady.

"Look at you," he said softly. "You know, you're growing up, little one, into a woman. Do you know that?"

She laughed, eased him to the bed, and tugged at his clothes until he finally yanked off the last of them and pulled her and the robe she wore over him like a tent. Hers was the power: she was sure of herself and of what she wanted. In time her ferocity ebbed and left her with an aching vacancy, abandoned her to the rising and settling, pulling and flowing of her need. So this is it, she seemed to gasp; so this is it. Again; at last. This. This.

When Ari gently touched her belly she shivered all over with enervated sensitivity. She blinked her eyes and discovered they were drenched with moisture. She was stuck like a wet leaf to the sheet. He murmured something affectionate and apologetically fell asleep. She lay inert for a long while, and then finally, both proud and subdued, reached over him to turn off the light. The darkness instantly seized her as one of its own.

29

She felt that every inch of her body, inside and out, eyelids, chin, the undersides of her breasts, had been painted with a slow-drying glue. Ari was jostling her, chuckling. From deep inside her gluey, unpleasantly shuddering cocoon, she wished he would just go wherever he wished and leave her a note. But still he shook her insistently.

"G'bye," she groaned, "see you later." But a nerve began to quiver at the bottom of her throat; now she might have trouble falling back to sleep after he had gone.

"No no, Hannah!" he laughed. "I thought today you will come with me to work. I try to get off early so we can go to a movie, but even if I cannot, at least we are together all day."

She blinked at his unaccustomed use of her name, and with grave reluctance, forced herself to a sitting position. The world swayed. She cleared her throat. "Okay. Do we have to leave now?" She squinted at him and realized he was already dressed. She was sure she could move no faster than a worm through cement.

"I do. In fact, I am already late."

Stiffly, she turned to confront the clock. No wonder she had felt so stunned! The obscurity in the room wasn't bad weather: it was just that the sun had only begun to rise. She could discern it creeping over the windowsill.

"Hannah?" Ari tapped her again. "I have left a paper with the address and telephone number of the Club, okay? Why don't you just go back to sleep for a while, and come to meet me there when you are ready?"

She nodded assent and he moved toward the door. "The paper is there by the phone," he said. "See you soon."

After half an hour's dizzy discomfort, Hannah admitted unhappily that she was not going to sleep: the pit of her stomach was obsessed with awakening, dressing, and locating that place. A shower relieved her hot skin, and her balance gradually reasserted itself as she moved about.

She found her jeans and camel sweater, choked down a swallow of juice, and painted her swollen eyes. Not that she greatly cared how she looked: somehow the information in the mirror seemed oddly unrelated to how she felt about herself.

The new sun was so tender that even the bruised garden took on a pale freshness. The flickering milky light reminded her of all the mornings of her early childhood: the fragrant kitchen, the lilt of the radio, her yawning, cotton-clad mother pouring cereal and calling her family to come and eat; and Hannah's own eagerness to run outside, and once outside, to run forever. Then all mornings had been one morning; their touch and texture were as deeply engraved as the whorls on her fingertips, yet she had no differentiated memory of them. The lemony kitchen, the opal squares of sky at the windows, the shiny counter with multicolored boxes and bottles, the burbling coffeepot and the smoking toaster, all were seen from the floor up; even Jenny's flowered robe swept up like a pyramid of roses.

She rechecked the paper in her hand, swallowed down her nervousness, and reached for the door of the "Moment to Moment Club," a coffeehouse that catered especially to members of the nearby Actor's Studio. The door was locked. Bewildered, she was looking around for a stoop to wait on when the knob turned in her hand.

"Are you a customer, or might you be the friend of Ari's?" asked a cheerful voice. "We're not open for business yet, I'm afraid, although we could conceivably make an exception for you if you can present documented evidence that you're a starving orphan. You don't look starving, though."

The voice belonged to a pleasant young man attached to a broom, the first person Hannah had met in days who seemed to come from her world, to banter in a language like her own.

"It's too early to be starving," she said happily. "And I'm not an orphan. I'm the friend. Does Ari live here? Can he please come out and play?"

"Yes he does, but no he can't. You'll have to come in and play with us."

She entered obediently, but what struck her first, and continued to strike her all afternoon, was that, despite the waiter's friendly invitation, Ari was not at play. Only when she saw him at work did she realize that she had not believed his claim to be part owner of this coffeehouse, to be a boss. But here he was, fully preoccupied with the role and apparently comfortable in it. He sprang up from a table to interrupt the waiter's mild flirtation, established his own proprietorship by placing a hand on each of her shoulders and pronouncing her name, and coolly ordered his employee back to his broom. Still holding one of her shoulders, he steered her back to the table where he had left a large pile of papers covered with figures, introduced her to another waiter and to a not-unattractive red-haired waitress with whom, to Hannah's astonishment, he was not flirtatious; procured her some eggs and muffins, said apologetically that now he must return to the business at hand, and to her further astonishment, did just that. He pored over the figures with great concentration and, it would seem, comprehension; he rearranged them, added and subtracted, and occasionally grunted with satisfaction. When he did at last stack the papers into three neat piles and fasten them with clips, it was not, as Hannah had anticipated, to lean back in his chair and return his attention to the people present, but rather to spring up even more emphatically to issue instructions to the cook, then to command the other two to finish their sweeping and table-setting, turn up the lights, and open the doors for business. As if in illustration, he unlocked the doors with great ceremony himself, pulled up the awnings that had covered both large picture windows, and then, on his hurried way to the kitchen, stopped to pull up the chair next to Hannah, who had been watching all this organization with quiet awe.

"Little one," he said tenderly, "I have picked a bad day, I am afraid, for your visit here. Only one of the cooks show up—the other does not even call. I don't know if he comes in ten minutes or stays away all day; he's an actor, like everybody else here, so he probably goes to an audition, but if he think—! Anyway, what this means is that I must help in the kitchen, since today I am all alone here. If you want, I give you the keys to go back home, but I rather you just stay at a table somewhere so I can see you now and then, since soon we cannot see one another at all. Do you want something, a Coke, a humburger? You will stay for me, as a present to me?"

He brought the Coke to the booth in the farthermost corner where Hannah had secluded herself with her book, kissed her fondly but absentmindedly, and disappeared into the kitchen. Hannah leaned back and yawned.

As the morning melted into afternoon, she began to wish more and more sleepily that she were able to nap in public. Finally, no longer able to concentrate on the swimming print in her lap, she leaned back to watch the customers wander in and out. Most of them seemed young, though even the youngest were five or ten years older than herself; most of them, male and female, wore blue jeans and turtlenecks and sunglasses which they kept on indoors. They seemed to know one another with the casual intimacy of strangers who cluster regularly in the same corners. Hannah was content to be invisible. She tensed only when one of the men glanced her way a second time or when the too-solicitous waiter inquired again if she was comfortable. She wanted only to observe, not to take part.

But the waiter, who introduced himself as Frank, would not relent. She sighed with dismay as she saw him leave a table where he had been passing time with two men and approach her determinedly. "C'mon," he pleaded, "you've got to reenter civilization. Some people over there are eager to meet you." Seeing her hesitate, he added, "They're friends of Ari's too, regular customers, actors like everybody else. C'mon, you must be hungry."

She shook her head.

"Thirsty? How about another Coke?"

At last tempted, she stretched and followed Frank to the center table, where he gestured in a circle and muttered names she made no effort to catch. Grinning enthusiastically at her were a slender, bespectacled boy and a muscular man with long black hair. She had been wishing she could escape to wash her face and brush her teeth, but concluded from their calculated charm that she must not look as frazzled as she felt. She fabricated a polite nod and took the glass that Frank slid toward her with assurances that he hadn't touched it. She sipped thirstily, then patted her cheeks and forehead with the cold condensation the glass left on her fingers.

The smaller man, she realized, was not a boy; he was at least as old as his more dominant companion, who in turn was somewhat younger than she had at first surmised: probably Ari's age. After their assault of flattery their interest in her faded, and they chatted together with the easy boredom of people who see one another too often to have anything new to say. Frank left at frequent intervals to take someone's order or relay food, which left Hannah feeling rather marooned, though even then the other two made no attempt to include her in the conversation. Mostly they bemoaned the dearth of jobs. The more unctuous and handsome one had just returned from California where he claimed to have worked briefly on one of the medical shows then popular on television, until the star, whom he resembled, had grown envious and purged him.

"I'm his type, you know what I mean? Physically, I'm his type, only a lot of people seem to think maybe I'm better-looking. What the hell, I can't really blame him—I mean, in this business a guy's got to protect his ass. In his place I'd of probably done the same thing. He's insecure, too. Nobody knows how he got that job in the first place, except maybe that he's Italian, if you know what I mean, and rumor has it he's into Vegas for a lot of bread. A hell of a lot of bread. Like, he's gotta keep that job for at least a couple of years: nobody wants to be fucked over by those boys—Oh, excuse me, Miss." He bowed earnestly toward Hannah, who, flabbergasted, made a vague gesture of pardon.

The actor's conceit fascinated her, since she had never even found the television star attractive, and this fellow struck her as at best the Lerner's version of the Gimbel's copy. She did have to admit, though, that the bulging muscles under the carefully ripped jersey, plus the plastered curls and greedy little boy's face, must prove winning in some circles, because their conversation was continually interrupted by pretty visitors. Flirtatious girls, alone and in pairs, kept wriggling self-consciously up to the table to say hello, and many of them must have spotted him from the street, since they didn't stay to eat, only lisped their messages and skittered away. The actor's responses were uniformly brusque and condescending; only when they were gone did he turn lascivious, lowering his eyelids and muttering knowingly about the anatomy and insatiability of each, then solemnly apologizing to Hannah. His friend rarely spoke at all.

After an hour of playing credulous audience, Hannah grew very bored and began to search for plausible excuses to return to her novel. She prayed to be rescued by Ari, but though he did emerge from the kitchen when an unusually thick crush of people descended on the cash register, he always hastened right back again, too harried even to glance in her direction. When at last he did pick up his head and look curiously around, and saw where and with whom she was sitting, he instantly joined them. He greeted the swarthy fellow by name, nodded at the other, and stood and conversed amiably with his hands planted firmly on Hannah's shoulders. But soon his name was called from three directions, and though he stroked the nape of her neck regretfully, he had to leave.

The instant Ari was gone, the other actor regained his interest in her. He grunted knowingly and pointed toward the counter with his thumb. "You gotta be careful with him, you know what I mean, princess?"

Hannah smiled. "I think I have a notion."

"Yeah? Well, he's a real heartbreaker." He watched her expectantly, as if imagining she might leap to her feet, hand clasped to a broken heart, and pledge allegiance to himself.

"So I gathered," Hannah said.

He continued to stare at her, calculations moving in visible creases over his brow. "Are you an actress?"

"No. I'm interested in acting, but right now I'm a freshman in college."

"Huh. I wouldn't have guessed that: you look older, more suave, you know what I mean? The reason I asked is you look sort of like an actress."

Startled and a little flattered, Hannah raised her eyebrows curiously.

"Well, sort of actressy, you know, dramatic. But I also wondered on account of you have big legs, big muscles, and I thought maybe you're a dancer."

In a mixture of alarm at having unfeminine legs and pleasure at being mistaken for a dancer, Hannah mumbled something about swimming and horseback riding.

"I guess that explains it. You hardly ever see a girl so muscular unless she's a dancer. I notice that, you know, 'cause I'm interested in working out myself. Physical fitness. After all, when you get right down to it, that's all we are. Bodies. Do you live around here?" he asked flatly.

"No. Right now I'm visiting on my way to my parents' in New Jersey."

"New Jersey?" He brightened. "Just out of town? Where?"

"Oh no," she explained. "The other Jersey. Hours away. By the ocean."

"Oh." Immediately he dismissed that possibility, and as if to signal his fading interest, yawned, stretched, and addressed a series of rhetorical remarks about the insensitivity of agents to his friend. This time when he swore he didn't bother to apologize. Yet when Hannah at last saw an opening to make a polite escape and went to rise, he exerted his toothiest smile, demanded that she stay, and to insure her compliance, fired a volley of unrelated questions, hardly giving her time to answer.

Only when he knew he had her pinned did he again allow his attention to flag. Then, just as Hannah was deciding to force the issue, he again yawned, mentioned the time resentfully, shrugged into his motorcycle jacket, polished his hair, and instructed Hannah to tell Frank they would see him again tomorrow. "You gonna be around again then?" he frowned, dimly sensing another option.

"I doubt it."

With an uninterested glance across the restaurant, he ambled to the door, his sidekick following in his wake. As he placed his hand on the knob, a covey of girls pulled open the door from the other side and, when they recognized him, called out his name; then, instead of entering, wheeled around and escorted him down the block, past the long front window.

Hannah lingered a few minutes longer, making her straw gurgle in the dregs of the soda. Why, she wondered, did she find that fellow loathsome, yet succumb so readily to Ari, when in truth they weren't all that different. Ari was equally vain, boastful and selfish, equally cruel, even if he did have the good taste not to slaver grease on his unruly hair. They were equally obsessed. Yet somehow in Ari obsession seemed mixed with uncommon joy, with a kind of purity of sensuality, the difference between a cat and a bull. She sighed in dismay and rattled the remaining shards of ice. Maybe he had that purity, that grace, only with her; maybe she evoked it—or invented it. Maybe she aimed the spotlight that transformed his act to ceremony, to ritual and dance. Well, that didn't matter; she didn't care about the state of his soul when he was alone. She cared only that his driving need to mesmerize her, to awaken and seduce her until she reflected the vision of himself he so desperately needed to see, somehow, momentarily, transformed them both. Or so it seemed at the time. Was she falling in love with him? Was she willing to trade her rather abstract goal of shared vision and mutual respect for his very tangible charm? As is usually the case, his charm had very little to do with the merit of his character—it lay in the graceful way he crossed the room, the unreasonably appealing contrast of his ascetic cheekbones with his generous mouth, and most of all, in the arrogance with which he invaded the private space of others. Insinuating with subtle smiles and gestures that he knew what women wanted, he moved startlingly close to them, touched them, teased them, evoked an air of secret understanding—and since nearly everyone is a bit uncertain of what she (or he) most wants, and treasures a childish hope that someday a stranger will come to enlighten and gratify her (or him), this trick of suggestion allowed him to march into women's fantasies as though he possessed the master key. Though a trick, it was by no means altogether a lie, for if he did not know and naturally could not gratify the full array of a human being's needs (even his own), he did know that everyone needs to be touched and indulged, to be made happy without effort or will, and he could, when he wished, dispense this happiness like a stranger handing out candy to children. His charm was potent and real. Had Hannah lied to herself? Had her traitorous emotions slipped heedlessly out from under the cautious restraints of her words?

Customers were now nearly filling the room and she began to feel conspicuous sitting alone at a center table. To wake herself up, she pulled her jacket over her shoulders and went outdoors. Too lazy for one of her epic walks, she strolled happily around the neighborhood, watching and being watched.

When she returned, she toyed with the paragraphs of her book and squinted at the people who came and went. The indoor lights brightened as the day dwindled. Occasionally words from the jukebox interrupted the vague flow of print under her hand. Ari emerged once to touch her and bring another soda. She suggested going home to wait for him there, but he urged her to stay, and she was too torpid to demur.

Her attention stirred when a pretty young woman with bleached hair massed at the back of her neck darted in, perched by the counter, and peered myopically about. She seemed tense but determined, perky in her black stretch slacks. She tapped at her twist of hair with one pink-tipped hand, then spied Frank and waved eagerly. His tactless but instinctive reaction was to glance at Hannah, who smiled to herself.

After the blonde whispered to him, Frank shook his head, leaned into the kitchen for a minute, then winked at the girl and resumed his business, this time avoiding Hannah's gaze. Soon Ari appeared at the inner door. He paused a moment to contemplate the stiffly nonchalant back the girl had posed in his direction, sighed, and walked rather wearily over to lean on the counter in front of her. Even from a distance Hannah could see the girl's entire expression dilate. She quivered expectantly, fluttered her hands, and finally, as though reminding herself of her purpose, began to speak with great solemnity. Ari's answer was brief. He bent over to kiss her rather chastely on the cheek, then gestured in a businesslike way at a table near Hannah, to which the yellow-haired girl quickly scampered and sat. There she rummaged in her rhinestone-clasped bag until she had unearthed papers, notebooks, checkbooks, paper clips and pencils, at which she then frowned in a kind of bewilderment, as if she was astonished to find that sort of thing in her purse. She vaguely sought to organize it all, poked, shuffled, sighed, opened a compact, inspected herself, and at last decided to paint her mouth a shinier pink. For a moment she blinked vacantly into space, like a bird on a telephone wire, then, as if she had been timing herself, swiveled around to locate Ari, who was again operating the cash register. Realizing she was doomed to more waiting, she hopped up to fetch an ashtray and held it in her hand as she smoked in tiny, nervous puffs. When the line at the counter seemed to diminish and Ari glanced her way, she instantly stubbed out the cigarette, but when more people promptly approached with checks extended, she relit it. She never noticed Hannah's undisguised scrutiny.

Two cigarettes later, Hannah followed the blonde's eyes to the doorway, where she saw a tall, wide-hipped, fleshy woman in a grimy trench coat and a striking, slouchy purple hat stride in and halt, self-conscious but poised. The other girl's promiscuous gaze darted elsewhere, but Hannah's lingered on the woman, whom she instinctively liked. Her bearing was massive but stately; her unstylish hourglass figure was bluntly female in the tightly belted coat. Slowly, she removed her sunglasses and maintained a commanding pose near the door while her eyes grew accustomed to the light. Her face was broad but her features surprisingly small, especially the little sparrow's beak of a nose. Even from across the room her eyes looked bruised, puffy; and without the protective and glamorous screen of the glasses, she looked older.

As soon as Ari saw her, he waved brightly, and as soon as he could manage it, he hastened over to say hello. She waited with erect composure, smiling to herself. Hannah admired her, admired the irony in her private smile, and though slightly jealous, was mostly glad that Ari hugged her so warmly. He slung his arm around her broad shoulders, led her to a table, and sat down across from her, ignoring Frank's irritation as he scampered double-time from his customers to the cash register. From their short bursts of laughter and sharp gestures, Hannah guessed they were sparring in an affectionate and ritualistic duel. The woman tapped Ari on the arm and made as if to rise; he caught her hand and bent over to kiss it, but she laughed and pushed him away.

Soon after the thickening crowds forced him back to his post, the woman rose, took out her wallet, and went over to the already-blaring jukebox. Obviously familiar with the selections, she quickly punched out her choices and returned to her seat. Meanwhile she smoked long and steadily, resting her tired eyes in the rising spirals. Frank once broke her reverie by affectionately calling out her name, which Hannah couldn't make out. The woman jumped in a quick beat of alarm, then recognized Frank and waved back, calling him honey in a throaty voice, but as soon as he turned away, her face regained its severity. She pulled off her leather gloves, and Hannah saw with mild disappointment that her nails were painted red, a little chipped and ragged. Frank eventually brought her coffee. She grinned and said something that made him laugh and pinch her cheek before she could elude him. She pushed him away playfully, but strongly enough to make him wobble backward with surprise.

Looking increasingly harassed, Ari glanced impatiently at the clock, hesitated, and finally decided to join the blonde, who was now gaping strickenly at the woman in the purple hat. He turned to the mountains of papers the blonde had built and talked to her for a long time, apparently with great patience. She handed him pamphlets which he dutifully skimmed and paraphrased back, meanwhile drawing her lists of figures on separate sheets of paper.

Bored, Hannah resumed her scrutiny of the older woman, who now, in her turn, was with some resignation but considerably more amusement, eying the blonde. Hannah breathed thanks that she was in a sense invisible to the other two, since they didn't know she was in the script. The woman sighed, shook her head, and carefully removed her splendid hat, placing it on the seat beside her like a floppy and mute little friend. Hannah was tempted to introduce herself—how they could laugh together at this silly situation! She admired the way that, while obviously caring, the woman could still smile at the whole mess and at herself; she admired her ability to shrug and go on stirring her coffee.

Only when the blonde at last rose, giggling a little, and swung off to the bathroom, did the woman allow herself to glance up at Ari. But to everyone's surprise, he walked hurriedly over to Hannah and beckoned her to follow. Astonished, and a little dismayed at having her anonymity demolished, she glanced apologetically at her rival, but the woman was again staring down at her cigarette.

Hannah turned the corner to find herself alone with Ari in the short and secluded hallway that cloaked the service entrance to the kitchen.

"We'll be squashed if anyone comes sailing out of there," she noted over the clatter of dishes and pans and the hiss of hot steam.

"They won't." He tilted up her face and swayed close enough that she could feel the gravity of his torso. "Listen, lovely," he said tenderly but rapidly, as if rehearsed. "I'm having a little trouble out there—"

"—Yes," she interrupted, "the problem's obvious. You don't have to explain."

Nonplussed, he blinked at her, then continued more thoughtfully. "The blonde one does not so much matter; it's just that she is a nice person and I hate to hurt her more. I tell her when we break up that we can still be friends, and so now"—he leaned his head wearily back—"she come to me with all her financial problems as if I am her banker. She ask me how to fill out her taxes; she is stupid about these things. In fact, she is stupid about most things, but she is very sweet."

He sighed tragically. Then, unable to resist Hannah's steady smile, he began to grin, chuckled helplessly and tucked his face into her hair. One hand fell gently on her spine and stroked it absently. "But the other, the other is an agent and I cannot afford not to be nice to her. Besides, I would be nice anyway, because I like her very much, I respect her. But she says she is in love with me. You see?" He brushed the hair from her forehead to rest his chin there. "This makes it difficult for me. You understand?"

"Yes, of course I understand. I like the older one, by the way."

"She's a very good woman, a strong woman. I admire her, and she knows me probably better than I know myself. But she loves me. She say she doesn't know why, and neither do I—all I do is hurt her, and I don't want to do that. I don't want you to fall in love with me, lovely: I don't want to hurt you. I was afraid when I bring you back here I see you cry. And instead you laugh. You aren't sad?"

She allowed herself to touch his chest, wishing they were alone. "I would much rather be home with you, I admit, but I'm not about to burst into tears." She relaxed against him and helplessly noted a low throb beginning to drum in the center of her.

"Ah," he breathed, welcoming her into his arms. "You are such a lovely little girl; I too wish we are at home right now. You always surprise me, you know that?"

She murmured noncommittally. She didn't want to think. She closed her eyes in the fabric of his shirt.

"Why don't you stay a few more days, little one? Tomorrow is too close. I want to keep you. Then we could spend your last evening together."

Hannah was entirely taken aback. But as her feelings sorted themselves out, she realized that postponing her visit even another day would disappoint her parents more than was conscionable. Moreover, she felt in an indefinable but certain way that this was long enough. One day more, now, would be a kind of spiritual gluttony. Yet his invitation, his unexpected generosity with the self he usually portioned out like the last drops of water in a drought, made her pink with astonishment. "I can't," she said firmly. "I'd like to, but it would be impossible."

Interested, he watched her face, tried to cajole, then postponed the question until later. He sighed and straightened up. "Look, little one, do you want to go home now or wait for me here? I'll be awhile still. I could give you the keys—"

Despite her best judgment, his withdrawal made Hannah flinch. She ached to touch him again, to fall back into that yielding warmth that had overcome them both for a moment; her submission to the warmth had left her open and vulnerable. She sensed he might prefer her to go and leave him with one fewer responsibility, but she was too curious to comply. Besides, it was growing dark out and she wanted to walk home beside him, following his hand, not having to calculate the streets for herself. "No," she said, "that's okay. I'll wait."

"All right, and when we get home, you will have me all to yourself for a couple of hours before I have to go out," he whispered seductively —both as a promise and a warning. Hannah cuddled closer.

"Aren't you going to ask me where I'm going?" he asked with real curiosity.

"No, Ari," she said patiently, amused. She leaned back and looked up at him. "I'm not stupid, you know."

"I know you're not," he said. Businesslike again, he issued instructions. "Now listen, lovely, I want you to go back to your table alone, because I don't want the big one to see us together. Okay? I'll try to hurry; you look tired."

His caution struck her as superfluous—and indeed, as she reentered the room, she saw that she was right. Their small deception had been futile: the woman had seen them leave together, and despite Ari's attempted nonchalance, had easily surmised the rest: she wasn't stupid either. Her face was grim and set.

As Hannah was resettling in her booth, the blonde also minced back to her seat, a little flustered at being on display under the cool eyes of the seated woman, but jaunty too, conscious of her youth and perky step. She averted her eyes bashfully but lowered her slender girdled hips with a twitch of defiance. Ari resumed work on her bookkeeping.

With a jab of irony, Hannah realized for the first time that the three seated women formed a perfect triangle. She was chuckling to herself when she glanced up to find herself briefly caught in the older woman's wide, bruised eyes, but before she could signal a greeting, the other looked away. Hannah grimaced with frustration. How could she engineer a meeting with her comrade-in-arms? She was certain the two of them could share a cruel delight in this tableau they had unwittingly made; perhaps they could even discuss Ari and his dangerous appeal. Surely they had more in common with each other than either had with him, this magic stranger, this shaman washed to their shores by foreign storms. How she admired that dashing purple hat!

Hannah raised her head expectantly, eagerly—then sank back into her seat in shock. She saw that the woman's thick face was bulging and sagging like a bag of potatoes falling off a shelf. She was crying. Mottles erupted all over her cheeks. She spread her chapped fingers over her face to hide the evidence of her defeat, but her broad back continued to shudder, tormented by terrible gulps.

Through her astonishment and pity, Hannah gradually realized that the stricken woman was concentrating on some element in the atmosphere: indeed, that she was listening. Suddenly the music struck Hannah's ears so loudly she thought the volume must have doubled. Records had been superseding one another all afternoon so that she had ceased to distinguish one from another, but now she heard Garland wailing forth her eternal anguish over the man—that one good man—who got away. She sighed. She too could weep, but her loss was not a man, it was her admiration for a woman who could capitulate so soggily to that song, and to Ari. In undesired contrast, she all at once felt very young, very free, and cruel. She suspected the woman of having chosen that record herself, with the same instinct that sends a tongue to prod an aching tooth; she suspected her of relishing the pain as her way of demonstrating sensibility, of identifying herself with Garland, the center of attention, the star, glamorous in her suffering, the martyr who stands alone in the spotlight only because no man has proved solid enough to support so much weight, so much gravity. Look, the tears begged, I may seem to be large, strong, smarter and richer than you, I may seem to intimidate, to hold you at arm's length, but it's all illusion, beneath the surface I'm still a threatened maiden, a lady of tears. I am in need of rescue; I am lost; I am lovable. Take me. Take me in.

Right now the woman was probably lamenting to herself that the men who respected her, whom she could talk to, were invariably unexciting, while all the exciting men turned out to be sadists like Ari, undomesticated animals who had scarcely learned to read. Where had all the real men gone? Most men of her acquaintance probably took for granted that any woman as impressive as she was must be invulnerable, but Ari took for granted that even impressive women would melt to needy children in his arms, and because those women were bewildered at finding loneliness their reward for competence, and because they still yearned for that safe seat on the back of the strong white steed they had been promised as children, they gratefully cuddled in his arms and proved him right.

Hannah was grateful too: she had never known how to cuddle. For all his complicated cruelty, Ari was far more sensitive than most people to the ebb and flow of emotion in others. He was almost magically able to intuit vulnerability, to draw out anxiety and even transform it to joy. For all his disclaimers, she didn't doubt that he had survived his own childhood by anticipating every fluctuation of mood in a complicated mother. He had acquired his sensitivity through a childish subjugation to an adult, and now he used it to subjugate other adults, to demonstrate that they too were children, needy and impressionable. But one doesn't have to learn the exact lesson a teacher wishes to impart. If, with Ari's help, Hannah was learning how to accept that part of her that was a child, full of wonder, spontaneity, and uncertainty, if she was learning how to surrender at times to forces much more powerful than any self she could construct, forces that were also part of herself, that didn't mean she would surrender herself to Ari. The test of her openness to natural awe and ecstasy would not be her willingness to weep in coffeehouses over the likes of him. There must be some other way for a romantic and intelligent girl to be a leading lady.

She watched with sad curiosity as the woman first peered out from the shelter of her hands, then lifted her eyes desperately to the ceiling and drew a deep breath. Gray and unevenly swollen, her face looked like dough beginning to rise. She scrounged in the pocket of her coat for a wadded tissue to apply to the puddles in the folds under her eyes, and then, hands shaking, lit another cigarette. Now she turned to see if Ari had noticed. Hannah guessed that he had, for while his own eyes were fixed resolutely on his work, those of the girl, now covered with pink glasses, flinched with confusion at the questions swimming in the puffy eyes of her rival.

The windows looked like sheets of gray metal. The clatter of dishes and voices grew more jagged as the dinner crowd grew and the customers' impatience increased. The artificial light was harsh. Hannah tightened. Her earlier drowsiness had gone, leaving a cold stiffness in her muscles, as though she had tripped in a puddle and been left to dry in a draft. It was, she concluded, time to go, but since she could hardly rise once more and demand the keys without being misunderstood, she was doomed to wait.

As if he had heard her unspoken complaint, however, Ari also stretched and pulled back his chair, looking down at his companion in clear expectation. With an air of sulky disappointment, she swept together her clutter, elaborately fastened her bag, and patted her lackluster clump of yellow hair. Pouting, insistently taking her time, she removed her glasses, wiped them with a napkin, and tucked them into a sequined case, while Ari frowned, arms crossed. At last, exuding great dignity, she began a stately voyage to the exit, but Ari called her back. He reached down in the booth where she had been sitting and picked up a manila envelope, and handed it to her with an aggravated shake of his head. He let her tromp alone to the door, but waved in impatient goodwill.

Then he turned to the agent. She leaped cumbrously to her feet, jostling the table: having waited until she had his full attention, she would now proudly withdraw. She had already shielded her face with the dark glasses and protective sweep of her brilliant hat. Now she hastily pulled on her gloves and fumbled with her wallet. As soon as Ari reached her, however, he calmed her trembling hands in his, removing the gloves, then reached to the table for her bill and tucked it in his back pocket. Hannah recognized this ritual of pretense and reassurance as a caricature of her own ambivalence, and felt depressed for all three of them. Tenderly, Ari went to touch the woman's cheek where the skin was still damp and mottled, like the beach after persistent rain, but she flinched as though he had raised a hand to strike her. Apparently that exasperated him a little, for he began to speak—probably consolingly, Hannah surmised, but also a little methodically, as though he had been on the road in the same play too many long months in a row. He hung his arm over her stooped shoulders and walked her to the door, then out into the street.

As soon as they left her sight, Hannah pulled on her own jacket, picked up her bag, and prepared to leave. But when Ari returned, he bade her wait a little longer, then once again disappeared to the kitchen. The minutes dragged by; Hannah traced her fingertips discontentedly over the scarred wood of the table. The intensity of her regret that they were not to spend this last night together surprised and displeased her.

At last he reappeared in his own jacket and signaled her to join him at the counter where he was issuing instructions to the help he was leaving behind. Abstractedly he drew Hannah close and cuddled her as he spoke, and she nestled in his arms, vaguely dispirited, understanding little of what he was saying, and again noted the strangeness of Ari's so casually assuming such authority. She almost expected the rather resentful quartet of employees, especially Frank, to snicker and walk away, but instead they listened respectfully and nodded. The contrast between the clipped tone of Ari's words and the warm pressure of his arm, interested her.

Outside, the spring air was chilly, damp and sullen with broken promise; she was glad she had waited for company. She peered at her watch and saw with surprise that it was past dinnertime.

"That's a nice watch," Ari commented, taking her wrist. "It's gold?"

"Yes, it was my grandmother's." And how surprised it must be to find itself here, she thought, kidnapped by gypsies, lost and afloat in a world its Philadelphian makers could never have envisioned. "It's later than I realized," she added.

"Yes, we could have eaten there, but I think you are probably tired of sitting, and I am tired too. I want to go back and take a nap."

Hannah almost pouted. If he napped, he would probably have to leave as soon as he awakened, which meant that she was not going to see much more of him before she left tomorrow. Maybe she should just take the late bus home tonight.

"Do you want to go to a movie tonight?" he asked.

"No," she said with a rather glum sigh. "In the city I only go to the movies alone in the daytime. At night I feel like a walking target."

"No no." He grinned tiredly and pulled her closer to muss the top of her head. "I mean with me, stupid. I never let you go out alone."

"B-but—" she stammered. "You're going out—"

"I was. Well, not out, exactly, but I thought I have to work there all night because the man who is supposed to manage the second shift call in sick and the other cook never comes—a real mess. But then I decide I want to stay with you, so I call someone else to trade me for another night, two nights, in fact. That's why I am so long in the kitchen before we leave, making phone calls."

"Oh," she said, more than a little amazed. "I thought—the agent woman—"

"I know you did." He watched her rather smugly. "So, you want to go to the movies?" When she nodded, he took his arm from her shoulders to fasten his coat. "Brrrr—cold, yes?" Then he softly added, "Why don't you stay another day, little one? I still have so much to do before I leave, but maybe you can help."

Hannah refused again, and continued to refuse even under his surprised cajoling, but soon she began to shiver, not so much from the wind as from an amorphous excitement nibbling at the base of her throat; she almost giggled. Instinctively they both began to walk faster. All at once Hannah was deliciously, incalculably happy, and when Ari, still fumbling with his last button, stopped to do the job correctly and released her hand, she turned her surprise and shivers and happiness into a comic little dance step beyond him, twirling with her arms spread, laughing to keep her teeth from chattering. An ineffable gaiety, too deep and free to reach with her mind, expanded in her chest. Simply and helplessly, she danced for joy. When Ari called her to wait for him, she danced back but eluded his attempts to catch her. Suddenly the streetlight overhead snapped on. "Aha," she teased, "God has turned on a spotlight for you."

He pulled the cowl of his jacket over his ears, shaking his head with mock forbearance. "Crazy, you are crazy. You get drunk on all the sodas I give you, yes? Here, come closer and we warm each other up."

As she went up the stairs in front of him, Hannah was conscious of the play of her body in his vision. She stylized her walk; she enjoyed the strength of her thighs passing like twin pendulums marking unkept time. She felt her ascension become a kind of dance, flirtatious yet formal in its preordained rhythms. She could hypnotize with her body. When his hand sought her she leaned aside, and back again, and laughed. She was the swaying watch suspended in the mesmerist's hand; hers was the golden lure of time refusing to pass, of time repeating. She stood still. She turned and watched him follow in her wake.

They laughed together in hungry joy and peeled off their clothes, and, in answer to his challenge, she arched fearlessly and offered herself until both were succulent with her juice and with his. When at last he rolled from her, she shimmered with silent laughter. She lay flat, spread, open, motionless except for the surface tremors of her deep amusement. She laid her palms on her belly as if to reassure herself that she had an exterior, a boundary to her shifting tides.

To her distant surprise, he pulled himself back up and over her as though he were a drowning swimmer reaching for a half-submerged rock, and once again sought her moss-slick recesses. She continued to lie almost motionless, her head thrown back as if discarded, yielding to an inner pulse too powerful for muscles to imitate. He dashed across her again and again like a succession of straining waves, each time melting back into froth and falling away. Once she opened her eyes and touched his cheek, as if she could ease whatever pain seemed to wrack him, but at last she could only slip back to her own blind and grateful suffering. Finally he shuddered and slumped across her, and she tried to lift a heavy arm to stroke him, almost afraid that he might, after all, have drowned, and from oceans away she smiled with faint relief at hearing him breathe.

Then, reassured that he was suspended over her, above danger, she drifted back to wherever she had been. The pull, the lure, the peace of that dark remove had the merciful power to deliver her from sensation and knowledge and self. It was as ruthless and as irresistible as the call on water of the moon—which was as sightless as the sky that surrounded it, for it could find no light to reflect. Its own reflection shivered on water like spilled ink. There was no light anywhere. There was no movement and no sound but emptiness. The face of the sky lay against the sea as a crow's wing folds against its breast. Deep, down, buried, forever inscrutable and blind; there she would wish to stay, always to stay. There was simplicity. She gave herself up to it; she abandoned herself to the blackness that swam through her veins like blood and calmed her until she was as heavy as a stone, sinking. There was no bottom; she would fall forever. She knew nothing at all.

Damp with sweat and tangled unpleasantly in the sheet, she peered out into a strange room. Ari lay awake beside her, smoking, the candle on the bedtable flickering brightly.

"What time is it?" she whispered, rubbing her eyes which mascara threatened to glue shut.

"Not quite nine. I'm sorry if the candle wake you, but soon I wake you anyway. I thought we eat the chicken that's left and go out, and then if we are still hungry after the movie, we can go to a restaurant. Yes, that is okay with you?"

"Fine." She heaved upright, her vision swimming nauseously. "I think I'll shower. I must have had weird dreams."

As Hannah pulled her green turtleneck over her damp head, she watched herself emerge in the mirror piece by piece, a drawing in process. She brushed back the damp strands of hair that clung like weeds to her forehead and joined Ari at the counter where he stood munching chicken.

"I think this last forever," he mumbled through full mouth.

They finished it that night, however, and Hannah neatly washed and put away the platter. Flushed with steam, she turned from the sink and found him watching her reflectively. Wordlessly, without passion, they touched, held each other tenderly, then drew on their coats.

The night, unlike their moods, had not mellowed. They drew on gloves and tied scarves around their necks. They strolled in affectionate silence, arm in arm, following Ari's suggestion that they walk down likely streets until they saw something that caught their interest, and when they finally turned into an enormous, old-fashioned theatre, they were almost sorry, for their quiet pace had been so pleasant. The building, however, delighted them. It was like a gingerbread palace built for children, with gilt cupids and scrolls and winding staircases and ragged crimson velvet hanging everywhere. The long, capacious halls snaked out in all directions, all finally converging in a many-tiered cavern with a bright screen shining like an altar at the far end. Clearly the theatre had once housed something more glorious than retreads of old movies.

They entered midway through the picture, but that didn't seem to matter. They snuggled in their coats and each other for warmth, since the massive old tomb was apparently impossible to heat, and gobbled candy. Ari said he wished it were a double feature, and Hannah agreed, for it was hard to leave such a cozy nest. As it was, they lingered long past the scene where they had come in, and troubled to bestir themselves only when a wily usher caught them with their feet on the seat backs in front. He flashed on his light and scowled to see them so entangled, their hands traded under one another's clothing, mouths full of chocolate, buttons loose, legs sprawled, blinking up at him like sleepy puppies. Ari snarled back his annoyance at some length, lecturing grandly on the American right to privacy; Hannah chuckled into her coat and tried surreptitiously to zip up her clothes. Then, before the furious usher could evict them, they rose majestically under their own command, scattering crumbs, papers and boxes everywhere, and with great dignity, fastened each other's belts. Hannah assumed her most regal manner and prayed that the rest of her clothing would hold. Miraculously it did, and hand in hand, giggling happily, they ran down the long halls, snaked back for the fun of it, explored staircases, emerged through mysterious doors, and finally landed in the lobby.

Outdoors, however, their frivolity dissipated. Ari said remorsefully that he hadn't planned to go to sleep at all on her last night, but that he was tired. Hannah knew what he meant. There was so little to be said together, so little that they could share. Their business with one another had nothing to do with words or friendship. In a way, it had nothing at all to do with who they were. They walked back home quietly, deliberately choosing a longer route. In the seclusion of their obscure garden he held her for a moment, then stepped back to yawn and scrounge in his pocket for the keys.

Inside, they undressed separately, Hannah putting on a nightgown for the first time and Ari reclaiming his robe. She watched him as he made himself coffee, then moved over to make room for him on the bed. For a long time he sipped and looked into space. She thought about going home, about sleeping in her own bed, about the people she would see again after so many months. When he finally raised his head to speak, she expected him to make plans for her exit in the morning.

"You make me very peaceful, you know," he said reflectively. "I wish you did not have to leave me. Or I wish I not have to leave you, because it isn't just another day I want for us. I want to meet you all over again a year ago, or before that. Although"—he smiled teasingly and toyed with her hand—"although I guess a year ago you were not legal, yes?"

She puzzled a moment, then grinned. "No."

He put down his cup and wiggled closer, still tenderly holding her hand. "That's better; I like to touch you when I talk. So, a year ago you were only a child."

"Well, legally speaking. But like a lot of kids, I had other ideas."

"No, it's true. You were too young then and at the same time too old for those stupid boys you meet. But what I want to say is this, little princess: I am thinking of how much I want you to visit me in Tel Aviv."

Hannah hardly knew how to answer. "Well—thank you. But—I guess—well, of all the obvious difficulties that leap to mind, the main one is that I would be so colossally dependent on you. It wouldn't be so easy for me not to mind where you were going and what you were doing."

"I know; I think of that too. I will have to take care of you more there. I even—" His voice waxed expansive as he warmed to the fantasy he was painting; his eyes danced. "I even be faithful to you for a whole week—no, two weeks!"

"My heavens!" Hannah gasped. "A full two weeks? Be careful what you're committing yourself to, Ari. I might hold you to it. I mean, do you think you're psychologically capable of such a sacrifice?"

Amused, but also serious, he bent over and parodied a sweeping bow. "For you, lovely, it is easy. Well, almost easy, anyway. But if it is so easy, it would not be a sacrifice, yes? But for you I will do it. So—you will come then? Even after the first two weeks I still take care of you and not let you be lonely."

For the first time Hannah understood that he was in earnest—at least for now. "Well," she stammered rather shyly, "why don't you give me your address?" She found her book in her suitcase and handed it to him, but even the name of his street, scrawled in his large sliding print, was completely foreign. She had him repeat it until she could pronounce it, then wrote out hers for him.

"We cannot get married—I mean, I am not able to marry you in my country—did you know that?"

"Don't worry, I didn't think you were proposing—"

"No no!" He caught the hands that she had begun to hold up. "I only mean that if we do want to, still we cannot, because you are not Jewish. We would have to go across the border to another country, you see."

"Really?" She found it hard to imagine herself so unwelcome anywhere.

"Yes, it is true." Then he added, "It would be very good to get married to each other if it always was like this, yes?" And before she could answer that nothing stayed the same, he slid off the bed and went to put his cup in the sink. On the way back he turned off the lights. "I hope you will come, lovely," he whispered. "Really, very much I hope it."

Like an old married couple, they held one another chastely and sweetly, then slid separately into bed. Hannah lay on her back, tracing patterns among the obscure shapes visible in the darkness, and wonderingly explored her feelings. He had given her, she thought, a splendid gift, and she was grateful. Now if the fantasy stole into her mind of herself in a vague foreign country, standing under a stronger foreign sun, arm in arm with an Ari dressed in safari white or sheik's capes or gypsy jewels, she would be free to entertain it. He had given her that permission. Now she could pride herself that he too had imagined it. She stretched against the sheet and felt it press against and define her outlines. Paradoxically, she felt, somehow, both more open and more self-contained than she remembered ever seeming before; she felt that somewhere changes were being made, of which she would be informed at some later date. She fell asleep suffused with peace.

30

But she awakened in a clench of anxiety. As soon as she recognized the sunlight, a fierce need to hurry sent her upright in bed, staring at the clock. She crawled over Ari as quietly as possible, tiptoed to her suitcase, and rummaged through it for her bus schedule. After staring uncomprehendingly at the wrong side for minutes, she flipped it over in a frenzy, and decided on the late morning bus.

In the bathroom, as she drew lines around her eyes with trembling hand, she perceived with grim satisfaction that tension had drawn her skin so tight against the bone that she had the taut, chic, contemporary look she could so rarely manage. If the top of her head shot off like an exploding cork, she wouldn't be surprised. She smudged out the shaky line with her finger and began again. Her wide eyes were as deep and reserved as an owl's. She began to dress.

How would she manage to pass the next hour? All she could see of Ari was a mountain range of blankets. Too jittery to sit and concentrate on a book, she quietly opened the refrigerator and poured some juice, but it sizzled in her stomach like acid.

So she carried her last things from the bathroom to her suitcase and tucked them neatly into the side flaps. Inspecting the room one last time, hands on hips, she spied her almost-demolished loafers under the bed and painstakingly pulled them out without a sound, only to drop one with an awful clunk. Seeing that Ari didn't stir, she released her breath and packed them; but when she rose and turned around, she started in alarm at the sight of him reaching for a cigarette.

"What are you doing?" he scowled.

"Packing," she said. "I'm sorry I woke you, but I'll be out of here soon and you can go back to sleep."

"Why, where are you going?"

"Home!" she almost cried.

He dropped the recalcitrant lighter and stumbled to the bathroom, commanding her over his shoulder to wait a minute. She obediently sat on the edge of the bed, folded her hands in her lap, slipped on her high heels, and waited blankly. After the usual crash of cataracts and bleats of a drowning man, he reemerged, dripping and squinting, his face still damp and speckled with soap, and with a disgruntled groan, sat beside her on the bed. The contrast between her spruced and tailored costume and his disheveled, sleep-swollen nakedness, jarred her. He reached again for lighter and cigarette, seemed stupefied that the former still refused to ignite, and fumbled through the pockets of his pants, which he kicked out from under the bed, for a bent and rather linty match. His body brushing against hers upset her; he was so thin and taut, so closed from her. Behind her eyes her head buzzed like a camera with open shutter. She wondered miserably why the act of leaving always so unnerved her.

He heaved backward and crossed his legs so that he was facing her, which was unusual for him, given his preference of touch to sight. He asked how long her trip would take, and when she said just a few hours, frowned and asked impatiently why she had to leave so soon. His annoyance seemed to flap around her head like malevolent birds. She stammered into her lap that she had assumed he would be going out soon, and she would prefer to be on her way. When he touched her knee, she involuntarily shuddered.

His eyes widened and his drawn brow cleared. Almost laughing, he said softly, "You are so tense. You thought I want you to go early."

"I thought—I thought you'd have errands to run as usual, and I didn't want to be hanging around in your way—"

"Silly baby, why does it take you so long to understand?" He fell back against the pillow, pulling her over him. "Oh, we could have slept for hours more." She laughed with surprise, then choked with embarrassment as she realized that her nose was running. Sniffing, she lunged awkwardly across him to reach for a tissue, but he pushed her back firmly and handed her one, pulling the covers over both of them. She felt ludicrous in her skirt, girdle and high heels, yet she also began to relax in his arm.

"Silly, lovely," he murmured soothingly, holding her. "Didn't you believe me last night? Do you think I want you to visit me in Israel but don't want you here for a few more hours?"

"I—" She hesitated because that had been only part of her reason for haste, but she was too moved by his solicitude to explain.

"Ah, you are such a child, I always forget. You look so calm when you are sad. I was angry that you want to run away so soon, without even waking me up to say good-bye."

Under the covers, tucked against him, she began to thaw. She lay passive and still while he sucked the flame to the nub of his cigarette, stubbed it out, and deliberately knelt over her to undo all the dressing she had so tensely accomplished. At first his hand and mouth tickling her skin were both tantalizing and oddly annoying, like being nibbled by a swarm of delicate insects, and she had to resist an impulse to swat, but soon she realized he was softening her as effectively as a sculptor kneading new clay.

"I'm afraid I make your sweater all sweaty," he said apologetically as he slipped from her to the mattress. "Now you will smell of me on the bus."

Amused, she smiled and answered tenderly, "Well, that's nice. Maybe we can find some way to bottle you up and sell you as perfume. I'll buy a case."

The pleased glow her words brought to his face startled her. "You don't mind smelling of me?" he asked with a simplicity, a seriousness, that was new.

"No, of course not," she said affectionately, turning so that her head rested on his shoulder. "I like you."

"Do you love me?"

She turned over again and hid her face between his neck and shoulder, tasting him gently, like an unweaned kitten. "I like you a lot," she whispered softly.

Soon, since they were both awake and too distracted to doze, Hannah got up and took out the schedule. Ari decided on an early afternoon bus, then gathered his clothes from their various positions on the floor. On a sudden impulse, Hannah changed her clothes and pulled on her jeans again. Ari brought her juice, which she now found she could drink without metabolizing it into acid, and watched as she made one more inspection of the room for lost belongings and began to close her bag.

"You still have those pictures of me?" he asked suddenly.

"Of course."

"Then wait, I give you one of the big ones too, I think they are better—"

"Thank you," she said with surprise as he handed her one of the large glossies. "I'll hang it on my wall at school and all the other girls will come in and admire it. My reputation will go up fifty points. And it'll give me something to contemplate as I try to fall asleep at night; maybe I'll say my prayers to it."

He sat down happily beside her again. "Yes, you look at the picture of me, and I will look at the ones of you in my camera when I have them developed at home. I will hang them on my wall too, or on my ceiling—"

"Oh no! Promise you won't do that: half the civilized world passes through your bedroom! Keep them under the mattress or something."

He patted her affectionately. "Okay, I will take them out from under my mattress and look at them, and that way we can both go to bed thinking of one another, yes? You have a pen? I sign it for you."

"I suspect your bed will be rather more crowded than mine," she said wryly. "I hope gazing at pictures of me won't annoy your other friends."

"I will think of you after they are asleep." He stared at the photograph in his lap for so long that Hannah became curious. Finally he printed the date and place, and resumed his study. At last, with great concentration, he began to write. He beheld his achievement with evident satisfaction, and proudly handed it to her.

A little embarrassed, she deciphered it hastily. "To lovely child-woman Hannah. Eli Arieli. April, 1963. NYC." Because he seemed to expect some kind of response, she thanked him, and carefully tucked it with the other pictures under her sweaters.

They looked at one another fondly, each a little mystified and a little sad, then Ari leaped up, stretched, and began preparing to leave. "Since you are all ready," he suggested, "why don't we go out to lunch? We can go back to where I take you the other night, where you try to run away from me. It is very near Port Authority."

She retrieved her coat from the closet and ran her hand over the gold owl with jade eyes that Jenny had bought for the collar. She slung her bag over her shoulder and went to lift the suitcase, but Ari laughed and took it from her. Its stiff creases jabbed both of them as he heaved it through the door. Hannah wished she could leave the clumsy bag behind and go off with Ari free of encumbrances; even more she wished she could tactfully make her own way from here. Though she was grateful he wanted to keep her, in a way she wished she were already gone. It felt unnatural to watch as he lugged her parents' baggage; it was incongruous, like watching a cat fret under a dog's leash. She wanted to free him again and watch him run.

In daylight the theatre restaurant was altogether different, like an actress robbed of makeup and spotlights. A few clumps of people sat eating at prim distances from one another, absently leafing through newspapers. The floor was visible, and its black and white tiles were a little shabby. The wallpaper, embossed with felt and gilt, formerly so lush and elegant, was now rather scrubby, and worn spots showed. With no brilliant light to refract and shimmer, the glasses behind the counter were merely containers again, dull with steam.

Her watch promised almost an hour before they need think of leaving, but she was surprised when Ari ordered a full meal with a first course of soup. She had planned only to sip a Coke, but at his urging, finally asked for a sandwich. Ari kept shifting nervously across from her, evidently undecided how best to arrange himself in the booth, whether or not to take off his jacket, what to do next. She was relieved when he excused himself to make a phone call. Her sandwich came with his soup and she began to nibble at it unenthusiastically, but midway through, began to wonder where he was. Perhaps she should have ordered milk since the Coke sloshed hollowly against the walls of her stomach. When at last she saw him striding back, however, she thought he seemed more settled, less inwardly coiled, and she too relaxed a bit. He sat and looked at her alertly.

"Do you remember the waitress at the Club yesterday, the one with red hair? Well, I just call there, and they say they almost have to close up early this morning—late last night, really—because of her. She had a fit." He attacked his soup with gusto.

"A fit?" she prodded. "What does that mean?"

"How can I say it—you know, she start to go crazy, screams and cries and just—" He shrugged, gulping another mouthful. "Naturally this disturb all the customers, so Frank and the others drag her into the kitchen and throw water on her, like a cat. That make her stop laughing and screaming and being so loud, so then they don't have to send her to a hospital, which they don't want to do." He stirred his soup thoughtfully. "This is good—you want some, after it is so cold out?"

She shook her head. "Did someone finally come get her?"

"Yes, her mother and her husband. I see them once before; they are ugly." He lifted his bowl to drink the remainder, then sopped up the spillage with his napkin. "They have a mess to clean up there. Before she start to scream and they notice her, she teared up a whole lot of napkins and spilled out glasses and plates and broke them, and in the kitchen, the same thing before they can stop her. Too bad."

"What will happen to her now?" Hannah asked, more curious to hear how Ari would respond than to know the answer. "Will you fire her?"

"I think she quit anyway. And then when she get over it, maybe we take her back."

"Do you think she'll get over it, though? I mean, it sounds like she's on the verge of—or the middle of—some kind of breakdown."

Again he shrugged. "But that doesn't mean anything will change. You take it too seriously. More than she does, probably. She's an actress; she shows her feelings. She hopes acting like a baby change something, but when it does not, then she will get used to things, or she will get another man."

They sat in silence, waiting for the rest of Ari's meal. Periodically, Hannah, who could feel anticipation rising along her spine, checked her watch. Even if he received his food right now, he would have to gobble it if she was to have time to buy her ticket and walk the length and breadth of the terminal to her departure gate.

"I probably forgot to mention that I haven't bought my ticket yet," she said nervously.

"I know. Don't worry about it. Take off your watch. I get us there in plenty of time."

"Well, actually there's no reason you have to come. It would be silly to waste a good steak just to—"

"You are being silly," he said sternly, annoyed. "You never nag before. Take off your watch so it not make you nervous." Seeing her settle back in her seat, he reiterated, "Really, take it off. I watch out for us. There's a clock behind you I can see from here."

Time, of course, was not a matter to be decided by the most authoritative voice, but Hannah didn't want to bicker, and the word nag irritated her. She unclamped the watch, dropped it into the zippered compartment of her wallet, relaxed, and looked around the room.

Apparently pleased with his assertion of leadership, Ari signaled to the waiter and scolded him for the delay. The waiter apologized, mumbled about a misunderstanding, checked with the kitchen, came back to apologize again, and finally, after two more checks and apologies, returned with the steak. During the interval Ari's good humor was restored, and he chattered pleasantly about his numerous plans for now and later. Since he was talking more to himself than to her, Hannah nodded at the end of paragraphs and allowed her mind to wander. She pictured her home, her entrance, her parents' warm greeting, her own bedroom, the walk she would take on the beach tomorrow with Matty. She tried to prepare herself for the abrupt wrench of going from here to there in a few hours. It was always strange, and this time would be even stranger.

Ari chewed through meat, potato, bread, lettuce and tomato, one at a time. Then, sighing with satisfaction, leaned back in the booth and gestured for coffee. Hannah suppressed an anxious wince.

"I'll put milk into it to cool it, because soon we must leave," he said, studying her expressionless face with approval. When the coffee finally arrived, he did sip it steadily, eyes turned inward. Then he rose, asked for the check, paid, unearthed the suitcase, and at last they left.

Relieved of responsibility, Hannah was calmer. Scowling at the elements, they ducked their heads in the saturated wind and plunged forward, neither of them looking up until they came under the protective shadow of the bus station. "Here," Ari spluttered, holding open the door for her, then banging through in her wake.

"Ugh," she laughed, wiping her face. "What a ghastly day—the omens must be against my leaving!" Relief at having begun the first stage of her trip buoyed her spirits. "If you'll watch that thing, I'll get my ticket, then I might as well leave you here—" She broke off as she saw him stare in comic dismay at one of the large clocks that dominated the ground floor.

"What time is your bus?" he asked mournfully.

She followed his eyes. "About twenty minutes ago."

"What time does your watch say?"

She unearthed it and strapped it back on. "Same thing as the clock."

"I guess that other clock must be slow, almost an hour slow." He dramatically pressed the back of his hand to his forehead and moaned.

Hannah was silent, soothed by the thought that all she had to do was wait. "Well listen," she said finally, "there's a five-thirty bus. I'll just buy a magazine and get settled upstairs at the gate. I really don't mind." She didn't: waiting was something she did well.

"I do," he said unhappily. "I hate bus stations. We go back home instead."

"Oh no, I meant—there's no reason for you—we might just as well say good-bye now."

"All along you must know how late we are," he said, putting his hands on her shoulders.

"Well yes," she stammered guiltily. "Or no, not after I took off my watch, then I didn't. I stopped thinking."

"But still you let me scold you and you take off your watch like I ask and you wait for me, and now you don't even say you told me so." He shook his head. "You are very sweet, lovely. To me, this is a wonderful thing you do."

Such praise took Hannah by surprise: it struck her as a very curious interpretation. If she had protested, they might have made the bus, but she was cowardly and cared more for peace.

"And now you think I mind having you with me for a few more hours when I want to have you for much longer than that?"

"But you have other plans now."

"But I am not in such a hurry; now I can finish my coffee." He tipped back her chin to study her eyes, then kissed her gently. "Since we are here, though, you go to buy your ticket, yes?"

"Yes," she agreed, and went off to the counter. As she waited in line, she decided that Ari deserved credit for consistency: many people, including James, would have turned around and berated her for allowing them to make fools of themselves.

She returned to find him flirting with two teen-age girls, who seemed to her very young and ingenuous. Hannah smiled teasingly and took his hand, savoring their crestfallen looks, then suggested storing the valise in a locker. Freeing herself of that burden considerably lightened her mood: she checked to be certain her ticket was still in her wallet, then smiled at Ari, prepared for anything.

Hand in hand, they retraced their damp trail to the apartment, pausing now and then to nuzzle in the drizzle. Neither spoke nor felt any need to speak until Ari, fiddling with the lock of the lower door, said that Hannah often confused him.

"Me? But I feel I'm transparent," she protested.

"No, darling, to me you are a mystery always, a lovely mystery." He slipped off her coat and hung it in the closet. "Before I was very hungry for hot coffee after that wet walk," he said pulling her closer by the zipper of her pants. "But now I think it is not coffee I am hungry for the most."

She recognized with surprise that his haste was more emotion than lust, but before she could consider that insight, an answering need burst through her so brutally that her knees almost buckled, and she gasped with shock at her loss of control. "Hurry," she pleaded softly. "Please."

Galvanized, he caught his breath and in swift choreography yanked off his clothing, pulled back the blankets, freed her long enough to reposition her, and moved into her as simply as a pen into its cap. Her head pitched back as though she needed the whole sky to breathe in, and she suddenly clutched him more in fear than fondness, for she was fighting desperately to hold something back from the awful release that threatened to empty her of everything she owned. She was wild with strength and appallingly weak at once, and everywhere she melted, flushed. Everything flowed from and back to her; she was blissfully but dangerously open, a sluice gate and a drain. Her skin ached with need to absorb, and a frenzy of incompletion brought tears of frustration and something close to anger. Finally, because she feared she might fly apart in this struggle to fill herself again, she forced herself to lie still and allow it, and him, to happen to her. The panic eased somewhat, but the awful flux worsened, and even more cruelly, the more she let herself go awash the less she could feel him, the more he became a frictionless force she couldn't take hold of at all. Every time he came to her he left her. At a far remove of despair it occurred to her that this might never end, that she might be forever abandoned to what she was now: a bald pulse of shameless need, a tooth drilled to nothing but naked nerve endings. The prospect made her mouth open to scream. Suddenly her spine arched back like a drawn bow and she felt all resistance rip and shatter until she was bashed inside out, squashed like a beetle; splat, soaking into the sheet. Slivers of wing, shards of bone. He fell beside her.

After a dead space she opened her eyes, and immediately closed them under the sweat that poured in as if her lids were leaky rain gutters. Her hair was soaked against her skull. She felt like a pot of boiling water after the burner is switched off, abruptly motionless but still soundlessly vaporing. When he reached over to touch her breast affectionately, she shuddered so pervasively she had to beg him to stop.

"You are still excited?" he whispered hoarsely.

"I guess." Her mind was too limp and soggy to form words or thoughts. Intense but hopeless longing still paralyzed her muscles. And after today, she was never to see him again. Perhaps it would be possible to lie perfectly still and dream under glass like Snow White until it was her time again. Until someone came to her again. She thought she might endure the wait if she stayed absolutely still, so that not the slightest flutter of air would agitate her skin. Somehow she must be alone until this uncontrollable need seeped back from the edges of her body.

He surprised her by leaning over to kiss her, but only when she at last understood that he would come to her again did she allow herself to focus. They touched this time and saw one another. She felt as if they were strangers thrown into sudden intimacy by a storm, huddling together and taking comfort from one another's touch. She stroked him with open palm wherever she could reach, seeking to memorize his texture as though to reproduce it somewhere else, some other time. This time she opened her eyes and watched his face while he watched hers. His was perfect, and perfectly foreign to her, the imperious bones robed in velvety curves. Was he really somewhere within, or did he only seem to be there, as a voice seems to be in a radio? He would not be there if she broke in to find him. Was she the same enigma to him, hiding behind her eyes? She touched his face and tasted it, but she couldn't have it. She knew, achingly, that the parting didn't matter, for there was no way, even if he stayed, for them to have one another. She again lay very still, now pierced with sorrow that it was over, radiant with pleasure that it had been.

"Do you love me?" he asked softly.

"No," she answered automatically. Then she stopped and tried to think. "Not love," she said. "Something else—but I don't know a word for it." Love had something to do with what you said to one another when you were awake, with the ways you understood one another as the particular people you were, who you were struggling to become. With friendship. This was entirely other. It was hard to imagine this happening for a lifetime with someone whom you also loved, consciously affirmed and loved, but she hoped it was possible.

He moved over to kiss her again, then leaned on his elbows to look down at her. His desire for intimacy right now confused her. What they were feeling together and separately had nothing to do with what could be said to one another.

"I do love you," he said very clearly, kissing her again. Then he fell quietly back beside her.

She went rigid with shock. Obviously the next step should be for her to answer in kind, but she could not. Though his words represented a kind of victory for her, she took no pleasure in it; she didn't want to hurt him. Her entire body still spun after him, but that had nothing to do with commitments. There was no way feeling as she felt, that she could say anything. If he had given her anything at all, he had given her silence. So she gratefully touched his hand.

She didn't dare look at him. Instead she thought she must try to accustom her body to the fact of their parting. He rolled over and tucked her tenderly against him, not angry as she had feared he might be—perhaps tantalized.

"Will you come see me in Israel?"

"I don't—it seems terribly unlikely, but I'd like to. I hope so."

"We are very good together, yes? We get along very good, don't you think so?"

"Yes. Oh yes. We get along very well. I've never felt like this about anyone; I've never felt like this at all." That she could say with absolute honesty.

"Do you ever think of getting married?" The ambiguity of the question made her hesitate, and he added, "I mean, do you think someday you will? Get married?"

"Oh—sure, I suppose so. Everyone seems to. But no, I don't think about it often, if that's what you mean. I can't imagine it, really. But then I'm only eighteen; give me another eight or ten years."

He chuckled. "Not so long as that, I bet. You will make a very good wife, I think. I know."

"But I can't cook!" she protested. She had never thought of herself as in the least wifely, even feminine.

"I can teach you that; anyone can. It's very easy and you learn especially easy because you are sensual and like to eat. But that's not what I mean, cooking and sewing; I mean you are very good to come home to. I would like to keep you always in my home"—he smiled—"in my bed. To have you there for me always, waiting for me to come home to you." He leaned over to look at her again, half teasing but half very serious. "So, you like to wait for me there also?"

"Well," she laughed, "I'd like to be there when you get there, yes. But I'd like to be allowed out now and then myself."

"Ah," he groaned with a languid stretch. "I wish I could stay home all day and all night, but soon I have an appointment, and we are both soaking wet. You must wash, I think, before you go home to your parents, yes?"

Without thought, she reached between her thighs to spread the liquid like an unguent across her belly. "I like being wet with you," she said.

His breath contracted with feeling, and he embraced her and whispered something in her neck she couldn't hear. And then, before she could contemplate what had moved him so intensely, he pulled her to her feet and into the bathroom, where, in what had become a ritual, she ran the tub and poured in the bubble bath while he went to the kitchen to prepare the Turkish coffee. When he carried in the ornate tray like an offering, she was waiting for him in the billowing water. Legs linked under the foam, they regarded one another happily.

"I almost wish you do not have your menstruation this month," he finally said. "I like to make a baby in you."

"God!" she exclaimed, more than ever glad for the painful cramps that had earned her the pill. "I can't say I share the sentiment, thank you just the same."

"Then we have to get married, yes?"

"More likely, I would have to go through a very unpleasant experience, so let's not talk about that."

"But you not have to. I am serious. If I make you pregnant, I want to marry you."

"Well, thank you for the thought." She smiled more gently, then changed the subject by teasing him with her toe, and in turn he explored her as though they had never seen one another in daylight.

* * *

They dressed slowly and quietly, affectionately touching yet separate again, marooned in their private lives. Outdoors the same sad drizzle hummed accompaniment to their more leisurely return to the restaurant. They sat in the same booth, Ari ordering coffee for himself and hot chocolate for her.

"This time let me have your watch in front of me," he suggested, holding out his hand, and Hannah, though a little dubious, complied. "I must warn you of one thing," he added after a moment, removing his hand to stir his coffee. "This appointment I mention before is with a woman. I wish I can phone her and tell her not to come here, but when I talk to her this morning, she says she is just about to leave to go shopping and won't be back home. I hope she is late, but I think she will not be because she is in love with me, and this is the last time probably I will see her. Will you mind very much? We leave her here when we go to get your bus."

Hannah shook her head, a little regretful, more than a little curious.

"Ah, you are so good; you make me so grateful. Her name is Beth, and she is my best friend in this country until you, and probably the one woman I meet then that I truly love. She tells me about myself. Sometimes I don't always like that, but I think it's a good thing for a friend to do. And she is very smart, which I also like. She understands people." He frowned reflectively. "I don't think she always understand me—some things, maybe, but not everything. She thinks she does."

"Is she the one you have a picture of in your drawer, the one with the long blonde hair?"

"Yes," he said with some surprise. "That is Beth."

He deftly moved the conversation to a monologue on his anxieties about packing: finding boxes, finding the cheapest means of shipping, deciding what to take, and a thousand other things that didn't interest her. Finally she suggested that it hardly mattered because, in the end, he would probably convene his harem in his apartment after he had left, to do the work for him. He howled in comical dismay and envisioned his belongings arriving in shreds, threatening notes tucked inside each box. Next she advised him to get one girl to take care of everything by persuading her it was an honor.

"Can I persuade you? You will stay here and pack for me?"

"No, I make it a rule not to fall for my own tricks. Besides, I hate chores like that as much as you do."

"Yes, I remember that afternoon in the rain when we are supposed to go to look for boxes and you suggest something else instead—yes? You remember too?" He smiled affectionately, and she was about to answer when she saw his attention shift to something advancing over her shoulder.

"Ah," he beamed as a very small girl with long bleached hair stomped up to their table with a fierce scowl. "Beth, you are early."

"So I see!" she snapped.

"No no," he hurriedly explained, "I don't mean it that way. Ah, Beth, this is Hannah. Hannah, Beth."

They nodded, Beth very curtly. Hannah smiled as warmly as she could, hoping by her expression to say: "This is absurd and difficult for us both, so we might as well laugh at the situation, and especially we might as well laugh at him." But the other girl's narrow face was stony.

Ari motioned toward her ingratiatingly and slid toward the wall to make room. "Please sit down, Beth."

"Oh, how cozy! You mean the three of us are going to have a little tea party together?" She remained standing, glaring down at them.

"Hannah is going home to her parents' house in a little while, but we just miss the first bus. It is my fault, I—"

"I'll bet it was," Beth snapped again.

Ari seemed innocently startled by her vehemence. "Yes, it is my fault, or the fault of the clock up there that doesn't work. So I thought we sit together until I take her to the next bus." He widened his eyes ingenuously, and then, as if he had suddenly had enough of explanations, said firmly, "Please sit down now."

Beth very stiffly complied, holding her body aloof from his, and Hannah found herself confronting them both: the trick of seating had turned them into a unit, which was faintly unsettling. But she was consoled by the fact that Ari's earlier estimate that Beth was not as pretty as her picture, was correct. Her hair was too conspicuously bleached and abused to retain the childlike allure of the photograph; her complexion was too scraped by nerves and bad food. Hannah admired her body because it was tiny and muscular, but in outline it had the shape of a narrow plank. She must feel to the touch like a parakeet clinging nervously to a finger: jittery, sharp and gristly. Nonetheless, Hannah liked her: she liked the coiled resilience of her step and the feisty set of her delicate jaw. The city had bleached and bruised her, but it hadn't managed to drain the alert intelligence from her quick eyes. Hannah respected Ari for choosing this one to love.

"What do you do, anything?" Beth challenged. "An actress, I suppose, supported by Daddy."

Nonplussed by such open hostility, Hannah wasn't sure how to answer, but Ari rescued her. "Hannah is a college girl," he said.

"In that case she must be able to speak for herself!" Beth glared at him furiously, betrayed by his instinct to protect her rival from herself.

"Yes," he answered coolly, "Hannah is very intelligent."

"You don't say! All that and brains too, how unfair to the rest of us. Where do you go to school?"

"Bennington."

"Oh, sure, I know all about Bennington." She turned sarcastically to Ari, on whom all her energy was focused, even when she ostensibly addressed Hannah. "Then you're right, Ari, she must be a very smart girl. Lucky for you you're too dumb to know when you're out of your league."

Disturbed by such unalloyed bitterness, Hannah protested. "Oh, that reputation is just a myth. Actually we're not very intellectual, just stylishly neurotic."

"Well you haven't got any monopoly on that, believe me. In fact, there are some real sickies right here in this very room, aren't there, Ari sweetie?" When he looked at her blankly, she turned back to Hannah. "Do you know a girl named Janine, by any chance? She's a senior dance major, I think—"

"Oh, you're that Beth!" Hannah exclaimed in spontaneous delight at having something besides the awkward link of Ari to connect them. "Sure. At least, I know her to say hello to. In fact, last time a friend of mine spoke to her, she mentioned you—uh—in the context of Ari."

"I'll bet she did. Are you a senior too?"

"No, I'm a freshman. I met Janine through acting—"

"Oh no, Jesus God!" Beth smacked her fist on the table. "Now you're robbing the goddamned cradle, Ari! I'm used to competing with geriatric homes, but now it's nurseries! Shit. So how old does that make you, nineteen?"

"Eighteen," Hannah admitted.

"Oh." Beth buried her face in her hands and laughed weakly. "I've never had to cope with ingenues before. In fact, I thought there was a law against this sort of thing. Ari, don't you know the young bruise easily?"

"Well, but you can't be much older—" Hannah said in some confusion.

"Old enough to be my mother," Ari chirped.

"Oh God, that's perfect; that says it all in a nutshell, right out of a textbook." Beth raised her hands helplessly and looked around for confirmation from an unseen audience. "I'm twenty-nine," she said finally to Hannah.

Her parents had been about that age when they purchased her bicycle, but Hannah couldn't connect those two grown-ups with these two young people. She absentmindedly studied Beth, thinking that she looked no older than her friend Janine, then suddenly focused on the serious anguish beginning to congeal the childish features. Shocked, then angry with herself for having been so tactless and dense, she scrambled out of the booth and excused herself.

Hannah tried to linger in the bathroom a generous length of time, but as soon as she slid back almost apologetically, into her side of the booth, Beth, who had been staring ahead in bludgeoned silence, got up. Her eyes, Hannah noticed sorrowfully, were pink. The moment she was out of earshot, Ari leaned eagerly forward. "She told me I am a sadist," he said with considerable interest. "She say I like to torture people, to see them suffer, that it gives me sexual pleasure. Do you think this is true?"

Amused by his reaction—or lack of it—to such a diagnosis, Hannah didn't know quite how to answer. "Well," she began honestly, "I do think you enjoy the sense of power you get from being able to make people suffer—but on the other hand, you also enjoy the sense of power you get from making them happy. I'm not sure you enjoy the pain itself; sometimes I think that's just a regrettable side effect. I must admit, though, that you do cause a lot of it." She studied his face, wondering if that made any sense to him, assuming it did not. Then she blushed. "I don't really think you've been cruel to me—though I suppose you would have seemed cruel had I wanted other things from you. I think you've been honest with me, and I've never felt tricked."

He had looked a little blank, but at the last remark he reached tenderly for her hand. "I don't want to be cruel to you; I want to make you happy. You think that is because I want power over you? When you have pleasure, it give me pleasure. I love to see your face change when I touch you."

Her face changed and she ducked her head shyly, but she tried to answer in a typically composed voice. "Well, I've thought about it, and I honestly don't think you've ever been gratuitously cruel just to see if I would stay around. Of course, I do think you're, well, as crazy as anyone else, probably more. But anybody who thinks you're a sadist and still hangs around, must be a masochist herself."

"A masochist? This is a person who fall in love with a sadist?"

"More or less. A person who enjoys the pain the sadist enjoys inflicting, but also a person who finds pain where someone else might not, who needs to be hurt, for various reasons. You see what I mean?"

"Yes." He meditated on that for a moment, and Hannah wished she could picture how thoughts shaped in his mind. "So tell me, lovely," he asked gently, as if it were the logical next question. "Since I am not such a sadist with you, did you fall in love with me?"

She sighed and smiled at him. "I have loved every moment of the time we've spent together," she finally said; then she impishly grinned. "Especially between the covers."

He was delighted, as she had known he would be. Apparently relieved to return to his familiar preoccupation, he promptly got up and switched seats, sliding in beside her to hold her for a moment, then to tease her leg. Though she was pleased and warmly flustered, Hannah thought of telling him to move back in order to spare Beth any further pain; and, as if she had spoken aloud, Ari said, "She will not like it. But I will be with her all night, and this is the last time I see you."

"Yes," Hannah agreed ruefully. "The logistics of these games are very complicated, aren't they?" She went to reach across the table to slide her watch to his new place, but he caught her hand.

"No," he said softly and pensively. "I change my mind. This way I cannot see you, and I want to see your face."

Again he changed seats, and as he did, Hannah saw Beth coming up the aisle, tautly observing his readjustments. But when she sat beside him, she said nothing. Hannah was absorbed in the floating sensation that such a brief contact with Ari had induced in her stomach, and was regretting his final arrangement, for right now she would far rather touch than see him.

Ari, however, leaned complacently back and cleared his throat. "Hannah thinks you are wrong," he announced. "She thinks I do not like to hurt women, but they ask for it. I am only being honest. She say you want me to hurt you—"

"Oh no!" Hannah protested, horrified. She flushed with embarrassment, but forced herself to look directly at Beth. "What I did say is that if Ari is a sadist, which by certain definitions he probably is, then anyone who falls in love with him must be a masochist. I'm not certain, though, whether his cruelty is inflicted for its own sake, or whether it's more a by-product of his—uh—Don Juanism, or whatever you want to call it." She winced and stole a look at the subject of all this analysis, but he seemed smugly unperturbed. She was angry that she had used that term, for the theory behind it seemed to her to leave out all the difficult and mysterious elements in sex that might make someone's obsession with it more than a mechanical displacement. Ari's obsession and his search, while certainly confused and probably futile, had their own ineffable grace, or why would so many women, herself and Beth included, be so profoundly drawn in? The pat words seemed to her a betrayal of him, or of her vision of him, and their implicit vision of what people should be instead, depressed her.

Beth, however, stared at her with dawning recognition. Hannah realized that this was the first time the older girl had seen her as an autonomous person, rather than just another instrument Ari had devised to torture her with. "This is a bright girl, sweetie," she finally said. "Congratulations. I don't know if this makes it easier or harder." She coughed sharply. "Give me a cigarette, will you?" He held out the pack, and she groaned caustically as she took one and lit it with her own match. "None of this flashy gallantry for Ari—his women get through doors under their own steam and they damn well better keep their matches handy. Here, want me to do that for you?" She offered her match to the cigarette he had taken out for himself.

"Thank you." He leaned forward and coolly forced her to go through with her sarcastic gesture, and from the impatience in his frown, Hannah guessed this was a running quarrel.

"Anyway, getting back to Don Juanism," Beth drawled heatedly. "That really hit the nail on the head, you know, Ari. It's just what I've told you so many times: the fellow was really homosexual, and he screwed so many women because he was terrified he'd wake up and find himself in the sack with a man some fine morning, right?"

Ari only laughed. Then Beth, to Hannah's surprise, threw back her head and laughed with him. "So—" Ari said with a perplexed smile, "I am like those people in the Village, you mean? With my hair like this—?" He puffed his hair with suddenly prissy fingers, pursed his lips, batted his eyes, and wiggled his shoulders as though mincing down the street.

"Right!" Beth howled, her mirth rapidly gaining momentum.

"And that is why I like to fuck women so much, you mean?"

Beth caught her breath, only to convulse in giggles all over again. She nodded helplessly. "Only you don't like it all that much," she finally wheezed. "That's the point."

Ari considered her for a protracted minute. Then, in an abruptly objective tone that made Hannah stiffen, he asked, "You think I don't really like it with you? You think when I fuck you I rather be with a man?" Clearly not trusting herself to speak, Beth began very deliberately to smoke. Ari turned to Hannah, his face bright with ostensible curiosity. "And you, Hannah, do you think I like to make love to you?"

She ducked her head, not wanting to be implicated. "You think I like it with you, yes?" he insisted. She nodded glumly.

"Ah, this is interesting, then. Maybe it is only with you that I wish I am homosexual," he announced gaily to Beth, then watched her expressionlessly. "You think that can be?"

In her place, Hannah would have run from the table, but Beth waited a moment, then answered with composure. "I don't expect you to admit it—that's the point, of course, that you have to keep it subconscious. If you could accept it, you would be homosexual instead of a Don Juan."

"And then you would be happy?"

"No," she answered seriously. "I'd be happy if you would go to a psychiatrist and work some of this out, as you know."

"Hannah, do you think I need to go to a psychiatrist?"

"I suppose we should all go sometime or another," she muttered. "It helps us clarify what it is we want."

Ari still gazed remorselessly at Beth. "And then, you think, I will not want to fuck so many girls, and I will settle down and marry you—that's what will happen if I go to a doctor?"

"I don't know about marrying me, but in general, yes, something like that."

"But you see," he said sternly but not meanly, "I don't want to want that. I don't want to settle down or get married the way you mean it, or any of that. The things I do, I do because they give me pleasure. Understand?"

"Well," Beth agreed wearily, "you can't be helped if you don't want to be."

All three sat in solitude, staring at the table. Hannah wondered why

Beth accosted him that way. The pain under his anger was visible, and it made her sad, as sad as she had felt earlier for Beth. But then it occurred to her that perhaps Beth's vituperation indicated that essentially, she respected him far more than Hannah did. Beth thought he could change, and tried to persuade him to, but to Hannah he was simply an episode in her life, a character in her drama, fixed in his role. Most people, she suddenly and unhappily decided, were probably doomed to be supporting actors in someone else's play; very few could write interesting scripts of their own. She didn't think Ari could. She only wanted part of him, the best part. Beth wanted him all.

But then she squinted, vexed, as if the complexities of the three of them hurt her eyes. For, in another sense, she respected, or at least accepted, the part Ari had chosen for himself, and Beth did not. Short of having a magic wand turn him into the very embodiment of her fantasies, Hannah would not choose to change him. If he were different—well, then he would be different; he would lose his magic. If he were different, he would no longer squander the best of himself in this compelling ritual to which others so eagerly submitted; he would be occupied elsewhere, being responsible and steady and fixed. He might be more admirable, but it would be at the sacrifice of the gift that had drawn her to him in the first place, and for the moment, it was that gift she needed. It was magic; it was grace.

She glanced up rather wearily, and to break the silence, said that judging from this conversation, it was Ari who was the masochist. Both of them laughed, relieved to have an excuse. The waiter brought coffee for Beth, and like a good sport, she then chattered pleasantly and wittily about the play she was in, which, she kidded, was farther off Broadway than Alaska. To get them through the remaining afternoon, she graciously performed a repertoire of practiced but amusing anecdotes about the difficulties of a five-foot-two dancer in a towering line of show girls, and Hannah, listening appreciatively, was sorry they would never be friends. It would be nice to meet her again in some other time and place. But though Beth's tone was friendly, her eyes were those of an actress too frightened to focus on anyone else on stage.

Their relief was almost audible when Ari got up to pay. Hannah put on her jacket and strapped on her watch while Beth fiddled with the ashtray. When he returned to the table, Beth too stood up to go.

"The weather is horrible," Ari suggested diplomatically. "Why don't you wait here for me—I only be a minute—have another cup of coffee—?"

"No," said Beth grimly, "we'll make better time afterward if I come with you. I have a raincoat." She pulled her long hair out of her coat collar, then looked up resentfully. "Unless, that is, you two mind my company."

After a conspicuous pause, Ari said that of course they did not, and though Hannah was disappointed, she didn't blame him, for the alternative would have been to humiliate Beth unconscionably. She thought that in Beth's place she would have volunteered to stay behind, but then, Emily Post had not yet codified the rules for situations such as this.

Halfway to the terminal, Hannah shouted over the wind that she was sorry to subject Beth to such a nasty day, and Beth replied that it was quite alright, she was used to it. Otherwise, no one spoke as they grimly ploughed through the spitting air, each absorbed in his own discomfort. At the door, Hannah suggested the pair of them might leave her here, and Beth promptly turned around, but Ari declared that of course they would see her off properly. His refusal to abandon her touched Hannah, but on the other hand, they made a rather strained trio, and she might have been glad to shed her glum escort.

Beth visibly flinched when they drew Hannah's valise from the locker. Ari told her he would meet her in the bookstore in a few minutes, but she again staunchly refused, undaunted by his frank look of disgust, and they floated up the escalator in a line, Hannah leading, Beth planted in the middle, and Ari and the suitcase bringing up the rear. At the gate they moved in a line to the plastic benches. Beth had taken Ari's free hand and now went to insert herself again between the others, but he deliberately repositioned her and removed his hand. All three stared speechlessly from the clock to the gate to their feet. Hannah's awareness that in a short time she would be in transit to another and altogether separate world, distracted her and removed her from the couple beside her. She felt no great pain at leaving them together—indeed, she was eager to be gone. Her chief disappointment was Beth's manipulations. She had again taken Ari's hand and was clearly bent on flaunting their propinquity; Hannah had thought her braver and more gallant, and some of her former respect disappeared.

Uniformed men approached the bus and prepared it for boarding. Diverse passengers trailed up to the gate from various directions and formed a haphazard line. Hannah began to rise, but Ari placed a hand on her knee and said tersely that it still wasn't time. At last the driver flung open the bus door, and Hannah, sighing with relief, swiveled politely in her chair to say good-bye to them both, but Ari insistently carried her bag up to the door, and there, to her confusion, embraced her. She froze in his arms, conscious only of their undoubtedly stricken audience, and she had the feeling that Ari too was forcing himself to go through with the ritual for her sake, which she appreciated but regretted. When he hugged her tightly, she closed her eyes, less from sentiment than to block her clear view of Beth scrunched wanly on the bench, clasping her pocketbook as though it were a pain in her belly.

"Good-bye, little one," he whispered in her ear. "You will write me a letter, yes?"

"Yes," she whispered back, and for a moment she forgot everything but the warmth of his breath, and wanted to close her eyes and let him dispose of her at his will.

"And you will come visit me in Tel Aviv? I love you, sweet little princess."

To her confusion, she saw Beth actually get up and walk stiffly over to join them, like a dour chaperone, and she could only moan speechlessly, touch his cheek, pick up her suitcase and flee. She handed over her ticket, stumbled aboard and found a seat in a daze, and only when thoroughly settled did she dare look back at the gate. To her amazement, the couple was still there. Truly, Ari was determined to see her off. Beth's face was blank, but she was speaking rapidly, while Ari, holding her hand, watched the bus. Eerily, they resembled upset parents bidding her farewell.

When at last the bus belched and began to back up, and Hannah, her vision of them rapidly receding, watched them link arms, still talking, and turn to go, she for the first time felt a stab of regret. Suddenly she was left behind, left out. She wondered what they were saying now in apparent comradeliness. They would walk arm in arm down familiar streets, they would make love in the familiar apartment, their drama would ensue, while Hannah was being smoothly swung backward, swept through a long black space and into a series of spiraling and descending ramps, carried ineluctably away. She was leaving; they were staying. It came to her then—as it now and then so sharply does—that everywhere life went on without her, that her absence would make no difference at all.

But after the initial wrench and a deep but brief stab of loss, the scenery that she knew so well began to soothe her. It passed along her window like a silent movie rerunning for the hundredth time, and filled her with anticipation of being home again, herself again, back to normal. Her chest began to lighten with a dawning sense of pride. She had done it. She had gone through with it after all, and she was glad. This was how an explorer must feel on the return voyage, she mused, with the thrill and excitement and the danger left safely behind, and a deep conviction of accomplishment now growing in their stead. The bus swooped and sailed into the long tunnel, and its darkness, modified only by the rhythmic swish of passing cars and the regular flash of colored wall lights, embraced her. The pearly light on the far side filled her with joy. She was going home, and this time she felt she had earned her passage. She had earned the right to feel at home, to make herself at home for a time, because, at last, she had begun the journey of her leaving.

EPILOGUE

"Doesn't anything ever change around this house?" Hannah snapped. "You know I won't go to church with you, Mother, Easter or not. Don't you think I'm old enough by now to make up my own mind?"

"Yes," said Jenny patiently. "I do. You know we've been marveling over that all week—how much older you seem, not only what you say, but even in the way you walk across a room. I have no intention of bullying you into doing something just because it's good for you—as if you were still the little girl whose whole future I used to be responsible for."

Hannah let the magazine in her lap fall shut. She felt obscurely guilty, less for the irritable way she had responded to her mother's innocuous request than for this change that everyone agreed was so striking, so flattering. Her parents had been sentimentalizing over it all week, and their insistence had begun to make her nervous: in order to admire the picture she made they seemed to be holding her out at arm's length, pushing her away, which she resented. Yet at the same time they seemed to be waving good-bye from some receding island, abandoned, which made her grieve. Why wouldn't they just drop the subject? And now here was Jenny rattling on about God, a battle Hannah thought she had won years ago.

"I only wanted to explain what it would mean to me if you came tomorrow," Jenny went on. "That is, I wanted to tell you about myself. Lately, I feel as if I've been going through some changes too, you see. And you've been one of the reasons. You've been so much help to me, you know, Hannah. It's very strange. I imagine you'll experience it for yourself someday. You and your husband will have a baby partly to extend yourselves and your feelings for one another, and instead, you'll end up sharing your home with someone who for years won't even know you exist as a separate person, with needs of your own. Someone who, in the course of getting her own way—or finding her own way—will change you. Change you for the better in many cases—maybe because you've tried to give her the best of yourself. I guess that's really the reward. Looking at you, thinking about what you've meant in my life, I feel so rewarded.

"Anyway, I didn't mean to nag. Just the opposite. I only wanted to share with you this new sense I have of—of coming together, somehow. On the one hand I've finally realized that it's safe to be myself, to have whatever odd thoughts and feelings I want without looking over my shoulder to see if a reporter is taking notes. You know, my father used to tell me that I should never do anything I wouldn't want published on the front page of the *Inquirer*. But on the other hand, I also realize none of it's such a big deal—not myself, or what I do or don't do. I know that sounds contradictory—to feel more honest and brave at the same time that you realize you're pretty insignificant, that it doesn't matter much in the end whether Jennifer Erikson was brave or not. But I always used to worry so much about being good." She sighed. "It's times like this I wish I were as articulate as you and your father. You could say it so much better if you were me. But you're not; I am. That's one of the things you—and your going away—have made me understand. You see?" Jenny stood up, her smile brimming with the same detached affection that had been unsettling Hannah all week. "I'll let you read now. That's quite a pile of magazines that collected while you were away."

But even when left alone, Hannah couldn't concentrate. These occasional mystical effusions of Jenny's always left her irritated, but this one disturbed her even more deeply, left her quarrelsome and tense; she had to restrain herself from bursting out in rational debate. Arguments still kept forming in her mind, obliterating the print of the magazine.

"Your mother said you were feeling a little agitated," announced James suddenly from the doorway, making Hannah jump.

"Maybe if people didn't sneak up behind me and shout I could relax," she said sharply.

He laughed. "Why don't we go for a short ride in the boat?—Good for exactly what ails you."

"I'd be better off going upstairs and doing some homework."

"Do that afterward."

"I procrastinate enough by myself; I don't need any help. You won't be there to write out an excuse for me when the term paper is due."

"You'll work better after a half hour on the water. Right now you're

Epilogue

so rigid the pages in your hands are shivering. You're back to your old trick, you know—trying to snub your own confusion as if it were some outside intruder and not a member of the family."

She turned from the magazine to glare. He too looked infuriatingly detached and loving. They were robbing her of her triumph: she had come home expecting them to spin in their habitual circles while she watched from an Olympian remove. Instead they were perpetually watching her, applauding the differences they found, jostling her with hugs of approval. Worst of all, they were taking her by surprise. "Well, I certainly agree that confusion is a member of this family," she said coldly. "Which is exactly why I'm going to march upstairs and get my own affairs in order. Thanks anyway." Determined to act the role she had planned even if her parents were abdicating theirs, she rose abruptly and moved toward the stairs.

"Hannah!"

Despite herself, she spun around, tears welling at his tone.

"Come."

"But I don't want to. Christ! I don't want to go to the damned Episcopalian church to hear that lamebrained bigot preach; I don't want to go out in your damned boat; I don't want everybody forever grabbing at my feelings; I don't want—"

"Forget about what you want for a little while and come out anyway."

Fortunately for her pride, Hannah was able to hide her emotion out on the bow of the cabin cruiser. Wind and the loud chant of the engines absorbed the sound of her crying. She wept not because James had forced her to go, but because he had been right: the familiar sunswept planes of blue all specked with white, the hot wood she sat on, the upthrust power of the boat that made her hold the railing tightly and grin with answering power, worked their usual magic. She calmed. Then she continued crying because she felt so full.

On their return, James expertly slipped the crusier between the docks, while Hannah hung over the bow to hook the rope that hung from piling to piling like a child suspended from her parents' hands. Anticipating the quick jerk and backward lunge of the boat as it braked, she deftly caught the line, wrapped it around the metal cross between her knees, then fastened the side and stern lines. James checked the knots and nodded approvingly. She warmed with satisfaction.

Afterward, as the two of them sat side by side on the top of the steps, which James had lowered back into the lagoon the day before as a ritual of trust in the coming spring, he tactfully refrained from pointing out the happy color in her cheeks, the brightness of her eyes. In gratitude, she made no attempt to hide the change in her mood. She thought how deeply she loved this home, this land: how attached she would always be.

As if in response, James said, "Next time you come home to us, it may be to a very different place."

"What?"

"Well, I'm exaggerating a trifle, but a year from now maybe. . . . Would you mind very much. . . ?"

Hannah looked at him uncomprehendingly.

"It's what your mother was trying to prepare you for. We've been making up our minds to do what you've been arguing for all these years —sell our portion of the bank to my brothers, move away from the whole family cemetery—the business, Philadelphia, even this house. Jenny and I feel—somehow—much as we love it, the house has the power to scold us, belittle us, as if we were still the children it used to know." He looked at Hannah with concern, then touched her knee. "It's one reason why we've been so glad to see you all grown up and self-possessed. Sometimes it takes a separation before people who have been so close can see one another as they have become."

She had thought they would regret her growing up, her leaving the past behind with them locked in it. But they were not content to stay in it: they were coming too. Perhaps Hannah's weight had even held them back. For all their nostalgia, they were relieved to see her move toward independence. Hannah was stunned. But no longer angry.

Seeing her expression turn welcoming again, James said, "Of course it will take time, and there are a hundred problems still to be worked out, plus a hundred more that can never be worked out, that'll be with us wherever we go. We're well aware that part of the old baggage we have to lug with us is ourselves. That's why—that's the reason I hope you do go to church tomorrow with your mother—because for her, faith is a way to comprehend uncertainty. Her kind of faith isn't your way, I know, but that's not important. What is important is that you be willing to help her grow on her own terms. That's the best adults can do for one another. Don't you think?"

His own expression was cautious. Clearly he expected a hot indictment of organized religion, disorganized belief, and the imagery of capitalism in Reverend Bain's weekly advice to his flock, for such scorn had always been Hannah's response when James acted as Jenny's attorney in their trials with their daughter. Yet when Hannah only stared into the murky green depths of the lagoon as if it were a lover going off to war, leaving her behind, then turned back to her father and hugged him, he looked almost disappointed. When she stood up, smiling, and said she wanted to ride down to the beach with Matty, he continued to hold her hand. But he did not ask to go along.

She wheeled her bike to the front of the house, then held the gate open for the ecstatic dog. No one could resist such radiance. The vibrant sun made every patch of white on the long street shimmer so brilliantly that some houses seemed to join hands over their duller neighbors and break into dance. Cottony puffs of cloud had deserted the sky to nest below, disguised as picket fences, bait boxes, shutters and lampposts. It was a day to air out winter, to throw open windows and doors.

With Matthew hurtling along in figure eights across the lawns of empty summer houses, Hannah headed for the boardwalk. There was little that either of them liked better than these races high over the beaches that followed the curve of the ocean's lip. Since the time when the road of wood was erected, decades ago, the thirsty sea had drunk up more and more of the adjacent land until now there were blocks where water slurped directly underneath, spitting through the widening cracks, stinging Hannah's ankles. The loose boards made a clunking, clicking melody as her tires passed over them. Glancing down, she saw whitecaps seething patiently below, and heard the ocean sucking at the corroded pilings stuck like decaying teeth in its mouth. Then, gradually, the waves fell back again, a full beach away.

This time of year there were few people to disturb the meeting of sky, water and land as Hannah sped along their eternal edge, only a dreamy old woman on a three-wheeler, an occasional child escaping the nearby school. Matthew stopped to sniff the interesting end of a dachshund, but when the irritable dog yapped in protest, he vaulted over the length of her back and resumed his gallop to freedom.

At the boardwalk's end they stopped to rest. Only then did Hannah notice the stench enveloping the long esplanade, intensifying with every minute of heat. The gulls had their own version of a clambake to celebrate the coming of spring. Having unearthed a burrowing shellfish and shaken it loose from their neighbors, they took to the air, aimed, and dropped it to break on a hard surface below, revealing the tasty flesh. Bridges, cars, roofs, sidewalks, all were put to use as giant nutcrackers, but this wooden banquet table that spanned the beaches must have seemed built for the purpose. The birds lent it back to humans only grudgingly: the fetid aroma of rotting fish was their revenge.

Recent storms had dredged up wads of treasure. Huge conch shells, usually so rare, lay everywhere, a city of hotels for hermit crabs; Hannah stripped off her shoes and headed down the mildewed steps to gather some. The sand was hot, but when she plunged down to the ripples they seemed to slice her feet like the side of metal, fiercely cold. Her ankles went red and throbbed.

Finally, arms full of shells, she turned around lazily to see where Matty was, and howled with fury. The elegant setter was rolling blissfully on his back in a pile of decaying animal, long feathered legs jerking shamelessly in the air as he strained to absorb all the perfume he could. By the time he came obediently to Hannah's side, his gleaming fur was pungent with old death.

She sat with him a moment then, aching with a peace that was a kind of pain. At one with the landscape she loved, she was also apart from it, made separate by her self-possession, the very quality that let her survive, made her Hannah. In this flat sun-steeped panorama of dog and fish, of armies of sandpipers and solitary gulls, having left the old woman and tricycle far behind, she was unique. Mortal.

Though she had long ago accepted that her parents were too lost themselves to tell her how to go, she had thought at least they would stay in that position, marooned on their familiar island, one stable point in the geography she must learn to navigate. Her guilt at abandoning them had been all the greater for the flattery she had taken from the contrast, as if only she could swim. Now she could no longer use them to push off from. They too were on the move. The tides would roll over, sighing, and their lonely island would go under, no more her guide to the shallows and the reefs.

Nothing stays the same, warned the voice of her worst anxieties. Even a marriage destined to endure cannot stay the same from year to year, for as two individuals unite to shape work, children, home and adventure, perceptions and philosophies, those creations will in turn reshape them and their love in ways impossible to calculate, so that in the fu-

Epilogue

ture, neither will love in the same way the same person he or she had cleaved to in rapture some time in the past. Her parents would endure, but not as the same young Jenny and James who had indulged their small daughter with a gleaming behemoth of a bicycle a decade ago. Her own romance with Ari could not endure beyond grateful memory. Nor was his gift any more a magic solution to the decisions that must comprise her life than her former isolation had been, for grace is only an easement, an added strength in a long journey, not a destination.

There was no lasting refuge in the happiness she and Ari had so briefly created. He had already abandoned it, doomed to search for the same thing elsewhere, everywhere, in everyone, like a sailor spinning around the world in circles to keep the sun from setting. But that only meant the night was forever behind and before him. Nothing lasts. If she stayed in the ocean, she would drown; she would become the tide, though the tide would not be Hannah. Or, if she clung to land, the sun would suck her dry, then leave her beached, whittled down to ivory slivers by the wind, until finally she was sand. With all her might she must take hold. And let go.

Suddenly lonely, she tucked her face into Matty's soft warm fur. Not understanding, he returned the affection with an energetic lick that said how eager he was to be on the run again, free. Hannah did understand. Smiling, she took her hand from his collar and watched him race back to his happy, futile pursuit of birds. Then, still smiling, she looked over him to the faraway line where the end of the sky bled into the sea, her eyes wide open.